A CHANCE TAKEN

Robb's anger was like a wedge that kept them apart. Laird MacPherson was right. Someone had to bridge this gap. Taking a deep breath, she smiled and looked up into his eyes.

The harsh gaze that met hers nearly silenced her, but she would not be intimidated. "My laird, dinna ye think it time we put our differences aside?"

"Differences?"

"Aye. 'Tis foolish to start a life together with animosity harbored between us."

"What are ye proposing?"

She swallowed her fear, for his eyes were cold and harsh. "Yer father wanted this match. I honor his name as I will honor yours, but we canna make a marriage succeed when there is no trust or respect between us."

His chuckle was snide. "Ye not only enjoy trapping a man, but ye want him to be happy with it. I would never have married ye. If not for the vow I gave my father, ye would be out in yon field, left to fend for yerself. I have no love for ye, and never will."

Terror raced through her. Would he harm her? She raised her chin. "I carry your child," she whispered.

Books by Marian Edwards

HEAVEN SENT
A PRAYER AND A PROMISE
HEARTS VICTORIOUS
A YEAR AND A DAY

Published by Zebra Books

HEAVEN'S REWARD

Marian Edwards

Zebra Books
Kensington Publishing Corp.

http://www.zebrabooks.com

ZEBRA BOOKS are published by

Kensington Publishing Corp.
850 Third Avenue
New York, NY 10022

Zebra, the Z logo and Splendor Reg. U.S. Pat. & TM Off.

First Printing: October, 1999
10   9   8   7   6   5   4   3   2   1

Printed in the United States of America

For Christopher, congratulations.
We are so proud of you.

And to my favorite aunt for sharing both
her love of reading and her books.
Thank you, Aunt May.

PROLOGUE

Scotland—1189

Ariana stood at the top of the cliff and watched as a seabird screeched overhead, riding the currents of air before diving straight down into the sea for a meal. The waves crashed against the rocks with a violent force, spraying foam upward in a frothy plume. The taste of salt permeated the air as the wind whipped her clothes and tangled her hair. Glancing down at the angry whitecapped sea over half a league below her, she shivered, dragged the strands from her eyes, and turned to look back at the tree-lined path.

"Where is he?" She crushed the missive in her hand. *I should leave,* she thought, but the crinkled edges of the parchment cut into her palm. She could not.

Suddenly, amidst the roar of the crashing waves, a deep husky voice hailed her. Bushes rustled and branches parted as he appeared through the deep foliage. Strong and muscular, he walked with a steady gait. His vivid plaid slapped about his thighs; his distinctive blond mane was unmistakable. Even in this stiff wind his two braids hung straight from the temples, while the rest of his golden hair flowed free in the breeze. Anger shone in his light blue eyes. His stare, as unforgiving as a stormy sea, chilled her.

"What have ye done?" he challenged.

"I?" she choked. Heart pounding, she held out the missive. "Why did ye send for me?"

"What trick are ye about now?" He ripped the parchment from her hand and scanned the words. His eyes widened as he finished reading the message.

"I did not send this."

She raised a brow. "Who then did?"

He flung the parchment at her. "Ye would do anything to get back into my good graces, would ye not?"

"Robb MacGregor, I will never forgive ye for abandoning me and our child. I came because the missive warned it was important."

"Ye expect me to believe ye have no feelings left in yer heart for me?" His hand caressed the side of her cheek. When her eyes closed, his fingers softly traced a path to her collarbone, slipping under the edge of her tunic to skim over her swelling breast.

Her eyes flew open as instant heat ignited in her, and she slapped his hand away. Her topaz ring sparkled in the sun as she held him at arm's length. "I am a married woman now. I belong to someone else and I will honor the vows I have given him. Robb MacGregor, ye may have given my bairn life, but 'tis my husband who has given my child a name."

His face darkened. "I would have cared for both ye and our child."

She laughed, her voice a hollow sound. "As yer mistress and bastard."

" 'Tis all I could offer.''

"Ye could have given us a place at yer side. But ye thought ye could have us as yer whore and by-blow. Nay, I would rather die than put my child through that hell."

"Ariana." His voice softened for an instant. "Can ye tell me ye harbor no love in yer heart for yer child's father?"

His words cut to her heart. "I loved ye once and ye deserted me."

He laughed. His voice was harsh. "I made love to a foolish naive girl, who thought I would get down on my knees and beg her hand when she told me she carried my bastard."

Her chest tightened as she heard his selfish condemnation.

"Ye are the prettiest flower I have known," he went on. "But when ye thought marriage was part of the arrangement, I knew ye were like all the others who tried to trap a man."

"Ye are not trapped. Ye are free. I want no more to do with ye." She removed his medallion from around her neck and flung it at him.

He slipped it over his head. "Ye have forgotten that yer marriage has thrown us together."

"Nay, I have not forgotten, nor will I ever. Angus is an honorable man. He offered me a home and life when ye would not."

"He meddled into an affair that was none of his business. Ye would have come around to my way of thinking had he remained out of our lives."

"Ye know so little about me. I would have never agreed to those terms."

He laughed. "Ye would have."

Tears burned her eyes, but she raised her chin and shook her head. As he stared down at her, she caught a shadow moving toward them. "Robb," she whispered, but he silenced her with a wave of his hand. His expression closed and withdrawn, he turned away from her, staring out to the sea.

Suddenly she felt a hand push her.

"Robb," she cried, stumbling back, losing her balance. Her fingers grasping fistfuls of air, she stretched out her hands for Robb as she tumbled backward over the cliff. Hearing her cry, Robb turned and reached out to grab her. For a moment she thought she was safe, but he was also falling. He clutched her to his chest and in the downward rush he turned his body, placing himself beneath her. "Ariana, forgive me. I love ye," he whispered, and pulled her to the cushion of his chest.

Tears pricked her eyes as she clung to him. "I have always loved ye," she breathed.

They hit the ledge that protruded just above the rocky sea caves. The bone-crushing impact she felt must have shattered Robb's back. Excruciating agony shot through her. Raw pain burned every nerve and fiber as her body died piece by piece. Then suddenly the unbearable suffering ceased as she floated upward with her beloved and their child. Now they were three souls soaring through the sky, each glowing bright as a sunlit cloud, rising toward heaven. A peace she had never known filled her. Soft harp music and harmonious singing filled the air as she studied the soft clouds and bright light. She absorbed all the sound and light as her loved ones merged with her.

All was peaceful until she felt a great rush of wind pass her as three swirling mists of silver-edged light streaked earthward. She looked back to the ledge and saw herself and Robb lying still, their bodies broken and bent. Two mists entered her physical body, and the broken bones miraculously healed and the woman on the ledge slowly moved. First a finger twitched, then an arm lifted as she rolled off of Robb, and her eyelids fluttered open. The other silver-mist hovered overhead before slipping into Robb's lifeless body. As sure as Ariana was that they were dead, she knew other souls were now inhabiting their mended bodies. "Avenge us," she whispered. Her invocation was half prayer, half blasphemy as the earthly image faded.

Wales—1068

Christophe's sobs were a tortured sound he refused to acknowledge as his own. "I cannot live without you. Come back," he begged as he gathered Bronwyn's unconscious body in his arms. She had suffered a chest wound, and shortly after had lost consciousness. *This can't be happening,* he thought. To lose both his beloved and their unborn child was too cruel. She hung in his embrace like a lifeless doll. He rocked her limp body in his arms, and the grief tightened in his chest. His world had shattered.

"Christophe," Nicolas said, laying a hand on his shoulder.

His brother's voice seemed to come from far away. Christophe turned, and met the worried gaze. "She has left me. I cannot wake her."

"Let the ladies tend her." Nicolas motioned to Nesta.

Christophe could not let go of Bronwyn. He allowed his brother to help him lower her back on the pillow, but he would not release her hand. She looked so vulnerable, lying on their bed. Her dark-blonde eyelashes fanned across her pale, soft skin. Her lush lips were pink and closed. So rested, so motionless. He strained to see her chest move. It barely rose, then fell. If only she were asleep, and he could waken her with a kiss. But this was not a fairy tale and he was not Prince Charming. As ridiculous as it was, he leaned forward and brushed his lips across hers. Her mouth remained still beneath his.

He pulled away and studied her serene, cool features. How he wanted to feel her warm response. He just wanted her back. He stared at her so long that he thought he saw her eyelashes flicker. But they had not. When Nicolas tried to pull him from her, Christophe flung his brother's hand away.

"Non," he cried, hanging on to her lifeless hand. "I will stay."

Nicolas sighed. "I will see to your duties."

Christophe nodded, too choked to speak.

Night fell on the castle and the candles and fires lit the gloomy darkness, but the light did not chase away the sadness, nor the fear.

Bronwyn lingered in that state, neither gone nor there. By morning she seemed closer to death. He sat by her side, unable to hold back his tears.

"My lord, might I try?"

A voice, vaguely familiar, intruded on his thoughts, and he looked up to see a nondescript friar.

"What is it you want?"

The heavily robed man stepped into the light. "Might I pray over her?"

"She is not gone yet, Father."

"I know, but I wish to pray for her health." The friar held out his folded hands, a Bible in their midst.

Christophe stepped aside, allowing the man room by his wife's bed.

"Friar, have we met?"

"It is possible. I meet many of God's children."

Christophe nodded, but he thought that this was no casual meeting. As he kept hearing the prayers of the friar and the tone, the intonation struck a chord deep within his memory.

"The angel," he whispered, remembering the heavenly spirit who had sent them back in time after they died in the fiery plane crash.

He knelt down and whispered to the friar. "Send us to our time. I don't care if I must return to an old body and she a crippled one. I cannot bear to live without her. If she is to die, then let us be together."

"Your time has not arrived, my son."

"And neither has hers," Christophe declared.

"She gave you the ultimate sacrifice. She put her love above her very life."

"Is she to be rewarded for this?" Christophe stared, terrified of the answer.

"Aye."

Relief swept through him, then anxiety as a thought suddenly occurred to him. Was her reward life or heaven?

He tried to ask, but the friar silently prayed over Bronwyn, not allowing another disturbance to distract him from his prayers.

Christophe bowed his head and added his own prayers. His hand reached out and covered hers.

Beneath their bedchamber, in the great room, Lucien's anger and hatred were beyond consolation. He was pleased that Lady Bronwyn was dying. Avoiding everyone, he lowered his head and let the wicca talk as he pressed the dagger point into the witch's back. Together they made their way to the tower. He crept up the stairs, and when a maid or guard passed he lowered his head, letting the cowl of a Druid monk fall over his features. Every step of the way he savored his coming revenge. He would kill Christophe Montgomery.

Bronwyn felt a burning pain. It was unpleasant and she wanted to go back to the cool restful sleep, but something pulled her away from the comforting slumber. Noise intruded and she was angry. There had been no sound, nor movement, nor color, just peace and the gentle current of the air she floated on. She tried to protest, wanting to return, but more intrusions occurred. Light filled her mind, painful and intense. Voices drifted in and out of her thoughts. She heard prayers, low murmured chants, as if she were in church. Her eyelashes fluttered open and she saw Christophe. He knelt beside her bed, his hands folded and head bowed. He was praying.

Suddenly, she remembered. Poor Christophe, he must be wracked with worry. There were others, including a friar. She could hear and see them all, but no one mattered but her beloved. She reached out her hand to touch him, grazing her fingers through his hair.

He looked up and for an instant just stared at her. Then he gently gathered her in his arms. He trembled. She felt the shudder pass through him.

Caressing the side of his face, she tried to ease his tension. "It's all right, Christophe. Please, tell me what is wrong."

He pulled away, tears glistening in his eyes. "I thought I had lost you. I thought I had lost you and our child." He cradled her face. "I love you. I always have and I always will."

He kissed her. His mouth moved over hers tenderly, as though he were afraid to bruise her. Her arms wrapped around him, and she kissed him with a hunger he soon met. She had just realized that they had been given another chance. *Thank you,* she whispered silently. His arms crushed her to him. The kiss deepened and she responded, needing to give as well as receive. She savored the taste of him. Every sense came alive in his arms. She inhaled his masculine scent and reveled in the musky aroma that was his alone. His lips traveled to her ear and he whispered her name in a husky voice that would live in her memory forever. The sound sent shivers up her spine. His lips traveled back to hers, and she kissed him with all the passion and love in her heart.

She could hear the others moving from the room to give them privacy.

She nestled closer to him, enjoying the warmth of his body, needing to feel the closeness.

He touched her face reverently. "I should let you rest," he said, but made no move to pull away.

"I don't need to rest," she breathed, wanting to draw him back, but he was already pulling away.

Fang, her pet wolf, whined, and she turned to see what had disturbed him. On guard, Fang stared at the wicca and the robed monk who entered and stood in the shadows. "My lady, I have come to humbly beg your forgiveness, again." The wicca's face was drawn, and she kept slanting her eyes to the side.

Christophe ordered the wolf from the room. Fang whimpered, but obeyed.

"I have forgiven you," Bronwyn said as a shiny flicker caught her attention. A blade shone in the torchlight as it traveled in a downward arc.

"Look out, Christophe!" Bronwyn pushed him away and the blade meant for him pierced her chest and her heart. The room receded and she tried to speak to Christophe, but a blackness engulfed her.

An unearthly cry tore from Christophe and he turned to face Lucien. In a rage he dove at the attacker, and beat him mercilessly, striking blow after blow, while ignoring the wicca's pleas for mercy. The pain and agony in his heart could not be contained. Bronwyn had been taken away from him just when she had returned. His bellow of rage was heard throughout the castle.

Though Lucien tried to escape him, Christophe tackled him and held him in the room. He pulled him to his feet and smashed his fist into his face. "You will die for murdering her."

Without mercy Christophe beat the life out of Lucien. When the assassin swayed on his feet, Christophe moved closer to deal him a death blow, but from within the confines of Lucien's tunic another dagger was unsheathed. Unaware, Christophe moved forward. Suddenly the blade appeared and the blow was delivered. Christophe's eyes widened as he saw the blade in his stomach. He wrapped his hands around the assassin's neck and squeezed the life from him, then staggered toward his love.

Now the room was quiet as the castle occupants filed in. Gasps immediately went up as Lady Bronwyn's body was seen, but no one, except Christophe's brother, intervened.

Nicolas reached out to help him, but Christophe shook his head. He fell on the bed and reached for Bronwyn's cold lifeless hand.

"My beloved," he breathed, "I will join you soon."

The friar looked shocked as he shook his head.

The wolf ran into the room and began to howl, long mournful notes that filled the air with sadness.

Christophe felt a bone-chilling cold. His eyesight faded in and out and he knew his time was short. Fingers numb, he raised her hand to his lips. "Once upon a time there was a love so great, the lovers traveled through time to be together," he whispered, then kissed Bronwyn and collapsed.

Suddenly the light and sound receded as he hurtled through time. Flashes of color once again whizzed by him as it had when he, as Drew Daniels along with Regan Carmichael, had first traveled from the twentieth century back to the eleventh where he had become Christophe Montgomery and she, Bronwyn Llangandfan. He sensed his beloved ahead of him.

Never doubting that their love was eternal, he whispered, "Believe in love, Bronwyn. I will find you."

CHAPTER ONE

Bronwyn awoke to find herself dressed in a strange tunic and lying at the bottom of a cliff. Her clothes were tattered and stained. Branches and twigs clung to her long red hair. She immediately felt her abdomen as a quickening occurred. She sighed in relief; her child was safe. Tears of gratitude stung her eyes as she looked heavenward. "Thank you," she whispered.

Next to her lay a man, his Nordic ancestry revealed in every sharp angle and hollowed plane of his face. The bold features looked harsh, unyielding, cold, as if chiseled out of ice. Though he looked every inch the Viking, his rugged attire declared him a Scot. His plaid kilt covered very little of his muscular legs; the tartan sash and open shirt displayed his strong chest. *A brawny Highland rogue,* she thought, as her gaze explored his impressive physique. He was golden all over, from his long hair, the color of hay, to his bronzed skin, to the shiny medallion nestled in his thick, crisp chest hair. She reached for the medallion, then glanced to his face. His long fringed lashes lay closed, as if dreaming, but he was lying too still to be asleep. Her heart skipped a beat as she leaned over him and pressed her ear to his chest. He wasn't breathing.

Without thought, she started CPR. *Damn you, don't die,* she silently screamed as she worked over him. After only a few moments he responded. Sluggish and disoriented, he came to.

His eyelids opened, and blinked several times, revealing vivid blue eyes, brighter than a June sky. For a few moments he stared at her, drawing deep breaths to fill his air-starved lungs.

"Are you all right?" she asked.

He grabbed her hand, his grip digging into her fingers as he looked at her topaz ring. "Bronwyn?" he whispered.

"Oh, Christophe," she cried, and threw herself into his arms.

He held her tight. "Where are we?"

"I don't know."

"What time is this?"

She looked down at her dress, noticing the strangeness of the lines. "I don't know. The twelfth century perhaps?"

Then she looked at his attire and hers. "But I appear to be a lady and you a formidable Highlander. And we both seem to have been thrown off a cliff," she said, with a mixture of amusement and trepidation.

"It doesn't matter, we are together. And our prayers have been answered."

She smiled. "Once upon a time a lady wished for a true love. She found him, only to discover that he had been at her side always—and would remain there for forever."

"Wife," a gravely voice rasped out from behind Bronwyn.

Her breath caught in her throat as she lay stretched out upon Christophe's chest. He stiffened at the imperious demand, and wrapped his arms protectively around her.

"Wife." The summons came again, and a lump of apprehension thickened within her. Bronwyn turned in Christophe's embrace to look over her shoulder. A burly old man with white hair and wizened features had just climbed down the cliff. Letting go of the rope, he came to stand over her, his light green eyes clear, his gaze penetrating.

"Come." The old man extended his hand to help her up.

Her heart raced. Unlike the last time-travel, she had no memories of the life she had apparently inherited.

She got to her feet uncertainly, followed by Christophe. Her husband gripped Christophe's hand. "Thank ye. Ye have saved my wife from a bad fall. I willna forget that ye put aside yer animosity toward her and offered aid." Then to Bronwyn he said. "Before I take ye home, show yer stepson yer appreciation."

Bronwyn closed her eyes. *Dear God, was Christophe her stepson?*

"Ach, canna ye at least put aside yer dislike and give my son the kiss of peace for saving yer life?"

She leaned forward and stood on tiptoes to kiss Christophe. "What will we do?" she whispered.

"Believe in love," he murmured in reply. Then he stepped back, bowed, and lifted her hand adorned with the ring that carried the hopeful inscription. He placed a soft kiss in her palm. "I will see to your welfare always."

She smiled and stepped back from him. Immediately the old man grabbed her hand. "Tell me what happened."

Suddenly a vivid memory flashed through her mind. " 'Twas no accident. We were pushed."

"By whom?" her husband asked.

Bronwyn shook her head. "I didna see him." She turned to Christophe. "Did ye?"

"Nay." His features had hardened to stone, and his regard was now devoid of emotion. But his gaze slanted to her ring as her husband dragged her away, and his lips formed one word. "Remember."

A pair of coal-dark eyes hidden in the brush atop the cliff watched the rescue of the young woman as she climbed up the stiff incline, her long red hair dancing out behind her as the wind whipped her plaid skirt against her legs. The young man on the cliff below held the rope, watching the woman's progress before he started up. His long blond hair identified him as Angus MacGregor's son.

"Curse their lucky stars. How could they have survived that fall?" Alastair Frazier spit a thick stream of phlegm onto the ground. He wiped his mouth with his sleeve as he watched his victim's rescue in disgust.

"Next time ye will not be favored by fate."

A cold shiver raced along Bronwyn's nerves as she climbed up the rope to safety. Her heart beat faster even after the men helped her to solid ground. Her legs trembled and a wave of nausea assailed her as she looked back down the cliff to watch Christophe climb up the rope. Big plumes of sea foam outlined his ascent as icy waves crashed against the treacherous, rocky shore below. A chill coursed through her as her gaze traveled to the ledge that had broken their plummet to the sea.

"My lady, this way." A huge silvery-haired warrior interrupted her thoughts. "The laird will stay behind and search the area." He bowed before her, then extended his hand for her to precede him. She glanced longingly in Christophe's direction, then sighed and nodded. Lord, she didn't know in which direction to walk, didn't even know her name in this time. She walked in front of the burly warrior on the well-worn path that wound through dense foliage. Sunlight filtered through the trees up ahead and the bushes thinned, showing the fork in the narrow footpath. She panicked; she didn't know which trail to take. Preoccupied, she stumbled and fell. Immediately, the soldier was at her side, assisting her to her feet. As he helped her up, an idea formed and she sagged against the warrior's side. "My ankle," she cried out as she gingerly placed her foot down.

"My lady, with yer permission?" the soldier asked. "I will help ye back."

She nodded, feeling a moment's regret. This kind man was easily thirty years her senior, but his strength belied his age as he easily picked her up and carried her down the right path.

The magnitude of her precarious situation washed over her, leaving her drenched in fear. One mistake could expose her and Christophe to danger. Before hopelessness could take hold, Christophe's words echoed in her mind. "Believe in love." An inner glow warmed her. Oh, yes, she believed in love. They had traveled through time to be together before, and she knew nothing could ever separate them. Not now, not ever. She fingered her ring. The amber topaz glittered in the sun, its multifacets capturing and housing the light like a golden flame shining within the gem.

" 'Tis odd, is it not, my lady, that ye owe yer life to Robb MacGregor, the laird's son?" the soldier asked.

"Aye," she whispered, not knowing what to respond, but relieved to have heard Christophe's name.

The soldier carried her out of the foliage into a lush green meadow that stretched out like a thick carpet across the valley. A sparkling brook bisected the land, guarding an enormous estate. She gasped at the sight of the magnificent castle. Rich golden sunlight made the tall gray stone walls into amber columns that seemed to pierce the sky. "Good Lord," she whispered.

"My lady, dinna fret, I will have ye home soon," the soldier said, misinterpreting her exclamation. She wanted to talk to the man, but knew neither his name nor his title. For now she must be satisfied to listen and learn. She had no choice. How ironic. She had lived as Regan, an outspoken political candidate, and as Bronwyn, a rebellious freedom fighter, and in both lives patience had never been her forte. Who would she be here? Only time would tell.

The soldier carried her beneath a stone archway with a raised iron portcullis, across a stone courtyard, and beyond two huge, double oak doors with black iron hinges.

"Laird Angus's lady has been injured," he bellowed, stomping upon the herb-scented rushes as he marched through the great room. The sweet aroma of basil and thyme filled the air as he set her on a massive trestle table. Footsteps echoed in the cavernous area as the castle occupants came running from the kitchen and upstairs. Several women crowded in, their voices a crescendo of questions.

"What have ye managed to do now?" a shrill voice rang out, silencing the others as a sour-faced woman walked through the crowd and stood with her arms folded. Hatred shone in her pale blue eyes as she looked down her narrow nose. "My poor brother must rue the day he brought ye here."

"Lady Morag!" the soldier protested.

Her pinched features narrowed into a withering look that silenced the soldier's defense. With her pale hair scrapped back into a topknot, the thin mane hanging to her waist, she looked like a prim spinster. Turning, she walked around Bronwyn. "Tell me, Ariana, what trouble have ye wrought this time?"

A secret smile lit her heart. So Ariana was her name now. Knowing her identity eased her distress. She studied Lady Morag, and decided that neither the woman's manner nor her tone could be tolerated. "Yer Christian spirit is sorely lacking," Bronwyn told her. "I have been injured in a most foul deed. Yet ye berate me." She waved her hand in the air. "Be gone with ye if ye canna offer solace."

Morag sucked in sharply.

"Aye, the laird's lady has the right of it," one servant called out as the women crowded in again.

Morag's cheeks flushed with anger. "How dare ye reprimand me?"

Just then Angus's deep voice rang out from the doorway as he entered with his son and men. "Morag, leave be. I willna have ye harassing my bride."

Morag's lips moved several times, but she censored herself until only a harsh gasp sounded.

Bronwyn closed her eyes as she caught Christophe's solemn look.

Angus quickly crossed the room and picked up Bronwyn's hand to gently pat it. "What is it, my dear?"

She opened her eyes and stared into the kindest gaze she had ever known. Did he know about the child? she wondered. "I tripped on the walk here and injured my ankle." She pointed to the warrior. "Yon soldier gallantly carried me here."

Angus sighed, and touched her cheek. "I feared after yer fall the child had been unseated."

"Nay, my lord, my child is firmly planted," she said, relieved he knew she was pregnant.

"A woman does not lose a bairn from tripping," Morag scoffed.

Angus turned on her. "I am not talking about tripping. If not for my son's quick actions, my wife would have died from the attempt on her life."

Dumbfounded, Morag stared at her brother as she pointed to his son. "He saved her?"

"Aye." Angus nodded. "And it cost him dearly. Robb canna remember the past."

Several gasps filled the silence; then Angus looked around at the surprised faces. "Thank God both my wife and son are well."

Morag's smile thinned.

"What, pray tell, by all that is holy, happened to yer dear little bride?"

Christophe arched a brow at the sweetly couched sarcasm.

"She was pushed off a cliff, and if not for my son's heroic action she would have been killed."

"Pity," Morag murmured under her breath.

Angus rounded on Morag as his anger flared. "What did ye say, woman?"

Morag took a step back. "I beg yer pardon, my laird. I canna help speaking my thoughts."

"See that ye hold yer tongue from now on. It is no secret ye dislike my wife, but I willna have her shown disrespect."

Though Morag bowed before turning to leave, Bronwyn noticed her tense body language. Apparently, the woman resented reprimands, and was not as humble as she pretended to be.

After Morag left the great room, Angus rested his palm on Bronwyn's shoulder. "My lady, courage." He bent to examine her ankle.

She held her breath. Would he see through her sham?

" 'Tis not swollen," he said, gently probing the area. "But there are cuts and bruises." He looked up at her. "Rest, my dear."

He turned toward the servants. "Send for the healer."

While the women turned to do the laird's bidding, Bronwyn's gaze locked with Christophe's. A bittersweet longing overcame her. The poignant need to feel his arms around her made her quiver. She sighed.

"Nay, brother," Morag's voice called from the balcony. "I will treat her with yer permission." Morag descended the stairs with a tray of her herbs and linen strips balanced on her hip.

Angus nodded. "See ye do the job right."

Morag bowed before the laird, then placed her tray upon the table. As she folded back her sleeves, she kept her gaze downcast.

Bronwyn watched Morag closely. She wanted to pull back her leg when Morag reached for it, but the woman's touch was surprisingly gentle as she felt the ankle. Then, without warning, she exerted enough pressure to make Bronwyn cry out if her ankle were truly injured. Though she felt like a fraud, she winced and jerked her ankle out of the cruel hold. "Ouch."

"Have a care," Angus warned.

Morag's gaze locked with hers. "Ye did indeed injure yer ankle."

"Aye," she said, hating the lie as she looked over Morag's head to Christophe, silently begging his help.

"Forgive me," Morag murmured. "I willna be so heavy-handed."

Christophe walked over to watch. "Where were ye this morning, Aunt Morag?"

The woman paused in her binding of Bronwyn's ankle, then blinked as the question's significance became clear. "I was here, nephew, and ye wound me to infer I had anything to do with this." Her voice wavered and her eyes moistened.

"Tears?" Christophe mocked; then he shrugged his shoulders. "Aunt Morag, if ye persist in yer sour ways, others will suspect ye."

She straightened from her task and jabbed her finger

into his chest. "Ye, of all people, now champion this lady's cause? Did ye injure yerself in the fall so badly that ye forgot the hatred ye hold for this woman?" she asked.

Silence descended on the room.

Bronwyn held her breath as she watched the faces nod in agreement to Morag's words. She silently prayed Christophe could carry off the deception.

Christophe smirked as a dark chuckle filled the air. "Whether I hate the woman or not is not the point. I owe my laird my loyalty, as do ye."

"My son is right, sister," Angus said.

Morag lowered her gaze, but not before Bronwyn caught the outrage the woman quickly concealed.

After the ankle was bandaged, Morag turned to the gray-haired soldier. "Malcolm, carry Lady Ariana upstairs."

As the soldier lifted her in his arms to do Morag's bidding, Bronwyn shot Christophe a panicked glance.

"Wait," Christophe ordered Malcolm, then turned to Angus. "My laird, in light of the attempt on the lady's life, it would be prudent not to leave her alone tonight."

"Ye are right, Robb." Angus turned to Malcolm. "Stay with my lady, until ye are relieved."

His reassuring words about her safety helped, and she relaxed as the soldier named Malcolm carried her up the stairs, down a long hallway, and through the master's bedroom door. Her peace of mind fled the moment Malcolm placed her upon the big fur-covered bed. *Good Lord!* she thought, the full reality hitting her in the face. She belonged to Laird Angus, not Christophe.

The dark walls and heavy tapestries closed in on her, making her heart race. Would her husband want his connubial rights? She closed her eyes. What, dear God, was she going to do?

As Malcolm closed the tall window shutters, she clasped her hands, trying to get a hold on her fear. Her tight grip caused her topaz stone to dig into her flesh. The ring's inscription suddenly came to mind, and a quiet calm stole over her.

Two hours dragged on before the door opened and Christophe entered. "Malcolm, I will relieve ye. Yer wife Jessie has placed the dinner out. Go eat yer meal."

Christophe waited until the soldier left before sitting on the bed with her. "Are you all right?"

She flew into his arms, needing to feel his security and love.

"Bronwyn," he said, pushing her back to stare into her eyes. "Are you all right?"

She drew a deep breath. "Christophe, I am fine. I didn't hurt my ankle. I tripped, and because I didn't know which way to turn on the path, I let the warrior carry me."

He nodded in understanding and gently took her hands in his. "My name is Robb in this time. I think we will have to be very careful. If anyone discovers our masquerade, we will be in deadly danger."

She tightened her hold on his hands. "Christophe—I mean, Robb—I believe we are already in danger. Someone tried to kill us and our child."

"Not us," he whispered, pulling her into the shelter of his arms.

She leaned back and stared at him. "What do you mean?"

He sighed. "I think the intended victim was just you."

Her hands shook as she gripped his tunic. "What are we going to do?"

"First off, you are going to calm down."

"Calm down!" She tried to pull away, but he held her firm. "How can I calm down when someone is trying to murder me?"

He pulled her back against his chest and gently kissed

her forehead. "I'll protect you." His hands caressed her back. "We are alive and our child is safe."

His comforting words washed over her like a warm summer's rain, and the reassuring beat of his heart beneath her ear added a steadying security. She started to relax, until she remembered one thing and pulled free of his arms. "Christophe, I'm married to another man—your father! How will I avoid him?"

He blanched, and ran a hand through his hair. "I don't know." He drew a deep breath and looked directly into her eyes. "My love, you are a desirable woman. I'll try to keep him busy tonight, but if I fail, can't you plead morning sickness?"

"I'll try, but that excuse will soon wear thin."

His lips touched her forehead. "It will buy us time." He kissed her brow, then her temple. "We need to know more about these people and this time," he whispered, then traced a soft seductive path of sultry kisses to her mouth.

The moment his lips touched hers, she was lost in the magic of his embrace. His hands caressed her back and she moved closer to him. Heat flared within as instant desire overwhelmed her and she willingly gave herself to the wonder of his kiss. The taste and touch of him were as familiar as breathing. She needed him as she needed no other. Her hands roamed across his broad shoulders and down his back, caressing his glorious body. Robb was more muscular than Christophe or Drew, and it was strangely delicious, almost wicked, like making love to a stranger.

"Christophe," she breathed, "no matter what body you possess, I will never tire of touching you. Never."

He looked into her eyes. "A redhead," he mused.

Her lashes slipped down since she was unable to let him see her insecurity. It never occurred to her that he might find her not to his liking.

He chuckled softly. "I've known you as Regan, a provocative brunette, Bronwyn, a luscious blonde, and now as Ariana, a breathtakingly beautiful redhead. Whether your name is Regan, Bronwyn, or Ariana, you are a beautiful woman in any lifetime." He caressed the side of her face, pushing back a bright red curl. "I must say, you leave me as speechless as you did before. Never doubt my love." He kissed her then, and she thrilled to the sensual experience. He had the most exquisite way of expressing himself. He always had. Need flowed through her as his kiss deepened and she lost herself to his fiery embrace, giving back as much heat as she received.

He tore his lips away, his breathing labored, and rested his head against hers. "We must stop. No matter how much I want to make love to you, it's too dangerous." He took several deep breaths and looked into her eyes. "Do you understand?"

She caressed the side of his face. "You're right, but it will be hard."

He nodded and pulled her into his arms. "Hard? It will be impossible."

"We'll have to think of something," she murmured as she snuggled closer into his embrace, shamefully savoring the warmth of his muscular arms. "I will not be able to stand a long separation."

He stilled her movements and hugged her. The rise and fall of his chest were the only sounds for several minutes. Then he tipped up her chin. "Have you remembered any more since this morning?"

"No." She shook her head, then held his gaze. "Have you had any memories return?"

"Nay." He gently withdrew from her embrace and walked over to the window to open the shutters. "I can remember our other lives clearly, every minute detail of when we lived as Drew and Regan, and even as Christophe and Bronwyn, but nothing of this one." He raked his fingers through his golden hair. "It is like amnesia. I heard the date and over a hundred years have passed since our last life, yet it seems as only minutes to me." The bright sunlight poured in, and he stood there staring out over the land.

"I will miss Fiona and Nicolas," she said with a sigh.

"As will I." He looked back over his shoulder. "But your sister and my brother as man and wife will be capable of taking our place as lord and lady of the land."

She nodded. Then her smile faded as a thought occurred to her. "They are dead now."

"Bronwyn," he warned. "Don't cry. They lived their lives."

He was right, but she couldn't stop the sense of loss that overwhelmed her.

"My love," he said softly. "We can find out how they fared. All we have to do is look up their history."

She drew a deep breath, holding her tears at bay. "Then that is exactly what we will do."

He smiled. "You amaze me. Sometimes I think you have more courage and strength than I do."

She stared at him in wonder. Though Christophe had been tall, dark, and the size of a giant, with the muscles of a bodybuilder, Robb's Nordic stature dwarfed him. "Valhalla," she whispered, then shook her head as if to dismiss the ludicrous thought. "Well, my love, what of us?"

"I wonder if your ancestry has anything to do with this lifetime."

"I've pondered that too." She stared down at her ring. "I know very little about my family tree. I knew of Bronwyn because that is where the ring originated, and, I've heard scattered stories of a few others who wore it."

"Does the name Ariana strike a chord in your memory?"

"Since hearing my new name, I've tried to remember

if I've heard anything about her, but Ariana MacGregor is as foreign to me as this century."

"We will have to be very careful. From what I can glean, this clan makes their living from raiding and warring. They know nothing else. We have stumbled into a people whose families have warred for generations and who use their ill-gotten gains to survive."

"That would explain the absence of crops," she breathed.

"Remember to use the brogue, and you must adjust to the social customs. We are operating blind in this world, and until we know the mystery that surrounded these two, we are at risk."

She looked up, his altered appearance taking her breath away. "I think they were ill-fated lovers."

His movements were brisk, economical, as he digested her answer, then returned to her bedside. He squeezed her shoulder. "Have faith, my love. We will find a way to be together."

She stared up at him, needing to believe he would always be with her, holding her, protecting her. He lowered his head and brushed his lips against hers. Her eyes closed as the taste and touch of him invoked intense memories of their lovemaking. Only moments passed as his whisper-soft kiss enticed and enchanted her senses, building a familiar need within her, before he pulled away. His eyes darkened, and she knew he wanted to take the kiss further, but could not. Tears burned her eyes, and her arms ached to hold him. She reached out to him as the door handle rattled, tearing them further apart before Malcolm returned.

"Robb, ye may leave."

Bronwyn ignored the elderly soldier, and a thick lump formed in her throat as she watched Christophe walk away. Dear Lord, this adventure was going to be pure hell. To be so close and unable to touch!

* * *

As Christophe left Bronwyn's room, he turned and ran into Robb's Aunt Morag.

She gasped. "Robb, ye scared me."

He quickly steadied her so she did not fall. "What are ye doing here?"

"I am not snooping if that is what ye are so indelicately trying to imply. I thought the Lady Ariana might need something."

"Really," he said as his eyebrow arched. "I do not remember ye being so solicitous."

She reared back and a mean scowl covered her tight features. "Unlike the others, I do not believe yer fall has rattled yer brains and ye have forgotten yer hatred of Ariana."

Christophe frowned as he studied the bitter woman. "I dinna remember any hatred for Ariana."

"Robb, ye hate all women."

"How can I hate all women?"

She shook her head sadly. "How could ye not when it is common knowledge that yer mother abandoned ye and betrayed yer father for another woman."

Christophe's eyes narrowed. A wealth of emotions overwhelmed him as he stared at his aunt, suddenly feeling Robb MacGregor's physical pain.

"Ye see?" she cackled. "Ye canna hide yer feelings from those who raised ye."

The words formed in his mind and were out before he could stop them. "Ye have as much compassion as the bitch who deserted me."

Her cackle turned almost gleeful, her angular face crunching up into an expression of joy. "Aye, that I do. As yer father instructed me, 'Raise him to have no weakness for the opposite sex.' And ye do not."

Christophe knew this woman had succeeded in stamping out any tender feelings in Robb. He drew a deep breath to get his anger under control. Though he barely managed to contain his rage, he knew he could not let this woman know how she affected him. "Dinna push the matter with me again."

Still laughing, his aunt scurried out of sight, and he stormed off. Bits and pieces of Robb MacGregor's life slowly filtered through the murky void of his memory. Lord, he could never act like a man who hated women. Especially when he was so in love with his wife.

He left the castle and saddled his horse. In a confused state he rode out to find some solitude. The land fell away as he explored the boundaries of the MacGregor land, hoping something would further jog his memory, but he only succeeded in exhausting himself and his poor steed. It was long after dark when he walked his horse back into the castle stable. After seeing to his mount's needs, he trudged into the castle, exhausted and spent.

As he passed the great room, his father's raised voice caught his attention. He stopped and listened.

"What do ye mean?" Angus asked his trusted advisor, Lor.

The barrel-chested man nodded, his shiny pate reflecting the firelight. "My laird, 'twas exactly what I said, whether ye choose to believe me or not."

"Is it true?"

"Aye," Lor insisted.

Angus looked up, his gaze locked with Robb's. "Did ye know?"

Christophe felt his insides roil. "Know what?"

"That yer stepmother was meeting with another."

Unbidden, Robb's anger again returned. Christophe clenched his fists. "Nay."

" 'Tis true. Our man, Lor, saw the lady sneak out of the castle several times."

Lor stepped forward. "Aye, that I did."

"Whom did she meet?" Christophe asked.

"I didna follow her. I only saw her sneak out of the castle."

Christophe walked around the man. "I see. Who told ye to tell the laird that ye observed this?"

His eyes widened. "Why, the Lady Morag."

Christophe raised an eyebrow at Lor, then gave his father a sidelong glance.

Angus's features relaxed as he propped his feet up on the adjoining chair. "Strange, Robb, that ye, of all people, come to her defense."

"I have not said one word in her defense. But I know my father; he would want only justice."

Angus nodded his head and dismissed Lor. He extended his hand to the chair beside him. "Sit with me. We must make sense out of this incident."

"I agree, but I'll no be a party to a witch hunt."

Angus roared with laughter. "Ye have the right of it. Have ye remembered anything?"

Christophe's insides tightened. The large bump on the back of his head ached. He felt the goose egg and frowned. "Nay."

His father grasped his shoulder. "Try son. 'Tis important."

Christophe closed his eyes. Frustration curled through his veins as nothing, not even a hint of this life, surfaced. He sighed. "Father, I canna remember even the fall."

Angus leaned back and poured each of them a tankard of ale. "Here, drink this down. I have no doubt yer memory will return to ye in time."

Christophe thought otherwise, but said nothing as he accepted the tankard. He sipped his ale thoughtfully. Whoever had tried to kill them was at large. Mayhap, it was a member of their own clan. Until his memory surfaced, he would have to keep a close watch on Bronwyn. Thoughts of his wife and unborn child resurrected a primitive instinct, and he clenched the heavy goblet in his hand.

His father's chair scraped back. "Time for bed."

Christophe's thoughts scattered and his head snapped up. "Do ye no want another ale, Father?"

"Nay, too much muddles the mind." He walked out of the great room headed for his chamber above, and Rōbb felt his insides roil. "Father, do ye not want to talk about tomorrow?" he asked, grasping at straws.

Angus turned. "Aye, tomorrow will be a dangerous day. But we need our sleep if we are to attack the Fraziers." Angus waved good night and climbed the stairs.

"Attack?" The word swam in Christophe's mind. They were going to lead an attack in the morning? Why? His questions mounted, and he lifted the brew and swallowed his ale in a single gulp, then refilled his chalice and sipped his second drink more thoughtfully. It was another hour before he stumbled off to find his pallet.

The spirits did not dull his mind. As he passed his father's door an ache took hold, and he almost followed his gut instinct to shove open the door. But he forced himself to bury his pain. He had to believe that his woman could take care of herself for one night. He threw himself onto his bed. The moment his eyes closed, sudden images filtered through his mind. Was it the drink? Or was it Robb's memory?

Sharp images flashed with frightening certainty of his counterpart's life. Christophe felt his insides roil as he viewed the man's soul. Hatred and unbearable pain filled the man's heart. The poor miserable wretch knew only the hopeless existence of damnation. He saw Robb's anger, frustration, and final betrayal. The lonely boy who was forced to grow up the day his mother deserted her husband

and son for her lover. A chill passed through him as the painful memories flooded his mind. A mother's abandonment. His father's rejection. An aunt's coldness. A life spent in loneliness and misery, unable to reach out to another for fear of rejection. Never able to trust any woman, especially a beautiful one. Robb's pain became his own. Good God, how had the man lived with this bitterness? His life had been hell.

Christophe closed his eyes, eternally glad that he had found his beloved and vowing to find a way to be together. They had died for each other. Their love had survived the span of centuries. He would do anything to make sure they were together again. *Anything!*

CHAPTER TWO

Robb MacGregor, his yellow braids shining in the moonlight, kissed her shoulder.

"Oh, Robbie," she breathed, seeing desire burn in his pale blue eyes.

He kissed her hard; then his lips teased and tantalized a path to her breast. Her breath caught in her throat. She grabbed a fistful of his silky hair and tugged at his head, wanting, needing his lips, but he ignored her efforts, his lips and mouth fairly driving her insane as he worked a special magic on her body. She panted with need, her body writhing in half-pain, half-ecstasy, as her desire escalated. He kissed her navel and moved lower. She gasped when his mouth nestled in the soft red curls, and liquid fire shot through her as his tongue flicked across the tiny nub. Oh, God, he was driving her insane. "Please," she moaned.

"What is it ye want?" he rasped out as he continued to play havoc with her senses.

"Ye," she cried out.

He chuckled softly as his hands slipped over her stomach and he again pressed his mouth to her feminine core.

When his tongue slipped inside her, moving in and out, an incredible spiral hurled her toward heaven. "Please," she whispered, not sure if she wanted him to stop or not. The heat poured through her as liquid fire flowed in her veins, setting every nerve afire.

Her heart raced as though it would burst; then a thousand stars exploded before her eyes. She dug her nails into his shoulders and screamed.

As she gently floated downward from the heights of pure ecstasy, he held her close, whispering sweet words in her ear. Caressing her body when she moaned, he gathered her closer to his heart. The sheen on their bodies glistened in the moonlight. She touched his shoulder, awed by the incredible experience.

"Ye are a sorcerer."

"Nay, my lady, only a man who knows a woman's body."

His words were disconcerting. But before she could ask if he felt the same wonder, his lips were again working their magic as he kissed her neck. Shivers of delight traveled down her skin at his soft nibbles.

Her arms wrapped around his shoulders and she pressed her lips to his chest. The taste of salt teased her tongue as she kissed him.

His lips captured her. His kiss was carnal and hot. The tangy taste of salt and love on his lips. A rush of desire filled her. Her hands slipped over his broad back, needing to touch, needing to hold onto just a bit of this renegade.

He whispered against her lips. "Are ye sorry?"

For just a moment her fears surfaced. "For loving ye, or for disgracing my clan?"

"For loving me?"

"Nay, I have never regretted our love."

"By all that's holy ye should. Ye are an unusual woman."

Again, the unease surfaced, but the moment his lips touched her, her thoughts fled. His lips, his tongue, his body seduced her. Their movements were in tune, the rhythm and harmony blended as one. She knew his needs as he knew hers.

Her body responded to his. She trembled with need and he groaned with desire. Neither of them cared that their love was forbidden, nor thought of the consequences if they were found out. Love had become the most important mantra of her soul. She needed him as surely as she needed air to breathe. His hands caressed her, and she turned herself over to the pleasures of the flesh as she tantalized and teased him as he had her. Their bodies moved in a dance of music and might. Every thrust of his body brought her closer to fulfillment. She was both exhausted and exhilarated. Onward they moved as one, reaching for the stars and soaring higher and higher.

She felt herself soar and leave her body to burst into a thousand lights. "Robb," she cried out, unable to stand the incredible joy.

Moments later he gave one final thrust. "Ariana," he breathed as he found his release.

Lying in his arms sated and content, she softly stroked his chest, unable to stop caressing him.

"Do ye love me?" she asked.

He rolled over, taking her with him. "I will spend all night showing ye how much I worship yer body."

She raised up on her elbow and looked at him. "Do ye love me?"

He kissed her and all her fears dissolved. He would be happy about their child. Again she nestled back in his arms so content, so happy. He rubbed her back, his callused palm smoothing small circles down her spine as his fingers worked lower, creating a sensuous heat.

"Not that I am complaining about this tryst, but what was so urgent that ye risked discovery?" he asked as he kissed the small line of her collarbone.

She drew a deep breath as his finger slipped inside her, creating a need. Clenching her teeth to ignore the desire, she leaned back to watch his reaction. "I am pregnant with our child."

He stilled, his finger slipped from her, and his eyes turned cold. "Are ye?"

The indifferent words chilled her. "Robb, are ye not pleased?"

His face tightened as a muscle worked in his jaw. "Nay, in truth, woman, I am not." He pushed her off him and rose to dress quickly. Once he had his plaid belted, he moved from her.

Tears burned her eyes as she covered herself. Scrambling to her feet, she ran over to him, but he brushed her aside. And a horrible truth materialized.

"I will not be trapped by a woman. If I marry, it will be by my design, not some calculating bitch."

Pain sliced through her. She had thought he loved her. "Then I will have our child alone, without ye or my family, for they will cast me out."

He frowned. "Dinna try to soften me. I willna have any part of this ruse."

Though tears clogged her throat, she met his eyes. "Then begone. Ye will never have a say in my life, nor my child's."

He roared with laughter. "How will ye survive? If I dinna take ye as my mistress, ye will starve."

"I would rather starve than be yer whore!" She slapped his face and lifted her chin, her haughty stance ruined by her disheveled clothes.

He caught her arm. "I willna marry ye."

"I dinna ask ye to wed."

"What will ye do?"

"That doesna concern ye. I will do whatever it takes to protect our child."

He laughed at her. "Ye will accept whatever I give ye and be glad I am so generous."

"Nay, I will not." She spun around and ran from him. Tears streaming down her face, she blindly entered the castle. Her heart breaking, she swallowed her pain and threw herself onto her bed.

She could not be weak; her child depended on her. What a fool she had been to believe in Robb.

Bronwyn awoke in the middle of the night. Surprised to find her face wet with tears, she softly wiped them away. A cold shiver went down her spine at the painful images that still haunted her mind. Was it a dream or Ariana's memory? If it was her counterpart's memories, she pitied Ariana. Robb's callous behavior saddened her. How Ariana had loved him!

The door opened, and knowing it was Angus who quietly entered the chamber, she feigned sleep.

"Seek yer rest, Malcolm," Angus said, then barred the door after the soldier departed.

Her heart pounded as she forced herself to lie still. Moonlight poured into the room, outlining her husband's frame as he stripped off his kilt and smock. She held her breath, afraid he would awaken her, but he slipped silently into bed and it seemed the moment his head touched the pillow, he started to snore.

Thank God, she thought as relief washed over her, and she drew her first easy breath. As she cautiously listened to his loud snores, the disturbing images from her dream returned. Over and over the scenes replayed in her mind. Ariana's sadness and betrayal descended on her like a heavy coverlet, weighing her down beneath depression and pain.

Bronwyn ached to feel Christophe's arms around her, needing the warmth and comfort of his love to chase Ariana's heartbreak away. The bitter sadness lingered, making her heart ache, until her thoughts grew muddled and sleep finally claimed her. A white-colored mist swirled in her mind, pulling her deeper into slumber, and slowly a dream took shape.

She stood as straight as a statue before Angus MacGregor in a great hall adorned with rich tapestries. Her mother, Ruth, sat at the trestle table, her eyes filled with sadness, while Hamish, her father, paced furiously behind her.

"Understand, Angus," Hamish MacPherson said. "Even though Ariana refuses to name the father, I know yer son is the one. If ye dinna marry her, I will cast her out."

"Nay," Ruth implored, but was quickly silenced by Hamish's warning look.

Ariana stared straight ahead, refusing to meet anyone's gaze.

Angus ignored Hamish and looked from Ruth's frightened eyes to hers. "Why will ye not name the father?"

A deep pain curled within her, but even so she refused to crumble. "He wants nothing to do with the trap of marriage. I willna name him, nor will I marry ye."

"Aye, ye will." Her father's bellow shook the rafters. He walked over to her and grabbed her arm. "Listen to me, I will have ye whipped if ye dare disobey me."

"Take yer hands off the wee lass." Angus shoved her father away, then gently lifted her chin to stare into her eyes. "Ach, lassie, ye have very little choice."

Tears formed in her eyes as she saw his compassion. "I canna be a wife to ye," she murmured to Angus.

"If ye willna name the man, will ye tell me if yer child carries my blood?" His whisper reached only her ears.

She drew a deep breath, and shook her head. Holding back the tears, she nervously twisted her necklace, revealing the medallion Robb had given her.

Angus's features softened as recognition shone in his eyes, and he gathered her into his arms. Then he turned to her father. " 'Tis done. Send for the friar."

Slivers of pain pierced Bronwyn's eyelids. She awoke with a terrible headache. Groggy, she reached out to the form beside her, until she remembered it was Angus, and not Christophe. Instantly, she pulled back her hand. Thoughts swirled in her mind. Last night when she had fallen into a deep sleep, troubled by dreams filled with terror, her husband had not yet retired. Disjointed memories and fragmented images of Ariana's life had scattered in her mind like the shards of a broken vase. Only two dreams did she remember, and they might just be nightmares. Still, she hoped Angus had married her when his son would not. She closed her eyes at the tangled web of Ariana's life, and a sudden thought took her breath away. Could she be in danger from Robb? No, she thought, Christophe had taken his place. Apparently Ariana, the child she bore, and Robb had died in the fall off the cliff. But who'd pushed them? For over an hour she wrestled with her thoughts, but as the first rays of daylight streaked up from the horizon, she had more questions than answers.

Dawn's golden red fingers stretched clear overhead, coloring the sky a bright pink, when Angus began to stir. Her heart raced as he stretched. As she listened to his loud yawn, she frantically thought of an excuse, any excuse, to refuse him his husbandly rights. With the lie of a headache on her lips, she moved slowly, rolling onto her side, and opened her eyes. Delicately, she placed a hand to her temples and winced.

"Does yer head pain ye?"

She nodded, unable to stand the compassion in his eyes. He gave her a sympathetic smile, then a soft hug and a gentle kiss before he arose.

Sadness filled her heart. This brave and gentle man deserved a loving wife. She averted her eyes when he dressed.

After several minutes of listening to Angus pull on his clothes—his foot stomped into first one boot, then the other—she raised her head as his footsteps approached.

Haloed by the sunlight, his white hair shone in the bright light. His vivid plaid was belted and his sword in place.

"I am going to be late today, so dinna worry."

"Why?" she asked, suddenly feeling the terror that had gripped her last night.

"The clan is inspecting the perimeter. Every now and again the Fraziers think they can steal or kill our sheep. Our livestock's herd has decreased. Now, ach," he said, coming to her side. "Dinna worry yer wee head. All will be fine."

He kissed her brow. "I will be back before ye can have a chance to do any mischief."

She smiled. "Be careful, my laird."

He kissed her forehead, then extended his hand. "Let me help ye down to break-the-fast."

She panicked, then remembering her excuse, frowned and touched her brow. "I canna."

He took her hand in his. "I will have Cook bring ye some food. Ye must keep up yer strength for the bairn's sake," he said, before walking across the floor and leaving the room.

When the door closed, she threw back the covers to dress, but a wave of nausea hit her full force, causing her to fall back upon the bed. Her stomach rumbled queasily, and she began to fear her morning sickness had returned.

Finally, after the wave of dizziness passed, she slowly rose and dressed. Her reflection in the polished silver caught her attention and she stared in the mirror, seeing a stranger. Red hair, not strawberry, but more raspberry in color, flowed down her back in soft ripples, and amber eyes that resembled those of a sleek panther glowed warm and mysterious. She touched her face, awed by the porcelain quality of her white skin. A magazine model would kill for this complexion. She sighed. At one time she had coveted such exotic looks, but Ariana was far removed from the crippled twentieth-century woman Regan, who had traveled back in time to learn from her ancestor, Bronwyn, that true beauty came from within. Her amber stone flashed in the mirror. She stared at the ring. Apparently Ariana had also been her ancestor. She glanced up at her likeness once again. She would have trouble adjusting to this exquisite creature—so beautiful, so perfectly formed that she seemed a dream.

Shaking her head, she turned from the polished mirror. There were more important matters to contend with. Her child, and Christophe, had survived the time-travel and she must make sure that both were safe. Not only must she pass for a Scottish maid, but she must also discover who tried to kill her. The enormity of her situation sobered her. A slip of the tongue could expose her and Christophe as frauds, but an overlooked clue could expose them to danger. She played a deadly game.

When a servant delivered her breakfast, she took one look at the unappetizing fare and quickly turned from it and began to fix her hair. She braided her thick mane into a long braid, and then wrapped it around the crown of her head into a coronet. She stepped back and looked at herself. The effect was stunning, and gave her a measure of confidence.

She turned to the steaming hot mug of nearly scalded milk and the thick porridge sitting on the tray. Her stomach roiled at the strong aroma. Quickly covering the food with a linen cloth, she shivered. Her condition would not tolerate such heavy fare. She would have to see about making herself something else. Maybe she could find some rose-hip tea and hot biscuits.

A knock on the door startled her as Christophe peeked his head in. "Are ye all right? Angus said ye were suffering."

A wave of relief washed over her at the sight of his handsome face. "Oh, Ch—"

He placed his finger to his lips, then carefully closed the door and lowered the bar. When he turned, she saw longing and regret deep within his light eyes. He hurried over to her and took her hands in his. "Are ye ill?"

"I'm just a little unsettled," she said, trying to alleviate his concern, though a small part of her was still thrilled that he worried.

His face blanched. "Bronwyn, did Angus. . . did he hurt you?"

She shook her head. "Christophe, I have morning sickness." She reached up and touched his soft, bearded cheek. "Your fears are unfounded. Angus did not accost me."

He pulled her into his embrace. "God, I love you. Last night was a purgatory I cannot endure again. I imagined you fighting off his advances." He closed his eyes. "Forgive me."

Tenderness flooded her heart as she smoothed the frown on his brow. "Christophe, he married me to ensure his grandchild had a proper name."

Christophe's eyes widened. "He told you this?"

"No. I believe I remembered part of Ariana's life in a dream," she breathed. She cradled his face in her hands. "Besides, Angus is too concerned about the bairn to press his husbandly rights." Christophe's features softened into a smile. "Christophe, I miss you so."

"Not half as much as I miss you." He kissed the top of her forehead.

His arms slipped around her and she melted into his embrace. The man who held her had pale golden locks and bright blue eyes, his image so different from Christophe's black hair and dark eyes. But, she reminded herself, this man was her beloved. Though his light eyes and pale blond hair would take some getting use to, his body was every bit as magnificent as Christophe's. She closed her eyes and let her senses absorb the comforting warmth of his muscular embrace, the steady rhythm of his heart beneath her ear, and the husky timbre of his voice.

"I also had a dream last night," he breathed as he caressed her back.

At the sound of his voice, she leaned back and saw his frown. "What is it?"

"If my dream is to be believed, my counterpart has had a very bitter life."

She drew a deep breath. That could explain Robb's callous behavior in her dream.

He looked deep in thought, and she smoothed away the lines of worry. "Thank God we found each other so quickly this time," she said. "I can't imagine what kind of hell it would have been if we did not know who we were when we entered these bodies."

He kissed the side of her mouth. "I know in my heart that you could never hate me."

"Are you so sure of our love?" she teased, kissing him with a deep hunger. Her lips played across his, her tongue darting out to tease and tantalize him.

"We have died for each other, my love. I need no more proof than that," he whispered against her lips before kissing her with a passion that streaked to her heart.

When he raised his head, she smiled and placed his hand over her stomach. "And we have our wee bairn also."

A look of wonder came over his features. "I will never doubt the existence of miracles." His eyes met hers, and the light shining in them took her breath away. His lips took hers in a kiss of possession and need; then he tore his mouth away. "God, woman, you are like a potent drug."

Her arms slipped back over his neck. "Am I?" she asked, snuggling back into his embrace.

He removed her arms and sighed. "I have to ride with Angus." Regret shone in his eyes as he kissed her once more. "As much as I long to stay, I must leave. Rest while I'm away."

"Take care, Christophe," she breathed.

"Not Christophe. From now on you must think of me as Robb, and yourself as Ariana."

Her name would not be a problem; 'twas merely playing a part, a game of make-believe come true. But his new name would be difficult. She had fallen in love with Christophe Montgomery, and in her heart, Christophe lived. She frowned.

"Ariana?"

She nodded. Though she might speak the name Robb, he would always be Christophe to her.

"Ariana," he murmured, then leaned forward and stole one more kiss.

"I love you," she whispered, her heart aching as she watched the tall, broad-shouldered Nordic-looking warrior leave.

Christophe marched down the hallway. He had a duty to perform and while becoming Robb MacGregor, he had to find a way to be with his beloved.

He shook his head when he met his father. "Ariana is not well."

"Some women have a harder time than others carrying their first. Mayhap she is unhappy and that is why her pregnancy is difficult."

Christophe shot him a look, but Angus's face remained expressionless.

"I doubt she is unhappy," Christophe said. "After all, she married ye." A sudden rage filled him as he recognized Robb's bitterness. Christophe took a deep breath. "More likely she just isn't feeling well."

Angus merely grunted.

"Ye think it more than just her being with child?"

"Aye, Robb, I do. But I will leave it be for now."

Christophe ground his teeth together. Already he could feel the bite of his counterpart's pain. Unbidden, Robb's anguish reached out its talons to consume him as it had the previous night. Before he lost control, he abruptly changed the subject. "Where are we headed?"

"To the north. There is a report of foul play."

The sun was rising when they finished their meal and mounted their horses. Christophe felt an uncanny need to turn. He looked up and saw Ariana in the window, and it nearly cut his heart out to ignore her farewell as she waved and Angus waved back.

Angus chuckled softly.

"What amuses ye?" Christophe asked, glancing at his father in annoyance.

" 'Tis a jest ye have never understood." Angus smiled. "Son, I dinna envy ye, nor would I suffer the pangs of youth for anything. I have made my way and ye must make yers."

Angry, Christophe dug his heels into the horse's belly and rushed by the soldier in charge, galloping out of the castle. The men followed his impetuous breakneck pace until Angus caught up with him. "The horses willna stand the pace ye have set. Either slow down or leave."

Christophe pulled back on his reins. Never had he felt this kind of uncontrollable rage. Robb's anger and frustration were horrifying.

"Until ye come to terms with yerself, ye will be no good to yerself or the clan," his father warned.

Though Christophe nodded, the rebellious urge to lash out rose again. He suppressed the feeling, but it took its toll on him, almost as though he were waging a war and losing.

His heart raced and his thoughts swirled in a myriad of

images as he fought off Robb's personality. Drawing a deep breath, he looked away from his father and noticed some warriors on the ridge. "Look," he shouted.

Angus followed his direction. "It is they." Angus pointed to the hill, and giving a bloodcurdling scream, he spurred his horse around and galloped toward the raiders. All the MacGregor clansmen took off in pursuit.

In the distance an answering war cry sounded as the leader held up his claymore and the men on the hill turned to fight.

Christophe saw the distinctive plaid of the warriors and knew instinctively who they were. His heartbeat pounded in his ears, drowning out all other sound. An unholy malice rose within him, one he couldn't identify. Once again he battled Robb's embittered personality, fighting for his very existence as a darker spirit took hold, and he lost the fight to his counterpart. Eyes alight with the fire of retaliation, he pulled out his sword to charge into battle. His horse reared up, but he drove his animal into sword blades and lance tips. In the heat of battle, Robb's blood lust took over his thoughts and senses. He hacked his way to the leader, courageously, foolhardily riding into the heart of the enemy. Claymores clashed, the resounding crash of steel against steel filling the air as he wielded his sword with one intent. Red-hot hatred blinded him. He fought with the valor of ten men. After only ten minutes, his enemy's blood spattered his face and chest, and his sword ran wet with blood as he slashed, stabbed, and skewered anyone in his way. Through the enemy lines he caught a glimpse of Archibald Frazier. His mother's cousin, second in command to Alastair Frazier.

Sounds of death and pain followed in Robb's wake as he chased his nemesis. The MacGregors pursued his bloody path. Not a Frazier was left unharmed. Rage as hot as Hell and as black as death lived in his heart. He could not stem the hatred and vengeance that flowed through him, crying out to be released. This clan embodied all he held foul and lewd. The scapegoat for a lifetime of animosity and wrath burned in Robb's heart as he charged through the last line of bloody plaids.

Finally, he stood face-to-face with Archibald Frazier. As he advanced he could see the fear on the man's face. "Ye will die like the cur ye are."

Frazier raised his sword to parry the thrusting advance, but it was a useless ploy. A bloodcurdling war cry sounded as Robb raised his sword and delivered the death blow.

"Robb, 'tis over," Angus cried out, his voice sharp with reprimand.

The words reached Christophe as he tried to shake off his counterpart's hold, but even as he turned on his father he saw one Frazier who lived, struggling to stand as captives held his arms. A red haze possessed him and Robb Mac-Gregor pushed his father aside, aiming his sword at the man's heart.

Angus gripped his arm, his fingers biting into his flesh. "Nay, we need information."

"He lives," Robb shouted, trying to break free and end the soldier's life, but his father held him like a vise, his expression fierce.

"The clan means more than yer vengeance."

Robb stared at his father for several moments, then blinked. Christophe suddenly gained a measure of control and nodded. His stomach roiled as memory of his actions washed over him.

Shaken by his loss of reason, Christophe moved behind his father, letting him take over. But even when he looked at his enemy, an overwhelming hatred arose. He closed his eyes, blocking out the hated tartan, and listened.

In the heat of his rage he heard the Frazier clansman's words, and opened his eyes. "Ye will all die, and I dinna have to raise a finger. Now, yer clan will perish before mine."

"What mean ye?" Angus's harsh voice rang out.

"Look to yer guards in the north country. 'Tis God's retribution at hand."

Angus stepped forward. "Explain yerself, ye bloody cur."

The wounded, mud-covered Frazier wiped his mouth and spat at Angus's boot. "God will punish ye for yer treatment of our clanswoman, Lady Elspeth. Vows spoken and disregarded is yer sin, Angus MacGregor. The Mac-Pherson woman is nay wife, but whore. Ye will be in Hell soon."

Angus's face grew red at the mention of his wife. He drew several deep breaths as his hand covered the hilt of his sword. "Then ye will be there before me." Angus raised his sword and delivered the death blow.

After they buried the dead and gathered the wounded, the Scottish warriors rode north. At dusk they made camp, and as they supped, Christophe avoided the friendly camaraderie of the clan.

"Where are ye going?" Lor asked.

"I need to wash," he said, grabbing a clean plaid.

Lor smiled. "Ye were yer old self back there, Robb. I wondered if ye had forsaken us, when ye charged into the thick of things. Battle has returned our hero."

Christophe brushed past Lor, marching to the river to think. He could not explain what had happened earlier, but he understood that Robb's forceful personality had taken over. He washed his face in the cold, bracing water and took a long drink of the mountain stream. Troubled thoughts swirled in his mind as he sluiced the water over his neck and shoulders, letting the cold, calming fluid drain his tension. For just a few moments during the battle, Christophe had disappeared, and in his place had lived a bitter, vengeful man—Robb MacGregor's spirit incarnate.

Christophe stared at the blood that covered his plaid. Bile rose in his throat as the memory of the slaughter returned. When he undid his belt, his fingers faltered. He realized Robb had enjoyed the killing. Stripping off his kilt, he dove into the stream. Peaceful silence enveloped him, momentarily washing away the terror and fear. When he surfaced, he scrubbed the blood from his flesh, not stopping until every inch of his body was scoured clean. Only after his skin was nearly rubbed raw and the day's filth washed away did he swim off to the other side. The cold water engulfed him as he fought against the current and the knowledge that, for a time, he had vanished and been replaced by his counterpart. The knowledge that he was powerless to stop Robb from emerging had shattered his world. If it had happened once, he feared it could happen again.

As the sun sank beneath the horizon, the purple haze of night engulfed him, and bewilderment still clouded his mind. He lay upon the embankment and covered his eyes. "God," he whispered. "What is happening to me?" Silence met his pleas as he looked up to see a canopy of brilliant stars against a black sky and found no comfort in the serene beauty. He shut his eyes, blotting out the sight as he did his thoughts.

Slowly, the night sounds faded and he slipped into a deep, heavy sleep. Images filtered through the dreamlike state.

"Dinna blubber," Angus said to the young lad at his side. The laird's long, bright-gold hair flowed in the breeze as he watched the woman leave.

"Momma," Robb cried, trying to run after her, but Angus held him back.

"She has chosen." Angus pulled him along, denying him a chance to reach his mother. But there were no tears on her face as she took her maid's hand and walked away.

"Let me go," Robb bellowed, wanting to run after her.

Angus cuffed him in the head. "Dinna ye ken? She doesna want ye."

As Robb watched his mother leave, her voice floated back to him. Her joy in the midst of his heartbreak finally made him accept his father's words. He stopped struggling against Angus and stared after her.

Angus raised his fist high in the air. "Death to her and all like her. No Frazier will ever again set foot on our land."

Robb stood with his hand in his father's, and his chest hurt from holding back the sobs.

"From now on we will speak no more of her. And son, ye best learn now that ye canna trust a woman, especially if she be a beautiful one. Use them, for they be good for that, but never love them."

Robb nodded, swiping the wet tracks from his face.

Gasping for air, Christophe awoke covered in sweat. The images of Robb's hatred lingered in his mind. As he recalled the painful visions of Robb's life, terror shot through him. No wonder Robb MacGregor's heart had turned to stone. He swallowed deep gulps of air and his heart raced as he tried to calm his nerves.

His hands trembled as he slid back to the creek and sluiced more water over his face. Robb's personality intruding upon his thoughts was one thing, but again his counterpart had completely taken over. His own disappearance terrified him. He drew deep draughts of air before he made his way back to camp and rolled up in his plaid to sleep. When he did close his eyes and drift off, he was tortured by images again.

In the morning Christophe arose tired and drained, but he forced down a breakfast of oatcakes and wine. His stomach roiled and rumbled when the food hit his hollow belly.

He glanced around and noticed that the men were sluggish and out of sorts. He lowered his eyes and concentrated on finishing his food.

After the clan broke camp they rode further north, and found several guards dead at the perimeter of their land. Christophe's jaw hardened as he remembered Archibald Frazier's threat.

Angus shook his head. "The Fraziers will pay," he spat.

"How were they killed?" Lor asked as he dismounted and walked over to the men. "Their claymores and daggers are still sheathed." He bent down and rolled one corpse over.

"I dinna see a mark on him." He walked over to another and nudged the guard over.

Angus scratched his head as he stared at the dead men. "Are they all like that?"

"Aye," Lor said as he turned each guard over, then looked back at the laird.

"No doubt those Fraziers, the lying curs, poisoned our men." Angus pointed to the still bodies that carried not a mark on them. " 'Tis the only explanation."

Christophe's stomach again roiled as he watched Lor flip the men over. Their bodies lay faceup as small insects hovered over the corpses. A wretched look of pain frozen on their features, their eyes were wide open, as if they had helplessly watched their death. These men had not died peacefully in their sleep. Their horrific expressions were silent testament to their excruciating death. Every Scot in the patrol stared silently at their dead clansmen.

"Dig their resting place," Angus said, his voice weary, his expression hard.

The dead were wrapped in their plaids and buried. After

Angus said a few brief words over the lost comrades, the men mounted their horses.

They rode out on patrol, but none of the other clansmen had seen any raiders. Whoever had poisoned the men had escaped. Further north, the MacGregors found several shepherds lying dead on the ground with not a mark on them. Angus shook his head as he stared at the men. "My enemy has found a way to destroy us without even raising a sword."

"Robb, take several men and check the land to the west."

Christophe looked over the area, his suspicions mounting. There was no sign of a fight. How had the enemy delivered the poison? "My laird," Christophe said. "Mayhap, it is a sickness that has stricken our men."

"A plague," one clansmen breathed.

"Nay, not a plague," he said to stave off panic, though he feared just such a catastrophe. "Just a sickness."

Angus looked to the corpses. "Good Lord," Angus muttered. "How did Alastair Frazier send a pestilence on us?"

The men worked hard burying the dead shepherds and burning their effects. Then they left new guards with the flock and rode back to the castle.

If it was indeed a plague, the clan would have to be warned.

On their way to the castle, the village they rode through already had signs of sickness. Christophe spied the sick, and feared that by nightfall the numbers of those taken ill would increase.

Bronwyn heard the men return, and listened to their reports as they climbed off their mounts and went into the castle for a light repast. Her heart plummeted when she heard of the death of the guards. The servants brought the food and hovered as the news of a plague traveled like wildfire throughout the castle.

Angus discussed sending Robb out to patrol and aid any villagers that needed assistance, while he as chieftain called on their neighbors to see how they fared. The clanswomen shuddered at the thought of coming in contact with the disease.

Bronwyn's food sat before her untouched. Her gaze strayed to Christophe repeatedly. Every fiber in her body cried out to stop this folly, but she could not stop the men nor could she go to her love. Standing helplessly by while her beloved left was harder than she could bear.

Several times she felt Morag's censure. The pinched-faced woman stared at her, as though ready to pounce. The tension within her mounted.

"My Lady Ariana," Angus said when he finished his meal. "Ye must eat for the bairn."

She sighed and nodded as he turned to his aide. She pushed the food around, conscious of her husband's regard. At last she raised a crust of gravy-soaked bread to her lips, but the succulent aroma only made her stomach churn. Without even tasting the rich gravy or the chewy dough, she lowered the crust of bread to her trencher, then when no one was looking fed it to the hounds.

When the laird turned his attention back to her, he smiled, satisfied she had eaten. He stood and signaled his men. She held her breath. Christophe was only two feet away, but she could neither touch him nor acknowledge him. "Safe journey," she whispered to Angus as he bent to kiss her cheek.

"Now, wife, I want a smile when I leave. Can ye no do that for yer man?"

She swallowed her apprehension and nodded. Aye, she would do that for him, but could she do that for Christophe?

Angus turned to his son. "Bid yer stepmother good tidings."

Her eyes glanced to Christophe, and the longing in his gaze tore at her heart. She looked away, unable to stand his agony. He bowed before her, and when he lifted his head whispered, "Have courage, my lady."

She smiled. "Be careful," she admonished.

He nodded. "To be sure, my lady, that we will."

Satisfied, Angus turned and marched away. Christophe followed. Her gaze lingered on his broad shoulders as she walked out to the steps. Commands filled the air and soldiers snapped to attention, moving quickly to their places. She watched as Angus mounted his steed, and she waved to him. Her heart broke as she caught sight of Christophe ushering the men out of the courtyard.

Armed to the teeth, they were valiant warriors, but swords and lances were useless weapons against disease. She closed her eyes. It was possible that some would not return. She tried to put the thought out of her mind.

CHAPTER THREE

Unlike Morag, Ariana did not waste time while the men were away. She knew from her prior life as Bronwyn what a dedicated medieval lady's duties could and should be. Before the morning meal had begun, she checked the larder and wine cellar. Then, ignoring her status as mistress of the castle and against the servants' protests, she picked up a bowl of porridge and a loaf of bread from the kitchen and carried it to the trestle table.

Clearly horrified, the cook, Jessie, bustled after her. "My lady, are ye sure ye can help after injuring yer ankle?"

Morag sank her crooked teeth into a chunk of bread, and ripped it in half. As she chewed, she glared at Bronwyn.

"Aye, it is much better, thank ye." Ignoring Morag's frown, Ariana followed the plump cook from the great room. Once in the kitchen, she pulled out a chair for Jessie. "Rest yer bones while I make us some tea. There is time before the castle guards come to the table."

Jessie blinked, at first taken aback by the kind gesture;

then a broad smile crossed her ruddy cheeks and she readily accepted the offer. "Thank ye, my lady. That would be kind of ye indeed." She nodded to her kitchen help, pride glowing from her eyes.

The servant girls stared as Ariana prepared the tea. "Jessie, ye have the finest kitchen I have ever seen."

Jessie beamed.

"That she does," Malcolm agreed as he came in and gave his wife a peck on the cheek.

As Jessie blushed, Malcolm turned to Ariana. "My lady, though the laird has decided ye are over yer scare, know I will be near if ye need me."

Ariana smiled.

When Malcolm bowed and took his leave, Jessie pushed a platter of meat and cheese before Ariana.

The pungent aroma of strong cheese and cured meat made her stomach roil. As discreetly as possible, she pushed the platter away. "Jessie, I fear my stomach is not up to such wondrous fare."

The cook's full cheeks rippled as she chuckled softly. "My time was much like yers, my lady. But dinna worry yerself. The sickness will pass."

She smiled. "I didna anticipate being so ill."

When the tea was brewed, Jessie motioned for Ariana to take a seat and rose to serve her, offering her a few biscuits also.

When Ariana declined the biscuits, Jessie removed them, brushing a few crumbs aside. After wiping the table clean, she looked at the mistress. "Ye are different than we expected."

"How?" Ariana raised her cup to her lips.

"Forgive me, my lady." Jessie's rosy cheeks deepened in color, and she lowered her eyes. "My cursed tongue gets me in trouble."

Ariana placed her cup down and clasped Jessie's hand. "Ye have not offended me. I really would like to know."

Their eyes met, and Jessie stared long, mentally measuring the honesty of the plea. Trust lit her expression, and she nodded. "I believed when Robb MacGregor cursed yer name, that ye were an evil-tempered shrew." She pointed to the twin serving girls, her kitchen help. "We all wondered if the laird had made a mistake. I am glad the rumors were false. Laird Angus chose wisely."

"Thank ye," Ariana said, knowing that winning over the cook was the first step to acceptance. She took several sips of her tea, noticing the way the staff operated. The servants were busy preparing the morning fare. As her stomach began to settle with the soothing warm brew, they talked about the castle and its operation, but her gaze kept straying to the work station. She watched one of the young twins preparing a meal. The servant had cracked all her eggs into a bowl and was looking around for more.

Indecision and worry colored the maid's big brown eyes as she finally approached the cook. "Mother, there are not enough eggs to feed the men. And I promised my Gavin, he could have eggs today."

Jessie pursed her lips at the blond-haired girl. "Find something else, Iona, canna ye see I am busy?"

"I am Isla," the girl corrected.

"May I?" Ariana asked Jessie, pointing to Isla's task.

"Ye, my lady?"

"Aye." She chuckled. "I am no stranger to the kitchen."

Though leery, Jessie nodded as Isla and her twin crowded in behind Ariana to watch.

Ariana picked up the milk, but Isla stayed her hand. "My lady, I have already added milk to stretch the eggs. Ye canna make more eggs than we have."

"Trust me." She poured some milk into the bowl, and whipped the eggs. "How many men do we have to feed?"

"Ye need double the amount of eggs, but the chickens would not cooperate this morning."

Even though she had traveled back in time, and had had a life in medieval Wales before this one, her memories of the modern world remained. How simple it would have been to run to the supermarket for eggs. She had learned how much she had taken for granted.

"My lady, ye will not have enough eggs no matter how much milk ye add," the other maid said.

"Hush, Isla," Jessie admonished, although her expression held just as much skepticism.

"I am Iona," the maid huffed.

Ariana smiled at all the ladies. "I know how to cook."

"My lady, that may be, but if ye add more milk, all ye will do is make the eggs too runny," Isla said.

"O ye of little faith. My fine friend, when I am through ye will eat yer words, as well as my eggs."

The servant was taken aback by her manner and repartee.

Ariana chuckled. "Trust me." When she picked up the loaf of bread from yesterday, she noticed the raised eyebrows. But she overlooked their disbelief, tearing up little chunks of bread and dropping them into the eggs.

"Oh, my lady, now the bread is ruined," Isla wailed.

"Nay, it is not." She ignored the look of distaste as the servants mumbled among themselves.

"Soggy mess" and "pig slop" drifted to her ears, but she continued knowing the bread would be indistinguishable in the finished product while stretching the meal to feed the men.

Placing a large skillet over the fire, she added the eggs and bread mixture. Before she could finish making the dish, the cooking aroma hit her full force. She covered her mouth and motioned for Isla to take the pan. In her pregnancy, aromas bothered her as much as food. Unable to stand the smell, she moved away, directing Isla to scrape the wooden spoon back and forth to produce the fluffy scrambled eggs.

When the eggs were done, Isla scooped out the pile of light airy eggs onto a large platter. Jessie was the first to taste the results. She chewed thoughtfully; then her eyes sparkled. "My lady, ye canna taste the bread, nor can ye see it. How did ye know?"

"I told ye I was no stranger to the kitchen."

With approval shining in the cook's eyes, the twin sisters each tasted the eggs. Their nods of approval lightened her heart.

"My lady, is there anything else ye can show us?" Isla asked as her twin Iona lowered her gaze when Jessie glowered.

"Although I doubt any improvement could be done here, I remember how we split up the chores at home." She looked up at Jessie. "What do ye think, Jessie?"

A puzzled frown creased the cook's forehead. "Split the chores, my lady? Are ye sure?"

"Aye, let me show ye how it can be done," she said instituting the simple principles of teamwork and production that she had employed when she lived as Bronwyn in Wales.

The twins immediately saw the advantage of her ideas and pitched in with eagerness.

Ariana's queasy stomach continued to give her trouble during the day, and she refrained from eating.

When she attended the evening meal she sipped only her hot tea.

"Is not our food good enough for ye?" Morag sat at the evening meal eyeing Ariana's untouched plate.

Ariana smiled at the snide comment. "How charitable

of ye to be so concerned about my poor appetite.'' Morag's meanness seemed to increase when the men were away.

Throughout the dinner and during the late evening, several servants complained about sour stomachs. When two collapsed in the great room, Ariana rushed to their side, and was taken aback by their ashen pallor. ''Jessie, fetch me some cool water and a linen cloth.''

''Throw the ill of body out of the hall,'' Morag ordered, motioning the captain of the guard over to them.

Gavin, the young, broad-shouldered, auburn-haired giant, strolled slowly over.

''Nay,'' Ariana shouted as Jessie rejoined her.

Morag turned from the captain and looked down her pointed nose. Torchlight burned, throwing flickering light on her angry features. ''Ye dare defy my authority?''

Ariana handed the wet linen to Jessie and showed her how to cool their patients' foreheads. Once Jessie had started, Ariana stood up, placed her hands on her hips, and stared Morag straight in the eye. ''These good people are our clansmen and I will not repay their loyalty with abandonment.''

Morag's eyes grew large. ''Would ye endanger the whole village? 'Tis the plague, I say, and these people are evil if they carry it.''

Gasps echoed in the hall as servants cringed away. The news of the sickness linked to God's retribution had paralyzed the people with fear.

''Nonsense, God does not punish His children. He no doubt is watching us very closely to see if our hearts are charitable. If we are to survive this illness, then we must take care of each other.''

Servants knew all too well how expendable they were, and bobbed their heads in agreement but remained silent.

''I will have none of it. Let the peasants die.'' Morag turned to the captain. ''Gavin, take them from here.''

Gavin's steely gaze swept the laird's sister with scorn before he turned and bowed before Ariana. "My Lady Ariana, where would ye like our ailing clansmen taken?"

Ariana thought for a minute. "Take them to the armory." The guard nodded and the sick were taken there. "And Gavin, see to it that any others who come down with the sickness are taken there as well."

The armory was an excellent choice. It had good ventilation and was separate from the body of the castle. She prayed the sickness was not a plague.

The servants retched pitifully as they were carried away.

"Ye will rue the day ye have done this," Morag hissed.

Ariana paid her no heed as she turned to gather her tray of herbs. Thanks to her past life as Bronwyn, and her knowledge of herbs, she immediately recognized the powdered red root of Dragonwort and the grayish bark of the willow. Both were invaluable for diarrhea. Also present were balm and peppermint for stomach cramps, nausea, and fevers. She was pleased that the herbalist was well stocked.

Both maids were running low fevers, and Ariana made them as comfortable as she could. They were losing fluid with their vomiting and diarrhea, and Ariana feared dehydration. She prepared an herb drink of hot peppermint tea, and once it cooled, forced huge volumes of liquid down their throats. Then she made up a pint of Dragonwort medicine and administered teaspoons every few hours. Without modern medicine and diagnostic tools she was operating blind, using ancient remedies to treat the symptoms. But without any idea as to the nature of the illness, she was at a loss as to its cure.

By morning, four more maids and three guards had the ailment. "Help me, my lady," Iona moaned.

"Shh, I willna leave ye."

Isla hovered over her twin sister. "My lady, what ails her?"

"I dinna know, but we will care for her and those afflicted."

The moans of her patients broke her heart, but she instructed Jessie and Isla to give them the teas she had made, stating again how imperative it was to give them the liquids and keep them comfortable.

As the day progressed, a steady line of guards carried in the afflicted and put them to bed. Ariana stretched her muscles. Her back ached from changing soiled linen and making fresh pallets. Once the bedcovers were replaced, she instructed her servants to boil the linen and bathe the ill. Her patients were so weak they could not rise to use a chamber pot. Ariana gagged with the stench, and opened as many windows as she could. Thankfully, a breeze diffused the smell.

When Isla collapsed in the middle of the day, Gavin caught her. "My lady," he said, his face ashen as he laid the lovely young lass on a pallet.

Ariana patted Gavin's arm. "Stay with her, Gavin. I need all the help I can get."

By late afternoon half the castle's occupants were down with the ailment, while those who were not in their beds looked wan and weak. Ariana worked all that evening and half the night, her frustration mounting over the perplexing sickness as the numbers of her patients increased.

In the predawn hours it occurred to her that she was too sick to eat or drink, yet she had not come down with the illness. Could it be food poisoning? She wondered. Then she suddenly remembered the men talking about the sick guards. The shepherds would not have eaten their food, but they would have drawn their water from the same river. The only liquid she had drunk was boiled tea.

The water was contaminated.

Oh, Lord. She frantically looked around at the ailing men and women. What the devil was she dealing with? Dysentery, or cholera? Both were terrible, but pray God, it was not the latter. Cholera epidemics had wiped out whole villages. Her medical training seemed so long ago. She racked her brain, trying to remember each symptom, but her memory failed her. All she recalled was clean water and antibiotics.

Thank God she had boiled her water to make the teas and medicine. She examined the herbs in her packet, sniffing and tasting them, until she discovered one that contained a mild antibiotic. She brought her tray to the kitchen and set two caldrons to boiling. "Jessie, I will need yer assistance."

The rotund cook waddled over and nodded. "Aye, my lady." The cook's eyes were watery and her skin white.

"Are ye feeling poorly?"

"Nay, my lady, just tired."

Ariana sighed, knowing the cook worried over her daughters. She squeezed the woman's arm. "Yer daughters will recover."

"Aye, my lady," Jessie parroted, trying to smile, but her worry showed through.

"Truly, I think I have found the answer."

Jessie's smile brightened and she motioned Malcolm to join her. Arm in arm, the hopeful couple faced her.

Ariana sighed, praying she was right. "Malcolm, from now on I want all our drinking water boiled. Can ye see to that?"

"Aye, my lady, I will attend to it now." He kissed his wife and left.

"Jessie, I want ye to make a big kettle of soup. We will need it to nurse the sick." Ariana suddenly saw small pinpricks of light as a wave of dizziness assailed her.

"My lady, sit." Jessie steadied her, helping her into a chair.

"I am fine, I just need to rest for a minute." She took deep calming breaths to stave off the light-headedness. It occurred to her as the woozy feeling passed that the healthy needed protection. She couldn't remember the incubation time for the disease, but precautions had to be taken. After several minutes, she stood, waving off Jessie's concern as she reached for her herb tray.

"I am going to make some medicine and I want to see that the sick, as well as the healthy, take it."

"The healthy, my lady?" Jessie's eyebrow raised as she hovered.

"Aye, the healthy." She shooed Jessie away, and began boiling water for her medicine. Hope loomed, however tiny, on the horizon, and she felt a measure of peace. In a bowl she ground the tough black root into powder and poured the boiling water to dissolve it. The dark hue was not inviting, nor was the smell, but she knew it was the only antibiotic tonic she could make.

When the cook turned to start the soup, Ariana grabbed a village girl. "Go to the armory and make sure the pallets are changed as often as needed. Ye must make sure there is a good supply of clean linen."

The young girl's eyes widened. "Do ye expect more people to come down with the sickness, my lady?"

Ariana knew the villagers had gone into seclusion, terrified by the plague. "Mayhap, but we have the medicine to fight the illness."

"Aye, my lady." The girl curtsied.

Ariana had expected some rebellion from the village maid. After all, the castle servants were used to orders, but the farmers were not so amenable, and anyone would balk being ordered to care for the sick.

" 'Tis a pity her father is so ill," Jessie whispered as she watched the lass scurry off.

" 'Twill be a pity if any more become sick." Ariana rolled back her sleeves. "We have a lot of work ahead of us."

"Aye, that we do, my lady." Jessie's somber face turned toward the new girls who had come from the village to fill in for the sick kitchen help. "Be quick about it. We have our clansmen to see to."

Ariana sighed gratefully. Jessie had the constitution of a general and the determination of a warrior.

By that evening the men had not returned and the armory had several more patients. Fear for her beloved lingered in her heart as she treated the patients. She prayed Christophe had recognized the disease, and that their band of men were safe. But she could not dwell on her fears. She needed all her energy to handle this crisis. Her eyes scanned the armory and she drew a deep breath. In their weakened state, the sick moaned, their bodies suffering the same symptoms as the others. The new arrivals were as listless and weak.

"My lady, please look at my sister. I think she is better," Isla called out as she lay on her pallet, her hand clasped within Gavin's firm hold.

He stood when Ariana approached, and she waved him to be seated. Iona lay next to her sister's pallet.

Isla's cheeks were rosy and her smile, though small, was present. "Ye look better," Ariana said hoping she had stumbled on to the right cure.

"Oh, my lady, ye have saved me and my sister." Isla clasped her hand. "God bless ye, my lady."

Iona's face was flushed and her eyes bright as she reached out and covered her sister's hand. "Thank ye, my lady, for caring about us."

" 'Twas not I, but the Lord who cured ye."

Friar Peter cleared his throat, causing her to look over to his pallet. "Then the Lord had a good helper."

She smiled at the frail cleric, whose gnome-like features reminded her of an elf. " 'Tis good to see yer grin, Friar."

Gavin's mammoth hand swallowed the lady's palm as he raised it to his lips. "Yer servant always, madam."

Embarrassment crept up her cheeks. "Excuse me." She moved away, walking among those who lay on their pallets in pain, offering a word of comfort along with the teas and medicine. When the last patient was personally checked, she wearily sank into a chair.

"My lady, please, get some rest. We can tend to those who are ill," Jessie said as she spooned some medicine into a sick villager.

Ariana rose and patted the cook's shoulder. "If we are to have these clansmen healthy, every soul is needed. I will rest when I know our clansmen are recovering."

Morag snorted in the doorway. "Ye are a fool." She flung her cup of medicine on the floor. The goblet rolled across the stone floor, spilling out the dark liquid. "I willna drink this foul brew."

Several sick warriors looked at Morag, disgust showing in their eyes, before they rolled over on their pallet presenting her their back.

Ariana ignored the woman's aggressive behavior. "Please yerself. I dinna have time to cater to a spoiled woman. Ye can drink the medicine now, or ye can drink it later, when ye are sick."

Jessie hid a grin behind her hand, coughing loudly to conceal her chuckle, but her eyes sparkled at Morag's chastisement.

A vein bulged in Morag's face. "How dare ye curse me with ill fortune."

"Ye, not I, have set yer fate." Ariana moved to another pallet and helped spoon some medicine down a young child's throat. "Make yerself useful and lend a hand, least these poor kin die for want of care."

Morag's eyes grew round in outrage. "Ye canna mean for me to treat the sick. Nay, I will have none of it. Make yerself sick if ye choose to join their lot, but leave me be." Morag ran from the room as though the hounds of Hell were nipping at her heels.

Jessie put her arm around Ariana's shoulder. " 'Twill be a pity if Lady Morag becomes ill. The great charity she has shown others will be returned."

Ariana chuckled at Jessie, applauding the woman for her discerning taste. Though it certainly was unchristian of her, she agreed. Morag was a formidable woman, and if she were popular with the clan, it would only bode ill for Ariana.

She dismissed the disturbing thought, and helped Jessie and her kitchen staff care for the ill. They changed soiled linen and spooned medicine into each new patient. She slept intermittently, and by dawn the numbers of the sick had increased to nearly all of the castle servants. But the panic that had insidiously permeated the air that it might be a plague had waned with the recovery of those who had contracted the disease early on. They were already on the mend.

Ariana placed a hand on her spine to ease the pain. She stretched and looked around her. This had been an epidemic averted. Her thoughts went to the village. She feared they had also been infected. "Jessie," she whispered. "How many women and children are in the village?"

Jessie scratched her head. "There's a goodly number." She ticked off several families on her fingers. It became quickly apparent that she could not cipher, so as she spoke Ariana mentally added.

"So there are about fifty left in the village."

"Aye, my lady."

Ariana looked at the armory. There were thirty-five people already there. "I am going to take some medicine into the village and make sure those who have not become sick take it."

"My lady, think of yer baby. Ye must rest. Yon guard can see to yer instructions."

"I will rest after I see to the villagers. Dinna worry, dear friend. I slept some last night."

With Jessie pacified, Ariana called to Gavin, who followed her into the kitchen and carried the vats of medicine she had prepared into the village.

The sleepy village had just begun to stir when they arrived. Several women stood on their doorsteps as the guard went up to the first hut and knocked. A young woman opened the door, smothering a yawn. Her mouth dropped open and she stared as if struck by lightning.

"Lady Ariana has brought medicine for ye, Moire."

"How did the lady know we were ailing?" Wisps of red hair escaped the bedraggled braids as the woman stepped back, suspicion covering her features as it did with the others who had left their hovels and crowded in closer.

Ariana knew how critical this moment was. She looked pointedly at the villagers. Then drew a long breath and turned back to Moire.

"I dinna know if ye were ailing, but there are many in the castle who are." She paused and let her words sink in. When the women behind her stopped their murmurings, she continued. "I made this medicine to treat the sick and more importantly, protect those who are not yet sick. If ye do not want to take the medicine, then ye may be joining those who are already abed."

Frightened that she would be denied the cure, Moire shook her head. "I meant no disrespect, my lady."

Ariana nodded. Knowing everyone was watching, she

poured a portion of the medicine into a flagon. "Ye are to drink one glassful three times a day." The silence denoted the avid interest. "And I wish ye to boil all yer water before drinking it."

"Why, my lady?" a voice called out from behind her.

"Because," Ariana said, knowing she could never explain about germs, "where I am from, we have found it protects us from getting ill. I do not know why, but our healer is very adamant about this."

The women looked skeptical, but refrained from commenting.

"If ye would like the medicine, please bring yer flagons to be filled. I will see that each day ye are provided with fresh medicine."

The villagers scurried off, except for Moire. She touched Ariana's tunic sleeve. "My lady," she whispered. "My bairn is sick."

Ariana patted Moire's hand. "How long has yer child been ill?"

"Since last evening, my lady." Tears filled Moire's eyes. "I have done everything for her, but still she ails. She is so very weak."

"I will look at her."

Moire clutched Ariana's hand, and kissed her fingers. "Thank ye, my lady."

"There now, it will be all right," Ariana said, embarrassed by the display.

After instructing the guard, Gavin, to fill each container, Ariana followed Moire into her dark hut. At the threshold, she gagged at the fetid stench. "Open some windows, and let some sunlight and fresh air in," she ordered.

After Moire complied, Ariana covered her mouth and entered the hovel, taking slow, even breaths. Spying the cause, she nodded to Moire. "Remove those soiled linens."

"Aye, my lady," the villager replied as she scooped up

the offending clothes and wrappings and rushed out the door.

It was a baby of no more than a year. The little girl lay on a small soiled pallet. "Oh, the wee one is so weak," she whispered to herself, seeing the lethargic movements.

The mother returned and hovered anxiously in the background as Ariana felt the baby's head. The bairn had the same low-grade fever as the others. "I will try," Ariana said to the mother, knowing that the baby's recovery was doubtful. "Ye must do exactly as I say. I will need my herb tray to make up some infants' syrup. Ye must go to the castle and ask Jessie for my medicines." Ariana smoothed the child's matted hair. "Do not tarry," she advised.

Moire nodded and ran out of the hut to fetch the lady's supplies.

Ariana picked up the baby and rocked her. The poor thing was too weak to cry. "Please, God, help me." She knew the child's dehydration would have to be taken care of, but until she mixed up a lower dosage of medicine, all she could do was boil some water. Once the water had cooled she gave the infant some liquid. After the baby had finished drinking and rested in her pallet, Ariana started to pull a tub from the corner. Then Moire returned.

"My lady," Gavin said, following the servant into the hut. He took the tub from her hands and placed it on the table. "Ye have been up all night caring for the sick, ye must think of yer own rest."

"Nay," Moire begged, grabbing hold of Lady Ariana's sleeve. "Ye canna desert us."

Ariana looked into the frantic woman's eyes, then turned to Gavin. "I canna leave just yet, but ye can return."

He stared at her for a moment, then shrugged. "Nay, my lady, I will stay with ye."

Ariana almost sighed with relief that the guard did not push the matter. "I will need help," she whispered.

"What do ye require?"

"Can ye fetch more fresh water and set it boiling?"

He nodded, and picked up the cauldron to leave as Ariana turned to the mother. "The baby's pallet is soiled. I want ye to scrub it clean, then set it out in the sun to dry."

While the mother stripped and scoured the bed, Ariana removed the child's soiled clothes and filled the tub with tepid water to bathe the child. The poor wee mite lay in the lukewarm water like a lifeless doll. Ariana's heart broke at the listless response, but she quickly washed the baby and wrapped her in warm clean linen to stave off a chill. Once she was bathed, the child's temperature dropped slightly and Ariana handed the baby to her mother. With the baby clean and the hut smelling fresh, Ariana started to make up the bottled syrup by boiling dragon root, cloves, marshmallow root, angelica, and ginger powder. After the herbs had simmered, she strained the thickened mixture through a cloth. Once the dark syrup was free of any large particles, she added sugar and boiled it again. When the thick syrup cooled, Ariana measured out a teaspoon of the medicine. "I want ye to give yer bairn this amount at each feeding."

The mother nodded, and watched closely as Ariana poured the small measure of liquid into the baby's mouth. She brushed the baby's soft blond hair, then kissed the small forehead.

"Ye must not miss feeding the medicine to the bairn," she warned, then looked over Moire's shoulder to see Gavin motioning to her. He was pointing to the door.

"My lady, the cauldron of water is boiling. I will wait for ye outside." His gaze traveled momentarily to Moire and her child, and his expression softened.

Ariana nodded and turned back to the mother. Moire

rocked her child, crooning a soft melody to soothe her daughter.

After instructing the mother about the water, Ariana took her leave and checked on the remaining villagers. Several of the children had already taken ill. She repeated making the syrup for the young, then told the mothers how to administer the medicine and broth. With Gavin's help, she checked the food and water supply in each hovel, and again lectured the villagers on the importance of boiling the water to purify the drinking supply. Then she instructed the women on good hygiene before leaving the village. Once inside the castle, she went immediately to her quarters and collapsed in her bed.

At midday she was awakened by Jessie. "My lady, ye must come quickly."

Disoriented, Ariana stirred. "What is it, Jessie?"

"More have fallen ill, my lady."

"Our villagers?" Ariana asked, sitting straight up in bed.

"Nay, my lady, travelers. The guards refuse to permit them entry."

Head pounding, she threw on her clothes and rushed across the courtyard toward the walkways leading up to the gatehouse. Her heart broke at the sight that greeted her. The travelers stood below her just outside the castle. Their sunken eyes and vacant gazes had the hopeless expression of the sick and dying, their clothes soiled. The adults wobbled on their feet as limp children hung in their fathers' arms and the women cried.

"How many?" she breathed to the captain.

"I counted ten children and twenty adults."

Before the captain could stop her, she leaned over the battlements. "We will help ye."

"My lady." He grabbed hold of her arm. "They are not of our clan, nor kin."

"We will not turn them away," she ordered, staring at

Gavin until he removed his hand. Once free, she leaned back over the wall. "Be patient, I need to prepare lodgings."

"Thank ye," the leader yelled up.

"Ye can thank me when ye are well," she replied. Turning around, she brushed past Gavin and rushed down the stairs. She grabbed Malcolm and ordered him to follow her into the kitchen. "They will need medicine and care." She looked at Jessie. "Can we handle them in the armory?"

"Nay, my lady, we will need the room if others of our clan come down with the illness."

Though her words made sense, Ariana could not turn the travelers away. "Come with me," she ordered Jessie and Malcolm. She climbed to the top of the stairs and looked at the great room. "We could put them in here and use the armory for meals."

Jessie sighed. "Aye, it could be done, but Lady Morag will object."

Ariana crossed her arms. "Ye let me worry about Lady Morag. I am the mistress."

"Aye, my lady. But what will ye do when the master returns?" Malcolm asked.

Ariana paled. "I will handle that problem when I need to. Right now, we have enough of a crisis without looking for more trouble."

After Jessie and Malcolm left to do her bidding, she ran up the stairs to the ramparts and leaned over the wall. "I will allow ye quarters within the castle, if ye vow to follow my instructions to the letter."

The leader, a large, heavyset man, whose clothes now hung loosely on him, knelt down and bowed his head, his dark braids falling over his hollowed cheeks. "My lady, my name is Brodie Maclaren from the Clan Maclaren. And for yer kindness, I swear I and my kin will give ye allegiance all the days of our lives."

They were dirty and travel weary. No one said the obvious—that they had been turned away from other clans.

"Verily, I will hold ye to yer word. I will be down to help ye settle in."

"My lady, are ye sure ye wish to do this?" The captain's face was expressionless.

"I canna turn away sick children, and since we already have sick of our own, we are not exposing anyone."

A small grin appeared on the stoic features.

"Dinna tell me ye approve of my actions?" she asked, surprised by Gavin's acceptance.

"Aye, my lady, I do. Ye have cared for my loved ones."

"Ah, Isla," she said.

He smiled. "And my sister, Moire, and her bairn, Jenna."

"The sick bairn is yer niece?"

"Aye. I will do whatever ye wish, even if I disagree with yer judgment. However, Laird MacGregor may not look so kindly on yer actions."

"So I have been told. If we are lucky, by the time he returns our people will be healthy."

"God willing," the soldier whispered.

"Aye, God willing." She looked the soldier in the eye. "After these travelers are taken care of we will go back to yer sister's hut. If the bairn is strong enough we will bring them here. In fact, if the sick villagers can be moved, I wish to bring them inside the castle. Here their loved ones can take care of them, and we who are healthy can take turns relieving one another."

"A good plan, my lady."

'Twas nightfall before her hospital was completed. Everyone looked to her for guidance. With the recovery of half the castle, she now had plenty of hands to handle the new arrivals. She instructed them on good hygiene, and spent long hours with the sick.

"My lady, are ye not worried about catching the disease?"

The thought had crossed her mind, but she knew if she did not help end the epidemic, she would be in danger of being infected. "Jessie, we canna worry about what may be," she responded truthfully.

"Ye are a brave woman, Ariana MacGregor," Gavin, the captain of the guard, said as he helped carry in the cauldron of medicine.

She brushed her hands on her skirt and assumed a brusque attitude. "Gavin, I think we will have to find a new water supply. After everyone has recovered, I would like to see a well dug."

Though he raised an eyebrow, he nodded in agreement.

She closed her eyes and patted the hand of the child she sat near. Her thoughts traveled to her own child. God, how she prayed she could help these people and keep her own baby safe as well. Terror sliced though her at the horrors of this disease. She drew a long breath. Unlike the others, she knew the disease could only be spread by the foul water, and if they were lucky enough to stop the use of the contaminated water, they had a chance of halting the disease.

Christophe's image swam in her mind just before she dozed off. Her beloved was alone trying to fight this disease. Pray God he recognized it as she had. If not, he along with the other clansmen could be in grave danger. "May God keep him safe," she whispered as exhaustion claimed her.

The captain of the guard gently shook her arm, awakening her at dawn. "My lady, the men have returned."

She came awake instantly, joy in her heart until she saw the guard's solemn features.

"Do they also have the disease?"

"Aye, my lady. Only a handful have returned."

A painful band constricted her chest. "Dear God, my beloved," she breathed, thinking of Christophe.

"The laird is among the party, but he is very ill." The guard helped her up and accompanied her to the courtyard.

"Who else has returned?" she asked, wanting desperately to know if Christophe was among the men.

"Robb MacGregor, Lor . . ."

His voice droned on but she had heard the one name she needed to hear. Thank God.

". . . after the men are taken to the great room, I will take out a patrol and bring back those too sick to travel. My lady, if ye would make that medicine up for me."

"I will do that after I see to the care of the laird and his men." She rushed out of the castle, and her heart broke at the sight of the men. The poor soldiers looked ashen and weak as they literally fell off their horses. Her gaze traveled to Robb and his father; both were as ill as the rest, severely dehydrated from the vomiting and diarrhea, their features sunken, their bodies mere shadows of once-robust warriors. Tears gathered in her eyes as she rushed down the steps, yelling commands to Gavin and his men, which were instantly followed.

"Angus," she whispered, checking him even though she longed to turn to Christophe. But she had a role to play.

Angus tried, but failed to push her away. "Be gone before ye too are sick. Ye must think of the bairn."

"Angus, I am yer wife. Ye canna send me away when ye are sick." She turned to Gavin. "Take the laird to the great room." Once Angus was seen to, she moved to Christophe. His strong body was as limp as a rag doll. He blinked at her. "Bronwyn," he cried.

Fear gathered in her as others took notice of his address. With far more courage than she felt, she patted his shoulder. "Nay, I am not the lass Bronwyn, but yer stepmother, Ariana." Then she turned to the soldier at her side. "He is witless with the illness. Carry him to the great room."

Quickly, she checked on the other men. All were in severe grips of the disease. "Jessie," she called as she rushed into the great room. "Jessie, where are ye?"

The rotund cook stood up from the bedside she was working at. "My lady?"

"We need to bathe the men and get the medicine into them. They are so weak we must make sure they have plenty of liquids. Burn their soiled clothes." The condition of the clansmen frightened her. Most of them were in the advanced stages of this disease.

At once the maids started stripping the men, who were carried in and placed on the pallets.

Ariana quickly disrobed the laird, and bathed him, then dressed him in clean clothes and administered the antibiotic. All the time she saw to her husband's needs, her mind centered on Christophe, who was in the throes of delirium, lying on a pallet directly behind her. His moans and restless movings had her aching to tend to him.

"If ye must see to the ill, woman, leave me be and see to my son," Angus ordered.

Although his command was music to her ears, she finished her ministrations before turning to Christophe. She immediately stripped the foul clothes from his body, and washed the filth from him. But bathing him was an agony. Completely naked except for his golden medallion, his body bore the scars of battle. His massive chest had several long red healed scars that looked quite lethal. "How did ye survive this?" she breathed. The wet linen matted the soft blond curls on his chest as she tried to cool his flesh and lower his fever. After repeated wiping, his temperature cooled. She brushed the blond hair from his cheek, then carefully lifted his head to administer the medicine. He was much sicker than the laird.

"My lady," Gavin said. "I must have the medicine."

"Aye," she whispered, covering Christophe and rising. She looked longingly at Christophe and Angus before drawing a deep breath to face the captain. "Do ye want me to come with ye?"

His features softened. "Nay, my lady. Ye are needed here."

Relief soared through her. She would be able to stay with Christophe. She quickly prepared the medicine and gave Gavin her instructions.

Once the soldiers rode out of the castle, she returned to the great room. The sick from the village and new travelers were recovering. She checked on the warriors, and at their weak condition said a silent prayer. Their symptoms were much worse, but she consoled herself with the fact that the others were on the mend and these were hardened soldiers, their bodies in better condition than the peasants who had already fought the disease and recovered.

All day and into the evening she tended the sick, and was heartened by the recovery of more patients.

"My lady," a soft voice called from the pallet to her right.

She turned and saw Gavin's sister, the woman whose bairn had been so sick. "Aye."

"Thank ye, my lady, my bairn is better," Moire said. "She now nurses."

Ariana knelt by Moire and touched the soft down of the baby's head. "I am glad little Jenna has recovered."

Tears misted the woman's eyes. "If not for ye she would have died."

"Nay, 'twas in God's hands, not mine."

"I have already thanked God, my lady, for sending ye here."

Humbled, Ariana nodded, then rose and walked over to Angus. Finding that he slept soundly, she turned toward Christophe. His head lolled back and forth as he mumbled in his sleep, and his skin looked hot and dry. She sat down beside him and took his hand in hers, afraid to think of the future, afraid to think beyond this minute.

His mumblings made no sense to anyone but her. She heard him speak out as Christophe, a Norman warrior in Wales, then as Drew, a twentieth-century businessman. She glanced around, relieved that the others slept and were unaware of his ramblings.

"Shh," she whispered as she drew a wet linen over his fevered flesh.

His eyes opened and he stared at her with a vacant look in his eyes. "Regan? Regan, is that you?"

She leaned close and whispered in his ear. "Drew, I am here, rest."

He smiled and closed his eyes.

Her hand drifted to his forehead. His fever had climbed. She lowered the linen sheet and began to bathe him again. She could not lose him now. Repeatedly, she drew the wet linen over his chest and arms, making sure to let the cold linen rest on his neck and temples. After an hour his fever once again lessened, and she covered him up. She spooned the medicine into his mouth, and dozed off.

The next morning she awoke with a start. Her neck and back ached from falling asleep in the chair. Christophe's condition had not changed, and the men still had not returned.

Friar Peter, who had recently recovered, was sitting by a bedside and praying. He looked up and smiled as she passed.

After checking on the other patients, she made sure

enough medicine and bed linens were available before returning to Angus's side.

"My lady," Jessie hailed as she bustled in. "I need to get into the cellar to check on the wine," Jessie said.

Ariana checked Angus and Christophe before reaching for the heavy key ring at her side. She was about to hand Jessie the keys when she reconsidered. Only the mistress was entrusted with the castle keys. She rose and followed Jessie out of the great room. The cellar housed the wine and ale. She and Jessie inspected the supply, and brought up what was needed for the week.

After seeing to the food preparations and making sure even the water used for washing the pots was boiled, she returned to the great room several hours later.

She was dispensing the medicine when Jessie entered and left a tray of hot tea and biscuits. "Take time to eat, my lady."

As Ariana raised her tea, a high-pitched scream sounded from the balcony.

"Dear me," she whispered as everyone stared upward.

Morag hung over the rail, her hair askew and her rumblings as wild as a lunatic.

"I am the mistress, do ye hear me?" Her voice was shrill, her movements sharp and seemingly disconnected.

"Jessie, we have to reach her." Ariana replaced her cup and took several steps toward the stairs, with Jessie following in her wake.

"Sister, are ye mad?" Angus called out, but Morag ignored him and pointed a finger to Ariana.

"Stay where ye are, ye outlander."

Halfway up the stairs, Ariana froze, fearing the woman would jump. She frantically thought of something to distract her. "Jessie, go back down to the great room, and take care that Lady Morag watches ye."

When Jessie stumbled down the stairs and staggered

across the floor, Ariana made it up the steps. "Morag, listen to me."

Morag turned so quick she momentarily lost her balance, allowing Ariana to move closer. "Ye are the reason I have nothing," Morag said.

"But my lady," Ariana said soothingly, while taking another step forward, "I need yer advice. Yer people and land await yer sound reason."

"Ye come to me?" Morag swayed, dangerously close to the rail.

Ariana bowed her head, pandering to the woman's ego. "Aye, I am but a newcomer. If ye do not help me, then ye will be hurting yer beloved clan." Ariana slid another tiny step forward.

"Stay where ye are."

"I need yer council, for it is well known ye have run this castle and the demesne with prudence and foresight." She continued to inch slowly forward, her voice calm, her actions smooth.

Morag preened. "I have done an exceptional job." She turned on Ariana. "But no one appreciated my efforts."

"I do." Ariana carefully extended her hand as she smoothly closed the distance between them. When she reached Morag, she saw that her eyes were wild with fever. "Ye will come with me to oversee the castle."

Morag broke free of her hold. "Ye mock me."

Ariana tried another tack. She cleared her throat. "Nay, I do not. Verily, I am lost without yer guidance. Here." She held out the castle keys, hoping Morag would come to her. "Here, I canna handle the responsibility."

Morag licked her lips as she gazed at the keys, the coveted sign of the mistress of the house. She moved away from the banister.

"Aye, I will help ye." She lunged for the keys, and Ariana caught her. The woman's weight almost toppled them both down the stairs. Luckily, Ariana staggered back a step before managing to regain her balance. With the keys in her hands, Morag let Ariana usher her down the stairs.

"I am the mistress," Morag chanted as Ariana crooned soft words of encouragement.

Once Morag was put to bed on a pallet and given her medicine, Ariana motioned for the maids to see to the woman. She sighed as the candles were lit and a fire stoked.

Angus shook his head sadly as he watched his sister fight with the servants until she fell asleep.

"She is ill, Angus." Ariana handed the laird a drink.

He sipped his medicine, then lay back on the pallet as she went to check on the other patients.

An hour later Isla ran over and handed Ariana the keys Morag had taken.

She accepted the keys and smiled.

The light grew dim as night crept over the land. She yawned and returned to Christophe.

"He is very ill," Angus whispered, his eyes grave with worry.

"Aye," she agreed, rising to feel Angus's forehead. Her husband's fever was down.

"Can ye save him?"

" 'Tis in God's hands," she replied.

Angus drew her hand in his. "Ariana, ye of all people have less to be charitable about where my son is concerned. I willna forget yer devotion to him."

She swallowed the lump in her throat. "I will do everything in my power to save him, Angus. Rest easy."

CHAPTER FOUR

Rain pounded against the castle's roof with the intensity of a thousand drummers. The mugginess hung in the air like a damp blanket, enfolding everyone in a clammy embrace, while what little light that managed to filter through the high windows increased the gloomy atmosphere.

"My lady, ye wear yerself out." Jessie brought fresh linen into the great room and looked around at the empty pallets.

One by one, those who had succumbed to the cholera-like symptoms had slowly recovered. After a fortnight, more than three quarters of the villagers had returned to their huts.

"Has the castle guard started to dig the new well?"

"Aye, my lady," Jessie said.

Ariana stretched her back, then reached out for the fresh linen. Thank God, Angus had approved of her edict and taken charge of the digging the moment he had regained his health, putting not only his men, but the Maclarens, to work as well. " 'Tis a fine idea, lassie," he had said, adding loudly for those who listened, "If we are ever under siege, our water supply will be safe."

Ariana cared only for their health. War made her shudder.

Thunder sounded overhead, and she rubbed her eyes as she stared at the candlelit great room. Only several villagers and some of the castle guard who had accompanied her husband remained abed, but even they were already were on the mend. Her gaze focused on Christophe and tears burned her eyelids. Only he suffered the effects of the disease without signs of recovering. She removed a set of linen from the table and walked over to him.

She reached down and felt his brow. His fever still raged.

While Jessie, along with a few servants, changed bedding, Ariana washed Christophe in a attempt to lower his fever. Why hadn't he responded to the medicine as the others had? The scars on his chest attested to a hard, rigorous, life and a powerful body; yet he still languished in the throes of the disease.

As she dragged the wet linen over Christophe's fevered flesh, she discovered Robb's every imperfection. His body fought the disease as his temperature rose. She did not know what else to do for him.

"How does he fare, my lady?" Jessie asked, her voice hushed.

"He is weakening."

Jessie patted her arm. "After I help ye change his bed I will bring him some broth."

Ariana nodded, knowing she must get liquids into him. They carefully moved him to remove the soiled linen. He was oblivious to their efforts. When Jessie left to fetch some hot soup, Ariana spooned water and medicine repeatedly into his mouth. Most dribbled out, but she softly massaged his throat until he managed to swallow some.

"Bronwyn," he called out, his voice hoarse, but audible.

At the delirious name, the guard looked at her and shook his head.

Jessie returned carrying a bowl of hot soup, and also a bowl and meal for Ariana.

Ariana's eyes widened at the amount of food on the tray. "Thank ye, Jessie, but I am not hungry."

"Try, my lady. Ye must keep yer strength up also."

Ariana nodded, knowing her appetite had suffered greatly with this pregnancy. The rich aroma of the thick hearty broth wafted in the air and teased her senses. She smiled; chicken soup, the cure-all of the ages. She sipped a few spoonfuls of soup from her bowl, and had to wait until the broth cooled before feeding Christophe. He took so little, her heart broke to see him waste away with hunger and fever.

Unbidden, fear encircled her heart. What if this was their good-bye? Tears pricked her eyes as achingly sweet memories flashed through her mind of what they had shared together in two previous lifetimes. Like a fast-forwarded movie, she recalled every touch, every kiss, every time they had celebrated their love. How foolish she had been to take even one moment for granted. She took a deep breath as the faces of family they had each known marched through her thoughts and left her bereft and alone. She reached for his hand, needing to hold on to what they had now. His touch reassured her, and she clung to the memories they had and dreamed of the ones that would be made.

Several hours later, Isla and Iona, along with the castle maids, entered to set the great room up for the evening meal, their compassionate gazes straying to her as they pulled the trestle tables out. Many stopped to offer their help and express their gratitude for all she had done.

"Isla, will ye fetch my herbs?" Ariana asked.

"Aye," she said, putting down her end of a table.

Morag made her way to the tables and glowered at those who dared offer Ariana a smile or a hand.

Morag grabbed Isla's arm. "Bring me my fare at once. I am still weak and need to recover my strength." Morag released the twin and pulled her chair out.

"I will, my lady, as soon as I do Lady Ariana's bidding."

Morag froze halfway to her seat. Her hands braced the table as she stood up. "Are ye denying me?" Morag hissed.

Though her voice was low, the threat was clear. A hush descended on the hall as everyone stopped their tasks and stared.

Isla looked terrified and shuffled her feet, unable to return Morag's gaze. "Nay, my lady, I would never think to defy ye."

"Then be quick about it." Morag shooed the girl away.

Isla's eyes darted to her twin, but she stood still, obviously unable to decide who to obey.

Exhausted, Ariana started to rise to handle the dispute, but Jessie motioned to her to remain with Robb.

With her hands on her ample hips, Jessie stepped through the stunned maids and stood proudly before Morag. "Ye are no longer the mistress here." She smiled and pointed to Ariana. " 'Tis my lady, Ariana, who decides what is to be done."

A vein bulged in Morag's temple and outrage lined every feature of her face as she stared at Jessie, her expression lethal. "If ye persist in yer disrespect," she said, jabbing a finger into Jessie's chest, "I will have ye whipped."

Ariana had had enough of Morag's posturing. "I dinna think that will be necessary since she honors me and I am the mistress of this hall." Ariana walked over to Jessie and placed her arm around the cook's waist, showing her support, then turned to face Morag. "If ye persist in thwarting my authority, someone will be taken to task, but it will not be a loyal servant."

Murmurs of agreement softly rose from the maids as they whispered.

Morag looked at the assembly, subtly intimidating each maid into silence with an enraged glower; then her gaze returned to Ariana. Hate shone in the dark depths of her eyes as she fisted her hands at her side. "Ye have made a very dangerous enemy. I will not allow anyone to humiliate me." Morag stomped from the room.

"My lady, well done," Jessie whispered. " 'Tis time someone put that witch in her place."

Ariana raised an eyebrow. "Witch?" she asked Jessie.

"Aye, there are stronger words, but being a good Christian I canna use them."

Ariana hid her smile and nodded. Witch was indeed too mild for the likes of Morag.

She put the incident from her mind, but the threat refused to disappear. Morag was indeed capable of being vindictive. Ariana would have to make sure she gave the woman no chance to prove her vow.

After Jessie left, the servants continued with their preparations. An hour later Morag descended the stairs and took her place at the table, acting as though nothing untoward had happened.

The sound of the servants setting the platters out and the delicious aroma of the roasted meats and hot breads permeated the air as Ariana went to check on the last few patients. They had fully recovered and wished to return home. After Ariana gave them a list of instructions, their families helped them dress. Watching the patients leave, Ariana sighed in relief. They had beaten the plague. Then her gaze drifted to Christophe and her exhilaration evaporated. He still languished with the disease.

It was not until the laird and his men entered and took their seats that Morag spoke, though she talked only to her brother, her tone hushed and impossible to hear. Ariana sat by Christophe's pallet, her gaze straying to Angus when the dinner was served. Though he carried on a normal conversation with his men, she noticed he ate little, denoting his concern. Finally, he glanced her way and beckoned for her to join him.

She quickly felt her patient's brow, and though she was reluctant to leave him, she went to join her husband.

"He is no better, lass?"

She shook her head. "Nay, his fever has not broken."

Angus extended his hand. "Sit. Ye need to take a meal."

She glanced at the meal he indicated, and her stomach protested at once. "My laird, I fear I will not be able to eat."

"Then have some soup."

She nodded. Apparently the laird had noticed that soup was about the only food she could keep down.

Morag leaned toward the laird and again whispered in his ear. When Morag raised her head, her expression was particularly pleased.

"Ariana," Angus said. "I think ye should rest. Ye must think of the bairn."

Ariana smiled, realizing what had just transpired. "My laird, I submit that I know what I am capable of doing." She looked pointedly at Morag. "Perhaps Morag, who has never borne a child, is unaware of the energy and strength an expectant mother possesses." When her gaze returned to Angus, her look softened. "Dinna worry, husband, I am truly able to care for the sick. Trust me, I would do nothing to endanger myself or the babe."

"Morag is only worried that ye overwork yerself," Angus said.

Ariana raised a spoonful of her soup to her lips and paused as her gaze trailed to Morag. "It is very comforting to know ye care so much for me. Mayhap ye would like to care for your nephew in my place?"

Horrified, Morag placed a linen square to her nose. "Nay! Oh, nay, I could not!"

"As ye wish," Ariana said, unsurprised by the woman's response. When she turned to Angus, she was taken aback by the warm approval in his eyes.

"Well said, my lass." He looked to Morag. "I think from now on, ye should take yer lead from the lady of the manor."

"I only meant to help, my laird," Morag whined, and lowered her eyes.

Again Angus turned to Ariana. "Yer devotion to our clan is admirable."

Ariana allowed the praise to pass, sensing there was yet another concern the laird had not told her about.

"What is it, Angus?" she asked.

When his lips thinned, she placed her hand on his arm. "Please, do not shelter me. I am a woman full grown."

His hand covered hers. He gave her a comforting squeeze before he looked into her eyes. "I am going to take the men out to see if we can find where the water has become tainted."

Trepidation surged through her. "Do ye suspect foul play?"

"Aye, I do."

She felt his muscles tense beneath her fingers. "Be careful, my laird."

"Yer compassion is misplaced, Ariana. My son needs yer charity, not I."

Her eyes widened and she nodded.

He patted her hand as his gaze strayed to his son. "I will leave orders for a guard to stand duty with ye."

She started to protest, but he clasped her hands. "I would feel better if ye had help when ye needed it. I know ye will lose sleep tonight, and I canna sit up with ye."

Ariana understood. Angus felt helpless. "Thank ye, my laird."

After he finished his meal, Angus motioned for his men to follow him into the armory. She watched the men march out of the room to plan their strategy for tomorrow, and a chill ran up her spine. This was more than a mere inspecting expedition. As though Angus had read her mind, he gave her a comforting smile before he shut the door. He was not just looking for the tainted water, but for the men who'd caused it. She knew he would spend half the night with his warriors, then retire for the rest he needed.

"Worried?" Morag raised an eyebrow, her face a mask of pure vindictiveness as her gaze followed the retreating laird; then her spiteful expression returned to Ariana. "Ye should be. If the laird dies, yer importance diminishes." Her chair scraped against the floor and she rose to leave, her carriage straight, her manner victorious.

The servants made quick work of clearing the tables as Morag's warning rang in Ariana's ears. She ignored the curious glances and went to sit with Christophe.

Jessie finished her chores and approached her with a cup of tea. "My lady, can I get ye any food before I retire?" Jessie asked as the servants' footsteps receded.

"Nay," Ariana responded, gratefully accepting the hot tea. She stared at the cavernous room, void of patients except for Robb MacGregor. "Seek yer rest."

Jessie patted her hand. "If ye need me, send yon guard. I will help ye."

Ariana smiled at the offer, and watched Jessie waddle

off to her pallet. The only sound in the room was the distant voices of the men as they discussed tomorrow's events. Ariana listened, but nothing could be clearly understood. She could hear Angus's voice raised in anger as she walked over to Christophe.

The guard cleared his throat. "Do ye wish something?" she asked?

"Nay, my lady."

She did not recognize the guard, and bent to feel Christophe's head. His fever still continued, but it seemed no worse than before. With the hall empty, she turned away from the guard's watchful eye and let her desire surface. Her gaze feasted on Robb's dear features, softened in sleep. She brushed his hair back, noticing the two thin braids. He was handsome and wholly masculine in a primitive way. His features belied any weakness, and yet he lay helpless. As she covered his chest, her hand slipped into his and she rested her cheek against the pallet. The soft murmur of voices in the armory lulled her to sleep.

Several hours later, the candles sputtered out and only the logs burned in the hearth. The soft golden glow bathed the room in a gentle warmth. She yawned as the armory door opened and the men filed out. Angus's face was lined with worry as he bid his men good night. The warriors' solemn faces and the lateness of the hour boded the seriousness of the planned campaign. After the last man had left the hall, Angus crossed the room toward her. He felt his son's forehead and frowned.

Angus MacGregor's compassion made tears spring into her eyes. He was a good man, and she suspected he was going off to war.

A lump formed in her throat. "I fear for ye, my laird."

Then his gaze locked with hers and he leaned down to kiss her forehead. "Dinna worry so, all will be right."

Swallowing her fear, she nodded.

His eyes held hers as he smiled. "See to my son. If he were to die, my life would have no meaning." He patted her hand and retired.

The hall grew colder as the logs in the hearth turned to coals and the light dimmed as the castle slept. She remained by Christophe's side, the minutes slipping slowly past as she watched his condition worsen.

She dozed on and off as she kept her vigil. Sometimes she would awaken to find his fever burning and spend endless moments bathing him. But even though she worked to lower the temperature, the heat never left his body. What was wrong with him? The others had not spiked a high fever. Though she continued to bathe his feverish flesh, more often than not he remained in an incoherent state, his weak voice moaning as he struggled with the fever. When Christophe started mumbling louder, then began tossing and turning in the still hours of the night, she became alarmed.

"Regan, the plane is on fire," he babbled, his voice almost as loud as the guard's fitful snores.

"Shh," she murmured, hoping to reach him before the guard overheard. She knew superstition was just as deadly an enemy as the disease.

"I won't leave you; we still have time to free you," he insisted, thrashing his head back and forth.

"We are safe," she whispered, knowing he was remembering their death in the fiery plane crash. At the sudden silence, she looked around, but though the guard had stopped snoring, he still slept. Relief washed through her and she leaned close to Christophe's ear. "Listen to me, my love. We are together and safe."

His eyes suddenly snapped open, and she shuddered at the glazed delirious look within them. "You're not Regan, nor are you Bronwyn. Who are you?" he demanded, painfully gripping her arm.

Terror seized her as she covered Christophe's lips with her fingers. "Shh." Again she glanced to the guard, but he still slumbered. Relieved he had not overheard Christophe, she quickly reached for the medicine. She poured out a dose, but he knocked it from her hand. Determined, she measured out another portion, but again he fought her, causing the antibiotic to dribble uselessly down his neck. "Oh, ye must take this," she crooned softly. "Please. Ye simply must!"

But he fought every attempt she made to medicate him, and eventually she stopped, for the effort weakened him so. After she cleaned up the spilled medicine and adjusted his covers, she rested her forehead on the bed and dozed off with her hand on his arm. Only a small amount of medicine was taken; she prayed it was enough.

The long night passed without any sign of recovery. His fever burned and his delirium increased.

He thrashed about again in the early morning hours, his violent movements waking her out of a sound sleep. The faint light of dawn revealed his face covered in dry sheen.

"Christophe," she breathed, trying to hold him still, but even in his weakened state his size was more than she could overpower. "Help me," she called out, knowing a guard was posted.

Gavin came instantly to her aid from his post at the doorway, and relief flowed through her that it was someone she knew.

"My lady, let me." He easily brushed her aside as he held Robb MacGregor down.

"Thank ye," she said, getting a fresh linen to cool his fever.

Fear swept through her. Everyone else had fared much better. Why was he still so sick? She suspected another agent was at work, but what?

Jessie bustled into the room, setting Ariana's morning fare out before the castle's occupants began to stir. "Is there anything I can do, my lady?" Jessie asked as she watched, mesmerized by the patient as he struggled against Gavin's hold.

"Nay, Jessie." Ariana tried to make Christophe comfortable, but he was lost in his own world of pain and misery. She sighed, holding the wet cloth to his brow. The soothing cold brought him some relief from his fever, and his thrashing slowly ceased. Gavin released the patient as the sound of footsteps echoed from the hallway. Angus appeared in the doorway, and Gavin came instantly to attention. "My laird."

"What is wrong?" Angus asked as he entered the room.

Her head snapped up and she nearly gasped. In the predawn light of the shadowed staircase, the similarities between father and son were more pronounced.

"Ariana?" His head inclined slightly. "How does my son fare?"

"I dinna know. The medicine that cured yer ailment has not touched his. But I willna give up."

As Angus walked toward her, the torchlight played across his features, highlighting the lines about his eyes and mouth.

"Has he been like this all night?" His voice was hoarse, his words strained.

"Nay, my laird," Gavin replied. "His fever peaks, then ebbs." Gavin then bowed to Ariana and returned to his post.

Angus looked at his son's pale features. Robb MacGregor lay strangely still after his violent episode, his color so ashen that he resembled more corpse than patient. Angus reached out to feel his boy's head, but when his hand trembled, he quickly withdrew it. Turning to her, he cleared his throat. "Is Robb's life waning?"

She couldn't respond, and shrugged. Angus had spoken her own fears aloud, and her throat clogged as her gaze dropped to her weakened patient.

Jessie set some hot tea down, squeezed Ariana's shoulder, and whispered, " 'Tis a puzzlement, my lady. He has always had a strong constitution, but every healer who has given him medicine noted that he takes longer to heal."

Lord, could Robb's body be susceptible to allergies? She prayed it was not, for she would be helpless if he was sensitive to her medicine. She grabbed Jessie's hand. "Are ye sure?"

Jessie's face sobered. "Aye, my lady."

Ariana cried out and dropped to her knees beside Christophe. Had she been poisoning him? Tears welled up in her eyes as she felt his feverish brow.

"My lady, dinna fret so." Jessie handed her the flagon of medicine.

Ariana looked at it and her eyes widened. "Nay," she cried, pushing it away.

The laird raised a brow. "My lady?"

"I must try a new treatment."

"And what is that?" Angus asked.

She took a deep breath and turned to face him. "I will do nothing."

Angus grabbed hold of her arms and dragged her to her feet. His face darkened into a thunderous rage. "Ye are going to let my son die?"

"Nay, my laird." She felt the muscles in his arms relax. "I am going to let his body heal itself. The medicine I prepared has not cured his ailment. But I suspect he can overcome the illness with his strong will and our prayers."

Dear Lord, please let me be right! she thought.

Angus pulled her closer, his eyes narrowed. "Ye wouldna still be harboring a grudge, would ye, Ariana?"

Her heart nearly stopped at the soft-voiced threat. "Nay,

my laird, I will treat him as I would any member of our clan who was sick." Her gaze drifted to Christophe. "I could never harm him," she whispered.

She waited for her husband to make a comment, but he did not. Instead, he released her and nodded, then looked to Jessie. "Make sure ye assist the lady in every endeavor. She has the clan's well-being at heart."

Jessie curtsied as the laird grabbed a ration of food and looked at his son a last time before leaving the room.

All day and half into the night, Ariana stayed by Christophe's side. "Dear God, please let him live. No penance is too high to pay," she whispered. But his condition remained the same. He slipped no closer to death, but neither did he improve.

After the evening meal, Isla and Gavin approached.

"My lady, go to bed and get yer sleep," Gavin implored. "Isla and I will call ye if Robb's condition changes." The young maid nodded in agreement.

Ariana shook her head, looking first at Isla, then Gavin. "Thank ye, but I must stay."

Gavin clasped Isla's hand in his and turned to leave, then paused and looked over his shoulder. "God be with ye, my lady."

She seconded that wish, but it appeared the Almighty was busy elsewhere that night, for Christophe did not improve. When everyone retired, she rested her head against his fevered brow. Without modern medicine, her knowledge was useless.

Shadows flickered across the stone floors as the torches burned low in their holders, and the candles sputtered, but still his condition remained the same. She sighed. Did he want to live? "Try," she whispered in his ear. "I know you can fight this off. Try. Don't you dare give up, Christophe." She grabbed hold of his broad shoulders and gently shook him. "I'll never forgive you if you quit."

His eyes opened so fast it startled her to be suddenly staring into his sky-blue gaze. "I would no more give up than I would ever desert you."

Tears pricked her eyes at the solemn declaration. His love and devotion humbled her. Even in his delirium, he spoke his heart. "Oh, my love." She leaned close, her hands caressing the side of his face, and brushed a soft kiss across his lips.

"Aha!" Morag's voice dampened the night. "Wait until the laird learns of yer deceit."

Ariana stared at the woman hanging over the balcony. She wore a shawl over her thin, almost transparent, nightrail. She was a ghostly figure in the torchlight, and her arms flapped about her like a bird losing flight as she moved to the staircase. Her pale hair, usually so impeccably groomed, now hung straight and stiff, like tangled sea grass after a violent storm.

"Who's the bitch?" Christophe asked, his eyes bright with fever.

"Fornicators," Morag continued to shout, her high-pitched voice waking the castle's members. In various stages of dress, the servants came slowly into the room, knuckling the sleep from their eyes.

"There." Morag pointed to them.

The servants stared at Morag as though she had lost her mind. "Look at them! See their guilt!"

When no one responded to her accusations, she glared at the guard. "Did ye not see her kiss him?"

Ariana held her breath. She had forgotten about the guard. He must have seen them. Brodie Maclaren stepped forward. "My lady," he said to Morag. "There is nothing amiss here."

"Ah, she has bewitched ye all."

Ariana didn't have time to ponder why the guard had

failed to see them, but she silently thanked her guardian angel as she stood to face her sister-in-law.

"Morag, perhaps ye would be more comfortable in bed. No doubt ye had a nightmare that seemed real."

" 'Twas no dream." Her eyes narrowed. "I know what I saw."

"If ye persist in this, Lady Morag, people will think ye are unhinged."

"Throw the baggage out." Christophe's fevered voice suddenly sliced through the air like a deadly blade.

Morag's face paled as all eyes centered on her. She drew back from the banister. Overhead a door slammed shut as Morag took sanctuary in her room.

"Forgive her, my lady, she is not well," Brodie said, loud enough for all to hear him.

When the servants returned to their beds, Brodie leaned closer to Ariana, his face a wreath of concern. "My lady, ye must be careful."

Lord. He *had* seen her. "Thank ye. I am in yer debt."

"Nay, my lady, neither I nor ye are held beholden."

She nodded. They were now on even ground. The honorable warrior had repaid his debt. Her thoughts went to the spiteful Morag. Her accusations of adultery could destroy Ariana. Though Angus had shown compassion to his young wife, he could not be made a fool of before his people.

"My lady, I think since Robb MacGregor is the only patient left, ye should move him back to the smaller room. The great room has a great deal of commotion during the day, and he would rest easier in the armory." Brodie looked pointedly to the balcony overhead, his message clear. The armory would afford more privacy.

"Aye," she said, and allowed him to move her patient.

After changing Christophe's sheets, Ariana closed her eyes for what seemed a moment and fell into a deep sleep.

In her exhaustion an angry voice dragged her from her rest. Reluctantly, she opened her eyes to find bright daylight. Two trays rested by her side, and she was stunned to find she had slept through the morning meal. Christophe was looking at her, his gaze burning with a feverish light. "Disloyal bitch." His fingers bit into her forearms, making her gasp as he jerked her against him.

Her eyes widened in fear. This wasn't Christophe or Drew speaking. Rage dwelt in Robb MacGregor's sky-blue eyes as he gazed at her with contempt. "Bitch," he hissed, tightening his grip until she cried out. She wrenched free of his painful hold. Where was Christophe? As she stared at the vengeful mask Robb MacGregor wore, she knew Christophe's counterpart had returned.

Gavin stepped closer and rested his hand on her shoulder. " 'Tis the fever talking. Robb has always had a dark side."

She nodded as fear spiraled up her spine. Robb MacGregor may have had a foul temper, but not Christophe. She reached forward and felt Robb's forehead. The heat emanated from him like a human furnace, his body temperature had risen to fight the illness, but the longer he remained sick, the weaker his body became. If and when he recovered, would it be Christophe who greeted her or Robb? She sighed, and slipped her hand into his. "Ye must rest."

He pushed her hand away. "I will never claim yer bastard."

Gavin's hand squeezed her shoulder as his eyes met hers. "Robb MacGregor was a fool not to realize what a precious jewel he had, Lady Ariana." She nodded, knowing he meant to comfort her, but a chill enveloped her.

When Gavin returned to his post by the door, Ariana covered Robb up and brushed the hair from his brow. His fever raged unchecked, as did her fears. No matter how she tried to ease his suffering, he continued to thrash about, mumbling incoherently. His gaze locked with hers, and the intense wrath within his eyes made her shiver with fear.

"I will take a wife, Ariana. But it will be a woman who can bring me fortune and land, not one who tries to trap me with a child."

Her hand trembled as she placed a cup of cool water to his dry lips. She pitied Christophe's counterpart, but her heart broke as she watched him suffer. Though she held no attachment for Robb MacGregor, if he died, Christophe would be lost to her. "Drink," she whispered.

Robb swallowed but a small sip, refusing to drink any more as the water trickled down his chin and neck. She lightly blotted up the thin dribble and wondered how high his fever would go. Would he convulse? Dread hovered about her shoulders like an ill-fitting shawl.

He slept for an hour; then his features tightened into tense lines and his eyes flew open, showing the irrational light of delirium. She leaned forward to feel his forehead, and he grabbed hold of her tunic and pulled her close. Only inches from his face, she could feel the heat emanating from him.

"Ariana, if ye marry Angus, I promise I will make ye suffer. The very day ye bed him I will make a betrothal. And ye will have the pain of watching me take another into my chambers. Dinna force the issue of the child, for I willna be dictated to." Then he thrust her away, and she staggered back while his eyelids dropped and he slipped further from reality.

All day he lingered in this state. The bits and pieces of Robb MacGregor's life floated through Ariana's mind as she reached for the water. Her heart ached for her poor counterpart. What hell the woman had suffered to love such a spoiled, selfish man. With an exhausted sigh, she held the cup to Robb's mouth again. His lips were cracked, his skin hot and dry, and this time he swallowed even less. Doubt crept into her thoughts. Had she erred? Would the lack of medicine cost him his life?

After Brodie relieved Gavin, he walked over and knelt before her. "My lady, please take yer rest."

"Gavin, I am fine, I will rest here."

The guard sighed. "Ye are a stubborn woman, my lady." He rose and left.

"Aye, I am," she whispered, unable to explain her devotion. Her gaze strayed to Brodie and she smiled, thankful he had taken the evening duty. Under his watchful eye she felt safe. Her hand covered Christophe's arm as she sat beside the pallet and lowered her head to rest near his.

Bone weary, she stretched her back, then yawned before slipping into a deep sleep. In her restless slumber, her dreams began—distorted, nightmarish images of the past. "Get out!" a woman screamed, trapped inside a burning plane. Drew Daniels, a handsome gentleman with white hair, wrapped his arms around her. "I won't leave you, Regan."

She felt the strong arms enfold her; then a fire overcame them. She screamed as her flesh burned and crackled within the searing flames. His screams merged with hers and their souls joined. Horrible pain racked their bodies until they passed from the earthly world, and miraculously all pain and suffering ceased. They floated upward, toward a wonderful cool mist. They hovered between worlds, then rushed toward earth again, entering two bodies whose souls were just departing. Unbeknownst to them, they were still together and had been given life as a medieval man and woman. Regan rejoiced until she discovered the man next to her was her husband. A man named Christophe Montgomery, whom her counterpart, Bronwyn, had poisoned the night before.

Their lives together unfolded, full of trials and tribulations, and against monumental odds they fell deeply in love. They had found passion, but they had died trying to save one another. This time when they stirred, drawing their first deep breath, they lay on a ledge as Ariana and Robb MacGregor.

She awoke with a start, trembling, knowing she had relived her life through her dream. She reached over to touch her patient; his skin still burned with the fever. Her throat tightened. "Don't leave me, Christophe. Please don't leave me."

For three days she never left his side, but no matter what she did, he lingered within the fever's grasp. Each night fell and each morning broke, with no change in his condition.

When his delirium stopped and he lay as peaceful as death, Friar Peter came to administer the last rites. He was a small, thin man who barely reached her shoulders. He moved about the bed quietly praying. A lump formed in the middle of her throat as she watched the good friar bless her patient. Her husband, her love.

All through that day the castle's occupants came to the armory to pay their last respects.

"Gavin," she said, holding her tears at bay as she motioned for the guard early that evening. When he bowed before her, she drew a deep breath to ease the burning in her throat. "Send for the laird."

He looked at Robb MacGregor and nodded, then solemnly withdrew.

Alone, she racked her brain for any memory that would help him. Only one came to mind, and she feared it was too dangerous to try, but as she looked at him and watched his life slip away, she knew she had no choice but take the risk. Though Robb MacGregor was obviously allergic to the mild antibiotic she had made, there were two other families of antibiotics. He could be allergic to them as well, but she had to take the chance. It was that or lose him.

She ran to her herbs and looked over the assortment. She sniffed two pouches that she had overlooked before. They looked as though they might be the molds and fungus that she needed. Saying a brief prayer, she mixed a crude penicillin and carried the milky-white liquid to him.

Lifting his head, she gently spooned the medicine into his mouth. For once he did not fight her. Although there was no way to guess the strength or amount to give him, she decided to give him half the liquid. Then she wiped his mouth and gently lowered his head to the pillow.

"He looks like an angel," Friar Peter said as he entered the room and put his hand on hers. The short cleric, reaching only her shoulder in height, joined her.

She stared down at Robb MacGregor. His features were softened by sleep. His light golden hair and thin temple braids framed his face like a halo. He did indeed remind her of a picture she had seen hanging in a museum. All he needed to complete the picture were wings and a sword.

"Michael," she whispered.

"Aye, the archangel." The friar patted her hand, then knelt beside her to pray.

After Friar Peter left, she sat back down by Christophe's bedside.

He lay there for hours, neither gaining consciousness nor even moaning. Her fear escalated as she again spooned another quarter of the medicine into his mouth.

At eventide Morag stormed into the room. Her eyes narrowed the instant she stared at Ariana. "I am told ye now give him medicine that ye had refused to earlier."

She charged closer to get a better look at Robb MacGregor, then reached down to feel his brow.

"Are ye trying to kill the one person who can bear witness

against ye?" Morag demanded at the same time that Friar Peter reentered the room, carrying his Bible for evening prayers.

"My lady, please," Friar Peter warned, rushing to the bedside. His thin features were drawn in concern.

Morag rounded on the little man. Her thin chest puffed out in indignation. "Friar, how can ye dare to defend her?"

Friar Peter straightened to his full height and stared the woman in the eye. "Aye, I do. Lady Ariana has done all she can to help yer nephew. His fate rests with God, not with her."

Morag's eyes narrowed. "We will see how his father views this upon his return. That is, if he makes it home in time to see his child."

"Morag, he is not dead." Ariana stepped forward, then turned to Robb MacGregor and clasped his hand. "Dinna speak as though he were."

Morag whirled about and stormed from the room. Though Ariana sank to her knees and prayed alongside the friar, her hand never released Christophe's.

He became delirious that night. She bathed him, trying desperately to lower his fever. His angry rantings proved that Robb MacGregor was still with them. Ariana grasped Robb MacGregor's hand, trying desperately to reach her Christophe. "I'll never leave ye," she whispered. "Our love is eternal. If ye give up, my love, so will I."

His eyes opened, and though he looked straight at her, there was no spark of awareness. No recognition.

"Oh, no," she cried, feeling this was the last time they would be together. Tears streamed down her face as she softly caressed his hand. "Listen to me. You have to try. Please." Her eyes closed, remembering all the sweet moments they had shared. "Let him live," she cried, knowing Christophe had asked as much for her. They had been through so much, they could weather this, she told herself.

An hour later his fever broke. His eyes were free of the bright fever and his expression had softened.

"My love," he whispered.

Tears stung Ariana's eyes as she quickly covered Christophe to ward off a chill. "I'm here," she murmured.

CHAPTER FIVE

Christophe drew a deep breath, savoring the fresh scent and clean taste of outdoor air. Two weeks' recovery had nearly driven him mad. He was glad to be out of the castle, and riding alongside his father again. Though his muscles ached from the vigorous activity, he relished the pain.

"We will make camp after we check our water supply," Angus said.

Christophe nodded, knowing Angus had found and dredged where the river had been poisoned with sheep dung, but had not had time to find the perpetrators. Although they now used the well water for drinking, the river needed to be patrolled and protected against another incident.

After another two hours the summer sun was slowly setting and purple and gray painted the sky when they encountered the guards Angus had left to protect the river on the northern boundary of their land. "Any trouble?" He rode up to the men, his face anxious.

"Nay, the cowards have not shown their ugly faces."

Disappointed, Angus shook his head, then turned to his troops. "We will make camp and set off tomorrow." He dismounted and held Robb's horse.

"Father, dinna treat me like a bairn," Christophe said, feeling the weight of the men's gazes and knowing smiles as he struggled to dismount.

Angus slapped his back. "Dinna berate yer laird. Ye would do the same for me."

Christophe's frown turned to a smile. "Aye, Father, that I would, and ye would hate every minute of it."

Angus chuckled. "Ye have recovered yer sense of wit if not yer strength." He wandered off to converse with his guards, and Christophe struggled alone to the campfire. He gingerly sat down, carefully easing out his sore legs. A groan passed his lips as his muscles protested being stretched. Once his legs were fully extended, he leaned slowly back until his shoulders and back rested fully upon the hard ground. With a sigh he closed his eyes to relax for a minute.

Several hours later he awoke. Overhead, the stars shone in an inky sky as the pungent aroma of the evening meal filtered to him. The low rumble of conversation drifted around him from clansmen who had gathered in a circle around the campfire. He yawned, realizing he had slept until his empty stomach had awakened him. After a diet of liquids, the tangy scent of oakcakes and hot cider whetted his appetite.

The moment he finished stretching, Angus quickly thrust a meal into his hands. Though the food was plain, hunger enhanced the taste and he immediately tucked into the meal with gusto. Unfortunately, he could not do the food justice. After only a few bites, he felt full and shoved his plate away.

"Ye eat like a babe," Lor teased.

" 'Tis yer cooking," he responded.

"Aye," Malcolm said, accepting his plate of food and staring at it dubiously. " 'Tis nothing like my Jessie's fare." Then he looked up and his face split into a grin. "Ye were spoiled."

"To be sure." Christophe chuckled, then pointed at the farrier's food. "But in a few weeks, when I regain my appetite, ye best look out, for I will be stealing yer food."

The men laughed and settled back as each man took turns telling a wild tale. As Christophe listened to their accounts, the fire crackled, and a cozy warmth of fellowship spread through the circle. His gaze traveled to each war-roughened face, coming at last to his father. Firelight played over Angus's drawn features, making him look older. *The face of a Scotsman, a laird*, Christophe thought. There was little softness to the man. His heart was true and his soul free. Aye, Angus MacGregor seemed a simple man, but Christophe knew different. Beneath the gruff exterior lay a complex man. His behavior toward Ariana proved that. Christophe knew this man could not be fooled or manipulated.

Lor rose to tell the story of the loch, his bald head bobbing up and down as he described the monster and the ghost. Each man listened avidly to the story as the thick-chested warrior acted out the tale, embellishing the scary details.

Christophe rose to refill his tankard, and his legs wobbled from the long hours in the saddle.

"Ariana thought ye should rest longer." Angus chuckled as he extended his arm for support.

Others listened to their conversation, and Christophe thought of how Morag had berated Angus for leaving them together. Though he knew it would take weeks to fully recover, he addressed a more important issue. "Father, I dinna want to malign yer wife for she saved my life, but I couldna stand another moment of her gentle care." Christophe smiled, trying to relieve the suspicions that could have arisen about her devotion to him. "And Aunt Morag's bickering"—he shook his head—"would have driven any man away."

Angus nodded. "My sister is very unhappy."

Christophe understood. A laird had responsibilities, and any scandal weakened his position.

"Mayhap Aunt Morag needs a change of scenery, to cheer her up," Christophe said.

"I will think on it; mayhap a journey to court would please her," Angus said, then turned and stared into the fire, thoughtfully sipping his ale.

Christophe finished his meal and enjoyed the comradeship of the men. The deep male voices faded from his thoughts as an ache of sweet longing overcame him and an avalanche of memories returned. Ariana was more than two-thirds through her pregnancy, and their child would be born soon. He needed to find a way for them to be together. But he could not do anything until he figured out how to unravel this coil without hurting Angus.

After the clan had retired, Angus asked him to share a tankard of ale. "I have been wondering, son, have ye regretted yer decision?"

Christophe eyed Angus carefully. In the flickering light his father's weathered features seemed more pronounced, tired. "What decision is that?"

Angus lowered his tankard and sighed. "Ye should have married her."

Christophe sucked in a sharp breath. Was this the moment he'd waited for? Or was it just a trap? He took a deep drink of his ale and shrugged.

"I blame myself for yer bitterness." Angus tipped his tankard and drained it. Wiping his mouth with his sleeve, he stared off into the darkness and muttered, "But what is done is done."

Christophe's insides knotted as he looked at his father. "Do ye love her?"

"I respect her." Angus's voice was taut. The line of his jaw tightened as a muscle worked in his cheek. Several moments passed before he added, "And any woman who can win my admiration is a special lass indeed."

Christophe held his breath. Angus had not denied nor admitted his love. Had Ariana unwittingly captured the laird's heart?

Angus abruptly looked back, his eyes clear, his gaze harsh. "I will see ye in the morning." He stood and left Christophe with his thoughts.

His strength barely recovered, Christophe knew Ariana had not only pulled *him* through this sickness, but the entire village as well. It was gratitude Angus felt, gratitude and nothing more, Christophe silently told himself. It had to be. As to why they were here in medieval Scotland and now separated, he hadn't a clue.

The wood smoke curled heavenward as he closed his eyes and took the last sip of his ale before laying his cup by the fire. No. He would not think of Ariana as Angus's wife. Her heart and soul belonged to him. Him and only him.

A smile crossed his dark thoughts as an inner voice whispered. "You are alive and with your love. What more could you want?" What more indeed?

He put the troubling concerns from his mind and turned over to retire. He yawned and closed his eyes, pulling the end of his kilt over his shoulder, and slipping off into a deep sleep. No sooner had he closed his eyes than a dream unfolded. The fierce images flashed across his mind invoking strong almost primal emotions.

Rage lived in his heart as he rode toward his neighbor. How dare his father and Ariana marry. He'd warned her, but still she dared defy him. He was a man of his word. The road fell away as he remembered her formal posture when she told him. He could see the moisture in her eyes, but being stubborn and proud, she refused to shed the tears. How could she push him? Did she not know he would keep his word? Foolish woman! Her pride alone had driven them both to this impasse. The castle loomed up ahead. He had momentary misgivings, but knew he must follow through. The drawbridge lowered and the portcullis opened before him as a premonition of doom settled over his shoulders. He shook off the foolish apprehension. He was a MacGregor, and MacGregors kept their word!

The old chieftain, Laird Drummond, came out onto the steps. His tufts of white hair circling a bald pate spoke of age, but the dark, shrewd gaze belied any infirmity. "Robb MacGregor, what brings ye to my house today?"

"I have business to discuss."

The laird nodded and accepted his hand. "Then let us have our talk in private."

Robb followed the old man into his great room.

"Bring ale," *the laird shouted.*

An attractive brunette entered with a flagon. "Father, will there be anything else?" *She kept her eyes respectfully lowered as she reached for their chalices. Her hands trembled as she poured their ale. Though a timid creature, she was quite fetching.*

"Nay, Cailin."

She curtsied and turned to leave, never once letting her gaze stray to him.

"Yer daughter is well bred, as well as easy on the eye."

"Aye, that she is."

His heart racing, Christophe awoke with an uncontrollable anger and rage. The fury lingered as he stared up at the star-studded sky. Sweat covered his chest as he threw off his tartan, letting the night air cool his overheated flesh. Robb's life had unfolded to him in dream, and as crazy at it seemed, for a brief instant he had again lost his identity and become Robb MacGregor. Unleashed fear flowed through his veins as he gasped for air. In an effort to banish his dread, he threw his arm over his eyes and thought of Ariana, seeking the comforting presence of their loving memories. God, how he missed her. He wanted nothing more than to end this charade, but until he had more information about their lives, he could not.

The hours slipped away as Morag waited for her beloved to meet her.

She rose from the campfire the moment Alastair Frazier dismounted. "Dear God, why dinna ye tell me ye poisoned the water? I could have died too."

His eyes dark, his look nonchalant, he slowly walked up to her as though he were stalking his enemy. "Mayhap that is the only way we will be together. Ye spurned my offer of marriage."

Morag backed away from him. "Ye know I had to raise my nephew. My brother would not release me from that chore."

"So ye say." His finger grazed her throat, his nail pressing her skin slightly. "But a man who waited two full scores for his love begins to wonder why she did not join him when there was no longer a reason to stop her."

"I have labored hard. I deserve more than a thank ye from my brother. If ye had finished Robb and Ariana, I could have ended Angus's life, and we could have ruled both kingdoms. But no, instead ye botched the job. I wonder if I have chosen poorly."

His meaty fists suddenly wrapped around her throat as his expression turned frighteningly dark. "Ye dare to take me to task! Take care, woman. My patience with ye is almost at an end."

Morag peeled his fingers away from her throat, and drew deep breaths. "I have no fear ye will forsake me. Ye would have precious little if ye do."

Potent anger flared in his eyes, but he quickly suppressed it. "Because I waited for ye, I missed my opportunities. Ye will not cheat me from my desire."

Hostility and intimidation were his usual way, but she lifted her chin and met his angry gaze. "Good. We understand each other. I want ye to kill my brother and nephew. I will take care of the chit."

"Give me a kiss to seal the bargain." He pulled her roughly into his arms. When his foul breath assailed her, she tried to pull away, and he tightened his grip until she cried out.

"Do not act like my sister. Either convince me ye canna live without me, or else ye will find yerself alone."

Morag closed her eyes and kissed him with an ardor she kept reserved for her secret dreams. Her hands ran over his shoulders and she nibbled on his lips, her crooked teeth cutting his skin.

He shoved her from him. "Show me," he hissed, quickly pulling off his tunic.

A superior smile edged her lips as he ripped his braies loose, his eyes fastened on her. She swung her hips enticingly, and his nostrils flared. She chuckled seductively, running her hands up and down her own form. Slowly, she peeled her clothes away, feeling masterful as she shed her prim facade and watched his excitement. She licked her lips, drawing out every movement as she removed each garment from her body with achingly sweet strokes. When she stood naked before him she swayed to and fro, touching and caressing her flesh as if she were her own lover. As she fondled her breast she heard him suck in his breath, and reveled in her power over him. Her breathing became labored and she forgot about him as her fingers swept lower.

Suddenly, he grabbed her, his lips wet, his hands rough as he interrupted her body's little private party.

Her nails grazed his flesh, digging into the skin, not in passion, but revulsion.

"God, when ye put yer mind to it, ye are better than any whore I've ever had," he breathed.

Morag blocked out his spoken crudities along with his wet slobbering kisses. She knew how to manipulate him. Nothing was beneath her to gain power. Little did the dim-witted lout know that the moment she rose to her rightful place, she would find ways to deny him.

As he sweated and pumped into her, all she could think of was would he ever spill his seed.

In the morning Angus's men broke camp, leaving their land as they traveled farther north. By midday they rode to a small bend in the river along Dunn's land. It was there that they found another place where the water had been tainted.

Christophe shook his head as he stared at the sheep dung dumped into the water. "What madman would endanger every life along the river?"

"Remember Archibald's threat. It could only be the Fraziers. They have no respect for life or property." Angus said as he directed his horse around the fetid pile.

Christophe looked at his father, feeling a rage well up inside him. Robb MacGregor's anger had returned. He took several deep breaths in an effort to regain control. Though the episode only lasted a few moments, it left him shaken.

Angus pointed to the dung that would take more than a week to clean. "They will pay with every last ounce of their blood for this disgusting abomination." He turned to Lor. "Ride to Laird Dunn and tell him what has happened. We will need his men to clean up this filth. Also, be sure to tell him I suspect the Fraziers."

Christophe felt the rage rise in his soul again, and this time fought against the nearly uncontrollable anger as he changed the subject. "Mayhap ye should send directives to all those along the river, telling them of the poison."

"Aye, and I will have Ariana make her medicine and distribute it to all the clans who are my allies and have possibly drunk the water."

Christophe's concern immediately surfaced. "Are ye sure ye want to expose her to more sickness?"

Angus eyed him keenly. "Why do ye care if I endanger her or not?"

Though it cost him every ounce of control, Christophe shrugged nonchalantly. "Ye said ye respected her."

"Aye, I do. She will be fine." He sighed. "Besides, she is my wife, and I will see to her welfare. None other have that right."

The power of his words robbed Christophe of any defense.

Angus frowned. "The other clans will be very sick by now. But when they recover they will be beholden to us."

Christophe ran a hand through his hair. "If the Fraziers are willing to poison all who drink at the river, then they will stop at nothing to wipe us from the face of the earth." His rage returned. "They must be stopped."

When Ariana received the missive from her husband asking her to check on the neighboring clans that lived along the river, she was only too happy to comply. She needed to get away. Morag had made life at the castle unbearable. "We will leave at once," she said to Gavin.

Before he could respond, Morag pushed him aside to confront Ariana.

"Ye canna go," she snapped, taking the missive from her. "Ye are with child, and yer time is only a few months off."

"Would ye have me tell my lord and master nay?" Ariana asked, her voice cool.

Morag's face tightened as she read Angus's demand. "Let me come with ye then."

Ariana almost choked at the suggestion. "Nay. Ye have just recovered and are not strong enough. I will have yon warrior and I will be fine."

"A lady canna travel with only men." Morag said.

"Then I will take a lady's maid. Mayhap Iona or Isla would like the change from the kitchen and either could act as a chaperone." Ariana pressed her point home. "It is truly selfless of ye to put my health before yer own."

"Now that I think about it, Isla is a perfect chaperone. Isla," Morag called, clapping her hands until the maid arrived. After giving the woman orders to accompany Ariana, Morag turned back. "There, yer honor is assured and ye should be fine."

Ariana smiled. "Ye are, as always, too kind."

Gavin looked relieved as he hustled Ariana out of the castle. "My lady, ye worried me."

She chuckled softly. "Aye, for a moment I thought Morag was going to come."

Isla rushed after them, carrying several satchels under her arms. She quickly handed their bags and collection of medicine to the stable master, then lowered her eyes before Gavin. Ariana turned to see a soft blush cover the maid's cheeks when Gavin handed her a horse's reins. He then helped Ariana mount her horse. "My lady, I wish ye to understand that on this journey ye must obey me. I canna have ye being stubborn."

"Gavin, I am ashamed of ye. I always listen to those in authority."

His eyes narrowed. "My lady, ye will forgive me, but I have seen ye when yer mind is set. From the moment we leave MacGregor land, ye must listen to my counsel. Yer very life depends on it."

She smiled at him. "As if I would not."

He sighed and mounted his own horse.

When they rode out into the courtyard she was surprised to see a regiment of soldiers waiting.

She turned to Gavin.

"I have asked Brodie Maclaren to ride with us. His men will give us more protection."

She glanced around and saw that the castle would not be left defenseless, then nodded and rode out of the Mac-Gregor stronghold. The painstakingly slow pace Gavin maintained because of her advanced pregnancy set her teeth on edge. Even though she knew time was of the essence, it would be ludicrous and dangerous to argue with him to make haste. Instead, she resigned herself to his decision and tried to make the best of it. As they journeyed along the river, she looked at the beautiful land, a great change from her two previous homes. " 'Tis truly a slice of heaven," she breathed, overcome by the green hills and flowered valleys.

"My lady?"

"Nothing, Gavin. I was just admiring God's handiwork."

He grinned. "I have traveled much, my lady. Ye must take my word for it. 'Tis no place as beautiful as Scotland."

If he only knew that she had lived in a country not yet discovered. "Aye, I do believe ye have the right of it."

The first village they entered belonged to the Clan Douglas, a good neighbor and friend. The people there were very ill, and already many had died. Guilt washed over her. She had been so busy with her own clan that she had not even thought that others might be sick. Her heart broke at the sight of fresh graves, the sizes clearly denoting that many who had perished had been children.

Dismounting, she went to work, and immediately left orders that all drinking water be boiled. Those within the castle were very sick. And for those who were well enough to care for the ill, she showed them how to prepare the medicine and left instructions for not only the sick, but all the clan to drink the potion. Too soon Gavin came to fetch her. He would not allow her to stay and nurse the sick, and fairly dragged her and Isla out of the castle.

By early afternoon, they traveled to the second clan, the Hays, who also suffered greatly. She gave the same instructions as she had to the previous clan. By the end of the day she had seen three more clans all in the same weakened condition. When they made camp, Gavin brought her a meal, but she was so fatigued she could only pick at it. Yawning through the surrounding conversation, she finally excused herself and sought her pallet. Before Isla could help her undress, she was curled up and sleeping beneath a fur robe.

The next morning they passed a village to the right. Confused, Ariana looked to Gavin as they rode slowly by the still huts and tomb-like castle. "Gavin, are we not stopping?"

"Nay, my lady, the Ruthvens live there, and they are not friendly to our clan," he said simply.

She looked at the village. The lack of activity clearly denoted the illness had struck there as well. "Gavin, have I not obeyed all yer orders thus far?"

His gaze became guarded. "Aye, my lady."

"Please," she beseeched. "The sick are not a threat to us. Helpless children need our assistance."

He stared at her, and though his expression showed his

indecision, he frowned. "My lady, I canna place ye in danger. We canna trust what they will do."

Brodie Maclaren, the dark-haired chieftain of the traveling clan, brought his horse next to theirs. "My Lady Ariana, there is no danger in yon camp, for they are allied with us."

Her face broke into a smile as she looked back at Gavin. "Ye see, Gavin, they are allied with this fine clan."

"My lady, because they are allied with Maclaren's clan does not change the fact that they will not be friendly to us. Their kinsmen are our sworn enemy."

She pulled back on her horse's reins. "I canna let innocent children suffer."

He sighed, clearly not liking the situation. "Very well, my lady, but ye must allow us to enter the village and fortress first. Promise ye will wait here until we send for ye."

She gave him a docile smile; then the men rode off toward the somber-looking fortress, leaving her and Isla only a personal guard. An hour later Isla pointed to the castle. "Look, my lady."

Only one rider approached, riding his horse hard, as though every devil from hell chased him. The hair on the back of her neck rose as Brodie brought his horse alongside hers. "Where is Gavin?"

"The laird holds him and all the men as hostage for yer good word," Brodie replied.

Her guardsmen crowded closer, urging her to return home.

Doubt covered Ariana's heart as she realized the danger of their situation. She stared at the man whom she had trusted. "Would ye betray us?"

Brodie Maclaren's hand covered his sword. "Nay, my lady, I would give my life for ye."

She had no choice but to believe him. "Lead on," she said, silencing the protests of her guards.

Everywhere she gazed lay signs of the dreaded disease. And although there were barely enough men to man the walls, the defenders could still easily overpower their small party. Vacant, hopeless eyes met hers. "How many are sick?" she asked the guard who took the reins of her horse and helped her dismount.

"Many," the sober voice replied.

Isla stepped close and touched her arm. "Ye should have listened to Gavin, my lady." Her anxious gaze traveled to the fierce men who walked the battlements, their weapons drawn as they faced the inner courtyard.

"Isla, have courage," she admonished, although her knees wobbled. Taking a deep breath, she straightened her shoulders and took her medicine bag. "Where are the sick?"

A Ruthven warrior appeared at the door of the castle wearing full battle dress. Sword drawn, he pointed at Brodie and her personal guard, motioning them to join the men who were held captive in the dungeon. When Brodie hesitated, her guard pulled their swords from the scabbard, and Ariana rushed over and laid her hand on Brodie's arm. "Dinna draw first blood."

He stared at her, his face a mask of indecision, then reluctantly let loose of his sword hilt and motioned for the guardsmen to sheathe their weapons. The Ruthven soldiers easily escorted her men away. The huge Ruthven warrior nodded at her wise action, then lifted his sword, indicating their direction. He walked at her side, and too soon she and Isla were surrounded by members of the clan. The guard silently led her to the citadel, holding the door for her to precede.

Inside the dark and dreary room a fire burned low and she saw the devastation. She gagged at the assailing stench of the dirty, soiled pallets that littered the floor. She quickly noted that very few women were left standing to tend the sick.

She swallowed the bile that rose in her throat at the horrible smell. "Isla, assign some warriors to clean up this room."

Isla's face blanched. "But my lady, they will not listen to me."

Ariana put her hands on her hips and turned full circle. Everyone looked at her with suspicion and even fear. The guard who escorted her stared down his nose at her, as though she were beneath contempt. Dismissing him, she stepped out into the middle of the room. "I am Ariana MacGregor and I have come to help ye. If ye wish to recover and see yer kinsmen do the same, ye must listen to my orders."

The clan stared at her, as though they had been struck by lightning, but no one moved or gave any indication that they would.

She moved about them, touching a shoulder here and there, especially when she saw they tended a child or a loved one. "We have also suffered the disease. I can show ye how to cure those who are sick. It is up to ye. I canna do this alone."

Though their faces remained skeptical, several women stepped forward, and Ariana pointed to Isla. "She will instruct ye with the cleaning of this room." She turned to Isla. "Make sure they boil all the water and change the linen." Then she pointed to the warrior.

"Bring several strong men down from the battlements."

When he started to balk, she stormed over to him. "The women can barely stand, and I"—she pointed his attention to her stomach—"canna lift. I need yer men." When he still made no move to help, she poked her finger in his chest. "Ye have our men locked away, what are ye afraid of? Would ye stand by and watch the rest of yer clan die?"

His face turned red and his eyes narrowed.

"Help her," a woman's timid voice pleaded as she carried fresh linens into the room.

His gaze swiveled to the young maid who had implored his help. For an instant their gazes locked. Then he grunted, neither agreeing nor disagreeing, and turned on his heel.

Ariana swallowed her fear. For a moment she thought he would strike her for daring to give him orders.

When Isla left the room with several women, Ariana rolled up her sleeves and grabbed a woman who carried in a large cauldron of soup. Guessing her to be the cook, Ariana instructed her in the preparation and distribution of the medicine.

The woman listened patiently, nodding in understanding as several warriors entered the room. Ariana waited until Isla returned with the women, who held the fresh linen and clean tunics.

"Wait. Who dares give orders in my home?" A weak voice questioned. The women stilled in their chores and turned toward the voice.

"Come here," the hoarse voice demanded.

Ariana stared at the women as wariness entered their eyes and they backed away from her, pointing to a pallet at the far end of the room.

"Dinna trust a MacGregor," one patient whispered, then moaned.

Pray God the laird was not delirious, she thought as she stepped around the sick bodies and stood above an old man.

His gray hair was dirty and matted, but his eyes were clear, devoid of the feverish light. His jaw firmed as he struggled to sit up. When several women tried to assist him, he pushed them aside.

Her mouth went dry as his piercing gaze settled on her. Though he was weak, there was no diminished authority in his eyes as he looked her up and down in a slow appraisal. "Angus MacGregor is a wily old goat to send his young wife on a mission of mercy."

She straightened under his sharp perusal. "My husband did not send me here. In fact, I fear I will have much to answer for when he finds out I have visited his enemy."

"Ye expect me to believe ye?" he rasped.

She held up the medicine. "I expect ye to save yer people."

"How do I know that is not poison?" One graying brow arched in an emaciated face.

She stared at him for a moment, then tilted the flagon so all could see that she drank from it.

Murmured relief whispered through the air as she lowered the container of medicine. Approval glimmered in the eyes of the women who met her gaze.

"Ye would drink this?" Laird Ruthven asked.

"Aye. I have no fear of the potion. It is meant to help."

He struggled to sit up straighter. "Why would ye help yer enemy?"

His question hung in the air as she looked around the castle. The poor sick children lying on their pallets were answer enough. Tears sprang to her eyes. "Should the children suffer because their parents canna find a way to peace?"

He stared at her so long she thought he would argue; then with a sigh, he lay back down on his pallet and motioned with his arm. "Drink the potion," he ordered, then his steely gaze met hers. "And release her escort."

Murmurs of hope rose in the room as the servants quickly took the medicine.

Relief soared through Ariana that her men were free. She knelt beside the laird, and raised his head so he could drink down the liquid.

But he stayed her hand. "Nay, not until all my people have taken the medicine." He looked to the pallet next to him. "Have courage, daughter."

Ariana shook her head at such stubbornness, muttering, "Obstinate, thickheaded, foolish Scot."

"Aye, he is," the lady of the manor agreed. Then the frail woman turned to Ariana, and accepted the medicine for her daughter. "I am Lilias and we will follow yer instructions." She waved the servants forward. "Watch Lady Ariana give my daughter, Lorna, the medicine."

After Lilias and Ariana lifted the weak girl's head and Ariana administered the medicine, showing the women how to massage the throat so the patient swallowed, the women quickly measured out the allotted medicine and rushed to a pallet.

Ariana moved from bed to bed to check on the patients. The room was in a flurry of activity as servants distributed medicine, then pallets were changed and fresh air circulated in a sweet rush that made breathing easier.

"Here," Ariana said when she came back to the laird's side. "The last clansman has taken his allotment of medicine. Now, ye must."

He covered her hand. "Foolish Scot that I am, I willna forget yer kindness, Ariana MacGregor. My heart and sword are yers."

When they left the village, Ariana rode between Gavin and Brodie. She smiled timidly at Gavin, knowing he was quite upset with her. "Now, dinna ye feel better knowing that yer enemy is no longer yer enemy?"

Gavin leaned back in his saddle and gave her long calculating stare. "My lady, Laird Ruthven's promise is just words. When he feels better he will remember his hatred."

"Nay, he is a good man," Brodie Maclaren argued as he rode with them.

Gavin glared. "That good man could have had us all put to death."

She sobered and drew a deep breath. "Gavin, it all worked out for the best."

"For yer sake, my lady, I hope it did. Yer husband will not be happy with ye."

She had admitted as much to the laird, but held her head up high. "I will deal with that when the time comes." In her heart she could not believe Angus would take her to task for saving these people. He hadn't for helping the Maclarens, but then she did not know the history between these clans.

"My lady, if anyone can convince the laird, then I believe it to be ye." Gavin patted her hand, then turned his horse and galloped forward to lead the way toward the next settlement.

Isla immediately moved into his place. "My lady, I would not have dared to help the Ruthvens, knowing they are kin to the Fraziers."

Aha, Ariana thought, and turned toward her maid with a sweet smile. "Isla, what do ye know of the blood feud?"

" 'Tis common knowledge, my lady."

"Ah," she responded, frustrated, knowing she would have to be cagey. "Anyone can understand why the hatred exists."

"Aye, after what the laird's lady did. 'Twas an awful blow to a proud man. Imagine the pain not only to the laird, but the clan, when his woman left him and their child for another. . . woman. 'Tis a blood feud that willna be ever ended. And the Fraziers knew the woman's preference and knowing it, still deceived the laird."

Although Ariana was reeling from the information, she merely nodded in commiseration.

That night, Gavin poured her a hot mug of cider at the campfire. "I will allow ye to see several more clans before heading the band home, my lady. But we will only see those clans along the river."

"Aye," she whispered, knowing they could not travel to every clan. After dinner she closed her eyes beneath a canopy of brilliant stars and thought of Christophe's counterpart, Robb. The poor man had led a tortured life. Thank God Christophe had not inherited his hatred and pain.

In the weeks that followed, they traveled to each clan along the river and gave them the cure for the sickness. At each place, she stayed far longer than Gavin liked, helping the clans with the measures that had to be taken, and instructing them to pass the cure on to other clans.

"My lady, the laird's instructions were clear. Ye must only share yer medicine, not yer time."

"Gavin," she said, placing a hand on his arm. She tried to rise by herself, but her pregnancy made her movements awkward. "I canna leave them without showing them how to boil the water and handle the sick. Would ye do any less?"

"Aye, I would," he said, exasperated. "But I will help ye, if ye are so bent."

She smiled up into the craggy features. "I am so lucky to have such a friend."

A fortnight later they returned to the MacGregor castle. In the morning sun, the castle looked as impressive as it had when she first beheld it. The sight of home made her breathe a sigh of relief.

Pleased by the success of her venture, Ariana entered the gates, bursting to tell the good news to Christophe.

Her gaze immediately traveled over the welcoming faces, searching for him, but Christophe and Angus were not among the crowd that greeted her. Disappointed, she turned to Friar Peter. "The laird and his men have not returned?"

"Patience, daughter. With God's help they will return as victorious as ye."

"Friar Peter," she admonished. "I am far from a conquering hero home from the wars."

His eyes twinkled as he offered her his arm. "Nay, ye are not. Ye have accomplished far more than a warlord. Ye have merely solidified the surrounding clans."

"I have merely extended a hand in friendship," she countered.

He smiled. "Aye, ye have, and news of yer selfless deeds has traveled faster than ye think."

"Peace, Friar, would be welcomed no matter who brought it about. But we are talking about stubborn, thickheaded Scots, who canna sit at their own table and discuss family matters without arguments and dissension."

"Aye, 'tis true. But might I remind ye, ye are one of those thickheaded Scots."

"Indeed, I fear our lady is the most stubborn of the lot," Gavin murmured as he passed by.

She chuckled. "Aye, ye are both right." A smile on her lips for the retreating warrior, she turned back to her companion. "If ye will excuse me, Friar Peter," she said at the door to the castle.

"Where are ye off to?" he asked when she started to rush inside the massive stone structure.

"I have been gone a long time. I must see to my duties."

"Ye have earned a rest, daughter. The castle can run itself for a morning."

"But I have much to do."

"Stubborn and thickheaded," he said, repeating her words as he stroked his chin thoughtfully.

Again she chuckled. "Ye are right, Friar, I am a Scot, but I would no want to be accused of being thickheaded. I agree to have a small rest before I start my day." On impulse, she leaned down and hugged the short friar before entering the castle.

"Pure gold," he whispered.

After Ariana had risen from her nap, she heard a guard shout. A rider approached with a caravan behind him. She ran with all the women to look over the battlements. Ariana hoped it was news from Christophe. She strained to see who it was, but not until the rider drew closer did she comprehend that he was a stranger followed by an entourage.

Her heart sank. 'Twas not the men, nor word of them. Morag, however, wore a pleased smile the moment she noticed the approaching colors.

"Ye will not be the only noblewoman of the castle now." She brushed by Ariana on her way to the gates.

Ariana watched the gates open and the entourage enter. A young woman dismounted and looked around as if dazed; then her face split into a happy grin when Morag, playing mistress, opened her arms in welcome. "Lady Cailin, ye received my missive. Come, I am so glad ye are here."

"I had an uneventful trip." The young girl stepped back and looked around the courtyard. "Where are Laird MacGregor and his son?"

"On a raid."

The woman nodded, a frown upon her features; then her eyes lifted to the battlements and locked with Ariana's. "My lady?"

"Aye," Ariana responded, inclining her head.

The woman curtsied, her head bowed in respect.

A sigh of relief passed Ariana's lips as she descended the steps. Thank God this woman, unlike Morag, did not hold any animosity in her heart.

"Welcome," Ariana said when she reached the court-yard.

"I am so glad to be here, Lady Ariana. I canna wait for ye to inform me of my duties."

Duties, what duties? Ariana wondered as she took the lady's arm and ushered her toward the castle. "Ye have just arrived. We will talk later about duties."

A broad smile spread across the pale features. "I am glad ye wish me well."

"Of course I do," she said, wondering what the woman meant.

Morag stepped in their way. "Cailin, if ye would like to come with me, I will show ye the castle."

Cailin's eyes brightened, but she lowered her gaze. "The mistress has bade me to attend her."

Cailin's features were so crestfallen, Ariana patted her hands. "Go with Morag. We will talk later."

Cailin was tall and thin with dark chestnut-colored hair and a bad case of insecurity. The girl had a slight overbite that was not unattractive, yet she seemed to scurry instead of walk, as if used to getting out of the way of disapproving eyes.

"My lady." The soldier who had arrived with Lady Cailin bowed before her. He held a missive in his hand. "This is from Lady Cailin's father, Laird Drummond. Since my mission is over, I must return to my clan immediately."

She took the missive and nodded as he bowed over her hand and left. She watched the small party of soldiers mount their steeds and ride back through the gates. Her gaze strayed over the now-empty courtyard, which held only Lady Cailin's trunk. It amazed her that the soldier would not even stay to refresh his troops before starting off again. With a sigh and a shrug of her shoulders, she ordered her guard to carry Lady Cailin's belongings inside. She followed the guard as he lifted the trunk and struggled up the steps, wondering where she would put the woman and what exactly her station was. Remembering the missive, she opened it, hoping to find a clue. She scanned the note first, then unable to believe her eyes, studied it again, this time more carefully. The words jumped off the page, nearly choking her. Reaching out for support, she leaned against the castle wall.

Cailin was sent as a bride. Her intended groom: Robb MacGregor.

CHAPTER SIX

Ariana moaned and gripped the doorframe.

"Lady Ariana," Cailin called out as she ran across the great room and out to the stoop. "Yer face has gone as white as goat's milk. Are ye feeling poorly?"

Ariana straightened and patted Cailin's hand. "I am well."

Lady Cailin hovered, a picture of concern, while Lady Morag stood back and watched, an amused smile on her lips.

"Let me help ye in," Lady Cailin said, wrapping her arm securely around Ariana's waist and moving through the servants who gathered close. "Is there anything I can do for ye?"

Yes, Ariana wanted to scream, *Do not marry Robb.* Instead, she shook her head.

"Is it the bairn?"

"Nay," Ariana answered. " 'Tis merely concern for my beloved."

Morag's eyes narrowed. She walked around her as if inspecting for vermin. "Ye have no one fooled. Yer concern is as false as yer heart."

Lady Cailin gasped as the servants stared, speechless.

A hush settled over the room as Ariana's cool smile met and held Morag's venomous gaze. "Lady Morag, yer tongue is as sharp as the finest sword. But I have no fear ye will prick me. False words fall far from the mark."

"Ahh." Morag threw her hands in the air. "Ye think I do not know that the babe in yer belly is not the master's."

Cailin's eyes widened as she stepped back from the blasphemous words. Several soldiers who had entered the great room crowded in to hear more.

Ariana knew she could not allow the words to stand. Adultery was punishable by death. She struck the woman hard across the face. "Ye court disaster to slander me and mine. My babe is a MacGregor."

Lady Morag covered her cheek with her palm, but neither regret nor tears were evident. "Would ye swear on it?"

"Aye, I would."

The murmurs died down. For anyone willing to swear on the Bible would surely be believed.

Morag stared, her gaze cunning. "Send for the friar, ye will give yer solemn vow."

"My Lady Morag," Cailin warned, horrified by the unfolding scene. "A holy man would be most distressed to be included in this challenge."

"Ye must learn who is the real power here," Morag said. "I raised Robb MacGregor, who treats me as his mother. Do ye really think ye have sided with the right lady?"

The poor girl paled.

"Morag, leave her be," Ariana said. "Cailin is meager sport for ye. By all means, send for Friar Peter."

A servant dashed from the room to fetch the good friar.

Morag paced the floor, and the minute the door opened she met the cleric. "Friar Peter, this unworthy woman has said she will take a solemn vow to prove the worthiness of her child."

The friar looked down his long pointed nose at Morag and scowled. "Woman, ye call me from my prayers for this?"

Morag grew more adamant. " 'Tis important. We of the clan must know if she carries a true MacGregor child."

The friar pursed his lips. "The laird married her. Does he know what ye are about?"

The servants moved away from Morag, distancing themselves from the friar's displeasure.

"I willna ask the woman to swear on the Bible. 'Tis not my place, nor is it yers."

Morag raised her chin, and her eyes narrowed. "Ye are a man of the church and know nothing of the ways of the flesh. I tell ye, the woman is a common whore."

Collective gasps echoed around the room.

Ariana stepped toward Morag. "Ye have shown yerself to be a bitter woman. Dinna pursue this."

"Do ye not see the devil in her?" Morag pointed at Ariana. "She is evil."

"Enough!" Friar Peter stepped forth, his temper sorely tested. "Lady Morag, I bid ye, go to yer room. Ye have been sick. I fear yer bout with the disease has affected yer judgment."

Servants' whispers rose to murmurs of open accord and their stares centered on Lady Morag as a guard ran into the room. "The men have returned," he yelled. "They have wounded."

The women scurried into action at once as the servants ran to see what would be needed.

The castle was in a flurry of activity, but the chaos could

not conceal the animosity that still hung in the air between Morag and Ariana.

Ariana ran out into the courtyard toward the battlements, her thoughts, her hopes, with her beloved. The clansmen could be seen moving down the trail in the valley. She squinted, trying to make out the riders, but they were too far to identify. She did see the litters and her stomach roiled. Men were injured.

Lady Cailin joined her. "Who is hurt?"

"I dinna know, but we must prepare to tend them."

Lady Morag held up her hand. "This is not Lady Cailin's province, and I willna have ye treating her as though she must assist ye."

Ariana turned and stood toe-to-toe with the woman. "Lady Morag, I have tolerated yer belligerent behavior because I know ye miss yer position as head mistress in the household. But I will tolerate no more disrespect." She pointed to the caravan of men. "This is not about ye, but those poor wee men who have suffered in battle. All hands that can help will be used."

"How dare ye!" Morag stood on the battlements, her nose in the air as she surveyed the land and the litters being carried.

"I dare."

Morag pursed her lips. "I. . ."

Ariana cut her off. "I am mistress of the castle and ye will heed my instructions. Now, if ye wish to stay, make yerself useful or leave us be."

Morag stomped down the stairs, muttering epithets that made the cleric blanch.

Friar Peter laid his arm over Ariana's shoulder. "My dear, yer heart is in the right place and I will support ye."

"Thank ye, Friar. I fear Lady Morag is feeling sorely displaced. I pray she will come around when she has time to think."

"I think our laird chose wisely," he said, his voice loud enough for the men on the battlements to hear.

Lady Cailin stepped forth. "What do ye wish of me?"

"Have ye ever attended men who have been injured?"

"Aye, I can stitch their wounds."

"Good, then follow me." As she had done before, Ariana quickly converted the great room into a makeshift hospital. Several times, the terrifying thought that Christophe was injured or killed entered her mind, but she quelled it, refusing to give into the panic. She would not entertain the possibility that her beloved might be gone.

Ye could be stuck in this time all alone, an inner voice warned. She protectively covered her abdomen. "No," she whispered. "Not alone, never alone."

Her child had survived, and she would see that her strength and resources were devoted to the baby. Her love was safe for her heart would know if he was not. Yet even after the mental reassurance, a wave of fear washed over her. Something had happened. She drew a long deep breath. Whatever it was, she would meet it calmly.

The faces around her blurred. Robb MacGregor's vivid image flashed through her mind. The expression on her beloved's face changed; a harshness slashed every line of his features. She stared into eyes that chilled her to the bone. For a moment the impression that Christophe had vanished overcame her. Fear, as bleak and hopeless as death itself, filled her.

"My lady, are ye feeling poorly?"

At Cailin's inquiry the image faded, but not the feeling of impending doom. "I am fine." She directed the girl back to work.

The men returned, walking through the gates, carrying the bodies of the injured. Moans filled the air as injured men were lowered to the cobblestones and laid out in neat rows. Ariana moved from one soldier to another, assessing each injury, then preparing the right medicine. She instructed the women on how to treat each wound before having the injured soldier carried into the great room. Only a quarter of the way through the line, her clothes stained with blood, she looked up when a fresh wave of soldiers entered the gates.

She gasped at the sight of her husband staggering into the courtyard. She handed her tray and bandages to Iona, and went instantly to his side. Dried blood stained the thin wrappings across his chest, and his face was white and his breathing shallow. With an arm firmly about his middle, she helped him into the great room and pointed to a chair. "Sit, my laird," she commanded.

Though he gave her an annoyed look, he complied. Carefully she peeled back the stained bandages, and shuddered at the gaping slash. Her hands shook as she probed the area to assess his wound. Though the laceration needed to be cleaned and stitched, there was no major damage. She covered the injury and ordered Iona to fetch her tray of herbs and a large skein of whiskey to dull the pain of the treatment. Taking a calming breath, she looked to his son, Robb. She drank in his bruised, dirt-covered face, torn kilt, and the few minor cuts and scratches that crisscrossed his arms. Bits of debris clung to his light braids and beard. Sadness dulled his blue eyes as their gazes met and locked.

"What happened?" she breathed, silently rejoicing that he was not wounded.

Robb stepped forward, his hand resting lightly on his father's shoulder as his gaze lingered on the bloodied covering. "The Fraziers attacked us."

"Dear God, how many are wounded?" she asked, staring in horror at the wounded, bandaged men limping into their home, and the growing number of litters filling the area.

His jaw tightened. "Half our numbers."

Angus raised his hand. "Send out the fiery cross."

The term puzzled her, and her gaze shot to Robb's for enlightenment.

"I will send a call out for supporters now, Father."

"Wait. Also send a call to the enemies my dear wife treated."

Her face paled, waiting for Angus's displeasure.

" 'Twas a brave act, my lady. I am proud of ye. Though my son thought yer actions foolish and reckless, I am laird."

Robb's expression turned hard as he stared at Ariana. Then he released his grip on Angus's shoulder. "Lor," he shouted, calling to the warrior who had just carried in the last litter.

The heavyset bald warrior trotted over to him. "Aye."

"Send four fiery crosses out to call our clans and new allies together."

"As ye wish." He bowed, then turned and ran back out to the courtyard.

Robb looked at his father. "We will avenge our men."

Her eyes widened, and she grasped Robb's arm. "Yer going out to do battle with them?"

He rounded on her. "Once our forces are strong enough, we will mount a full offensive." The hatred in his eyes chilled her.

"Dear God," she whispered. Her heart pounded, seeing raw anger and revenge slashed in every drawn line that creased his hard expression. She recalled her earlier premonition, and her stomach curled with apprehension. No. Christophe was naturally distressed, nothing more.

Turning to Angus, she handed him the whiskey, then reached for her tray, intent on cleaning out his wound. She had just removed the remaining soiled linen when Lady Cailin sidled close, her eyes downcast, obviously waiting for Robb MacGregor to acknowledge her.

When he said nothing, Cailin seemed to shrink into herself.

Ariana sighed. "Robb MacGregor, do ye have no words of welcome for yer intended bride, Cailin?"

Angus sat up straighter, his gaze encompassing the shy girl, then slicing to Ariana.

Ariana's chin raised as she looked at Robb.

His eyes widened momentarily, but he took his cue from her.

Two thin braids framed a hard face as he turned his piercing blue gaze on Cailin. "Aye, I bid thee welcome."

Cailin trembled beneath his regard and drew into a deep curtsy before him, never once making eye contact. Before she rose, he had turned and left.

'Twas not much of a welcome, but then Robb was not known for his tact. Cailin blinked twice before her gaze followed the tall broad-shouldered warrior as he marched out of the great room.

The tension mounted within Ariana, and pinpricks of darkness flashed before her eyes as a light-headedness rushed through her, but the moans of the wounded captured her attention. Taking a deep breath to stave off the dizziness, she picked up the needle and thread. "Gavin, help us," she called out to the captain of the guard. He directed several men to follow him as he moved through the great room.

Angus stayed her hand, his gaze searching hers. "Lass, are ye all right?"

She nodded, afraid to trust her voice.

He smiled and patted her hand. "My wife is an extraordinary woman," he whispered, then raised his skein of whiskey and finished the entire contents. "Another," he barked. He raised the second skein and drained that one as quickly as he had the first. "Begin," he ordered, his voice thick from the harsh drink.

Before she could start, his gaze captured hers. His whiskey-glazed eyes held trust and understanding before the lids slipped down and his head lolled forward.

The moment he succumbed to sleep, she motioned for the servants to lay him on the pallet.

Gavin and the two servants held him as Cailin wiped the wound clean so Ariana could stitch it. She raised the needle above Angus's wound and prayed in earnest.

He had lost much blood, but the wound was not as deep as she had first thought. She swallowed her fear and pierced his flesh. Slowly, the gaping edges came together beneath her skilled efforts, but each pull of the thread brought her stomach closer to heaving. By the time she was finished, her hands trembled.

Angus lay unconscious, and she thanked God he had not awakened during the painful procedure. She examined him for broken bones or other injuries and fortunately found none. 'Twas the loss of blood and the grueling ride home that had sapped his strength. After she carefully placed a salve of her own making over his wound, she wrapped a clean bandage around his chest. The white linen stood out on the bronzed skin of his chest. Though he rested, helpless was not a word she associated with this man. He would, she knew, be up as soon as the effects of the whiskey wore off. She covered him with a light tartan wrap and brushed the white-streaked hair from his brow to place a soft kiss. The similarities between father and son struck her. She closed her eyes. This could easily have been Robb, but she pushed the thought from her mind. Robb MacGregor had survived the raid. Her gaze surveyed the room. Taking a deep breath, she rose. There were other men to attend.

Just as she washed and wiped her hands on a clean linen, a frantic voice rang through the air.

"Malcolm!" Jessie cried out, running to her husband,

who was being carried in on a litter. "What have ye gone and done to yerself now?"

Isla and Iona rushed over to their mother, their faces lined with concern.

The silver-bearded warrior was carried through the great room and placed next to the laird before the hearth. Ariana felt her stomach roil at the sight that greeted her.

A broken lance pierced the leg of the man who had first carried her into the castle. Even though his face twisted in pain, he balanced himself up on his elbows in order to stare at his wife. "Dinna carry on so, woman," he ordered, his voice gruff.

Ignoring him, Jessie looked at Ariana and wrung her hands before her ample chest. "My lady, would ye look at his leg?"

"Aye," Ariana said, handing the linen cloth to Cailin.

"What think ye? Is it bad?" Jessie hovered near, her anxious gaze darting between her husband and Ariana. Isla and Iona peered closer to see the wound.

Ariana's heart lurched at the injury. She tenderly probed the flesh, trying to ascertain the true extent of the damage. Fortunately, the bone was not shattered, but the muscles and tendons were sliced clean through. His leg was severely injured. She had suffered her own hell with a limp in a prior life. Some scars never healed. Dismissing the disturbing memories, she turned back to Jessie. "We will have to remove the blade, clean the wound, then stitch it. He is very lucky the blade did not pierce the bone."

Jessie blanched.

" 'Tis not serious," Ariana said to alleviate the woman's fear. Iona and Isla patted their mother's arm.

"Father will be fine, Mother," Iona said.

"Aye, we will be near if ye need us," Isla finished, and the twins returned to the men that needed treatment.

Tears pooled in the cook's eyes as she nodded, trying to be brave.

"Dinna fash so," Malcolm admonished, but his hand covered Jessie's and he gave it a gentle squeeze as the warriors moved away from the litter. "The witless Fraziers canna even kill their enemies."

"Hush now," Jessie reprimanded. " 'Tis senseless ye are if ye think I find humor in this."

He took his wife's hand in his. "Now Jessie, me love, all is fine. Ye will quit yer worrying or I will send ye away."

She nodded. "Ye are a hard man."

"Aye, but I will no have ye worrying over a scratch."

Ariana smiled, seeing the close bond between them. She handed him a full tankard of whiskey. "Dinna leave a drop," she admonished.

He grinned, "My lady, may I obey all yer commands so willingly." He winked at his wife, before he tipped the tankard.

Once the warrior slipped into unconsciousness, Ariana immediately started the procedure to mend the mangled muscles and torn ligaments. Cailin handed her whatever she needed and kept the wound clear. More than once, Ariana's hands shook when she rethreaded the maze of twisted flesh. She took several deep gulps of air to steady herself, then continued. When she had looped the last stitch, she sank to her knees, her tunic stained with blood. Her eyes misted over and she patted the fallen soldier's hand. "Rest easy," she whispered. "And pray God I did the right thing."

Cailin blanched at the sight of the soiled linen, and stepped daintily away from the bloody rags.

Gavin helped Ariana to her feet. "I will clean the mess, my lady."

Noticing Cailin's squeamishness, Ariana allowed Gavin to dispose of the soiled linen while she finished bandaging

Malcolm. Once done, she thanked Cailin for her help, then stumbled over to the table and sank into a chair.

Gavin knelt before her. "My lady, please seek yer rest. I will send for ye if ye are needed."

"Nay, I will rest when I am assured all the men are comfortable."

His lips thinned, and he waved for the friar to join them.

"Gavin is right, my daughter," the friar said. "Ye must seek yer rest."

When she refused again, Friar Peter pulled Gavin aside. "Robb MacGregor is the only man besides the laird who can make her rest."

Gavin nodded, and went to search for Robb as the friar walked back to the lady.

Though Malcolm's leg would need tending, Ariana was more concerned about infection. Of all the men injured only two were seriously wounded: Laird Angus and their farrier, Malcolm the blacksmith. And of those two, Malcolm's was the greater injury.

"I want several things done," Ariana said, grabbing Iona as the maid rushed by. "Ye and Isla must set two big cauldrons to boil. Do ye remember the herbs I used when the sickness descended on the castle?"

Iona bobbed her head.

"Good, then prepare that potion and bring it to me. All the men must drink the medicine," she said.

She linked her arm with the friar's. "Father, please see to their spiritual well-being while I see to their wounds."

"Aye, daughter. Together we are a formidable team."

She paused and stared at the cleric; his words of acceptance startled her. She fought the tightness that suddenly constricted her chest. "Aye, that we are." Blinking away the sudden moisture, she let her gaze travel over the wounded men. Suddenly, the futility of war washed over her. "Friar Peter," she rasped. "While ye are praying for the sick, add some prayers for the clan. I dinna like the sound of this raid."

He nodded solemnly. " 'Tis the way of it. If one side attacks, then the other retaliates. The fighting never ends."

The shameful waste hit her as she heard the moans of the injured men. "Is there nothing that can be done?"

"Lass, peace in Scotland would take a miracle. But miracles do happen."

"Do ye think God will send a miracle before the men go to meet the Fraziers?"

"Lady Ariana," he admonished. "We are the miracle. Without us, who would stay the Fraziers from their abominations?"

She shook her head. Only a Scottish cleric would see their clan as an instrument of the Lord. And who was she to say they weren't? But mayhap in time she could influence the good friar into delivering a sermon on the merits of beating their swords into plowshares, and their spears into pruning hooks.

Cailin sniffed the potion warily, as Iona and Isla began ladling out the cure.

Ariana put her arm around the young girl's back. " 'Tis very strong, watch me." She measured out a half a cup and held up a soldier's head so he could sip the medicine. Then she handed the cup to Cailin and watched her pour out the allotted liquid and administer it.

Satisfied that Cailin knew how to proceed, Ariana picked up her medicine and walked with Friar Peter down the row. She stumbled twice as she moved from patient to patient, and the cleric's strong arm kept her from falling. When Friar Peter noticed Robb MacGregor standing in the entrance, relief covered his features.

Robb MacGregor rushed across the room, took the medicine from her hand, and handed it to Cailin. Then, without warning, he scooped Ariana up into his arms. "My father would want ye to take care of his wee bairn."

Cailin gasped at the sight of her determined fiancé holding the mistress. She stumbled away from her patient, thrusting the medicine into Isla's hands.

"Friar Peter, help me." Ariana struggled in Christophe's arms. "I must see to those who need me."

Friar Peter ignored her while he blessed the warrior, then turned away with a grin.

"I can dispense this, my lady," Isla said, holding up the antibiotic.

Ariana shook her head. "But—"

"No excuses. Ye will rest." As Robb carried her through the castle and up the deserted hallway, she rested her head against his broad shoulder. She was so tired, and it felt so good to be taken care of for a change. Her child kicked, and she covered her stomach.

"Did ye feel that?" she whispered.

He shook his head.

"Oh, Christophe, what are we to do?"

He cradled her in the warmth of his embrace, and though it was comforting, it was far from what she needed.

"Let me worry about it. Ye need to rest and recover for yerself and our child. And . . ." He paused, his features growing tense. "From now on I want ye to stay in the safety of the castle."

She swallowed, knowing exactly what angered him. "I couldna leave the sick to die."

He sighed. "I know. But I was powerless to help ye." His eyes clouded over with agony. "I lived a thousand deaths when Angus sent ye on that mercy mission."

She touched his cheek. "I was never in any danger," she lied to ease his pain.

He quickly opened her chamber, and once they were

behind the security of the thick door, he lowered her to her feet and his lips met hers. The moment the kiss began, her worries ceased. She took solace within the strong reassurance of his arms. For now stolen embraces and forbidden kisses were all they could have.

"God, how I worried about ye. I need ye by my side," he rasped heatedly.

His words filled her with hope.

He cradled her face. "I will find a way." He kissed her again, his desire evident as his tongue mated with hers. The kiss was hard, carnal, and ended way too soon. Breathing hard, he lifted his face. "I must go."

His eyes held a longing that thrilled her, and reluctantly she slipped her hands down from around his neck, letting her nails trail over his chest and catch his medallion. He stilled her fingers. "Witch," he breathed, stealing another kiss before he tore away from her.

CHAPTER SEVEN

She slept soundly for hours, and when she awoke her spirits were refreshed. She had to trust her beloved. Taking care to look her best, she brushed her long hair until it shone, letting the red curls trail down her back. The end of summer made her choice of gowns simple, a lightweight lavender tunic over a white smock, both of which flowed loosely to conceal her burgeoning figure. She eyed her reflection critically as she turned before the polished metal. By her calculations, if she carried her counterpart's child, she was seven months pregnant, but if she carried her own, she was eight months along. Her size indicated the latter, and she cherished a secret hope as she patted her middle. "Soon, my little angel, I will have ye in my arms." A warmth of pleasure and strength overwhelmed her. She could face anything.

She opened her door and stepped carefully down the darkened hall. Odd that the candles and torches were not lit. But with the men's return, perhaps the routine had

been interrupted. In the unlit hall, the cold stone walls
and drafts chilled her to the bone. Suddenly, a shiver, one
that had nothing to do with the dank castle, climbed up
her arms. Evil lurked somewhere near. She could feel it.
Her steps echoed in the dim corridors and none other
sounded. "Stop it," she admonished. "You're letting your
imagination run wild." Her unease persisted, but she swallowed her fear and hurried toward the staircase. As she
was about to turn the corner to the long winding staircase,
she felt hands on her back and she tipped precariously
forward from the hard push. Footsteps echoed in her mind
as she careened forward toward the deep descent.

Hands flaying, she screamed. Her shriek echoed in the
silence as she stumbled headlong toward certain death.
Her heart pounded in her ears as she twisted her body,
trying to protect her unborn child. All her dreams, all her
hopes passed in her mind and she cried out at the futility
of it all. Then just as suddenly, a pair of strong arms caught
her before she hit the hard stone steps.

"My lady! Are ye all right?"

Tears in her eyes, she looked up into Gavin's concerned
features. "Thank God," she whispered, gasping for air as
her heart raced.

He gently helped her stand, holding her until she found
her balance. When he started to pull away, she clutched
his tunic. "Good God, Gavin, I was pushed."

Gavin's expression froze. "Wait here, my lady." He dis-
entangled her hands and charged by her, but darkness
and an empty hall greeted his ascent.

"Who could have done this?" she whispered. An eerie
premonition engulfed her. *Her counterpart had been pushed
over a cliff.* She trembled. The killer was here, the killer
was close.

Terror edged up her spine as she waited for Gavin. She
had heard the assailant's footsteps, and a chill encom-

passed her as she relived the terrifying moment. The minutes seemed endless and she hugged herself to stave off her fear.

When Gavin finally returned, relief washed over her.

He walked toward her, shaking his head. "Let me escort ye downstairs, my lady." His face solemn, he took her arm and led the way down to the lower level.

"Gavin, I thank God ye were there."

"Aye, my lady. 'Tis luck indeed, for I normally do not check on the tower guards, but my men are still busy."

As they neared the bottom, Ariana began to tremble again. She looked back up the steep incline and knew she would not have survived the fall.

"My lady, ye need a guard reinstated to watch ye day and night."

She did not argue, knowing he was right. Her accident had coincided with the return of the clansmen. Could it be that her counterpart's killer was among the men? She prayed she was wrong.

At the bottom of the stairs Gavin called Brodie and his man over. He pointed to the soldier. "Watch the stairs and take note of anyone who passes." Then he looked to Brodie. "Ye will not desert the lady's side until ye are relieved. An attempt was made on her life."

Gavin led her into the great room, to a chair just inside the entrance, then bowed before leaving her. Brodie took his position behind her.

Gavin grabbed another soldier. "Fetch Robb Mac-Gregor," he commanded, then motioned for another soldier to follow him up the stairs.

Her gaze took in the clan members within the room. Who was missing? The killer had to be abovestairs. She stared at the occupants, trying to memorize faces and discern who was absent. Servants bustled about and warriors talked to the wounded, while waiting for the evening meal.

Too many people circulated around the room, and in the confusion her concentration waned. She rubbed her arms, trying to stave off the frightening effects of the near accident. Restless, she rose, but Brodie placed a hand on her shoulder.

"Please, I only wish to check on the ill."

Brodie nodded and accompanied her.

She walked across the great room to the hearth to find Malcolm still asleep. Iona and Isla sat by their father. Angus napped, and she quietly covered him and moved through the room, checking on each patient. To some she gave water, and to others she merely offered a word or two. By the time she reached the entrance to the great room, she had seen over fifty men.

Cailin hurriedly crossed the room, her eyes wide as she joined her. "What happened?" she whispered. "The servants say ye were pushed."

Ariana sighed, seeing the avid curiosity. "I . . ." She stopped when the doors swung open.

Robb MacGregor rushed into the room. He talked to the guard posted at the bottom of the stairs. Satisfied, he entered the great room. His eyes took in her shaken condition. "My lady, are ye all right?"

"Aye, but 'twas a scare."

Cailin had been very animated until she saw Robb; then her features sobered. She curtsied before him, drawing attention to herself.

"My lady," Robb said, offering his arm.

Cailin rose from her bow and rested her hand on his arm as her eyes met his.

Seeing Cailin's pathetic trepidation burdened Ariana's heart, but the sight of the woman hanging onto her beloved bothered her more. Excusing herself, she went to check again on Angus. This time she found him awake. He rested comfortably by the fire along with the other patients,

unaware of the intrigue. She walked around making sure
her instructions were being observed, then sat beside her
husband. With a heavy heart, she picked up his hand.
"How do ye fare tonight, my laird?"

"No doubt better than ye." He patted her hand, and
his gaze strayed to his son.

She raised an eyebrow, trying to bluff her way through
his concern. She took a deep breath.

"Courage," he warned.

She smiled, though her throat tightened as she watched
her beloved noticing his betrothed. When Robb Mac-
Gregor smiled at his fiancée, the band around Ariana's
chest constricted further. Her eyes burned, and she drew
another deep breath.

"He is a fool," Angus's voice rasped. "But ye know that."

"Knowing it doesna make it easier." She looked at
Angus, his compassionate expression a welcome balm.
Though it was shameless to draw strength from an injured
man, she did.

His smile flowed over her like an ocean of relief. "Ye
are the special flower in this castle, have faith."

"Faith is all I have left," she breathed.

Suddenly, footsteps marched down the steps. A guard
herded Lady Morag into the great room.

"What mischief is about here?" Robb MacGregor asked.

The guard pushed Lady Morag forward. "She is the only
person upstairs, besides the tower guards, and they are
within sight of each other. Both men vouched for their
whereabouts."

The guard bowed before Robb, but Lady Morag's features thinned as she stared defiantly at her nephew.

"What is going on?" Angus asked.

Ariana helped him sit up. "Someone tried to push me
down the stairs. Gavin caught me, but could not find the
culprit."

Angus's gaze went to his sister. "Sister?"

Morag faced him, her eyes shining with indignation. "Stop this at once, Angus."

Robb took a step closer. His features tight, his eyes cold. "Ye are the only one upstairs. Lady Ariana was pushed from behind. How do ye explain that?"

"I have nothing to explain. Mayhap the lady tripped," she declared disdainfully.

He rounded on her. "Ye expect us to believe ye."

She stumbled back, but quickly gathered her composure. "Robb, dinna talk to me in such a manner. Since Lady Ariana's arrival I have suffered untold indignities."

"Robb," Gavin hailed as he ran down the stairs; in his hand hung a long coil of hemp. The thick rope slapped against his leg as he marched across the great room to whisper in Robb's ear.

For an instant, a smug smile reached Morag's eyes, but the expression vanished so quickly Ariana thought it a trick of light.

Robb accepted the rope from Gavin. "It appears, Aunt Morag, that another was responsible for the accident."

She sniffed delicately. "Is that an apology?"

He snorted with disbelief as he walked around her. "Until the culprit is caught I owe ye nothing."

"Angus!" She turned toward her brother.

"Robb—"

"Father." Robb cut off his father's response, and held up the rope. "Though the knave has fled"—he emphasized the last word, then faced Morag—"he could not go unnoticed."

Angus groaned as he leaned forward. "Son, yer Aunt Morag deserves yer apology."

"Did I neglect to tell ye the rope was found tied to her window?"

Angus's eyes narrowed. "Was it?"

"Aye," he said slowly, as he turned to face his aunt. "Did ye see anything, Aunt?"

Her gaze darted between her brother and nephew. "Nay."

Robb MacGregor shook his head. "I find it difficult to believe ye have no knowledge of this."

Her face blanched. "I am a heavy sleeper," she stammered.

"Really?"

Her frantic gaze settled on the guard. "Yer man had to awaken me."

He turned to his guard.

"Aye, she was fast asleep."

At his confirmation, Morag turned back to her brother. "Angus, am I not yer sister?" She dabbed at the corner of her eye. "Have I not served the clan loyally for years?"

Angus sighed and leaned back into his pillow. "Morag, ye canna fault yer nephew for being suspicious. He only has Lady Ariana's best interest at heart." Then he turned to his son. "Robb, I venture whoever gained entry to the castle hid in Morag's room until he could strike. If she was guilty, the rope would have been pulled up and hidden after the varlet escaped."

The logic was indisputable, and Morag once again regained her composure. "May I return to my room?"

Angus waved her away, then looked at his son. "Robb, question the sentries."

Robb stepped closer to his father. "I dinna believe her."

"She may be involved, but ye will need far more proof than weak suspicions. She has served the clan for years and though she can be cantankerous, many would take offense to her being accused of betrayal."

"Aye, Father, but her bitterness at yer marriage grows." He sighed. "I will question the guards, but I fear it will be futile. An alarm would have been raised if an intruder climbed down the wall."

The words hung in the air. The validity was indisputable.

"No matter, my wee wife is safe," Angus's voice rang out. "Assign a permanent guard to my wife, and this time make sure she has protection at all times."

"Aye, Father. I will also increase our castle sentries. If the man has managed to breach our defenses, then we will have to tighten our efforts." Robb rose and gave his father's shoulder a comforting squeeze. "Rest, Father. I will take care of this."

Ariana felt a shiver take hold. She rubbed her arms, and noticed that poor Cailin stood petrified in the middle of the room, her eyes wide, her face white. Though this woman presented a threat to Ariana's happiness, she knew Cailin was not the instigator of trouble, but an innocent pawn. Ariana again pulled up the covers around Angus's chest, then walked over to the frightened woman and clasped her cold hands.

Cailin's features relaxed, but her grip tightened and she painfully clung to Ariana.

Brodie took his position beside Ariana. She looked at him and could not hide her fear. His hand covered his sword to silently reassure her.

Robb checked the defenses. He stared at his aunt's window from the battlements. Though it was partially shadowed at dusk, it still could be seen from the guard's post. He conceded it was possible that an intruder had breached the defenses, but his suspicion centered on his Aunt Morag. Bits and pieces of his counterpart's life drifted through his mind, and the harsh memories did not endear him to the woman. But he had no solid proof. His father had agreed to send the woman to court. No doubt that would occur after the wedding celebration. He drew in a deep breath. The wedding. Lord, what would he do now?

He pushed the unsettling thought from his mind. He had a great deal of work to do today. He marched the whole length of the walkways, noticing where their defenses could be strengthened. Once he had seen to their protection, he made up a duty roster and gave the sentries their schedules. Some would have to pull longer shifts with the under-manned staff. He considered putting Brodie Maclaren in charge of a walkway detail, but hesitated. The man had sworn an allegiance only to Ariana, not the clan. Robb had loyal kinsmen around, and would wait to see Maclaren's mettle. After the immediate defenses were reinforced, he sent a hunting party out to restock the meat reserve in the larder. By nightfall he was assured that their water was safe, their food supply adequate, and the defenses strong. He took one last turn on the battlements to think out his options. A bright moon hung overhead and the stars twinkled in the dark night. His thoughts drifted to Ariana. How could he enter the castle and ignore her? He cursed his counterpart for his foolishness. Now, no matter how carefully he behaved, someone would be hurt. He sighed.

Robb entered the great room to check on his father. Angus slept soundly, as did many of the other patients. Robb looked around with admiration at the organized and efficient makeshift hospital. Ariana could move mountains, and had before, he thought. In any time, she was a wonder. The wounded had eaten their supper in here, and were comfortably settled in for the night.

Suddenly, the soft tones of a lute drifted from the armory, and his head snapped up. The image of the shy girl flashed through his mind. No doubt the music honored his betrothed, Cailin. He took a deep breath and entered the armory for the evening meal. His insides roiled. Ariana stood with his future bride and Aunt Morag. Behind Ariana, Brodie Maclaren stood watch. If he did not mistake his bitter aunt's expression, it was one of gloating, while his fiancée appeared terrified. Ariana looked calm and composed, but he knew her better.

Protocol demanded he address his fiancée. "My lady," he said, offering his arm to Cailin.

Demurely, she placed her hand on his sleeve.

Her downcast eyes irritated him, but he led her to the table with the ladies trailing behind.

"Dinna they make a handsome couple?" Morag cooed to Ariana.

"Aye."

After seating his fiancée at his side, he took his seat, conscious of Ariana on his other side and Morag next to Cailin.

"My Lady Cailin," Morag said, her voice bright. "Did I not tell ye our castle is beautiful?"

" 'Tis the most lovely place I have ever seen."

"Thank ye," Morag said, taking credit for the decor.

"Lady Ariana." Cailin leaned forward. "Did ye change much when ye came?"

Before she could respond, Morag chuckled. "Nay, Lady Ariana was already with child when she came. Decorating was the last thing on her mind."

The pointed jibe hung in the air.

Ariana sighed dramatically. "Aye, but I was sorely remiss, with the plague to fight and the neighboring clans in need of medical treatment." She paused and stared at Morag. "However, after our men are seen to, I will have to attend to my duty."

Morag sat back in her chair in a huff. "Really, Ariana, ye sound like a saint. If I didna know better, I would think ye were looking for praise."

"Morag. I am far from a saint. But ye, who have managed

to raise a fine nephew and run a castle on yer own, know very well the hardships any woman faces."

Morag managed to concede the point with a snobbish tilt of her head.

Ariana's smile thinned. "Although someone wishes to speed up my demise, sainthood is something I shall wait for."

"Aye, my lady. We need ye too much to have ye depart the world," Gavin said.

"Aye, who would see to our needs?" Lor added.

After a general chorus of agreement the meal progressed without further incident.

Robb smiled secretly at her response, taking immense pride in her wit. Congratulating himself, he nearly choked when she pressed her knee against his. His loin tightened immediately, and he saw the barest hint of a smile on her soft lips and the softest tinge of color on her cheeks, and knew tonight would indeed be a long night. God, she was lovely.

The platters of meat Iona and Isla served were roasted to perfection. He cleared his throat, trying to regain some composure as he accepted the platter. "Thank ye."

Cailin preened modestly as he put some meat on her trencher.

When he did the same for Ariana, she raised an eyebrow at the portion.

"Ye are eating for two," he said hoarsely, then added two more pieces to her plate.

Morag touched her mouth with the corner of a linen. "Verily, Ariana, ye should learn to eat as daintily as Lady Cailin or myself, else ye find yerself as large as a sow."

Although Cailin flushed, and lowered her eyes at the insult, she did not dispute the statement.

Ariana sighed, looking at her rounded stomach, then picked up the meat from her trencher and nibbled on it.

"My time grows near, Morag, but I thank ye for yer concern. When ye are blessed with a life growing inside yer body, ye will know that the most important thing is a healthy baby. All other considerations pale."

Robb smugly placed the fattiest piece of meat on Morag's trencher before passing the platter to Lor.

After Friar Peter blessed their food, Robb stood up and raised his chalice. "To my betrothed. We of the clan MacGregor are proud and honored to have ye with us. May ye be happy in yer new home."

Cailin blushed as everyone raised their chalices.

"Many fruitful years," Lor called out.

"Aye." A soldier stood and lifted his chalice higher. "May ye be fruitful as Laird Angus, and Lady Ariana."

Robb noticed that Ariana's smile looked forced. Red-rimmed, her eyes looked suspiciously moist. She took several deep breaths before she placed her chalice down untouched. He turned away unable to bear her pain.

Several more toasts followed, each one more suggestive than the last. When he glanced again in Ariana's direction, his heart sank. Every loud salute had to be a knife in her. Though brave, she refused to meet his gaze. Pain etched her delicate features as she ate sparsely and conversed with Gavin. Only once did her eyes meet his. The anguish shining in the amber depths cut him worse than any sword wound. He understood all too well the pain of seeing her beloved with another.

He noticed that Morag's beady eyes followed his every move. God, but the woman irritated him. He smiled in her direction, just to irk her.

After dinner, the musicians played several soft ballads. He asked his intended to dance and she shyly accepted. Her eyes remained downcast. She knew the steps, but her movements were stiff, and he concluded that dancing in his arms was excruciating for her. Shy or terrified, she remained silent. The music played and the melody washed over them, but she remained aloof, and distant. In accordance with protocol, he danced three dances with her, and all of them progressed in silence. After he escorted her back to her seat, he asked his Aunt Morag to join him. It did not escape his notice that Ariana refused to glance at him.

Though loath to comply with social rules, he led his aunt into a dance. His jaw set against his aunt's inane prattle, his gaze remained on Ariana as she talked with his man.

They had danced around the floor when Ariana joined Cailin. Pride filled him. Even though this night tortured her, she was magnificent.

"Ye will be very happy with this young girl," Morag whispered, her low voice fairly purring as she smiled at the union.

"Why are ye so happy, Morag? Ye act like this is yer wedding."

"Nephew. I did not enjoy seeing ye so miserable. This woman is not like yer mother. She will never desert ye."

Black rage welled up within him. The mention of Robb's mother turned his insides to hate. Once again, he fought the demon that haunted Robb MacGregor. With discipline honed on the battlefield, he willed himself to remain calm and finished the dance. Though the effort cost him every ounce of his control, he managed to see his aunt back to the table without her ever suspecting the nerve she had hit.

The moment he left his aunt, he made his way toward his stepmother. His heart raced as he tried to bring his temper under control. A light sheen covered his brow as he interrupted her conversation with Cailin. "Since yer husband canna dance with ye, would ye permit me the honor?" He bowed, then led her out to the dance floor.

The moment she placed her hand in his, a peace filled him. Like food to a starving man, she filled his hunger. He breathed in her fresh scent and ached to possess her. He noticed her lips quiver and pulled her to his chest, shielding her from prying eyes.

Once she was in his arms, he warned, "Don't ye dare cry." He twirled her away from Morag and let his lips lightly brush her forehead. He felt her tremble, and pulled her closer as he danced into the shadows. "Meet me tonight at the river, near the bend where the trees cover the shore, after the others have retired."

Her gaze met his. Tears glistened in her eyes. "How?" she whispered. "I am closely guarded. Brodie takes his duty seriously."

He drew a ragged breath. "Trust me, I will find a way."

Her red-tipped lashes fluttered down to fan out across her creamy cheeks as she nodded. "I believe in you, I always have." Softly, she rested her face against his chest.

His heart swelled and ached with her trust. He would come up with a plan. He had to.

As the soft harmony of the lute danced through the air, her warm body responded to the melody with a unique rhythm all her own. Her fluid movements reminded him of their lovemaking. Cherished memories surfaced playing over his senses as easily as the song flowed through her body. Tension built within him as his manhood grew hard. He wanted to love her, he wanted to lose himself in her. Suddenly, she looked at him and the love and wonder shining in her eyes took his breath away. He groaned. The song became a bittersweet agony to endure.

When the music ended, he sighed, turning to find Gavin motioning for him. Robb led Ariana back to the ladies before crossing the room to meet with his captain of the guard. "What is it?"

"The sentries have returned and are wishing to see the laird."

Robb considered his father's condition. "I will confer with the laird, then meet with the sentries in the courtyard."

Before Gavin could leave, Robb touched his arm. "Gavin, I wish only Brodie Maclaren to guard the Lady Ariana."

"As ye wish." Gavin withdrew, and Robb went to speak with his father.

Angus was resting comfortably, and hailed his son over. "How did yer celebration go?"

Robb eyed the old man carefully, but brushed off the question with a shrug of his shoulder. "Father, the men have returned. I will meet with them, then report to ye."

"Aye, I would appreciate it, son."

Robb MacGregor left his father's side. On the way out he overheard Morag's waspish tongue. "Robb MacGregor will make a strapping groom. 'Tis said a maiden is much happier when the groom is not an old man."

About to rebuke his aunt, he overheard Ariana's response and chuckled. "I would imagine a maid is happy to have any groom, be he old or young."

Christophe needed to see her alone. She waited until the castle was quiet and all the servants had retired, before she made her rounds to attend the injured men. Once assured all her patients were doing well, she turned to Brodie. "I need to walk outside. Would ye accompany me?"

He bowed and extended his hand for her to precede him.

The cool evening air wafted over her as they took two turns of the courtyard before Christophe met them at the gates. "I will walk the lady now, Brodie. If ye would wait for her here."

Brodie looked from her to Robb. "As ye wish, but I would caution thee." He turned to Ariana. "Remember, my lady, who has the most to gain to have ye and yer child discredited."

"Thank ye," she said, patting his arm. "I understand and share yer concern." She slipped her arm through Robb's. "My stepson will see to my protection."

Brodie bowed, but the shadows upon his face spoke his concern.

As Christophe escorted her to the river, the moon was high and the silvery light spread out before them like a magical glow falling upon the moors and water.

She walked out of the castle under the cover of darkness and clung to his arm, needing the closeness of his embrace. The flickering light of the castle's torches fell far behind them as they slipped behind the cover of the tree-covered bank. Soft-flowing water moved peacefully below them, and the arbor of leaves shielded them from any prying eyes. She slipped her hands up his chest and around his neck. Lord, but the touch and feel of him nearly drove her mad. His lips descended on hers and the kiss was pure heaven. She had secretly, though foolishly, wondered if he still found her desirable. Then without warning, he pulled free of her arms. His sudden defection left her bereft.

"I dinna know what to do about Cailin," he said. Moving toward the bank, he stared into the water.

She sighed. "If you do not marry her, the clan would have to go to war."

He ran a hand through his hair. "War is a way of life for this clan. I would risk it."

She walked up behind him and rested her face on his back as she hugged him. "There must be a way to dissolve this wedding arrangement."

"How?"

"Can you buy your way out of it?"

He turned in her embrace to touch her cheek softly. "If I had the funds I could, but that avenue is denied us. This is a poor hamlet."

She fought the tears that suddenly pooled in her eyes.

He wrapped his strong arms around her. "Never fear, I will find a way."

Ariana reveled in the comfort of his arms. It had been so long since he held her. So long. She nestled closer against him. "Please, whatever you do, dinna place yourself in danger."

Haloed by the bright moon, his hair fairly glowed in the silvery light. "I've known danger from the moment I met you. But I would have it no other way. You are my life and my death." He smiled as his lips met hers.

The taste and touch of him were so different, yet familiar, but Christophe's kiss was unmistakable. Even if she were struck blind and deaf, she would know this man by the sensuality of his touch. Her heart raced as he deepened the kiss, a soft exploration that awakened her senses. His kiss both warmed and excited her.

Her hands roamed over his broad shoulders, caressing every muscular inch of him. She quivered with need of him. God, it had been an eternity since they had made love.

His kiss ended and he rested his chin on top of her head. "Every hour of every day you have haunted me with memories of silken skin and sugared kisses." No matter what resemblance she took, this woman could stir him as no other. His beloved, her essence, had him cocooned in a velvet embrace.

"I love you," she murmured as she nuzzled his neck.

"God, woman, you drive me insane." He pulled back. "What of our child? I do not want to harm the babe."

A husky chuckle filled the air as she ran her hands up his chest, her fingers slipping beneath his shirt and brushing his medallion aside. "Dinna worry, the babe is fine."

Her nails grazed his flesh, and he groaned. His hands roamed over her back, smoothly untying the laces of her gown and slipping it from her shoulders to fall gently at her feet. She stood clothed only in a thin smock. Lord, she was perfection. His hand trembled as he caressed the smooth skin of her shoulder. His fingers slipped over the top of the smock to graze her breast, and softly rub the nipple.

Her moan drove him on. She covered his hand with hers and leaned into him. Her eyes closed and a look of pleasure and ecstasy crossed her beautiful features. He eased the smock off her shoulders and watched it slip down to her waist. His fingers stroked her full breasts, then slipped down to feel her rounded abdomen, sliding her smock over her stomach until it slipped to the ground. He touched her stomach reverently, knowing his child resided within.

The cool breeze caressed Ariana and she became exquisitely aware of her nakedness. Her figure misshapen with her advanced pregnancy, she suddenly felt self-conscious. She tried to pull away as her inner fears again assailed her. "I am so fat."

Christophe pulled her back into his arms. "You are beautiful. Motherhood only increases your allure." He smothered her lips in a kiss that stole her breath. If she had any doubts that he still found her attractive, they vanished when his lips trailed down her neck, kissing every inch of her skin.

Tears sparkled in her eyes. Lord, but how she loved this man. One unkind or insensitive word would have demoralized her, but he had bridged her insecurity with love. Caring and trust filled her as she cradled his face in her hands and kissed him with a carnal passion that surprised him. She could not get enough of him. Ever so gently, she smoothly undressed him, her lips trailing a path to his swollen member. Her fingers wrapped around his shaft, her lips covered him, and her tongue lathed attention around the circle as her teeth grazed the side of his shaft. A gruff moan escaped him and he reached for her. Panting, he gently picked her up in his arms and laid her on top of his clothes. He bent over her, his face lined with concern. "Are you sure I won't hurt the babe?" he asked.

"I am, my love," she whispered, marveling at the kind gentle heart of her lover.

Suddenly the baby kicked.

Wonder and love lit his eyes as he reverently touched her abdomen. "Our child," he whispered. He placed his lips to her stomach and softly kissed the spot where his child had kicked. As if the child knew it was his father, he kicked again and, awed, Christophe looked at her.

Tears moistened her eyes. "It would seen our baby approves of our union." She caressed his cheek. "The baby is fine."

His smile of relief made her grin. "I love you," she laughed.

The desire burning in his eyes vanished her humor. Her heart raced as he lowered his lips to hers. Tongues mating, his hand slipped lower down her body, caressing her breasts until her moans of desire filled the air.

His fingers slipped between her thighs to find the tiny nub of her womanhood. His thumb worried it until she was writhing in his arms. Then he slipped his finger inside, stretching her as they started a rhythm that had her legs tightening around his hand. He spread her thighs open, his lips following, his tongue darting in and out until her soft cries filled the air. Frantic with need, she writhed as tension flowed through her. The rhythm increased, driving her further, faster. Desire boiled within her. Her senses sharpened. Alert to every stimuli, they suddenly escalated to snatches of blinding light, dappled with vivid colors, as crescendos of music played in her mind and a profusion of flavors and aromas surfaced in her memory. A river of fire flowed through her veins as a raging passion burned out of control. A thousand stars burst behind her eyelids and she cried out his name, clinging to him as she soared through the heat to a cooling cloud of peace, then slowly floated down to earth.

He waited until her climax peaked and ebbed then he entered her slowly, starting a rhythm as smooth as a wave washing against the shore. Liquid heat rekindled her body, bringing her right back to fulfillment.

She gasped for air as her heart and body raced out of control. Her nails scored his flesh, her movements frenzied as her second release hung in the balance—touching and beautiful. She cried out, her excited moans drove him on.

"Please," she murmured, her voice a wispy plea.

"Sweet Jesus, but ye make me work."

She delighted in his throaty response. Her hand roamed over every inch of his thick muscles; their bodies were slick with perspiration, their kisses hot, their breathing short and labored. Finally, their climax took hold, rocking them back. She cried out and he followed her, with a deep heartfelt groan. He rested his forehead against hers. "My love, I die a little every time we make love."

She caressed his face, her palm stroking his whiskered cheek. Tears welled up in her eyes. "I love you so. I don't think I can bear to see that woman with you."

He gathered her close. "I will find a way. Trust me."

"I always have. I always will."

He pushed back strands of fiery red hair and stared into her eyes. The same amber-colored eyes that had stared at him through three lives. "I will never tire of looking at you, nor tire of seeing love shining through your beautiful eyes."

She nestled close to him, listening to his heartbeat, the sound reassuring in an uncertain world. He would think of something. Christophe would never desert her as Robb MacGregor had her counterpart. The thought gave her a sudden chill.

"Are you cold?"

"No. I just felt a shiver."

He pulled her closer. "Have I ever let you down, fair damsel?"

She smiled up at him. "Not ever. Not in any lifetime." Her heart tumbled in her chest. "I believe in love. I believe in you."

He hugged her to his chest, his muscular arms wrapping around her in a loving embrace. The warmth of his body enveloped her and she lay peacefully in the afterglow.

Safe in his arms, she almost fell asleep, but unbidden, the thought of their continued separation intruded on her happiness. Suddenly, a wave of fear descended upon her. She clung to him in desperation. "I couldn't bear a life without you."

He smoothed the hair from her face and kissed her temple. "We will be together."

Tears gathered in her eyes. She stroked his cheek. "Make love to me as though this was our last time."

His lips covered hers. Though his kiss was gentle, she returned it with a wild, frenzied abandon. The heat grew between them. Sparks of desire burst within her as she caressed him with frantic need, her hands literally devouring his muscular body. She couldn't get enough of him, kissing his lips, cheek, and neck, her teeth nipping here and there. She wanted him; she yearned to hold on to him forever, and never let go. Her movements inflamed him. Passion, red-hot and erotic, coursed through her, setting every nerve aflame. She felt desire curl in her stomach, winding tighter and twisting her insides for release. Suddenly they were both out of control. His powerful arms nearly crushed her as he lengthened the kisses, drugging her with intense craving. Her legs wrapped around him, her feet sliding up and down his calves. His body pressed her down, as his fingers slipped between her thighs and stroked her to near frenzy. Her body aquiver, she kissed his lips, sipping long and deep, drinking his love as she devoured him. Her tongue was tasting, touching, tantalizing every inch of his seductive mouth. Her heart pounding, she caressed his powerful chest, her fingers gliding downward to wrap around his manhood and squeeze. With an earthy growl, he pushed her hands away and entered her.

"Open your eyes," he commanded, his voice raspy and thick.

She gasped, watching his face as he made love to her. The desire in his eyes rocked her soul. She clung to him, meeting his every thrust. Suddenly, the world exploded. A thousand nerves shattered and her pulse raced in ecstasy as she found her release. Seconds later he cried out her name, gave one final thrust and collapsed.

She floated gently down from the towering heights, all the while held securely within his strong arms. After several minutes he kissed her long and lovingly, holding her to his chest. "I love you. I won't leave you."

Tears again formed in her eyes, and her arms wrapped around his broad shoulders as she held on to him for dear life. A primal need surfaced and mentally she clung to the moment, remembering his scent, the strength of his arms, the taste of his kisses, and the sound of his love-starved voice. Instinct took over, storing the memory.

* * *

The bushes rustled softly when Alastair leaned closer, his mouth watering as he watched the two lovers. His member was hard. His beady eyes glowed with unveiled glee. "Fornicating adulteress," hissed Alastair, but he still watched every stroke of her hand, thinking of the erotic things he would have Morag perform.

His breathing became labored and he swallowed with difficulty as he watched them couple again. He smiled, knowing Morag would do anything for this information.

Anything.

CHAPTER EIGHT

At sunrise, Ariana watched the men gathering in the courtyard to raid the Fraziers, while her guard remained in the background. A fortnight had passed since the fiery cross had been dispatched and answered. Now, a multitude of tartans filled the area with a sea of rich-colored plaids. As the clan's weapons reflected flashes of fire from the sun, she shivered and huddled closer into her mantle.

Though she had begged Angus to wait to lead the men, he had kissed her forehead and shook his head. "This can no wait."

Her gaze strayed to Robb and her heart caught in her throat when he ran up the stairs toward her. Anticipation mounted, then crashed as he slipped by her, heading toward Cailin. Briefly, his eyes met Ariana's before he leaned forward and kissed Cailin on the cheek.

Her face flushed. "Take care," Cailin murmured, her eyes unable to meet his.

Pain sliced though Ariana at Christophe's actions. She

quickly looked away, smiling at Angus as he mounted his horse to lead the force of men made up of MacGregors and warriors from several clans she had helped through the sickness. Robb MacGregor nodded to her, then turned and ran down the steps, then mounted his horse to ride out with the men. Though the sun shone and the birds sang, winter had entered Ariana's heart. After everyone had withdrawn to the great room, she remained standing on the stone precipice, watching the men until they were out of sight.

Her heart broke as two tears slipped past her eyelids. He was riding out of her life to certain danger, and she couldn't even call out a loving farewell to him. "Be safe," she whispered.

"Trust me," Christophe's sexy, deep voice echoed in her mind. She closed her eyes and let the memories wash over her. His easy smile sparkled in her recollections, casting out her fear. The warm embrace of the past enveloped her, reminding her of the lives they had known, the obstacles they had overcome, and the extraordinary love they shared. Each sweet memory filled her with hope. She drew a deep breath, gathering her strength about her like a well-worn shawl. Her child kicked and though the future was unsure, her faith was strong.

"Ariana?" Cailin tentatively called as she peeked out of the door.

Ariana sighed and turned toward the lovely young woman. "I am coming."

Brodie, her ever-present shadow, held the door for her and followed her into the great room.

She had only a fortnight before the wedding was to take place. With the raid, all plans to sever the marriage arrangement had been tabled.

The great room was full of servants, and Morag, in fine

spirits for a change, waved for the ladies to join her at the hearth.

Ariana wished otherwise, but in the interest of peace acceded. Since Morag made a concerted effort to be pleasant, the least Ariana could do was respond in kind. But it would be a difficult feat with her heart so full of worry.

Cailin placed her hand on Ariana's arm. She leaned close. "Dinna ye think that 'tis truly wonderful we will be related?"

"Aye, but ken ye no think of something better?"

"Better?" Cailin whispered.

"Aye better, dinna ye have dreams?"

"Everyone does, but I am a woman. I must do as I am told. I hope to be a good wife, like my mother before me. My father rarely beat her. I know what is expected of me."

Morag leaned forward. "Aye, like I told ye, Cailin, keep a man happy in the bedchamber and yer life is full of ease."

"I plan to. I do not want to anger him. He frightens me."

Morag chuckled. "Men are such base creatures. Dinna ye agree, Ariana?"

"Nay. I love my husband. And dinna think of my wifely duties as chores."

Cailin's face blanched. "How can ye enjoy being with a man?"

"Ariana enjoys bedding; look to her middle and ye have yer answer," Morag said, walking away from them to fill her plate.

Ariana smiled at Morag's barb. "I do indeed enjoy consummating my love."

"Really?" Cailin asked.

Ariana sighed at the innocent surprise and changed the subject. "What are yer dreams, Cailin?"

Cailin lowered her head. "I hope that if my lord and master allows it I will be permitted to pursue my passion."

"And yer passion is?"

"Painting. I love to make pictures come alive with the beauty of God's earth."

"Why do ye fear yer husband would not allow this enjoyment?"

"Most men would not allow their woman such frivolous pursuits." She leaned forward. "I am terrified of Robb MacGregor. Though he is well respected, and I am fortunate he offered for me, I nonetheless fear him."

Thinking she had found a way out of the marriage for Cailin, Ariana poured her a healthy portion of mead.

"Do ye think it wise to marry a man ye fear?"

"Aye. Robb MacGregor prefers a woman who is docile. I am known for that."

"But what do ye prefer?" Ariana pressed.

Cailin looked up, her face blank. "I have never thought of what I preferred."

Ariana's heart ached with frustration. This era did not allow for women's rights. "Would yer family support yer decision if ye decided not to marry Robb MacGregor?"

Tears formed in Cailin's eyes. "Nay, they would disown me."

Ariana sighed. "Well, since ye wish to paint, I think the first order of business is to approach yer intended and ask."

The woman fairly cowered. "I couldna."

Ariana leaned forward and patted the young woman's hand. "Dinna worry. I am sure Robb MacGregor would wish to please his bride."

Cailin's eyes widened. "Ye must not know him well. It is said he pleases only himself in all things. My brothers told me not to anger him, for he has a vile temper and low opinion of women."

"Mayhap he has changed."

"Nay, my lady. It is doubtful."

Morag raised an eyebrow at the conversation when she returned. "Are ye two planning an insurrection?"

"Nay, simply discussing possibilities." It occurred to Ariana that the conversation could cause talk among the servants. She stood up, pulling Cailin to her feet, then reached for her mug of hot cider. "I think it prudent if we retire to my chambers." She swept her hand across her skirt. "Join us." Though she had no love of Morag, every castle had its pecking order. If Morag was refused entry to the mistress's room, she could lose valuable prestige when other ladies came to call.

Morag's smile looked like a puckered frown. "Cailin, will yer brothers and father come for the wedding?"

"Aye, they will be here on the full moon." She shyly looked at Ariana. "Please, my lady, I am without a mother, would ye help with my wedding?"

Morag stopped at the top of the stairs and turned back to look at Ariana, a malicious grin on her face. "Would ye not be pleased to see Robb MacGregor happily married?"

Forcing a smile, Ariana led the way to her chambers and waved the ladies inside. "Lady Morag is right," she lied. "I would be only too pleased to help."

Suddenly, Ariana found herself crushed in Cailin's loving embrace. "Thank ye, ye are so kind."

Never had she felt more like crying, but the smug look on Morag's face was enough to stop her self-pity. Never would she give the woman the satisfaction of seeing how much she affected her.

Brightly, she put Cailin from her. "Do ye have a wedding gown?" she asked, summoning up all the cheerfulness she could.

"Aye, I will fetch it."

Several minutes later Cailin burst back into the room, her arms laden with a beautiful gown.

" 'Tis lovely," Morag said as she moved to the window and stared out at the autumn day. Her words were an understatement for the intricately embroidered dress. As she'd intended, the halfhearted comment effectively robbed Cailin of her joy.

" 'Tis not lovely," Ariana corrected, her voice kind. " 'Tis exquisite."

Cailin's face brightened as she held out her gown for inspection. Silver and gold threads crisscrossed in the pale blue over-tunic, while an unadorned full white tunic hung elegantly beneath it. Ariana felt a nostalgia as she fingered the fine gown. Not once in all her time-travels had she wed her love. Someday, she vowed, I will have a real wedding.

Cailin flipped the dress out, shaking out the wrinkles, and held it up to herself. She preened in front of the mirror. "How should I wear my hair?"

"Down, I should think, with some fresh flowers or jewels woven into the curls."

Cailin grabbed her hand. "Ye are wonderful."

Though Cailin's enthusiasm was to be expected, Ariana found herself wishing the woman would cease her chatter. Every time the woman exclaimed her happiness, Ariana felt a knife in her heart.

By dinnertime she was thoroughly sick of the wedding plans, but no one had an inkling.

"Come, let us go appease our hunger," she announced, heading for the door.

She ushered Cailin out of the master room, waiting for Morag to precede them from her quarters.

Once they were at the table, Friar Peter stood and said the evening blessing. Before anyone could eat, he offered up several more prayers for the clansmen on the raid. The dinner tone now greatly subdued, all those present ate their meal in silence.

Ariana welcomed the respite from the enthusiasm of the young woman. She closed her eyes and remembered her beloved's promise. Then, without another thought, she lifted her chalice and proposed a toast. "To our brave and valiant men, may they be victorious and return to us safely."

Everyone raised their chalices and drank.

"Enough of this maudlin behavior," Morag announced. Ignoring the censure of the few sentries, she turned to Cailin. "After dinner, Cailin, come to my room and I will share several stories of Robb's childhood," Morag offered. She raised her eyes to Ariana. "Ye must come too."

"Thank ye, Morag, but I am tired. I will see ye both in the morning."

During the next few days, Cailin's trunks arrived along with a bevy of servants.

"Why did the servants not travel with ye?" Ariana asked, surprised by the lady's arrival alone.

Cailin blushed. "My father received a missive. He wished me to come at once and informed me he would send the servants with my belongings later. He only allowed me to take my wedding dress."

Ariana merely nodded, though she sensed there was more to the story than offered.

At midday the gifts for the wedding couple began to arrive. When Ariana saw the amount of costly presents sent, her heart sank. Apparently even the ruler of Scotland approved of this match. They could never buy their way out of it.

From the traditional to the extravagant, the gold, silver, and brass dishes and ornaments arrived. But aside from the fact that they would never be able to purchase Robb's freedom, there was the indisputable fact that powerful families might go to war over the affront if she and Robb tried to barter their way out of the ceremony.

How could they purchase their happiness in trade for the clan's danger? Even as she posed the question, she knew the answer. They could not, nor would they. Happiness never flourished from misery.

She sighed. There were always options. They would just have to find them.

"Is something amiss, my lady?" Morag's cold pointed question cut into her thoughts.

She smiled. "Nay, nothing at all." She would rather die than give Morag reason to gloat. With chin held high she turned full circle in the room. "We will need to decorate the hall for the wedding."

"My lady, what have ye in mind?" Cailin asked.

"I thought we would give the castle a thorough cleaning. Sweep the rushes out and replace them with scented ones."

"Oh, that sounds wonderful," cried Cailin. "What else?"

The joy in the woman's face filled Ariana with regret and guilt.

"Pray tell, what else do ye suggest?" Morag sidled closer.

Ariana pointed to the rafters. "We can drape gaily colored banners and"—she held up her hand so Cailin's exuberance did not interrupt—"mayhap ye can paint one."

Cailin squealed in delight. "I would love to."

Ariana directed their attention to the corners. "We can place baskets of fall flowers about."

Cailin's eyes shone with pure joy. "Ye are too good to me, my lady."

Jessie entered and came to stand with her hands on her ample stomach. "What dishes would ye like me to prepare for the feast?"

Tears formed in Cailin's eyes. "Whatever ye think is appropriate, and I will see my servant takes yer direction."

Jessie beamed. "I will be glad to supervise yer servant."

Ariana laid her hand on Jessie's shoulder. "Mayhap a few of yer scrumptious tarts, along with a huge cake to celebrate the event. What do ye think?"

Jessie considered the request. "A huge cake?"

"Aye. I thought ye might decorate the cake with sweet white frosting and dried berries."

Cailin's eyes sparkled at the description.

Ariana smiled and pointed to the area before them.

"I thought we would have the ceremony here at the steps. Perhaps we could build a bower of autumn flowers as well."

Cailin twirled around. "Even I would appear beautiful in such a setting."

Ariana's heart broke at such self-deprecation. "Ye are a lovely woman."

"Thank ye, my lady, but I fear only ye believe that."

" 'Tis not important what I believe. Ye are the one who must believe in yer worth. If ye dinna believe in yerself, no one else will."

"Aye," Jessie agreed.

The ladies busied the entire staff that day, and even though it was painful, Ariana discussed every aspect of the wedding from the music to the ceremony itself.

Cailin approached her after Morag had retired long after the evening meal. "Forgive me, my lady. I am guilty of believing some of the spiteful things said about ye."

Ariana did not have to ask where she had heard the malicious gossip. The fact that the woman had waited until Morag was absent spoke volumes.

"I should never have entertained such lies," Cailin went on.

" 'Tis over, let be."

Cailin clasped her hand and kissed it. "Never has anyone shown me such kindness. I shall never forget ye, nor yer different ways."

Ariana could not help but be moved by the woman's heartfelt admission. Guilt assailed her, but she tapped it down. It was neither her fault nor Cailin's that fate had placed them in this impossible situation. Christophe had told her to believe he would find a way, and she would not question his love or his strategy.

Within a week, the hall had been transformed. The tapestries had been cleaned, the rushes changed, the sweet scent of herbs filled the air, and the constant aroma of baked goods filtered through the castle. Ariana interviewed musicians and made arrangements for the guests who started to arrive.

Gavin approached her at the midday meal and told her Cailin's family had arrived. Cailin's gaze widened and she slowly sighed. It did not escape her notice that poor Cailin suddenly became quiet.

"I will see to their welcome." Ariana stood slowly, feeling her cumbersome weight, but Brodie's arm suddenly appeared, assisting her. "Thank ye."

Brodie bowed and took his ever-present position behind her.

Cailin rose, but her shoulders were bowed and her eyes downcast. "My lady, I will accompany ye."

Loud boisterous language fit only for a men's barracks met their ears and continued as they entered the courtyard.

Laird Alec Drummond's hair was a snow-white fringe of uneven spikes, but his two sons had the same coloring as his daughter, but where she was petite, and polite, they were unkempt and crude.

Ariana was not impressed. 'Twas not their physical appearance that put her off, though that was rather unremarkable, but their ill manners that formed her low opinion. After meeting Cailin's family, Ariana realized her timid manner made sense.

"Cailin, ye worthless girl, see to our needs at once," her father commanded.

Cailin's head bobbed as her shoulders cowered in on her body.

"And make sure there is plenty of ale," one of her brothers added, stopping his sister in her tracks.

Cailin again nodded and turned to leave, but Ariana held her fast, raising her chin to Alec. "Ye are welcome at Castle MacGregor. When ye have washed the travel filth away, ye may share in our midday meal."

Alec glared at her, from the top of her head to the tip of her boots. "And ye are?"

"I am Lady Ariana, mistress of this castle. I bid ye welcome."

Brodie stepped forward, his hand on his sword, making his presence known.

Alec snorted and turned to inspect the walkways. Then his narrowed gaze settled back on her as he leaned forward in his saddle. "Where are the men?"

"They are in battle." She smiled brightly. "Do ye wish to join them?"

"No doubt they find more comfort on the battlefield than here."

His sons chuckled rudely.

They were exactly like their father. Large, ill-bred men sporting long scraggly beards. She swallowed back the insults forming on her tongue and brightened her smile. "No doubt they do. I repeat, do ye wish to join them?"

"Mayhap we will. But first we will quench our thirst." He motioned to his sons, and they dismounted. Laird Drummond marched up the stairs with his sons in tow and brushed by her, nearly toppling Cailin over, but Ariana did not give an inch. Her hand on Brodie's arm to restrain him, she clasped Cailin's hand and followed. Head held high, she walked slowly into the room and returned to her seat. She noticed that Cailin's family ate nothing, but that they emptied three skeins of ale.

"Cailin, when ye are through eating, will ye help me gather some flowers for the arbor?"

Cailin bobbed her head once, but did not utter another word. Her eyes shifted several times to watch her family as they imbibed.

Ariana's heart broke to see Lady Cailin reduced to a cowering woman. She looked at the three men, and her anger grew as they drank too much and became obnoxious during the meal.

When she arose to finish her preparations, she pulled Cailin after her. Morag hurried after them, leaving Laird Drummond and his sons in the great room. Brodie followed quietly behind as he escorted her safely on her rounds.

Ariana, Morag, and Cailin were busy until the evening meal, drawing up plans with the farrier, Malcolm, for the arbor they wished built, conferring with Friar Peter in the late afternoon, then walking into the village to consign the sewing of the special banners to the best seamstresses. They did not return to the castle until after dark.

The moment they entered the great room the mouth-watering aromas of roasted meats and baked breads tantalized their hunger, but the boisterous noise of their guests, clamoring for their dinner, spoiled their appetite.

"It would seem they have drunk all afternoon," Brodie whispered as he escorted her in.

Ariana glared at her guests, then quickly bowed her head so Friar Peter could say grace. He said a long prayer as he eyed Laird Drummond's impatience.

The moment the blessing was finished, Cailin's family passed platters at an alarming speed. They speared food, leaving very little for anyone else. Servants hurriedly filled and refilled goblets.

Alec pounded his fist onto the table. "More ale."

His sons joined in, each sending their mighty fists crashing down on the table. Platters clanked and goblets overturned.

Ariana's cider spilled, gathering in a pool that sloped toward her lap. "Look what ye have done." Her eyes burned with angry fire as she jumped to her feet and threw her linen onto the spill to soak it up.

Alec Drummond looked at her as though she had lost her wits.

"Enough!" she cried, placing her hands on her hips and moving out from the table. When the servants entered with more flagons, she raised her hand in the air to halt them. "No more ale will be served in this hall until manners are observed."

Instant silence descended. It was obvious that no one had ever challenged the Drummond men like this before, let alone a woman.

Alec Drummond's eyes narrowed, but she stood her ground.

"Woman, ye dare take me to task!"

"Aye, I do. 'Tis my home, not a tavern. Ye will observe my rules or ye will leave."

"What are ye asking, my lady?"

"That ye stop acting like boors. This is a gentle home with the fairer sex in attendance. Since I know ye are neither dim-witted nor lack-headed, I ask ye to observe the common courtesies that knights reserve for their ladies. Ye are not on the battlefield now."

When Alec rose, a hush fell over the room.

Brodie raised his sword in plain view.

Oblivious to Brodie's protective action, Alec advanced on her. "Ye expect the courtesy of court, lass?"

"Aye, I do. Ye will show respect in my home as my husband would in yers."

"Or what?" he asked, coming to stand before her, his massive arms folded.

"Or, sir, after yer departure, ye will be known far and wide as an ill-mannered brute who takes his foul mood out on those who canna fight back and yer sterling reputation of a warrior will be damaged."

"Ye mean to put me out of yer home when I've come to see me child wed?"

She took a step forward. "Aye." They stood toe-to-toe. His eyes narrowed fractionally.

Ariana's heart beat faster as the gleaming metal of Gavin's steel caught her eye when he stepped forward.

Brodie tried to pull her behind him, but she stood her ground. Alec's lip twitched ever so slightly; then he threw his head back and roared. Though his laughter ceased, his eyes shone with a shrewd light. "Such courage belongs in a man." He turned to his daughter. "Daughter, be careful of this woman. She is dangerous."

Cailin bobbed her head dutifully, tears rimming her eyelids.

"My Lady Ariana," Laird Drummond mocked. "I humbly beg yer pardon. I and my two sons will attend to our courtly manners."

She raised an eyebrow at his tone, but nodded graciously, grateful that he had not pushed the matter. Clans had gone to war for less.

With the tension gone, she took Laird Drummond's offered arm. "By God, ye are a woman a man could truly admire."

"And ye, sir, are a man who could truly turn a woman's head if ye put yer mind to it," she mocked.

He chuckled. "Now I know why Angus married ye. Had I known such a woman existed, I would have given him competition for yer hand."

"Then we can all be thankful that no contest existed. I detest such displays."

"My lady, ye continue to amaze and surprise me." He looked briefly at his daughter, his disappointment evident. "I would ask ye to befriend her."

Though his hypocritical words angered her, she smiled. "Cailin is easy to like."

He sighed, adopting a parental concern as he held a chair out for her. "I can only hope Robb MacGregor carries his father's wisdom."

So did she, but not for the reasons Laird Drummond pretended. Her heart lurched at the thought of her Christophe.

Time was running out.

A week passed without the men's return, and her misgivings increased. Suddenly, it was the morning before the wedding. Ariana feared for her beloved, but tried to put all worry from her mind. She dressed and went down to break-the-fast where everyone was seated. Though her appetite was still poor, she joined the morning meal, taking her seat between Morag and Cailin.

"My lady, do ye think they will return in time?" Cailin asked.

Before she could answer, Alec leaned forward, his dingy white tufts of hair sticking straight out in stiff spikes. "If they are not back for the ceremony, ye will still be wed. Men have their business, woman."

Cailin shrank back, food forgotten, and nodded to her father.

Ariana glared at Alec Drummond's overbearing tone,

knowing Cailin's mental backbone would never stiffen under the weight of his condescension.

"Laird Alec, I believe yer daughter's wedding is her business."

She ignored Alec's raised eyebrow and patted Cailin's hand. When Cailin offered her a small smile, Ariana's thoughts centered briefly on her love. Pray God that he had a solution. Tomorrow eve was the wedding.

Distracted, Ariana raised her cup to her lips and did not notice Gavin enter. "My lady, yer father has arrived."

Fear coursed through her, and her hand trembled slightly as she set her cup down. Without any of Ariana's memories, she only had a vague recollection of a dream. Her father was a stranger to her. How would she recognize him?

Satisfaction gleamed in Alec's eye as he toasted her. "Ah, yer father is here. I would see if ye take him to task for his manners."

Pleased, Morag nudged her. "Hurry and greet him so we can meet yer illustrious father."

"Aye." She rose from the table with Brodie's strong arm beneath hers and followed Gavin out of the great room. Mayhap, Laird MacPherson would be dressed in finer garb than his men, she thought, trying to calm the butterflies that fluttered wildly in her stomach.

The men were just riding into the courtyard, dressed in battle garb. She had no idea who her sire was. Knots formed in her stomach as she squared her shoulders. Her eyes quickly scanned the men, but if she wished one to stand out more than the next, she was disappointed. The men were warriors, and all had the stoic facade. She drew a deep breath. How would she bluff her way out of this?

"My lady?" Gavin questioned as she held back from taking a step toward the stairs. "Are ye all right?"

Fainting occurred to her, but she didn't think she could

get away with it. She nodded to Gavin and waved for him to precede her as Brodie waited for her to take a step.

At the bottom of the stairs a gust of wind kicked up, stirring the dust and debris. She covered her eyes as the particles bit into her skin.

"My lady?" Brodie asked.

"I have something in my eye," she lied, and rubbed her eyes.

Suddenly big brawny hands gripped her shoulders and pulled her into a bear hug. "Daughter, 'tis been too long."

She looked through watery eyes to see her counterpart's father for the first time. His long, stark white hair and neatly trimmed beard were vaguely familiar, but not his expression. The joy shining in his wide smile and bright eyes touched her heart.

"Father."

The warmth of a genuine embrace was her undoing, and she clung to him without hesitation, as if he were indeed her own sire.

"I am sorry," he whispered.

Confused, she stared up at him.

"Robb is truly taking another. Life is not how we wish. But yer child is safe and mayhap someday ye will receive yer heart's desire."

She swallowed. Her father was aware of her abiding love for Robb MacGregor and had come to comfort her. "Father, thank ye."

He smiled and brushed her tears away. "There, there," he soothed.

" 'Tis only the dust."

Respect shone in his eyes as he ushered her up the stairs. "Ye have weathered harder things, my dear."

"Laird MacPherson," his man-at-arms called out, stopping him.

"Aye." He turned her around with him to confront his man.

"Do ye wish us to stay in the stable or should we make camp outside?"

He looked down at his daughter. "How much room do ye have?"

" 'Twould be better if ye made camp at the river, but I fear the water may still be contaminated."

"Aye, I know." Then he looked to his man. "Fife, be sure to take precautions."

He wheeled her around. "How are ye feeling?"

"All is well, Father."

"Yer mother and I are very proud of ye."

"Me?"

"Aye, all up and down the river the people are singing yer praises. Ye have stopped a plague."

"I was fortunate the potion I prepared worked."

"Nonsense. Ye are a hero. In fact, ye are famous."

"Verily, Father, I was merely lucky."

"Dinna be modest, daughter. Ye deserve the praise, and more."

She let the matter drop. She could see she would not win an argument with this man. He was self-assured and very fond of his family. She liked him. Thank God he was not like Cailin's father.

The moment they entered the hall the mood of the room changed. It was clear to her that her father commanded respect, even from the blustering Alec.

He was the first in line to greet her father, followed by Morag. She made the introduction.

Laird Drummond extended his hand to Laird MacPherson. " 'Tis a pleasure to meet a man who raised such an outspoken daughter."

Why, the nasty tattletale, Ariana thought as she stared

at Drummond's smug features. He was hoping to see her reprimanded.

Morag stepped closer. "Aye, yer daughter crossed the bounds of good manners more times than I like to mention."

Her father raised an eyebrow at Morag's opinion, then reached for Ariana's tightly clenched fist and deposited a kiss upon her white knuckles. After releasing her hand, he stared at the people before him, his eyes narrowed.

"Ye have no doubt been taken to task. Knowing Ariana as I do, ye probably all deserved it."

She could have kissed him.

He wrapped his arm around her, hugging her close as they moved through the embarrassed people. "I thought I was doing the best for ye. Forgive me, daughter. Had I known, I would have never forced ye to wed Angus."

So her dream was indeed real. "Ye did what ye thought was best."

"Aye, I willna desert ye again. Ye need a protector, now more than ever."

His words sent a shiver through her.

The morning light brought the call of arms. Robb watched his father walk gingerly out across the camp and mount his horse. If a human frailty existed in the laird, it was not allowed to show. Robb had grown close to the old man, and worried that Angus had not regained his strength.

His father sat straight in his saddle and waved goodbye to Laird Hay, who had joined them last night with information that the clan Frazier had fortified their ranks with Campbells. Unable to join them, Laird Hay had left his clansmen.

Unbidden, another farewell came to mind. When they

had left the castle, his father had stood on the porch with Ariana, then descended the stairs to mount his horse. Christophe's gaze had hungrily taken in her appearance. She had waved to his father, yet her gaze had strayed to him, a hint of a smile in her farewell as she waved her good-byes. The sun had kissed her cheeks and set her pure, creamy skin aglow with the fresh wash of daylight. How he had longed to take her into his arms and kiss her with all the passion and longing in his heart. Instead, he had dutifully kissed his betrothed, Cailin, and watched the light in Ariana's eyes die.

Now he sighed and mounted his horse. But the image of his beloved repeatedly returned to him long after they had marched out of their encampment.

Christophe rode by his father's side. The estrangement between them was an odd combination of pride and conviction.

How did a man breach such a gap?

Angus turned to him. "I have been thinking of Ariana." He sighed. "Men often recall their loved ones before a battle."

Christophe's mouth went dry as his father's words mirrored his thoughts.

Angus smiled. "I'm glad ye have softened toward her. She did not betray ye when her father insisted she name her child's father."

"Then why did ye marry her?"

"Because she needed a friend. 'Tis a cold world to be alone in, especially when ye are responsible for another."

Christophe stared at his father, knowing he had a role to play. Robb had a stormy history with this woman, but perhaps this was the opportunity to heal the rift between father and son.

"Canna ye no forgive her?" Angus asked. "She saved yer life."

"As I did hers."

When silence followed his response, Christophe looked at his father. What else did the man expect him to say?

"Aye," Angus finally agreed, his face drawn by the weight of his thoughts. "But that is not forgiveness."

"It is a start."

"Aye." Angus drew a deep breath, then leveled Robb with a parental stare. "Son, ye must learn to have forgiveness in yer heart. I made a mistake in forcing ye to share my bitterness."

"Father, I can forgive if it is warranted. My counsel serves me well."

"I am talking about yer mother. If ye never forgive her, ye will never find peace."

At once Christophe's soul filled with Robb's hatred. Overwhelmed by the feelings of bitter pain, he fought against the chilling hate, but could not relieve it. "The past is dead, leave it buried. My mother harmed ye, me, and all our clan when she left. I willna ever forgive her. Nor will I trust any of her sex."

Resignation deepened the lines in Angus's face. " 'Tis her clan we fight. Are ye ready?"

"Aye, I am."

Christophe pointed to the matted grass left by the Fraziers' retreat. "Look."

Angus studied the tracks left in the soft ground, then noticed the rocky terrain next to the clear trail. "They could have concealed their tracks. Either they are careless or overconfident."

Tavis Dunn rode up and heard the end of Angus's remark. "The Fraziers are many things, but dull-witted is not one of them. Their clear trail was done for a reason."

"Aye, they are cunning devils," Angus agreed.

"Father, I think we should let them think we are none the wiser. The Fraziers are unaware that Laird Hay sent reinforcements, or that several clans have joined us. I can take a brigade and follow the trail, while ye and Laird Dunn ride ahead on the flanks."

"Aye, ye are right," Tavis agreed.

Angus pursed his lips, his gaze returning to the tracks. Christophe's plan troubled his father and although the military logic was sound, an eerie premonition came over him, but he ignored it. "Father, I know we have always fought at one another's side, but it occurs to me that should our luck fail our clan would be without a leader."

"I would still prefer to have my sword guarding yer back and yers mine."

"As would I, but we have to put the clan first."

Angus sighed. "Very well, but I will lead the men in the diversion. Be at the fork in the road where the table rock splits at noon."

"Then, I pray thee, let me lead the diversion," Christophe begged, knowing Angus was still recovering.

Angus studied his son. Though fierce pride shone in Laird MacGregor's eyes, several conflicting emotions crossed his features.

"Father, if we must put the clan first, ye must show yer trust in me."

Slowly, Angus nodded. "Take care."

Christophe smiled. "Aye, Father, and ye."

As Tavis moved his clansmen off to the right, Angus raised his hand for the column on the left to follow him.

Christophe did not like the thought of a trap. But they had the best strategy. He silently wished his father well as the old man rode off.

"Robb, is it not wise to see to the horses now?" Lor asked, looking around the terrain.

"Nay. We need to be at the appointed place at noon and by heaven we will be."

Christophe rode his men hard, following the well-laid

trail. He was at the point before noon, and sent out scouts ahead. They reported back that the Fraziers had an encampment just over the next rise. After he had assured himself that his father and Tavis were in place, and informed them of the Fraziers' position, he charged down into the enemy's camp. It was a daring but deadly attack. The element of surprise gave them the added edge. His father could not attack until the trap was sprung.

Far outnumbered, Christophe's army fought like men possessed as they slashed their way into the enemy's midst. Just as he could taste success, the Campbells, the Fraziers' allies, charged them from the cover of the forest. 'Twas a bloodbath as the overwhelming numbers poured onto the battlefield.

"Close ranks!" Christophe ordered, dismounting, and the MacGregors held position, fighting in a tight circle. Loyal men all, they each fought two and three soldiers, waiting for Angus and Tavis to charge behind the enemy's reinforcements.

The MacGregors sustained heavy casualties in the thick of battle. Screams of wounded men filled the air as hacked bodies bled and fell. Christophe fought two soldiers, his skill tested to the limit as he parried the sword blades. While he wielded his sword, he yelled encouragement to his men. Their determination filled him with pride as they stood courageously in the face of impossible odds. They continued to fight with bodies pierced and limbs bleeding. Minutes seemed like hours as MacGregors fell and the enemy rushed toward them.

Finally, the blood-curdling MacGregor war cry sounded as Angus's force poured onto the battlefield from two fronts, surrounding the enemy and trapping them.

Immediately, chaos reigned in the enemy ranks as frightened men broke and ran, leaving their line defenseless.

The tide of the battle turned and the Fraziers found themselves outnumbered.

Angus and Tavis fought like demons, driving their men into the ranks to rescue Robb MacGregor's forces. Swords ran red with blood as MacGregors rallied and met their rescuing clansmen halfway through the fight. They had successfully divided the opposing forces and easily held victory.

"Where is Alastair Frazier?" Angus asked, looking at his son over the bodies of fallen men.

Christophe wheeled around and saw the Frazier laird running from the ranks.

"There." Christophe pointed as he hacked and slashed his way after his enemy, fighting through the remaining resistance.

Angus wielded his sword in a wide arc and kicked his horse's flanks to narrow the gap between father and son. His steed leapt forward, eating up the distance that separated them, when an arrow pierced Laird MacGregor's ribs. Holding his bloody side, he still rode on, yelling orders to his son, who fought against the last wave of retreating Fraziers.

Christophe maneuvered through the growing bodies to grab a fleeing horse. He swung up into the saddle, pulling the animal around and driving him into the fray, his example bolstering his men. He slapped the horse's flank and managed to break through the soldiers. Once clear of the lines, he had just caught a glimpse of Alastair Frazier's retreat when a thick club smashed into the back of his head. The heavy blow knocked him from his horse. Pain exploded in Christophe's head as his sword slipped through his fingers and he hit the ground hard, somersaulting over onto his back.

Defenseless, he struggled against the black hole yawning ˚ore him. He blinked, trying to stem off the dizziness.

Suddenly, a blade shone above him as an enemy soldier stood ready to kill. Though every instinct screamed to move, Christophe waited until the soldier lunged forward before rolling over to avoid the thrust. He turned, but unfortunately, his reflexes were sluggish. Cold steel sliced his arm, and a burning pain shot through him.

Christophe tried and failed to gain his feet as the soldier drew back his sword to strike again. His heart roared in his ear as he watched the sword thrust.

Suddenly, the soldier's eyes grew wide and his sword dropped from his hand. He looked down at his stomach to see a blade emerging from his back. The soldier dropped to his knees, dead before he hit the ground.

Christophe recognized Angus's sword hilt sticking out of the enemy's back. If not for Angus's true aim at hurling his sword, the soldier who had unseated Christophe would have finished him.

Christophe lay there, his thoughts spinning as stars shone before his eyes. Groggy, Robb's memories flashed through his mind, as they had the night before—the hatred and insecurities, the misguided judgment, every thought, every feeling. He closed his eyes to stem off the dizziness, and he felt his own thoughts losing ground.

"God, no," he whispered as he realized he was losing his identity. Terror seized him as he fought against the force pulling him from this body. "Bronwyn," he cried out, but no sound passed his lips. She was leaving his conscience. A black wave of forgetfulness slowly covered him as he fought the loss of his identity. But everything was moving in slow motion, his memories, his thoughts, his very personality slowly seeping from him like a wound that poured his essence into the ground. A silence engulfed him as he floated above this body.

Robb MacGregor's spirit returned and he was reborn!

Christophe railed against the fates as he hovered helplessly and watched Robb MacGregor's eyes blink when he saw his father riding toward him.

Angus struggled forward, spurring his horse closer to his son. As the Fraziers dispersed and the fighting thinned, Angus managed to make it over to Robb. He was dismounting when a Frazier suddenly charged him, piercing his flesh with his blade. Bellowing with rage, Robb leapt up from the ground, hauled the opposing soldier from his father, and drove his dagger into the man's heart. Dropping him, he reached to catch Angus as he slid to the grass.

Eyes closed, his father grasped his tunic and coughed, trying to hold on to life. He twisted the bloody fabric in his hand. "Forgive her," he rasped. "Promise me ye will look after her." He gasped for air, his voice growing reedy. "Take Ariana as yer wife, when ye take my place as clan leader," he whispered, his eyes opened wide and filled with passion.

Robb cleared his throat, knowing it would be the last words spoken between father and son. "Aye, I promise."

Angus's features relaxed and for a brief moment he looked at peace; then he went limp, hanging in Robb's arms like a lifeless doll.

Anger and grief grew in Robb's chest. He threw his head back and roared, his wrath as black as any sailing on the wind. He lowered his father to the ground.

Marry Ariana! That lying, scheming bitch who'd tried to trap him in marriage had finally gotten her wish. He had never forgiven that wench, but neither could he ignore his father's dying request.

The battle waned around him. Men shouted curses or cried out in pain. The noise of wounded and weary men intruded on his thoughts. He looked around the bloody battlefield. Bodies lay strewn about, bloodstains standing out in the thick green moors. Battle-weary, filthy warriors leaned over their comrades, anxiously checking their wounds.

The fighting was over. The Clan Frazier, now broken, had deserted the field. Shoving aside his grief, Robb lifted his father's body and placed him across his horse, then swung up behind him. He would take the fallen leader home for a proper burial. Sad solemn faces turned his way, understanding and acknowledging his pain without so much as a word being said.

Robb nudged his horse forward, heading his men home. He was their leader now.

CHAPTER NINE

Morag's quill made large curlicues and bold exclamation marks as she underlined her message. *Dear Elspeth, I will always think fondly of ye and still consider ye family. I would be remiss in my duties if I did not inform ye that yer only son is marrying. I know ye can claim the right to be here. So I have included the date of his marriage. Please come.*

She smiled. Alastair, the fool, thought her dull-witted. Elspeth's presence at the wedding would bring an unexpected gift more precious than gold—confrontation. Robb MacGregor hated his mother. After Ariana's treatment of the sick, Alastair needed to regain the sympathy of the border clans. After all, 'twas only her brother's word against Laird Frazier. No one had proof of the poisoning.

A shameful incident of a son denying his mother entrance to the festivities would do very nicely.

Ah, life was so very easy, she thought. Just when she despaired of ever finding a way to unite the clans with her faction, an option appeared. Laughter filled the air as she went to find her dear sister-in-law and offer her services.

On the day of the wedding, the castle decorations shone in the candle glow and firelight. The banners, especially Cailin's, were magnificent. The day's light streamed in from the doorway and high ceiling windows, but the fire's glow added a soft warmth. In the great room below, the wine and ale flowed freely as the guests waited, and no doubt speculated if the groom would be present for his own wedding.

Musicians began playing rowdy ballads, and the aromas from the kitchen filled the air.

In the master chamber, Ariana's stomach churned as she and the ladies attended the bride.

"Oh, how do I look?" Cailin asked, turning before the ladies. The soft blue tunic with the white underskirt swirled about her ankles as she preened before them. Her smile hesitant, she looked first at the ladies, then back at the mirror. "Ye dinna think the pearls are too much?"

A delicate strand of pearls was woven through her long curls, adding highlights and elegance to her dark hair. Cailin fairly radiated poise and beauty. How could the bride doubt her own appearance?

"Beautiful," Ariana said, giving her the little bouquet of flowers she had asked Jessie to pick.

"Oh, they are lovely." Cailin smelled the blooms, her smile as sweet as the bouquet. " 'Tis so kind of ye."

" 'Tis only a bunch of flowers," Morag groused. "The way ye carry on, one would think it a handful of gems."

"Hush," Ariana ordered. "Ye will not ruin this day."

"A wedding without a bridegroom is an ill sign," Jessie warned.

Cailin's smile crumpled.

"Balderdash." Ariana hustled Morag and Jessie out of her chamber, then hurried the bride along. "I will join ye presently." She needed a minute to compose herself. She shut the door and closed her eyes. Even if Robb MacGregor were not here, it would still be hard to know he would be beyond her reach, married to another. How could she possibly get through the ceremony? Her baby kicked, and a swift band tightened around her middle. She held her stomach and leaned against the wall, panting. By her calculations her counterpart's child was not due for another month, but she knew her own pregnancy was almost over. Though the pain eased, she expected her child's birth soon.

A knock sounded on her door. Taking several deep breaths to compose herself, she stood and turned. "Enter."

Brodie opened the door and Cailin stood in the doorway, her face white as a sheet. "Dinna leave me alone with Lady Morag."

"Ye will make Friar Peter angry if ye are late for yer own wedding."

Cailin grabbed Ariana's hand. "Please, I would wait for ye."

The poor girl looked as forlorn as she felt. Although Ariana doubted anyone could feel worse today than she, Cailin's fear was tangible.

"Ye must not be so frightened," she admonished, giving Cailin's hand a comforting squeeze to still her trembling, before looping her arm through the bride's. "Come, yer fate awaits."

Cailin stared in wonder. "How do ye do it?"

"Do what?" Ariana said, putting up a brave front.

"Appear always in command. Like a soldier or laird."

Oh, the bitter irony burned her heart. If Cailin only knew how hard this facade was, mayhap her own trials would pale. Ariana smiled serenely and led the way to the stairs.

At the top of the stairs, Ariana lifted her gown slightly so the hem cleared her foot. Brodie took her arm as she waited for the bride to do the same and wondered how to reach this foolish child.

"Cailin, ye must learn the world will seldom accommodate ye. Either ye adjust, or ye will be bowled over and buried by others."

"I dinna want to handle anything. That is what a husband is for. He will keep me safe."

"What if yer husband is the one ye need protection from?"

Cailin blanched and stumbled slightly on the stairs.

With Brodie's support, Ariana steadied the bride. "Not that Robb MacGregor is a tyrant," she rushed to assure her, though every nerve in her body screamed to lie so Cailin would beg off the ceremony. "But wouldn't ye be more secure knowing ye could take care of yerself?"

"Nay, I am not like ye."

"Aye, I've noticed."

" 'Tis our natures, my lady. I can no more change, than ye can." Taking the last stair, Cailin turned to Ariana. "I desire nothing more than to be married."

Ariana sighed. "Then, my dear, it would seem ye have attained yer dreams." They stood at the foot of the stairs and looked out into the great room with the assembled guests.

The hall's decorations crowned the area as boughs of evergreens and autumn flowers adorned the rafters, while fresh rushes filled the air with herbal pungency.

A hush settled over the crowd as they noticed the bride.

A lump formed in Ariana's throat. She took deep, even breaths to keep her tears at bay. Before them Robb MacGregor's sword stood embedded in the floor before the friar. How she wished this was her wedding. Though she had been married twice, she had never walked down the aisle. After each time-travel, she had awakened as a wife.

Unless a miracle occurred, Cailin would soon be Robb MacGregor's bride. "Please, God, stop this farce. I will do anything, suffer any trial, if you halt this wedding," Ariana silently entreated.

But no thunder crossed the heavens, nor did any lightning bolt shatter the roof as they walked closer to the friar, who would seal all their fates.

Ariana wanted to hold Cailin back from taking her vows, but instead her hand fell away and she stepped aside. Her throat burned as a painful band constricted her chest.

Two steps and Lady Cailin would be next to the sword.

Ariana's eyes stung as she watched the uncertain and shy woman look about for reassurance. "Don't go through with it," Ariana wanted to scream.

Friar Peter gestured to Cailin to take her place. She had taken one step when the doors flew open. In the entrance stood a warrior, his features hidden as his auburn hair wildly swirled in the wind.

"Wait!" Gavin rushed up to the friar. "Stop the wedding."

Ariana almost collapsed with relief. God had answered her prayers. She turned to Gavin, her hands shaking in the folds of her tunic.

His face solemn, Gavin turned toward the angry crowd and held up his hands. "The MacGregor's mother has come to witness the wedding."

A murmur of disapproval went up in the hall.

Ariana took a deep breath as she looked around at the stunned and angry faces. Only Morag seemed unaffected by the news.

"My lady," Gavin prompted.

She walked up to Friar Peter, and joined Gavin to face the angry congregation.

"Do not let that woman in here," one clansmen called out.

"Aye, she is the devil's spawn."

Suddenly, the room erupted in slurs as men raised their fists and women grumbled.

Rumors had clouded Robb's mother for years. Ariana spoke softly, intentionally, so the crowd would have to quiet to hear her. She smiled sweetly and drew her hand to encompass the gathering. "This is a celebration. We will have no dissension. Hospitality is the custom here."

Shocked looks mirrored the confusion as men and women alike stared at her. She turned to the friar. "We are Christians, are we not? Mayhap, ye should concentrate on reminding yon guests."

Friar Peter nodded, a hint of a smile touching his lips as he turned to sternly stare at those gathered before him.

In the deafening silence, Gavin bowed before her, then presented her his arm. She smiled and went to greet the new guest, with Brodie trailing in her wake. Passing through the doors that overlooked the courtyard, Ariana spied a small entourage with a slight woman dressed in gold sitting astride a white horse. She dismounted with regal grace, extending her hand to her guard.

Ariana waited as the woman seemed to glide across the courtyard and ascend the steps, never faltering nor giving any sign that her presence caused pandemonium.

"I am Elspeth Frazier, Robb MacGregor's mother."

"My Lady Frazier. I am Angus's wife, Lady Ariana."

Elspeth's eyes widened in surprise; then slowly her gaze lowered and she bowed. "I had hoped ye were my son's bride."

Ariana's heart skipped a beat. *Could the woman read her thoughts?* she wondered, staring at the bent fair head.

"Nay, I am his stepmother. I will call Lady Cailin." She backed up and peeked her head through the oak doors, motioning for Cailin to join them.

Laird Drummond held his daughter's arm, oblivious of her distress, and vehemently shook his head. "Until my daughter is married she is governed under my rule and I willna permit this introduction."

His voice easily carried to Lady Elspeth, and Ariana dreaded facing her. She glared at Laird Drummond, then with a tight smile in place she whirled around.

"I am sorry, Lady Cailin is unable to meet ye."

"Ye must wonder why I have come." Elspeth held up her hand when Ariana tried to speak. "I was informed I would be welcomed." She looked over Ariana's shoulder to view the silent crowd through the open doors. "It would seem the person who contacted me was wrong. But I didna believe the animosity had changed; still, I had to test the waters."

Ariana held out her hand. "Would ye come this way? Yer son is not here. His bride is to be married by proxy."

"By proxy?" The woman was taken aback. "It would seem I was greatly misinformed. I was told my son would be here, or I would not have journeyed this far."

"He may return today and yet make the ceremony."

"Nay, I am not welcome."

"No matter what ye have heard, ye are welcome in our home."

Elspeth shot her a piercing look. She studied her for several minutes before she offered her hand. "What they say about ye is true."

Her face flushed. "Excuse me?"

"I had heard ye were a saint, a true angel who walks among us. Until now, I doubted such a paragon existed."

"I assure ye, I am no saint," Ariana said as someone closed the doors behind her.

"I agree," Morag said, her voice sharp as she marched out onto the stoop.

Elspeth eyes narrowed. "Excuse me," Elspeth said, turning.

"Ye are going?" Morag asked, her face white with concern.

Elspeth turned back, her features tight with anger. "Aye, I have no use for the MacGregors. Only one interests me."

Morag glared at Ariana, then whirled about, walking back into the castle and slamming the door.

Ariana eyed Elspeth carefully. " 'Tis harsh words to levy on a clan."

" 'Tis a harsh world, my dear." She reached out. "But ye have been most kind to me, considering our status. Had I been in yer shoes, I do not know if I would have been so charitable. I thank ye." She turned and placed her hand on her escort's arm, then walked slowly down the steps and over to her horse. She looked back at Ariana. "Be careful, my dear. Ye are surrounded by enemies." With those cryptic words the slight woman mounted her horse and, without a backward glance, departed.

With her chin held high, Ariana entered the great room again. All eyes looked past her, searching for the Frazier woman.

"My lady, where is she?" Friar Peter asked the question on everyone's mind.

Ariana took Cailin's arm, rescuing her from her father's grip, then led her across the great room. "Lady Elspeth Frazier came to see her son."

"She left?" Laird MacPherson asked.

"Aye," Ariana said.

Cailin cried out, her face deathly pale. "I knew she would be offended because I did not greet her."

"I am sure she does not hold ye accountable," Ariana soothed.

" 'Tis not important, girl, if Elspeth hates ye. Show some pride," Laird Drummond admonished.

Large tears slipped down Cailin's face as she shook her head in denial, then ran from the room.

Ariana faced Laird Drummond. "Sir, if ye cause any more trouble ye will leave. I dinna want to hear one more disparaging word out of yer mouth. Do I make myself clear?"

He started to grouse, and she held her hand up. "If ye want this ceremony to proceed, ye will heed my words."

He fumed, but remained silent.

It took over an hour to settle Cailin down. The bride's eyes were red-rimmed and when she walked back into the great room she stared at the floor.

"Ahem." Friar Peter cleared his throat, indicating he wished to perform the ceremony.

Cailin blushed and took her place before the cleric.

After Friar Peter patted the bride's hand, he started the ceremony. Ariana's heart quivered as she watched the nuptials. Every word of the wedding service crushed her. *Stop! Please stop!* she silently cried.

"If there is anyone who hath just cause for this marriage not to take place, let him speak now or forever after hold his peace." Ariana's chest tightened painfully as she remained quiet.

When Friar Peter started in on the vows, a commotion was heard outside. The friar's displeasure showed as he stopped the wedding and waved to Laird MacPherson. "Can ye halt the disturbance?"

Laird MacPherson walked to the doors and met Gavin. He stood talking for several minutes, then suddenly waved all to follow him. "The MacGregors are returning."

Ariana nearly collapsed into Brodie. Robb MacGregor had returned. Her prayers had been answered. Relief rushed through her. Pray God her love had a plan. At once voices sounded as the warriors rushed from the great room along with the castle occupants.

On the battlements Ariana could see the band of men far off in the valley.

Laird MacPherson took Ariana's hands in his. "Courage. I will ride out to meet them." He ran down the steps and mounted his horse, waved at her, then galloped out of sight.

The guests had crowded into the courtyard, their voices rising.

She reached out to Cailin, whose tense features seemed frozen. "It will be all right. Robb MacGregor will return uninjured," she said fervently, needing to hear the words out loud.

Cailin nodded, her eyes as big as saucers.

Ariana rushed toward the gate. The horses were almost to the castle. With every step she took, her mind repeated a litany. "Let them return safe. Please, let Christophe be all right."

The faces of the castle's servants were drawn and somber as they jostled for better position, each one trying to see who had returned unharmed.

The hooves sounded on the drawbridge. The soldiers were dirty, bloodied, and haggard, but she rejoiced that they were alive. Her gaze searched the band, and curiously, two faces were not at the front.

Lor dismounted before her and she touched his sleeve. "Where are the laird and his son?"

His face tightened. "My lady, prepare yerself."

Prepare herself? For what? All thought, all feeling died. "Nay," she said, shaking her head. She did not want to hear him. She took a step backward as tears burned her eyes.

He reached out to her, but it was Brodie who steadied her as the men continued to file in. Some needed her healing skills; others were so exhausted they literally fell out of their saddles.

Lor followed her gaze. "Please, my lady, listen to me."

Then she saw the horses with the bodies strapped over them. They were wrapped in their plaids, their faces hidden. So many bodies, she shrank away.

"Oh," she cried, tearing out of Brodie's hold as horrible pain sliced through her.

Lor caught her. "My lady, yer husband died, saving his son."

The words penetrated the haze: Christophe lived. Her joy was short-lived as the men carried the laird's body over to her and uncovered his face.

She gasped at the sight of her husband, bloodied and dead. Tears filled her eyes at his passing. He was a good man and had offered her counterpart a sanctuary. After her thoughts earlier, shame covered her. An honorable man had lost his life. She would mourn his passing. Her own situation paled in the face of death. She looked over at the other corpses. Good Lord, they had lost more than a third of their men. "Gavin."

He rushed to her. "See to a burial detail," she rasped.

After he bowed, she took a deep breath and pushed out of Lor's arms. Her healing skills were needed. With renewed energy, she rushed through the sea of men toward the injured. Her heart stopped for a moment as she saw the carnage. Dear God, what had happened? "Jessie," she called out.

"Aye, my lady." The gentle cook stood up from tending an injured man.

"We will need to turn the armory into an infirmary to suit our needs. See that the soldiers do so."

"Aye, my lady."

She knelt by a soldier assessing his wounds. It was truly a miracle he had even made it home.

She patted his shoulder as she closed his tunic. "We will see to ye first."

"My lady, yer husband died bravely."

His words of comfort brought another wave of tears to her eyes. She nodded and moved away, knowing she would have to keep busy to stave off the grief that filled her.

Finally, after all the men had safely entered the courtyard, Christophe and her father rode through the gates. Though she wanted to run to him, she could not. In the span of a heartbeat she drank in his features, then turned to comfort the wounded.

Iona and Isla brought her tray. "What else do ye need, my lady?" they asked in unison.

"See that plenty of linen is ripped into strips. We will need them for binding."

"Aye, my lady."

Moving from one patient to another, she caught glimpses of Christophe as he walked and talked with her father, but he did not approach her, and she had little time to seek him out.

The castle guard lifted the wounded and carried them into the armory, after she assessed who needed attention first. After an hour, with her back aching and her tunic splotched with blood, she walked out of the armory into the great room. Laird MacPherson put his arm around her and gave her a hug. For a moment she clung to him, needing the comfort. She swallowed and looked up into his eyes. His compassion was nearly her undoing. She pushed free before she broke down and wept. The wedding decorations seemed to mock her as she stared at the guests. Their faces were downcast, and she suddenly sensed anger in the air.

Cailin stood in the corner, her face wet with tears as her clansmen gathered around her, their voices raised in anger. Suddenly Laird Drummond's attention slanted to

Ariana. One by one all the Drummond clansmen stared at her, their gazes filled with condemnation and fury.

A wave of apprehension washed over her as she weathered their censure and walked farther into the tense atmosphere.

Robb MacGregor marched across the room toward her, his eyes cold, his gaze harsh. Where was the warmth in his eyes? Had Christophe stopped the wedding? He took her hand in his, leading her back to the center of the room.

With all eyes on them, he lifted her hand. "Ariana MacGregor, I promised my father, if he died, I would take thee for my wife."

Drummond voices erupted at the announcement. Cailin's soft cries were muffled behind her hand as her clansmen raised their fists in the air.

Christophe's convincing act, though necessary, frightened her. Instinctively, she wanted to pull her hand free of his, but quelled her fears. Christophe would never harm her.

Laird Drummond stepped forward. "What say ye, woman?" He stood with his feet braced and his arms crossed.

Silence descended as all eyes centered on her. Robb MacGregor squeezed her hand in a silent warning.

Laird Drummond's wrath reached out to her. Her gaze briefly sought out Cailin's, but the girl refused to make eye contact.

Ariana drew a deep breath and lifted her chin, meeting the hostility in Laird Drummond's eyes. "I must honor my laird's last wish. 'Tis his dying will."

Enraged, Drummond clansmen issued threats as they milled closer together, squaring off against the MacGregors and MacPhersons. Laird Drummond's curses filled the hall, and he stormed across the floor.

" 'Tis an abomination," he said. Cailin's eldest brother

covered his sword as the younger one strode over to stand
behind their father. Laird Drummond jabbed his finger
into Robb MacGregor's chest. "I will see ye in Hell for this
insult."

A slow, satisfied smile slipped naturally across Robb's
lips. "Ye are tired of living?" His cool demeanor in the
face of such confrontation brought a string of curses from
the Drummond men.

Rage colored the laird's features at the taunt. His eyes
narrowed. " 'Tis not I who wishes to leave this world. When
ye taste the bite of my sword, remember yer foolish challenge." He turned and signaled his men. The Drummond
party marched out, dragging the lovely bride, her shoulders stooped and her eyes downcast.

Ariana's heart broke at the pitiful sight. Poor Cailin.
Jilted on her wedding day and returned to that uncaring
lot.

She could not stand to watch the girl's sorrow. With a
vow never to be at any man's mercy, she turned to meet
her beloved's eyes.

But Christophe had turned to his men. His bearing was
straight, his demeanor authoritative. He motioned for Lor
and together they walked out of the room, talking in low
tones as the men fell in behind them. She held her breath
and slowly followed.

Laird Drummond and his party marched out of the
castle, their voices raised in anger as their horses galloped
through the gate.

All the MacGregor clansmen gathered around the new
laird.

"This will mean war." He called Gavin over. "Prepare
the castle and see to the men."

"Aye, my laird." Gavin bowed. His gaze slipped to her
before he turned to fortify the walls.

A cold dread washed over her. War. Dear God. They

had survived a plague; now a war was forthcoming. She tried to calm her racing heart. Thank God Christophe commanded the castle.

He moved among his men. "Lor, see to the weapons."

Malcolm stepped forward, favoring his injured leg. "My laird, the well the lady had built is complete. We will have fresh water for the siege."

"Aye, if we defend, but I plan to attack."

"Attack!" The word echoed in Ariana's mind. Fear traveled along every nerve as she watched him issuing orders. They were safe within the walls. She wanted to disagree, but knew she could not until they were alone. A terrible dread filled her. He issued commands as Christophe had, but yet he seemed different, more seasoned, more ruthless. He was utterly in control, fearless, and his arrogance terrified her.

When Gavin and Lor had carried out the laird's bidding, they returned and called all the able men into the courtyard.

She stood mesmerized as the new laird lifted his arms to men assembled in the courtyard.

His commanding voice held the clan spellbound.

"We will never bow to another clan. 'Tis not in our nature and would shame those who have died for our freedom."

She listened to his inspiring speech. Her heart ached. He was every inch the Scottish warrior. Pray God he stayed safe. She turned, knowing the castle had more to do to prepare for the war. A siege always meant confined and crowded living quarters. Hygiene was imperative. She would talk to Christophe when they were alone. He would understand the problem.

After the laird finished addressing the men, she dashed to the kitchen to check the larder with Jessie. The food supply was good, but her herbs were greatly depleted. Tomorrow she would go out and gather what she needed.

Her heart pounded when she heard the laird bellowing her name from the other room.

She rushed out into the great room, and found the whole clan assembled again with Friar Peter at the head of the stairs.

Everyone stared at her as she skidded to a stop. Laird MacPherson's eyes held pity and compassion, and his expression confused her. She faced Christophe. His closed expression seemed chiseled out of stone.

"There is one unpleasant obligation I must see to before I leave."

"Unpleasant?" she breathed, wondering if Morag had told him about his mother's visit.

"Aye, I must take ye for my wife." His eyes were hard chips of ice, his stance unyielding as he held out his hand to her.

Heart beating faster, she swallowed her fear. This was Christophe acting, she reminded herself. Yet as she walked forward, there was not one glimmer of welcome or warmth in his cold stare.

"Ye must feel very happy ye have won what ye desired."

"Aye," she whispered back.

Again that cold smile appeared, devoid of warmth. He turned to the friar. "Have done."

He lifted her hand in his. When she trembled, his smile broadened.

"Nervous, my dear?"

"Aye."

"It is as it should be."

She lifted an eyebrow as the friar began the ceremony. A niggling of fear crept into her heart, but she refused to give her imagination credence. This was her Christophe, and he, like she, had a part to play. She took a deep breath and silenced the doubts. Christophe had never betrayed her. He had died for her. A measure of calm stole over her, until just before the vows. Then a premonition of disaster took such hold that she felt her whole body tremble.

"Run," an inner voice screamed. "Do so now, escape."

The plague, the war, the time-travel, she was understandably overwrought. She silenced her fear. Christophe had found a way for them to be together and she would not let her fears stand in the way of their happiness.

She tried to glance at him, but he held his head straight, and his eyes focused on the friar. If only he would turn and offer her a little reassurance. If only he could let her know that he understood her fears. Suddenly, he did turn and a silent gasp sounded in her mind. Robb MacGregor's blue eyes shone without light, soulless windows to an angry man. Dread filled her, and she took a mental step back. Where was Christophe?

CHAPTER TEN

"Do ye take this man for yer lawful wedded husband?" Friar Peter asked.

Ariana looked at Christophe, and the name Robb imposed itself. She must now swear that she would love, honor, and obey him.

Her hand trembled as she placed it upon the Bible. Her heart raced. *No! Stop this foolishness!* her mind screamed. This was Christophe, not Robb! 'Twas merely a trick of light.

Then she watched Robb. Every muscle in his face was taut, his expression hard. Doubt surfaced. Was this an act?

Robb looked directly into her eyes. "What are ye waiting for?" His voice was low, deadly, the lack of volume all the more frightening.

She drew in a deep breath. Her heart pounded in her ears. Again the fear returned, but she forced it aside. This was Christophe, not Robb. He had to act so, in order to fool the clan. She gathered her inner courage, wrapping it around her like a warm protective mantle on a cold winter day. But still a chill invaded her soul as she faced Friar Peter. "I do swear to honor my laird in all matters."

The clansmen nodded, as did the women. All but one was satisfied.

Morag stepped forward. She pointed her finger at Robb. "Stop! 'Tis unseemly to marry yer stepmother."

A hush settled over the room as Ariana's stomach roiled at the challenge.

Robb MacGregor turned around. His eyes filled with outrage. "Ye dare forbid me?" His angry voice echoed throughout the room.

All eyes focused on Morag as she took a step backward, before she raised her chin. " 'Tis my right."

The air hung thick with tension, and Morag began to squirm beneath Robb's gaze. "I will rule the clan until my sibling comes of age to help," Robb said. "I will now marry the woman that is my stepmother. My father's last wish will be honored."

"Nay, 'tis shameful. I know ye have lusted for this wench while she masqueraded as yer father's bride."

A deafening silence blanketed the room. Clansmen moved away from her as Robb MacGregor stepped toward his aunt. "What say ye, woman!"

Morag lifted her pointed chin. "Ye heard me! Ye and she are fornicators. Praise God, Angus died without the knowledge and Elspeth left before she witnessed such shame."

"Elspeth Frazier was here?" Robb asked.

A collective gasp rose up as Morag, satisfied with the clan's reaction, smugly smiled into her nephew's face.

Robb MacGregor backhanded his aunt, sending her sprawling to the rushes. He turned and stared at his clansmen. "Is there anyone else that objects to this marriage?"

When their solemn expressions met his, he looked at

his aunt. " 'Tis time ye were sent away. My father suggested court, but I think a convent would do more to improve yer disposition."

Morag cupped her cheek, and slowly shook her head. "Ye canna mean this."

"Begone." He motioned for a soldier. "See ye that she arrives safely at St. Kathryn's convent."

Morag's eyes narrowed to murderous slits. She raised her fist as the soldier lifted her. "Is this the payment for all my loyal years of service to yer father and ye?"

"Nay. 'Tis for yer sour disposition. And for daring to mention that woman's name in my presence. Ye may return when ye have learned some humility."

Morag's indignant curses rang in the air as the guard pulled her out of the room.

Ariana looked into his eyes. Her heart fluttered at his harsh, condemning stare. The niggling of fear she had denied suddenly took hold. This was not her beloved. Robb MacGregor had taken Christophe's place.

Panic assailed her. Her heart raced as she watched his hard, unemotional features. *Christophe,* she silently cried, *where are you?* She swallowed her terror, refusing to surrender to hysteria. Christophe would find a way back to her. He had to.

Robb MacGregor made no move toward her. He was waiting for her to come to him.

She stepped forward. "I will accept thee as my husband."

His eyes narrowed. "The decision was never yers."

Although his words were curt, nothing prepared her for the hatred in his gaze. He turned to the friar. "Finish the ceremony and have done."

Friar Peter cleared his throat and motioned for them to once again take their places.

Cupping her elbow, Robb forced her forward. She stood by his side, every nerve afire, panic descending like a shroud. In the sudden silence, she glanced around only to find solemn faces meeting her gaze. Her mind rushed, frantically seeking a solution. "Wait," she cried softly while freeing her arm from his hold.

Disapproval lit his eyes as he looked down at her. "Do ye have an objection?" he asked ominously.

She sensed the clan's pity, and caught the friar's warning look, but even so she raised her chin and nodded. " 'Tis my wedding, sir. I will have one concession."

His eyebrow raised. She knew she had angered him more, but she could not stop herself. She must buy herself some time. "Friar, would ye not wait until our king could be sent for to witness this auspicious occasion? Then there could be no claim of dishonor, nor talk of annulment."

At her reasonable request, the cleric looked to the new laird. "Would ye permit a short delay?"

"Nay." He clasped her hand in a crushing grip that brought instant tears to her eyes. Holding her firmly at his side, he said, "Friar, say the words that will bind us together in a trap."

She gasped at his high-handedness, and though she tugged and pulled, he held her fast.

Not once since the cleric began his ceremony did Robb look at her. His total indifference during the wedding ceremony gave her a moment's respite, and she tried to gather her thoughts.

Flustered, the cleric repeated the vows. "Will ye have this woman for yer wife?"

"Aye," he thundered.

Thoughts of running, of turning around and leaving the big, hulking stranger, raced through her mind. The appeal grew as her fear took hold. Then the friar turned to her.

His kindly features were the needed measure of reassurance. "My lady, will ye have this man as yer husband?"

Though every instinct in her body cried out to run, she

knew she could not escape. "Aye," she said, silencing her fear and sealing her fate.

The friar smiled at her, then turned to Robb. "I pronounce thee man and wife. Ye may give the kiss of peace to yer bride."

Robb turned to her then, and a quiver of pure fear went through her at the loathing in his eyes.

Though she trembled, she refused to cower before him. She raised her chin.

He smiled. "The kiss, wife." He lowered his head to hers, slowly, so he could watch her reaction. Then his lips touched hers and nothing was slow. His brutal kiss ground her teeth into her lips. She tasted her own blood under his crude carnal display that humiliated her before all.

When he raised his head, he wore a satisfied smile. She swallowed under his arrogant, pleased look. He had meant to make her suffer and he had succeeded. A distant recollection of her dream drifted back, giving a little snatch of Ariana's life that was all too telling. Her counterpart had loved this man.

But the memory of her Christophe surfaced suddenly. She would find him within the man she had married. She would find him and bring him back. She simply had to.

Serenity flowed through her as she bowed to her husband, surprising him by her respectful gesture. His eyes widened as he watched her. *Good*, she thought, *better to keep him guessing than play into his hand. Let him question his earlier perceptions of her.*

Laird MacPherson gathered her in his arms and kissed her cheek soundly. "Ye make me proud, daughter. Laird Angus MacGregor would be too."

All around her voices exploded in a sudden profusion of smiles and good tidings. Gavin slapped Robb MacGregor on the back. Lor offered him a cup of whiskey. "Well done, my laird." The men circled the laird and congratulated him, as did the ladies her.

The music that she had chosen surrounded her.

Robb MacGregor stood with several men and bent his head to hear Friar Peter and Jessie's husband, Malcolm. His face solemn, he nodded to the men, then turned to face the crowd.

A shiver went up her spine at his cold expression. She smiled at those around him, then joined her husband, conscious of the sudden pall that hung in the air. Robb MacGregor held up his hands. The musicians stopped, and the clansmen came to order. "Before we celebrate, we must honor those who have fallen. The graves are dug and the bodies prepared. Now, before we lose the light, we will put our men to rest. Friar Peter will pray over the graves."

Silence descended, the festive mood forgotten as the castle occupants walked outside to honor their fallen men. In true Scottish fashion, the mourning began with the plaintive cries of the widows and orphans.

Her father beside her, Ariana walked from her wedding to a funeral. In a daze, she stood by Friar Peter.

"Send for the pipers," Robb MacGregor ordered.

At dusk, the mournful wail of the bagpipes filled the air as Friar Peter blessed and prayed over each grave. The wounded who could attend stood silently as women mopped their faces and children stared at the dark mounds. Friar Peter ended his ceremony at the laird's grave. The bagpipes stilled, the dying notes of the emptying bag a fitting tribute to a full and rich life struck down.

Ariana bowed her head, her heart heavy with pain.

"Good-bye, Father," Robb said. His gaze settled on her. The import of his words sliced into her heart. Her champion was gone, leaving her alone with Robb. Her stomach roiled at the prospect of dealing with her vengeful groom. *No*, an inner voice whispered, *Robb MacGregor loved you. 'Tis only that he felt betrayed. You must find the man who would die for you. He exists.*

She closed her eyes. "Christophe, where are you?"

After Laird Angus's funeral, the clansmen returned to the hall. A great heaviness hung in the air until Robb MacGregor stood in the center of the great room. "We will honor our dead, their hard-won victory, and this wedding with merriment."

Those clansmen who could dance pulled their ladies onto the floor and twirled them around. The MacGregors had learned death could come in a heartbeat, which made every second of life precious.

Laird MacPherson led her into a dance. "Daughter, if ye are to survive, ye must make peace with yer husband. He is a proud man."

Ariana thought of her counterpart. "Aye, Father, I will try."

"Ye love him. It should not be too much of a trial." He smiled down at her.

If he only knew, she thought. "Father, he is not an easy man."

Laird MacPherson's gaze shifted to the subject. "I know. By the scowl on his face, I would say ye are about to be led into the marriage dance."

A shiver stole up her spine as her father handed her over to her groom. The music flowed around them as Ariana danced with her husband. Others watched their fluid steps, but a cold chill separated them. His anger was like a wedge that kept them apart.

Laird MacPherson was right. Someone had to bridge this gap, and by the tense muscles beneath her fingertips, she knew it would have to be her. Taking a cleansing breath, she smiled and looked up into his eyes.

The harsh gaze that met hers nearly silenced her, but she would not be intimidated. "My laird, dinna ye think it time we put our differences aside?"

"Differences?"

"Aye. 'Tis foolish to start a life together with animosity harbored between us."

"What are ye proposing?"

She swallowed her fear, for his eyes were cold and harsh. "Yer father wanted this match. I honor his name as I will honor yers, but we canna make a marriage succeed when there is no trust or respect between us."

His chuckle was snide. "Ye not only enjoy trapping a man, but ye want him to be happy with it. I would never have married ye. If not for the vow I gave my father, ye would be out in yon field, left to fend for yerself. I have no love for ye, and never will."

Terror raced through her. Would he harm her and her child? Her instinct cried out to appeal to his vanity. She raised her chin. "I carry yer child."

"Aye, ye do. And it is for my seed that I tolerate ye. Nothing more, nothing less."

His voice cut through her fears as relief flooded her. He would not harm her child. "What do ye expect of this marriage?"

"Nothing." His voice turned flat.

An inner smile lit her heart. She pulled out of his arms and calmly retreated from the room with Iona and Isla following in her wake. In the master chamber she allowed them to change her gown and pull back the blankets.

Delicate herbs and dried flowers had been sprinkled throughout the room, and the subtle scent wafted in the air with the delicious promise of sensual pleasures.

"My lady, the laird willna be able to resist yer charms." Iona combed her hair, spreading it out across her shoulders and back like a windswept curtain of red silk.

Ariana smiled wanly at the servant. 'Twas not lust Robb MacGregor sought, but revenge. Protectively, she covered her swollen abdomen. Thankfully, she did not have the figure to entice a man's desire.

"My lady, dinna fret, ye are lovely," Isla offered, seeing her concern about her advanced pregnancy.

"Thank ye," she said, remembering how her dear husband had rejected her. Though she had been relieved, her pride now ebbed to its lowest point. Then her babe kicked and she roused herself from self-pity.

Though she wanted to cry when they left, she did not. A vengeful groom would soon appear—her counterpart's troubled lover. How in the world would she ever reach him? *Christophe*, she silently cried. *Where are you?*

Stop it! her mind screamed. *Ye are alone and ye must rise to the occasion. Your new husband is stubborn and proud and ye know how to handle that,* an inner voice counseled. Indeed, she did. But what about Christophe? She fretted over his disappearance. Suddenly, an angel's voice she remembered from her travel through time echoed in her mind. "Once Robb MacGregor is at peace, he will rest and Christophe will return."

"But how?" she whispered.

Silence met her plea and she closed her eyes, praying for an answer. A terrible loneliness engulfed her. What if Robb never found peace? Would Christophe be lost to her forever? An ache gripped her as fear and despair filled her heart. She needed Christophe. She wrapped her arms around herself, and rocked gently forward trying to assuage the terrible hurt. *Christophe, what am I to do?* Fleeting memories returned with a force that overwhelmed her. His hand clasping hers as they walked through the meadows. His lips whispering his love, his soft gentle voice caressing her in the middle of the night. She shivered with aching delight, remembering his arms enveloping her in his embrace. She could almost smell his manly aroma of fresh air and honest work. Lord, her memories were so real, she could almost imagine him with her. But her arms were empty, her lips unkissed, and her body ached from the absence of his love. Her breath caught in her throat as her raw recollection, lush with love and heartache, washed over her.

Before she could entreat the angel again, the door flew open with a resounding crash, and Robb MacGregor stood in the doorway. His eyes devoured her diaphanous gown of sheer white, which shimmered on her bare skin like a soft mist.

"Come here," he breathed as he stepped inside and barred the door behind him.

Her heart raced as she slowly moved off the bed. "I thought there was nothing between us but the vow to yer father."

This time his smile reached his eyes, but still there was no warmth dwelling within. She shuddered from the calculating expression.

"There has always been, and always will be, a fire between us."

She tried to move away from him.

"Do ye deny it?" He backed her up to the bed.

"My laird, ye wanted nothing from this marriage."

He took her in his arms.

She turned her head to evade his kiss, but his lips descended to catch her gasp.

Christophe, her mind cried as Robb's lips crushed hers in a carnal kiss.

His kiss was hot, wet, and wanton, but she did not respond. Then he suddenly pulled back. "The fire in yer soul has burned out."

Fear sliced through her; he could sense something was amiss. Her counterpart would welcome him. " 'Tis my condition, my laird. I am not the same woman ye knew." She stroked her rounded belly. " 'Tis hard to be a temptress when ye are heavy with child."

He studied her. "I have heard that a woman changes during her time." He caressed the side of her cheek.

Lord, what would she do now? To sleep with a man she knew was not her soul mate was impossible. She drew a deep breath. "My laird, if ye could wait until our child is born?" she ventured cautiously.

"Ye ask me to start over, then ye ask me to wait?"

"Mayhap we need some time to decide on how strong our affections are."

His knuckles grazed her lips. "Ye have always wanted yer way. Willful and strong ye be."

She decided to gamble and meet his challenge. Her chin lifted, her gaze locked with his. "Ye fell in love with my ways and I risked all to be with ye. Is it so much to ask?"

"Aye, it is." He pulled her back into his arms. His lips took hers again, but this time there was a softening, a warmth that slipped past her defenses.

She struggled, tearing her mouth free. "What do ye want of me?"

"Ye, my dear, little wife, used to warm my bed without the blessing of the Church. Do ye now find that once the vows are said, ye no longer have a desire for lust?"

" 'Twas not lust," she denied.

He chuckled. "Oh, it was indeed lust. Ye were the

most ardent lover I have ever known. Ye made my nights bearable.'' He caressed the side of her face. "I have never known a woman with such instinctive moves. 'Tis hard for a man to admit, but when ye wed my father I hated him, for I could not bear the thought of ye two alone.'' A darkness entered his gaze and the expression chilled her.

She trembled. "Do ye think to make me suffer for giving my child a name when ye would not?''

His gaze narrowed. "Do ye have no idea what purgatory ye put me through?''

She swallowed at the hurt that colored his words, and took a protective step backward, only to hit the edge of the bed. "I loved ye.''

"Ye know nothing of love.''

She looked him straight in the eye. "I know more about love than ye. I would never abandon ye.''

Pain flickered in his eyes before his face tightened in anger. "Ye did when ye married my father.''

"Angus rescued me from my father's wrath.'' She recalled the vivid dream. "Ye know he would have turned me out.''

"And I would have taken ye in.''

She knew very little about her predecessor's love affair, but she had already surmised that Ariana would be too proud to be his mistress. "I would have died first.''

"So ye said.''

"Robb.'' She touched his arm. "For our child's sake, canna we call a truce?''

He shook her hand free. "I can never forgive, or trust ye again.''

Her heart clenched at the fury in his eyes. Her poor predecessor, Ariana thought. To love so arrogant a man.

But her counterpart must have seen his heart. Only a wounded spirit would spout such anger, an obvious defense against being hurt.

She had few options. The man's soul needed saving, her child depended on her, and her beloved waited to be rescued. What should she do? *Peace,* she thought, *and charity.*

"I have forgiven ye, and I have forgiven yer abandonment. When ye forgive, ye will know true peace. If ye let this slight fester, it will poison yer soul."

"Ye twisted my insides until I thought I would never be whole, and ye have the insolence to forgive me? I canna, I willna forgive ye. Will ye have me lie?"

"Nay, I respect the truth. But until there is trust between us, there will be nothing of value. If one of us should die without resolving this, our spirits will be haunted for all time. I would not want that on my conscience. I love ye, and I always will."

For an instant uncertainty crossed his harsh features. She began to hope she had reached him. He moved away from her and ran a hand through his hair. Her words had hit a nerve. But then he shook his head in denial. "Witch," he breathed, wheeling around. "I believed ye once. Never again."

She sighed. "Then we are doomed by yer pride."

She could see a myriad of emotions cross his handsome features in the space of heartbeat. She held her breath, anticipating he would consider her request.

When he turned to face her, his eyes were shadowed, making it impossible to read his thoughts. "Ye will accept what I am willing to give, even if it is less than ye wish."

Even though it was an order, she heard the edge in his voice and knew he was having difficulty, as though he was fighting a private war with himself.

She sighed. "It is a start," she said, disheartened that he offered so little.

"Then come here," he whispered, removing his smock and reaching for her. "Be the mistress I have missed."

Her heart nearly missed a beat at the wide expanse of broad chest with the golden medallion nestled among the thick curly hairs; then she looked up into the desire burning in his eyes. Terror surged through her as his muscular arms pulled her into his strong embrace. Their bodies pressed full against each other, his desire evident. She closed her eyes. *Christophe,* she silently cried. *Help me!* His lips descended on hers as she wildly thought of excuses. She pushed on his chest trying to get free, but all she managed to do was scratch his flesh.

A whimper formed in her throat as his kiss turned rough, demanding, insisting she respond to his caress.

A pounding sounded, an incessant drumming that she thought was her heart. Releasing Ariana, Robb MacGregor swore softly and went to the door, his voice a low growl. "This had better be worth yer life." He swung the door open, and Ariana's father stood outside.

" 'Tis worth it." He pushed the door in slightly and took hold of Robb's arm. He turned to his daughter. "Ye will forgive us, my dear, but yer husband and I have unfinished business."

Robb pulled his arm free. "What business?"

"Angus and I had a business arrangement that must now include ye. If ye will come with me, we will see to the details."

"Are ye daft, man? 'Tis my wedding night."

Laird MacPherson looked sharply at his son-in-law. "Are ye the laird? Or a lovesick lad?"

Robb's face burned crimson. Grabbing his smock, he pointed to the hallway. "Lead on," he said, and followed the man out of the chamber.

As soon as the door slammed closed, Ariana's shoulders sagged as she slumped to the bed. She had little choice but to make the best of things. She closed her eyes, and at once her thoughts went to Christophe. Two tears slipped through her lashes. "I love you," she whispered. "I always will."

CHAPTER ELEVEN

Christophe walked through a thick, soundless fog, and an eerie foreboding engulfed him. He had passed through this filmy cloud before. " 'Twas the mist of time," he whispered, his voice a lonely echo in the still void.

Memories suddenly flooded his mind. The rich full-bodied taste of wine upon the pallet, the vivid colors that painted the sky and soothed the soul at each birth and death of a day. The earthy musk that permeated the land after a rainstorm had washed the air clean, and the most painful memory of all, the touch of his beloved. Her gentle fingers caressed him with a soothing life that fulfilled every need. Each memory took him back, stealing his heart as he recalled the sweetness of life. Though an agony, he summoned and embraced his memories, concentrating on the one he'd just had before encountering this fog.

Oh, God, the fight. He had been knocked from his horse with a blow to the head that had left his thoughts spinning. As he'd lain on the ground, he'd felt the sudden merging of Robb MacGregor's thoughts into his head. Christophe had fought the transition, but his own personality had receded, eventually leaving as Robb MacGregor took possession once again. It had happened before. Brief, terrifying periods when Robb MacGregor's will had forced itself into his dreams. But this time he had not been dreaming, and he wondered how long he had been separated from his counterpart. "Ariana," he breathed.

As though his wish had been granted, the mist slowly parted like the sea and he floated into the great room of Castle MacGregor. He gasped when he saw Ariana up ahead. He moved closer. Terror seized him. She stood next to Robb MacGregor, their heads bowed before Friar Peter. "Dear God," he whispered, watching their wedding like an uninvited guest.

When the friar asked if anyone knew why the marriage should not take place, he yelled, "I do." But his voice was only a silent protest.

Morag objected, and his heart soared. Though he could not abide the woman, this time she aided his cause.

Robb MacGregor silenced her with a savage blow. Fear clawed at Christophe's gut as he watched his beloved vow to honor such a man.

"Don't! It's not I," he yelled to her, but she couldn't hear him. He tried to touch her, but she gave no indication she knew he was there, although apprehension glimmered in her eyes.

What was happening? Why had Robb reentered his body? A terrible frustration filled him as he helplessly witnessed the ceremony.

Christophe knew Ariana thought she was marrying him. *He had promised he would find a way for them to be together. Trust shone in her eyes as she gazed up at Robb MacGregor. He watched Ariana give herself freely to his counterpart. It was obvious that she thought his strange behavior a mere act to fool the clan. But then she eyed Robb MacGregor, doubt momentarily flickering in her eyes, when Robb's head was turned.*

Christophe's heart ached as he watched his beloved seal her fate. He tried several times to break through the barrier separating them.

And each time he called her name, the light of uncertainty would flicker in her eyes, but she did not falter in her vows.

Christophe knew the exact moment she realized an imposter had taken his place. 'Twas during the kiss of peace.

The panicked look on her face tore into his being. Lord, how could he help her? How could he protect her? "Send me to her." He railed against his fate. Pain sliced through his every sense as he helplessly watched his beloved fight the stranger in her life. Restless, he circled her, knowing her life was in peril. Cries from the deepest, darkest part of his soul raged forth. An agonizing sound filled with grief and torture. "She needs me," he whispered, until the very essence of his spirit collapsed in despair.

A golden light enveloped his spirit. "Robb has unfinished business," an angelic voice suddenly washed over him.

Heartened by the answer, he rallied. "Send me back," he begged, his heart breaking. He watched her with Robb MacGregor. The memories of the flesh were too fresh, too poignant as another would savor her touch, her kiss, her love. His anger grew, and he turned away, unable to bear the pain of his beloved trapped with a stranger.

"When Robb MacGregor finds peace, you will return."

His senses thundered with impotent anger. "But that could take a lifetime."

"Pray it does not."

Frustrated, he held his temper. It would serve no purpose to curse at an angel. He concentrated with all his might, trying to communicate on some level with Ariana, but nothing helped. All he could do was watch her. And watch her he did. With his spirit free, he could listen, investigate, and infiltrate every life that was connected to his wife. The sensation of floating in and out of different lives was odd and akin to having a waking dream. He was totally aware of everything that happened, but unable to affect the outcome. Still, he did not give up. He swore that when the moment occurred that he could reenter his body, he would be ready. He ached for Ariana, but he would never be far from her. Never.

No sooner had he uttered the vow than a strong force suddenly swept him from the wedding reception. Enraged, he fought against his abduction, but the winds of destiny carried him to another castle. The structure sorely needed repair. The mortar in the walls crumbed, the unattended flakes revealing small tunnels between the massive stones. The stench of dirty rushes screamed not of poverty, but neglect.

The coldness of the dimly lit halls confirmed his impression as he floated through the rooms until he reached the great hall. Two people were in the room, a man and a woman. The man wore the Frazier plaid. The woman abruptly turned, catching Christophe's attention. Shocked, he winced as he recognized Morag. The traitor stood fully revealed.

Robb's aunt sidled up to Frazier.

"I have a plan, do ye wish to hear it?" Her shrill voice sharpened annoyingly at the end of her sentences.

"Aye, pet, tell me how ye propose to rid yerself of yer nephew and his wife," Frazier said.

Raw fury welled up within Christophe, unlike any he had ever known. He suddenly understood Robb MacGregor's black side. He reached and tried to wrap him fingers about Morag's treacherous throat, but his hands passed through her. He had no substance, yet he noted that her eyes widened.

Seeing her expression, Alastair asked, "What is wrong?"

She shivered, looking cautiously about. "Someone walked over my grave."

"Nonsense," he scoffed, throwing her cape to her. "Cover yerself, 'tis just a draft."

Morag wrapped herself in her cape. "Now, tell me of yer plan."

Suddenly, Christophe was pulled from the room. *Nay*, he shouted, needing to know the plan. He struggled, but the wind that brought him there carried him in an unbreakable flow, transporting him to the MacGregor stronghold.

He moved through the stone walls, knowing he had to reach his beloved and warn her. The music floated on the air as the revelers danced and drank in the main room. He searched the area, but Ariana was gone, as well as Robb MacGregor. His heart lurched. They had retired. This was their wedding night. He fought against the force that propelled him up the stairs toward the master's chamber. All his will could not change the direction, and he entered the room with fear clutching his soul. He could not bear to see her in another man's arms.

The fire in the hearth shed a warm golden glow over the room. The bed furs covered a scantily clothed woman. As he drew closer, a sigh escaped him. Thank God! She slept alone. He turned to search for Robb MacGregor, only to find he was not in the room.

He smiled. Ariana had found a way to keep Robb MacGregor at bay. Faith revived, Christophe's heart relaxed. He should have remembered how resourceful his love could be.

The memory of Morag and Frazier surfaced, and he flinched. He couldn't bear the thought of Ariana's peril. He swallowed his fear, racking his brain for a way to warn her. "Listen to me, my love. I am here. I will always be here."

She slept on, her breaths deep and even, her lovely face relaxed in repose.

Frustration built inside him and he tried again. "Ariana, please hear me. Ye must hear me."

The gentle rise and fall of her breast remained the same.

Peacefully, lovely and so very trusting, she slept unaware of him.

Despair filled him. God, how useless he had become. He fought against defeat; there had to be a way he could reach her. They were two souls who had joined together and weathered the test of time.

He hovered over her as she slept. Her lips were slightly parted in sleep, looking as though she waited for a lover's caress. Her cheeks glowed warm and rosy from the heat as she snuggled her pillow. He could remember the feel of her silken skin beneath his fingertips. Never had he wanted a woman more. He ached to take her in his arms, and seal his claim. God, he feared she might forget him. He floated nearer, her scent a familiar aphrodisiac that would haunt him forever. He needed to touch her, to kiss and caress her, to connect on some level. Her essence called to him, and he moved closer, surrounding her half-clothed form.

He absorbed her scent, the smell, the taste, and the sensations he had known existed—they existed again for him. Then he finally engulfed her, and she moistened her lips and moaned in her sleep.

He pulled back in surprise. Had he reached her?

"Christophe," she murmured, her voice throaty and breathless.

Elated, he recalled how he'd stroked her skin, loving and caressing every square inch of her exquisite body. She arched her back and wriggled on the sheets. He smiled. They had always communicated exceptionally well through the senses. Relief warmed him. Thank God. His warning could be delivered. Every delightful memory of their joining flashed through his mind. He made love to her through the power of his thoughts, his soul, his spirit, and the strength of his karma.

* * *

Ariana felt the butterfly kisses of her lover on her neck. Slow little nibbles that sent shivers of delight through her. A trail of soft little love bites that tingled until his tongue lathed the sting. A gentle river of soothing warmth coursed through her as his calloused hand roamed over her body. Loving, kneading, kissing. She quivered and sighed. Lord, but her beloved knew where to touch her. How to touch her. She shivered with desire and responded, the sensual experience robbing her very breath. His essence surrounded her. His masculine heat warming her heart and soul. She smiled. "Oh, Christophe," she whispered.

"Listen to me, Ariana, you are in danger. Morag and Laird Frazier are planning to murder you and Robb MacGregor." His warning swirled in her sleep-laden thoughts.

She moaned and began to toss on the bed. "You left me," she accused, her voice sad.

"I will never leave you."

His words echoed in her mind. His promise had traveled through time. He had given his life for her. She swallowed. "I believe in love. I believe in you."

His breath wafted to her. The gentle familiar scent of him surrounded her like the rich scent of coffee on an early frosty morn. She inhaled her beloved's distinct, comforting essence. She would know him anywhere. She responded to the hot, wild, carnal kisses, moaning in ecstasy as every inch of her flesh responded under the tender stroking caress of her lover's hand. God. She could feel his lips and tongue on her. His hot breath teasing and tantalizing. She gasped as his lips covered her breast, his touch like velvet heat. She grasped him to her, aching, needing more of the exquisite pain. The gentle tugging sent streaks of need to her core. Her stomach curled with desire and she arched her back upward. Grasping to feel him near, she nearly slipped off the bed when his hands trailed a path to her navel, then to the crease below. His lips and tongue followed the same path, teasing and tantalizing her with every delicious inch. She cried out, needing him to bring her to fulfillment. But he took his time. Slowly loving her body, bringing her to the brink and back in a loving litany of agony and ecstasy. Tears slipped past her eyelashes as her need and want overcame her. Christophe and only Christophe had the power to rob her will and drive her over the edge. "I love you," she whispered. Her eyelashes fluttered as she stretched on the bed; in her sleep she reached out to him. "Christophe, love me."

She snuggled into his embrace as he took her in his arms. His spirit entered her dreams, and the erotic fantasy that unfolded shook her.

"Oh," she cried out as the force of his love filled her. Gratitude and humility swirled within as love's caress awakened her heart to the joy of intimacy. She hugged the warmth, keeping his essence close. Her heartbeat accelerated as the timeless rhythm began. Liquid fire flowed through her as Christophe loved her. The utter abandonment and urgency sent her senses soaring. She gasped for breath as she climaxed. The shower of stars accompanied her slow descent. "Christophe." She moistened her lips as she wrapped her arms around the soft fur robes. "I love you."

Ariana awoke from her dream, her body covered in a soft sheen of perspiration. Christophe had come to her and made love.

She could still feel wondrous sensations and let out a shaky sigh. He had not deserted her after all. Tears filled her eyes. But where was he now?

"I love you," she whispered out loud, and in an instant a warm comforting sensation enveloped her. She snuggled into the covers as happiness engulfed her. She was not alone.

But something nagged at her. What was it? There was something, just on the edge of her memory. Danger, he had warned of danger. But no matter how hard she tried, she could not remember.

Later that night, Ariana heard Robb MacGregor return

and slip into bed. She held her breath, afraid he was going to reach for her, but thankfully his snores filled the air instantly. She looked over at the big sleeping warrior and a sigh escaped her. This was not her beloved. And the animosity Robb MacGregor harbored would be hard to overcome. But despite her trepidation of him, she had to try. She sensed danger, and not only was her life in danger, but her unborn's child was as well. She would not give up, not until she found a way to reach him.

Robb stirred in bed, and she could smell the strong fumes from the ale he had consumed. His arms snaked out and wrapped around her, pulling her close. With his eyes closed, his lips grazed her temple as he hugged her to his chest. She could hear his heartbeat, as her ear rested against his bare chest. Lord, what could she do?

"Christophe," she silently cried as she lay trapped in Robb's arms. "Help me."

Christophe's soul cried out in utter frustration as he watched his beloved's dilemma. He cursed the fates at his helplessness. Hovering over the couple, he concentrated, utilizing all his energy to communicate with Robb. For endless minutes nothing happened, and he despaired that anything ever would. Not until the warrior fell soundly asleep did Christophe experience some change. Suddenly, he entered Robb's alcohol-induced dreams, and found disjointed memories of Ariana. Robb MacGregor had no memory of falling over the cliff and admitting his love. "Poor fool," Christophe whispered, but even as he uttered the words, he found himself strangely relieved. Unable to understand why the man had lost sight of his love, he wandered in and out of Robb's every thought, every hope, every dream, trying to understand the man.

A mixture of love and hate permeated every recollection, and Christophe knew Ariana's danger. Pride and animosity trapped Robb MacGregor. His selfish and demanding love doomed him to a hellish relationship. Christophe concentrated on finding the source of the man's hatred, but the secrets lay buried under years of defenses. He renewed his efforts, concentrating all his energy into unlocking the mystery of this man's suffering.

Suddenly, an avalanche of pain washed over him as he relived Ariana and Angus's wedding. Robb MacGregor's memories were disjoined fragments of anger and retribution. How dare she demand his oath of love? How dare she marry his father? He wanted the woman, but only on his terms. He would not be dictated to. Rage, a raw mixture of love and hate swirled in him. More memories surfaced. Christophe gasped as deep resentment and mistrust overwhelmed him. Robb MacGregor relived the betrayal of another woman, his mother. Fury, hurt, and a deep sadness that soured the soul emerged. Christophe fled the man's spirit. He stared back at Robb, understanding the man's abused heart. Then his gaze shifted to Ariana. How will I protect you from him?

Robb MacGregor woke early with a head that seemed three sizes too small for the ache within; then he looked at the angel in his arms. Soft, warm, sweet Ariana rested on his shoulder with open trust and innocent purity. How deceiving looks could be. Her bright red hair spread out beneath her, like a blanket of flowers, the gold-tipped lashes fanned out on her soft rosy cheek. Even though he knew her treacherous ways, he ached to touch her. Memories of their lovemaking flashed though his mind.

His fingertip lightly traced her petal-soft lips, following the line of a soft-edged pout. Beads of sweat formed on his brow. He withdrew his fingertip. God, he wanted to love her. But he could never forget her betrayal. The anger and resentment rose up within, and his gaze narrowed as he stared at her flawless features. The soft little breaths that she drew as she lay in his arms made her appear helpless, but he knew better. He felt his child kick, and he slipped out of the embrace. The child was not part of his vendetta. Something nagged at the edge of his consciousness, but the elusive thought refused to surface.

He dismissed the unsettling sensation. It was time to rise. He had an army to lead. He looked back at her as he wrapped his kilt around his waist. *Tell her!* his conscience screamed, but a sudden anger overwhelmed him. His pride kept him silent.

Tell her what? That he loved her, that he could not think of an existence without her. Her betrayal, and his father's interference, still sent his temper soaring. He had trusted her once. Mayhap, someday, she would again win his confidence. But it would take a lifetime for him to forgive her.

A strange feeling overcame him, but he brushed off the premonition. Of course they had a lifetime. A disparaging smile turned his lips as he remembered her grand dreams, when she told him of their coming child. "Robb, we will have an eternity to love and laugh and simply lie in one another's arms as we watch our children grow."

Again a chill overcame him. He sighed at the eerie foreboding. Did a dark specter hang over his shoulders? He pushed the disturbing thought away. Of course there would be time. He had it all planned out. When he was ready, and not before, he would accept her apology.

With iron resolve he moved to the door, but with his hand on the latch he looked back over his shoulder. Her beauty took his breath and almost his resolve. Need crashed through him, his ache a powerful force that nearly threatened to defeat his will. He closed his eyes to her and opened the door. He had a task to perform. A laird did not shirk his duty.

The corridors were cold, and his footsteps echoed in the empty passageways. He could hear his heart pound as he left her behind. A voice from a distant dream called to him. "Avenge us." The words were a litany that circled his mind. Who had said it? A ghost of a memory surfaced and he pictured his sweet Ariana, whispering the words. A rage filled him again, and it was uncontrollable. He would slay the demons that haunted him.

Alastair Frazier chuckled as he watched the skinny ass of the MacGregor woman ride back to the convent where she had been banished. He had used her, and for once he felt more in control. He drew a long drink of his ale, then slowly wiped his sleeve across his mouth as Morag disappeared from sight. But he also had a plan. Morag would be pleasantly surprised. He would move his men into position when the MacGregors left. They would attack the castle with the men away. When the MacGregors returned, they would have to meet his clan.

Robb MacGregor marched out to the courtyard and gave orders to ready the men. He would take the whole clan. If he was to be successful in his campaign he needed every last man. He turned to Gavin. "I will leave a small force behind. Ye will be in charge. Make sure my wife does not leave the premises. I will not tolerate any breach in my orders."

Gavin frowned, then looked to the scarcely manned walkways. "As ye wish, my lord."

Robb's temper rose slightly as he read his man's thoughts and met his gaze. He drew a deep breath and agreed his castle was at risk. "Call Brodie Maclaren forth."

An hour later when the clan was mounted, Brodie Maclaren marched across the cobblestones. Manner proud, head high, he stood before Laird MacGregor. "Ye wish to see me."

Silence descended on the courtyard as everyone watched

the event. "I know ye, an honorable chieftain, have sworn yer life to my wife. But I would also have yer pledge."

"I give my bond only to those who have earned it," Brodie said.

Robb MacGregor smiled. "My wife has earned yer loyalty?"

Brodie straightened and looked the laird in the eye. "I would defend her with my life."

"I hope someday ye will feel the same about me. For now I will take yer oath that ye will protect this castle and all within whilst I am away. My man, Gavin, will be in charge."

Brodie Maclaren grinned, his dignity intact. Slowly, so all who witnessed the event took note, he covered his sword hilt. "I will protect them with my very blood."

Robb extended his hand "I know I have left my kin in safekeeping."

The tension in the air dissolved. Maclaren now had the same status as a MacGregor.

Robb nodded to his men and swiftly mounted his horse. He had a mission to perform. Unable to stop himself, he looked back at his room. There in the window stood his wife.

Laird MacPherson rode up to him. "Ariana will forgive ye for yer tardiness last night when she hears the financial details and lifetime truce that we discussed."

Robb's jaw firmed as he turned back to his father-in-law. It galled him that Ariana held the true power from what she inherited from both fathers. "I dinna have to explain my actions."

Laird MacPherson studied him. "Dinna take out yer poor humor on me. I am not yer wife and willna tolerate it." He slapped his horse and the animal shot forward, leaving Robb sitting in the courtyard. The thought of his wife filled him with an inner turmoil. She had manipulated his father into marrying her, and the thought still galled him.

He looked back over his shoulder. Lord, but the sight of her, the sunlight bathing her in a soft glow, haunted his mind and thoughts. Determined to leave with an unencumbered mind, and angry that the woman so affected him, he quickly turned from her. But despite his efforts, her image remained, floating in and out of his mind like a soft angel, reminding him of possible joy and a happier life. He thrust the thought from his mind like a soiled rag. He would not allow the woman to play upon his thoughts.

He raised his hand, and his men marched out of the castle behind him. Heavily armed, his warriors would follow him into Hell. Clumps of earth churned beneath the horses's hooves, eating away the miles as they rode to the Drummond fortress. Robb had set this travesty in motion, and thus he would set it to rights. Once he had been ruled by his foolish heart; now he knew only a warrior's spirit. Love and hate had no place in a chieftain's life.

They rode all day and far into the night. The moon rose in the dark sky, and the pale light cast a ghostly glow over the trees and road ahead. His thoughts of the upcoming battle warred within him. If he could spare his clan this confrontation he would. But Laird Drummond was a man of retribution. Pride, Robb conceded, would be the end of the clan.

He stopped his men about a mile from the castle and made camp. He knew the Drummond fortress inside and out. He needed the element of surprise. If they could get a small contingent inside the walls to open the gate, he could disarm and defeat his enemy.

Lor walked up to him. "What plan would ye have us use?"

Robb pointed to the battlements as Laird MacPherson

joined him. "The walls are not heavily manned. They would never expect us to attack."

"Aye, the fools are asleep in their beds," Laird MacPherson agreed as he stared at the poorly manned wall.

"Still, a siege will take weeks," Lor lamented.

Robb turned to Lor. "When I visited Drummond to contract the wedding, Cailin's brother Jamie showed me a side door his mistress used for their trysts."

"Ye mean the fool leaves the side gate unlocked?" Lor asked.

"Aye, every Sabbath."

MacPherson's grin split his face. "Ye see what a family of dolts ye would have married into if not for yer father's last request?"

Robb ignored the remark as Lor leaned forward. "My laird, the door may be barred."

Robb nodded. The possibility had occurred to him. "I will slip across the moors with a small band of men and check. If I find the gate unlocked, ye will, on my signal, send five groups of ten men across the fields when the battlement guards are at the furthest point of their patrol. It is important that no one make a sound."

"They will see the men," Laird MacPherson countered.

Robb looked to the heavens and noted the moon had slipped behind the clouds. "Nay, they are not looking for us." He looked at the wall, then pointed out every location to Lor. "After the men gain entry, have each group steal up to a wall with the fifth held in reserve for the gatehouse. Once on the battlements, have each group take the warriors out. They must be silent."

Lor nodded, and moved off to instruct the men. Several groups of well-trained men were chosen, then moved slowly out over the field. They blended into the night, their bodies hidden by the darkness of the cloud-cloaked moon. Soon they were in position as the remainder of men waited.

Robb led the main force into place on the ground. His strategy, a courageous, if dangerous, move, could only be called brilliant.

Silently, stealthily, he checked the side gate. The handle moved slowly under his pressure and the door creaked open. He froze, waiting to be discovered, but the sound went unnoticed. Quickly, he ushered his group in and waved the next group forward. MacGregors poured through the side door, until all the groups huddled in the darkened courtyard.

Robb deployed the main body of men up to the battlements, and led the last group to the main gate. Like clockwork, his men silently overpowered the unsuspecting guards. As soon as his group raised the portcullis and opened the gates, a smile slid over Robb's lips. Victory was assured.

When Laird MacPherson entered the main gates with the whole army, Robb sent a detachment of soldiers to the stables and barracks where the men slept, while he and Laird MacPherson went in search of the master.

Dawn rose over a captive castle as they burst into the master chamber. War cries sounded below, the noise of swordplay filtering through the castle as MacGregors engaged the enemy. Laird Drummond rolled out of bed naked and grabbed his sword. He blocked Robb's advance, working his way to the door, but Laird MacPherson cut off his escape.

For several minutes Drummond fought like a demon, but he could not outmatch his opponent. Suddenly, Drummond wounded Robb, a slice grazing his arm. Pain radiated through Robb, but he clenched his teeth and endured the searing agony. When Drummond threw back his head, bellowing a war cry, and charged, his weapon raised, Robb stood his ground and knocked the sword from his enemy's hand. Once Laird Drummond was disarmed, Robb grabbed him and dragged the man to the great room.

While Laird Drummond knelt in the rushes, his hands tied behind his back, Robb MacGregor wound a linen strip around his wound. The MacGregors had subdued the Drummond soldiers and Robb's men stood armed over the captives. With all present, Robb grabbed Laird Drummond by the hair and pressed his sword blade to the man's throat.

"Do ye surrender?"

"Aye," Laird Drummond croaked.

Robb's sword point pressed closer to Laird's Drummond's throat. "And do ye swear fealty?"

Drummond closed his eyes. "I swear my fealty to ye," he gasped.

Robb yanked Drummond's hair further back and pricked his enemy's throat, drawing a small trickle of blood. "And what of yer family?"

Drummond's eyelids flew open. "They as well."

Cailin's brother, Jamie, spat. Without so much as a moment's hesitation, Robb MacGregor released Laird Drummond and rounded on Jamie. His sword swung in a large arc and sliced into his arm. Blood dripped from the gaping wound. "Do ye truly wish to raise a protest?"

Though his eyes were filled with hate, the injured man covered his bleeding arm and shook his head.

Robb MacGregor turned to the waiting assembly, his heart racing as he brandished his bloody sword, daring them all. Conquest and battle were what he lived for. It made him feel alive. "Does anyone else wish to address me?"

No one said a word as they all knelt in the rushes before him. He moved slowly, weaving in and out of his captives. Stopping, he snaked his hand out and wrapped it around

Cailin's arm. "Ye, come with me." He needed a woman. She would become his mistress.

She stared at him, her eyes huge. She struggled, trying to gain her freedom. "My laird, please spare me, ye can have yer pick of anyone here."

"My taste runs to ye. If yer father had not pushed the matter, I could let ye go. Now, I canna."

He dragged her to the master's bedchamber and shut the door. He would take her in her father's bed. The man deserved it, daring to war with a MacGregor.

Suddenly an image of Ariana rose into his mind. Damn the woman, she was a witch. He could take any woman he wanted. It was his right!

Yet when he tried to bury his thoughts with another woman, he heard Ariana's voice cut into his thoughts. His conscience haunted him, forcing him to release the wench. "Go," he snarled. "I feel generous."

Christophe watched the massacre and the near rape of the lovely Cailin. He had whispered in Robb's ear. He prayed it was more than his suggestion that had stopped the vile action, that the warrior had done it on his own. God help him. How would he protect Ariana? How would he keep her safe from this angry man?

CHAPTER TWELVE

At noon Alastair lay hidden in the brush along the road, watching the MacGregors turn onto the fork leading north to the Drummonds' land. He smiled, envisioning his victory. He could have it all. Now, at long last, he would come into his own. His castle, his woman, and the respect he had craved for years. After a successful attack he would stop at the convent for Morag. Then, her attitude would reflect esteem. He waited until all the MacGregors marched out of sight before directing his men from their cover and onto the road. He led them toward the MacGregors' defenseless castle.

A less prudent man would storm the castle, but he had learned to be patient. It would take a full day to maneuver his troops secretly. Once they were in place, the undermanned castle would be at his mercy. No one would have time to come to their rescue. Yes, by evening, Robb MacGregor would be far enough away to leave a safety margin for Alastair. Then he would deliver his ultimatum. "Surrender or die."

Gavin and Ariana stood on the battlements listening to Brodie discuss the placement of the Maclaren men. With Brodie's new duties she no longer had a guard. It was a mixed blessing. A backache nagged her and she leaned against the wall to ease the pain. "I wish Robb had not chosen to attack the Drummonds."

Gavin sighed and turned from Brodie. "My lady, he had little choice."

Ariana looked at Gavin. "There is always a choice."

Brodie stepped forward. "My lady, though ye may not like to admit it, it was the only way. Laird Drummond would have attacked us the moment he could summon his men. Robb MacGregor's actions will save lives. With the Drummond numbers down, the clan will easily be subdued."

"Nothing is that easy," she said. "I hate the conflict."

"Aye, my lady, most women do," Gavin said. "But 'tis our way of life."

Men, she thought, vowing to change their way of life if she ever had the chance. She didn't want to raise her child in a war-torn country. She pushed away from the wall and fairly waddled.

Both men hurriedly lent her an arm, and she accepted their help on the stairs. Taking the last step, she sighed, and turned to her escort. "Gavin, are we safe?"

"Against an attack, my lady?" He looked around at the well-armed battlements, now manned by Maclarens, and smiled. "Only one clan would dare attack us, and they would have to think our strength is down."

"If an attack comes, my lady, we will be ready," Brodie reassured her.

"Aye, 'tis what we were discussing," Gavin said.

"Is there anything I can do?" she asked brightly.

"Nay," they both echoed, their eyes widened at such a suggestion. They both walked her across the courtyard to the castle and closed the door behind her, ending any further discussion.

The ultimatum came at dawn. Ariana lay resting upon the bed, her back aching, when the first shouts occurred. A flurry of activity occurred below her window, and footsteps echoed in the hallway outside her door, as servants scurried through the castle and more soldiers mustered to the wall.

Her heart racing, Ariana rose and quickly dressed. Wrapping a heavy mantle around her against the morning chill, she hurried through the castle to the battlements. Gavin's and Brodie's faces tightened when she appeared on the walkways.

"What is it?" She laid her hand on Gavin's sleeve.

"My lady, Frazier's men have surrounded us."

She grasped the rough stone battlement and leaned forward over the wall. Alastair Frazier stood beneath the walls, his face arrogant, his manner insufferable. "Lady MacGregor, if ye surrender yer castle no one will be hurt. I will allow safe passage for ye and all yer servants to travel and rejoin yer husband."

She felt the eyes of every MacGregor and Maclaren on her. 'Twas a test of her loyalty. There were those who would take the offer, she knew, but that was never an option.

"What will happen to my men?"

"They will be the property of my clan, my lady. Surely, ye understand that I am being more generous with ye than I need be."

'Twas true, but she didn't believe him. Still, she thought if she pretended to consider his offer she could buy the clan some time. She leaned forward to reply to Alastair, but Gavin touched her arm. "My lady, are ye considering his offer?"

"Nay, never. But in order to give Laird MacGregor time to return, I must delay Alastair. He will surely attack the moment he has my answer."

"My lady, forgive me for doubting ye."

"Gavin, I dinna trust Alastair, but even if I did, I could never desert my clan."

He smiled. "Then try to gain us time."

She leaned back over the wall. "It will take me several hours to gather my things and arrange for my servants to accompany me. Ye will wait."

"Nay, my lady, ye will let my men in."

"If this is to be done in good faith, ye will do it at my behest, not yers," Ariana replied.

"My lady, I dinna intend to wait out here in the cold, freezing my arse off, while I could be inside sitting by the fire."

"My dear sir, ye are the one who wishes to avoid a fight. My clan will give their lives for me and no doubt defeat ye or take most of yer men. Then there is the problem of hiding from my husband's wrath and that of the other clans I have saved. Why, they would hunt ye down like the dog ye are." She paused, and tapped her finger against her chin. "It seems to me, the more I consider it, that all the terms are on my side."

His face turned red with anger. "Very well, my lady, I will give ye until early evening and no longer. If ye are not out of the castle with yer entourage, then the truce is off. And I promise ye, if I have to storm the castle, I will not spare any inside."

"Understood." She turned away from his face and saw the wide smiles of her guards. She grinned at them and gave a small curtsy.

"Verily, my lady, remind me not to play any games with ye. Ye could certainly bluff yer way to victory," Brodie jested.

They used the extra time to good advantage. Inside the castle the ladies spent all morning boiling huge vats of oil and water to be transferred to the wall at the appropriate time. More often than not, Isla and Iona found a reason to be close to Gavin and Brodie.

At noon Ariana peered over the wall. "Gavin, can we hold out against them?"

"My lady, every clansman will give his life. It will depend on how many men Frazier has."

She sighed. "Well, then, we will have to quickly teach the ladies how to help."

He raised an eyebrow and started to protest, but she held up her hand. "Besides the oil and water, the ladies could use their mop handles to repel the ladders."

His skepticism remained as Brodie smiled. "Aye, they could, and that could free up the men to shoot more arrows at the advancing enemy."

She could have kissed Brodie, and turned to Gavin, who still seemed unconvinced. "It would almost double yer troops."

Brodie slapped Gavin on the back. "We will need every man to repel an attack."

Gavin at last relented, and nodded.

Brodie stepped up to her and lifted her hand. "My lady." He bent low over her hand and kissed it. "I am truly impressed. Are there any other ideas?"

"Aye," she said, noticing that Gavin paid close attention. "I think yer men should take their rest now and let the women, who I will ask to dress as solders, walk the walls." When he started to protest, she quickly finished. "With the women dressed as men, yer soldiers can get the sleep they need. I dinna know much about warfare, but I think

Frazier will see the advantage of attacking when our men are tired and half asleep trying to guard the wall.''

"My lady, ye astound me," Gavin quipped as he offered her his arm.

She blushed, unaccustomed to the praise.

"Where did ye ever learn about warfare?"

His question could spark other suspicions. " 'Tis just things I learned from observing my father."

He walked her across the courtyard. "I will have to remember that when I have a daughter. An intelligent woman is a dangerous prospect," he said solemnly.

Her head snapped up and she saw the amusement in his eyes. "Aye, best ye remember that an intelligent woman is also an asset."

He chuckled, then lifted her hand to his lips. "Thank ye, my lady."

"Thank me when we are out of this mess."

With her medicines mixed and waiting, she arranged the armory to best suit her. Thank God, the pains had stopped. A birth in the midst of battle would never do.

"My lady, dinna move the furniture, 'tis not good for ye." Jessie stood in the doorway, her hands on her hips. "I will have someone else do it." Jessie bustled in and took hold of Ariana's arm, forcing her to sit.

"I am fine," she protested as she looked around her makeshift hospital. "I hope there is no need for this room."

"Amen," Jessie whispered. "My brother died in a siege." Her eyes filled with moisture, but she quickly blinked her emotion away.

Before Ariana could comment, Jessie changed the subject. "The kitchen is ready. I wish the laird had not left."

"Aye, so do I, but we will have to be brave until he returns."

Jessie smiled. "Courage, my lady, has always been yer strong suit."

"What?"

"I remember how hard it was for ye to come to us as a young bride. Lady Morag didna welcome ye, nor did Robb MacGregor."

Ariana thought of how truly difficult it must have been for her counterpart to leave her family and live here among so many strangers. "But others welcomed me."

"Aye, but for a time ye were all alone."

She saw Jessie's concern, and a lump formed in her throat. "I have friends now," she breathed, standing up to loop her arm through Jessie's. "Come," she said, needing to break the mood. "I think I might be able to offer some ideas that will help ye in the kitchen." A project would help keep everyone's minds and hands occupied.

She showed Jessie, Isla, and Iona how to make a beef-and vegetable-filled pastry. "The men can eat it at their station, and for dessert ye can fill the pastry with berries."

Jessie watched, amazed. "What a difference from oat-cakes."

"Aye, and I can show ye some more recipes."

"Where did ye learn these?"

Knowing this was not available in medieval life, she hedged. " 'Tis an old family recipe handed down from generation to generation."

"How kind of ye to share it. Because ye have been so generous, I will share my famed haggis."

Her stomach roiled at the thought. "Ye would want to keep that in yer family, would ye not?"

Jessie smiled. "I know yer stomach may not be able to take the smell, but after the baby is born I will give ye my recipe."

Ariana smiled. "That is truly kind of ye."

When the kitchen was put to order, she had called the

women of the clan together for a meeting. After she explained her orders, they followed her out to the wall.

"We can help our men," one woman piped up.

"Aye," Ariana said, showing them how she wanted them to push ladders from the wall.

" 'Tis time we were given more responsibility," Isla said, brushing by Gavin as though he were the village idiot.

Iona held up the kilts when Ariana signaled her. "Ye will have to dress as the men to fool the Fraziers," Ariana told the women, drawing Brodie's interest.

Not one woman balked at the idea; in fact, the ladies were excited about the part they were to play.

In a short time they had changed their clothes and relieved the guards. Brodie Maclaren spent an extraordinary amount of time showing Iona how to hold a sword.

Gavin only permitted half the men to retire, keeping the others to guard in shifts. "I would prefer to have some men at the wall."

"A wise decision," Ariana said, noticing that Gavin had trouble keeping his eyes from the shapely pair of legs Isla displayed in her kilt.

Frazier returned to the castle gates at dusk. "Lady Ariana, yer time is up. Come out," Alastair demanded.

All eyes watched her in the silence that followed. The rising wind whipped her mantle about her, and she pulled it tight to ward off the sudden chill. She actually grinned as she leaned over the side of the wall and stared down at the pompous ass. "Actually, Laird Frazier, I need another hour at least."

He shook his fist in the air. "Nay, I will wait no longer."

"Very well, then I guess I will have to give ye my answer."

She looked back at Gavin, and nodded.

Bloodcurdling war cries split the air as spears and arrows

colored the sky. Every member of the castle manned the walls. The women brought boiling oil and water to be thrown over the side. The men shot arrows into the advancing clan, but their numbers were sufficient to withstand the rain of missiles.

"My Lord," she breathed, watching the fearsome clansmen charge the wall. Wave after wave of men moved forward under the protection of their shields. She leaned over the wall mesmerized by the advance.

"Get back, my lady," Gavin shouted as he pulled her away from the wall and pushed her behind him. "Ye endanger yerself and ye endanger the lives of brave men. Let us do our job. Keep the castle running orderly. The men will need to eat at their posts. And, my lady, we will need a place for our wounded."

A sudden pain gripped her, but she concealed the contraction from Gavin. Men were trying to defend the castle, and she would not call attention to herself. The soldiers' faces showed the strain, and she would not add to their burden. She straightened, feeling the nagging ache plague her as she made her way down the steps.

Every step she took seemed awkward, as though her balance was off. She managed to make the great room and gather her supplies before another pain overtook her. Gritting her teeth, she sat for a moment. *Not now,* she cried. An inner voice warned, "Yer time has come." Her heart raced, but she knew if she rested, the contractions would subside. She softly massaged her stomach and stayed at the trestle table, panting, until the spasm passed.

Slowly, she gained her feet. When the contractions did not return, she carefully gathered her herb tray and medicine pouch. Thank God the pains had stopped, her skills were needed. The sound of war intruded on her thoughts. The noise seemed to be dying. She quickly moved to the door to help those who needed her.

The MacGregor soldiers on the walkways cheered. She ran up the battlements and watched the enemy withdraw. She nearly collapsed with relief, until she heard Gavin.

"That was only the first charge. They were testing us. Be ready." Her heart sank. This was not the end but the beginning. There would be more attacks. She immediately put the unsettling thought out of her mind and moved among the men, bandaging those who needed assistance. Surprisingly, the men were in good spirits. Few soldiers were wounded and those who were only had minor injuries.

The Fraziers did not attack again that evening. After the first wave had been repelled they retreated for the night. The men ate their dinner in silence, then retired. Ariana smothered a yawn. "Will ye be all right, Jessie?"

"Aye, get some sleep, my lady." Jessie pointed to the other women. "We can stand this duty until the men relieve us."

She started to protest, but in truth she was exhausted. "Wake me for my shift."

"Aye, my lady."

At dawn Jessie awakened Ariana. "My lady, they need help on the wall. The Fraziers are attacking."

Slinging on the small pouch of bandages and medicine she had packed earlier, she rushed from the room.

The clanswomen ran out to the walls still dressed in the kilts. The sun was rising when they took their positions next to the men. Ariana dearly hoped their other men were on the way.

In the weak morning light, war cries filled the air as the Fraziers charged. Men with wild colored paint on their skin, brandishing swords and clubs, ran across the fields in waves to swarm at the base of the castle.

Charge after charge assaulted the walls, but each time the MacGregors succeeded in defending the castle. Arrows showered the inner bailey as the Fraziers took position and fired. All day the MacGregors repelled the Fraziers' attacks. Exhausted, the men stood their posts. Her heart caught in her throat as night fell and the enemy began to climb the walls. Torchlight flickered on the dirt-streaked warriors who scaled the walls. Boiling oil and water were poured over the wall, but still the enemy pushed on over the boiled and burned bodies of their comrades. Her stomach roiled at the smell of burnt flesh. Terror ran through her veins as their screams filled the air, and others climbed to the top of the wall. The clanswomen handed the men whatever they needed. They picked up mops and pushed ladders away from the walkways.

Ariana used her mop to push one ladder from the wall, and felt her stomach muscles cramp. "Oh," she groaned, bending over to ease the pain. The spasm only lasted a minute, and she quickly picked up her handle to repel another soldier. In a matter of a heartbeat the battle had escalated. She looked about and saw some of the soldiers had climbed over the wall. Swords clashed as men swung their blades. She saw Iona and Isla sticking their mop in the face of a soldier who had climbed over the wall before they could shove his ladder away. His sword was drawn and raised to hack at them. Ariana immediately dipped her mop into the boiling oil, then rushed forward to stick the mop in his face. His screech of pain filled the air as the twins pushed him off the walkway.

Ariana had no time to congratulate herself as another enemy soldier climbed over the wall. Before she could raise her mop, he sliced the handle in two. With a mighty blow of his fist, he knocked her aside and moved on.

He raised his sword blade to the twins to run them through.

Scrambling to her feet, Ariana threw her bucket of boiling water at the man. He screamed and fell from the battlements, but Ariana found she could not straighten.

Her throw had pulled a muscle and the pain gripped her now.

Isla and Iona ran to her side. "My lady?"

She closed her eyes as tears formed. "Dear God, wait." The contraction passed, and she drew a deep breath. "I am fine. The pain is gone."

Concern covered the twins' faces. "I think ye should go inside," Isla said.

"Aye and lie down," Iona finished.

"Nay, every hand is needed." She pointed to the wall. "We must help the men until Robb returns."

Isla and Iona stared at her for only a moment before running to their post. They lifted the kettles and dumped the buckets of hot oil over the wall with renewed vigor. Cries of wounded men filled the air, and Ariana moved among those with injuries. She bandaged some right on the wall, for they could not and would not leave their posts. Her tunic was smeared with blood as she hurried to help whoever needed her skill.

The air rang with the sound of clanging swords as their men met the enemy who streamed over the wall.

Horrible screams rose as men sliced through limbs and pierced their opponents with cold steel.

She felt a stitch in her side as she pulled bandages from her pouch and dressed a soldier's wound. An enemy warrior broke through the fighting, heading directly at her with his sword raised. Suddenly, his eyes bulged as he fell forward, a sword sticking out of his back, and lay dead at her feet. She looked up at Gavin, who recovered his sword. "Ye must retreat to the castle, my lady."

She nodded at his solemn expression. The siege was not in their favor. She picked up her medicine pouch and quickly moved toward the stairs, the ladies joining her.

"Get into the castle and barricade the door," she yelled, directing the women down the steps. Just as she stepped on the stairs, a tide of enemy soldiers came over the wall in an overwhelming wave. *Dear God,* she breathed, watching the Fraziers clamoring over the battlements to engage the undermanned MacGregors and Maclarens.

Her breath caught in her throat when a burly guard ran up behind Gavin to thrust his sword. Without thought, she rushed down the walkway and pushed the man, fortunately catching him off balance, his sword glanced off Gavin's shoulder. The enemy turned on her enraged, and backhanded her with his meaty fist. She fell hard into the wall.

Stars flashed before her eyes as her sight receded and blackness engulfed her.

The darkness faded and slowly, the sound of voices surrounded her as the cobwebs in her head cleared. Pain replaced the numb void and she moaned.

"My lady, my lady," Isla cried, "Please come back to us."

"Hush, daughter, let her rest," Jessie said.

"Her labor has started," Isla said.

"Will she lose the baby?" Iona asked

Ariana's eyelashes flickered open. "Lose the baby? What are ye talking about?"

Isla's face brightened. "My lady, ye have awakened."

"What do ye mean? Lose the baby?" She grabbed hold of Jessie's arm.

"My lady, yer labor has started."

"Labor," she said, unable to piece together the meaning.

"Aye, yer fall started the labor."

"Fall?"

"Aye, when ye saved Gavin's life."

Slowly, her memory returned.

"I am well, my lady," Gavin said, gripping her hand. " 'Twas a foolish thing for ye to do."

"Aye, I canna believe ye did that," Iona said.

"Thank God, ye did," Isla responded.

"The castle." She turned to Gavin.

"We are delivered. We turned the tide just as ye lost consciousness. Maclaren stood over ye so no soldier could harm ye."

"Maclaren?"

"Aye, yer fall rallied the men and Brodie kept ye safe," Iona said proudly.

Her stomach contracted again as searing pain knifed across her waist. She closed her eyes, enduring the spasm until it passed.

Her hands covered her abdomen. "My baby?" Tears welled in her eyes.

" 'Tis early, but many early births survive." Jessie laid a cool cloth over her forehead. "Ye need rest," she said, shooing the others from the room. "Try to sleep, my lady, mayhap the contractions will stop."

She closed her eyes. She did not believe the birth premature, but she fervently prayed the fall had not injured her child. "Please, deliver my baby safely," she whispered.

"Amen." Jessie patted her hand, then took a seat by her bed.

Ariana swallowed her fear. Her child would be all right. Labor often started from trauma, then stopped. But she feared the era she was in. No one had the skill to deliver a difficult birth. "Dear God, help me," she silently entreated.

For several hours she fretted, unable to relax about the fall. When the pain continued, and then increased without the relief of a delivery, fear enveloped her. Her child could die. "God, take me, let my baby live." Despair surrounded her, and she could not stop the downward spiral as she cried for her unborn child and for herself.

Tears slipped down her cheeks unchecked as a roaring thunder sounded in her ears. She moaned as a sharp pain gripped her stomach and the contractions continued.

"My lady, please, ye must try to calm yerself. Think of

something, anything that will bring ye peace," Jessie said soothingly. "Mayhap Friar Peter can offer ye some solace." Jessie wrung her hands as she inched toward the door. "I will fetch the good friar."

Oh, Lord, she must be losing her baby if Jessie must summon a priest. A painful band constricted her chest as a sharp pain sliced across her stomach. The spasm lasted a full minute.

"Nay," she called out, but Jessie had already left.

In a few moments Jessie returned with the sleep-ruffled friar.

Ariana turned her tear-streaked face into the pillow, ashamed of her emotional breakdown. "Forgive me, Friar Peter, Jessie should not have awakened ye."

"Dinna fash, child, 'tis my job to see to troubled souls."

"My soul is in no danger, Friar. 'Tis my child."

"I know."

" 'Tis my fault. I fell."

He picked up her hand and knelt beside her bed. "But God listens to all prayers."

A fervor of reverence poured into her prayers as she entreated her God. Drained, she stared heavenward. "Let my bairn have this time, this life, this hope." *Oh, Christophe,* she silently cried. *I need you.*

Suddenly, Ariana felt a calming presence as peace settled over her. "Christophe," she whispered.

He was with her. The gentle serenity of his spirit diminished her anxiety. Her heartbeat slowed, and she knew her blood pressure lessened. She leaned back into the pillow and closed her eyes to savor his warmth. Slowly the spasms lessened in intensity and frequency. She could draw a full breath without a contraction cutting her in half.

"Friar, I believe God has answered our prayers." She smiled at him, needing to be alone.

He patted her hand. "I am glad. If ye need me during

the night, send for me." He arose, and Jessie escorted him to the door.

When the friar left, Ariana watched Jessie as she went about the room. "Jessie, ye may retire now. I feel much better."

Though Jessie looked as though she was going to argue, instead she surprised Ariana and curtsied. "Gavin is right outside the door. He or Brodie will be on duty. If ye need anything call out."

Ariana nodded, pleased that Jessie had acceded to her wishes.

The chilly night breeze wafted across her, cooling her skin and calming her nerves, until finally the contractions not only slowed, but stopped. She drew a deep cleansing breath, thankful God had answered her prayers. Christophe had reached out to her from wherever he was and calmed her. "I love you," she whispered. It was a bittersweet moment filled with both longing and fulfillment. Memories of their love, of their life, circled her in a warm cocoon that both comforted and distressed her. She snuggled down into the big bed and burrowed into the fur covering. Her thoughts traveled to her husband. *Please, be careful, Robb MacGregor,* she whispered, knowing his welfare would affect Christophe's. Then she heard a faint whisper in her mind. "Believe in love." She smiled and slipped off into a deep sleep.

Dreams immediately filled her thoughts. She heard so many voices. Familiar sounds from her prior life merged with those from her present. The swirling clouds of time parted and people took shape, slowly as they walked though a mist. *Christophe,* she breathed. How she loved him. He stood with his family and he reached out to her. Tears burned her eyes. She tried to run to him, but something held her back. When she turned to look, it was Robb MacGregor who restrained her.

She struggled, trying to get to Christophe, but she could not break Robb's hold. Christophe saw her distress and though he ran to her, he never seemed to reach her. She held out her hand to him, but even as he tried to grasp it he fell short of her hold. Robb MacGregor tugged on her hand, pulling her further away from Christophe. She looked over her shoulder and could not see him.

A thin woman suddenly took shape and appeared. It was Robb MacGregor's mother. She held out her hand to Robb, her eyes filled with need and regret, but he turned away. Elspeth then turned toward Ariana and again held out her hand, but Robb MacGregor pulled Ariana from the woman's touch. Elspeth turned away, but not before Ariana saw the dejection and pain.

Her dream continued to unfold. Many people from the past and the present wandered in and out. Little vignettes of her past life, the plane crash, her time-travel, her meeting with her beloved. She tried to reach those she loved, but each time was held back. Then, like an epiphany, it occurred to her: Robb MacGregor would have to release her. She turned to him and watched the mix of hurt and pain cross his features. "What is it that ye want?"

He stared down at her, as though puzzled by her, but he remained silent. Then he looked toward the mist and just pulled her along as though he were unaware of her until she tried to gain her freedom. When she stopped struggling, his hold lessened. She saw Christophe through the white fog. Tears sprang to her eyes. She tried again to reach him. This time she nearly pulled free of Robb MacGregor's hold. But he clamped his fingers tighter than ever around her wrist. Christophe started to fade. "Christophe," she screamed, and awoke.

CHAPTER THIRTEEN

Ariana awoke in the dead of night covered in a fine sheen of perspiration. The empty chair beside her bed gave evidence that Jessie had not returned. Darkness surrounded her as her heart raced from the terrible nightmare. She kicked off the covers and felt the first twinges of labor return. "Oh," she gasped. If she lay still, mayhap it would subside.

Though she tried to fall back asleep, the nagging ache kept her awake. Her thoughts drifted from one thing to another. Her husband, Robb MacGregor, puzzled her. Did he love or hate her counterpart? Although Christophe hovered near, his spirit so comforting, but fleeting, she longed for his physical presence. Her home and family had yet to be born. In truth, she was alone. The thought chilled her.

Dawn's greedy pink fingers stretched across the sleeping sky when another pain knifed across her abdomen, taking her breath away. Her time had come! This was not false labor or pain from trauma. She gripped her stomach, panting, while silently riding out the contraction. Her heart raced as she counted the minutes until her stomach again constricted in a squeezing tight band. Her labor ebbed and flowed, the gut-wrenching pains fast and furious.

She needed Jessie, Iona, and Isla. Clenching her teeth, she gripped the edge of the bed and lowered her feet over the side. Pain sliced up her back when her toes touched the cold stone floor.

"Oh," she groaned as she straightened and stood upright. Focusing on the rough stone floor beneath her feet, she held her stomach and stumbled toward the door. A spasm doubled her over, and she waited until it passed. Gasping, she leaned against the doorframe and closed her eyes as another pain gripped her. When the contraction finally ceased, she opened the door.

Perspiration dotted her upper lip as she reached out to Gavin and grasped his forearm. " 'Tis my time. Send for Jessie and her daughters." Fearing the healers of the time, she tightened her grip. "I dinna want anyone else."

He nodded and carefully supported her, holding her as another pain ripped across her stomach. His arm was a lifeline and her nails dug into his flesh. She moaned as a rush of warmth flowed down her leg. "Help me," she cried.

He lifted her in his arms, and carried her into the room. His features tense, he carefully placed her upon the bed. "Rest, my lady, I shall return quickly."

While he was gone, an exceedingly sharp pain gripped her. She cried out again. Her scream echoed in the empty room. Her labor increased, slashing across her stomach and through her womb. Pray God, she was right and delivering her child, not her counterpart's.

The door flew open as Jessie rushed into the room in

her nightclothes followed closely by her daughters, then Gavin.

At the sight of the bedraggled cook, tears filled Ariana's eyes, and she reached out to her.

"Poor wee lamb," Jessie said, grasping her hand, as Isla and Iona hovered by the bed.

"Help me," Ariana breathed.

"There, there," Jessie intoned, then turned to her daughters. "Fetch clean linens and leather straps."

Ariana's eyes widened.

" 'Twill help to tie yer legs and arms in place."

"Nay," she cried, looking to Gavin for help.

His eyes widened and he took a step forward.

Jessie held up her hand to halt his advance, then turned to Ariana. "My lady, yer time is near. Ye are wasting too much energy thrashing about. And when the hard pains come ye will need to hold on to something to bear down. Ye must trust me."

Ariana fell back into her pillow. *Hard pains,* she thought. *How much worse could labor be?*

Gavin's features crumpled into resignation; then he helplessly shrugged and beat a hasty retreat.

By midmorning she felt as though she was being ripped asunder. Tears burned her eyes and her screams filled the castle.

Her stomach hurt from the endless contractions. She felt so weak from the agonizing spasms that she didn't have the energy to push; instead she endured the pains, riding the crest until the torment peaked. Lord, this was too hard, something was wrong. "Christophe," she silently cried. "I need ye."

Every pain reminded her that she must bring this child into the world alone. She would, even if it meant that from this birthday until her death, she would raise their child without Christophe. The reality chilled her, but as her child took over her thoughts and energy, she had little time to dwell on her beloved.

By the evening meal the castle grapevine had spread the news that the Lady Ariana's labor had started. Everyone waited anxiously for the birth.

The night passed into a stream of agonizing hours for Ariana, and at dawn she labored still.

By the noon meal, Lady Morag arrived back home in an agitated state. "I heard the castle had been under siege," she told the admitting sentry. "I came as quickly as possible." She rushed into the main room and was annoyed by the servant's distracted air.

When she overheard their conversation, she rushed from the great room, leaving her food untouched. She ran up the staircase and pounded on the master's chamber door. "Let me in."

Though weak, Ariana raised her head and vehemently denied the request.

Gavin nodded and opened the door. He blocked the entrance as Morag looked in, a smile forming on her thin lips.

"Move out of my way."

"I am sorry, my lady, I canna allow yer entry. Lady Ariana has forbidden it."

Morag's face flushed an unbecoming red. "Why am I denied entry?"

Ariana struggled to raise her shoulders after the last contraction. "Because ye have not cared for one person in this castle in their time of need, and I doubt yer skill."

Morag's eyes narrowed. "Ye will pay for this insult." She glared at Ariana, then turned her pinched features on the guard.

Gavin shrugged his shoulders and closed the door. Her outraged scream echoed through the hall as he turned

toward the mistress. "My lady, would ye wish me to fetch
Friar Peter?"

"Nay, he canna help." *Foolish man*, she thought, and
waved Gavin away.

He bowed and instructed Jessie to lock the door after
him.

Her stomach muscles contracted and the pain sliced
through her. She pulled on the straps until the contraction
subsided. Her back felt as though it were broken. She was
in the midst of hard labor and knew any number of things
could go wrong.

"My lady, we can send for a midwife."

"Nay," she gasped.

Jessie would listen to her instructions, another would
not. She glanced to her bound arms and legs. Well, she
amended, most of her instructions.

When Jessie patted her fingers, Ariana clutched Jessie's
hand. "At a time like this I want only those I trust around
me. Ye are like family to me."

Jessie nodded her head, and quickly ordered her daughters to fetch more clean linen. As they left, Gavin returned
with his sister, Moire.

Moire gasped when she saw Ariana. "My lady, ye saved
my child, Jenna, and I willna desert ye."

"There is nothing ye can do for me."

Gavin leaned forward. "My lady, my sister is the midwife."

"Nay," Ariana cried.

Moire tightly gripped Ariana's hands. "Dinna be frightened. I am very skilled and I willna do anything to ye
without yer permission. I only wish to be here to ease yer
labor." Moire immediately untied Ariana's wrist. "Ye are
a skilled healer, my lady, but no one knows more about
midwifery than me."

Blood rushed to Ariana's fingers as she rubbed her hands

together. Relieved to have her hands free, she leaned back into the pillows. "Ye may stay."

Later that day, Isla sat next to the bed and handed Ariana a sturdy wooden cross. "For ye, my lady. Gavin had fashioned it for me, but ye have more need of it now."

Lord, were things that bad? She accepted the cross, hoping Isla was overreacting.

" 'Tis a shame the laird is not here," Jessie said. "Not that he could do much. But somehow, just knowing yer husband is near is a comfort."

"Aye, I wish the bairn's father were here also."

Jessie blanched. "My lady, even though Angus fathered yer child, Robb is yer husband now. And he should be here so ye could curse him out in place of his father for getting ye with child." Jessie held up her hand. "No use denying it, my lady, we all feel the same way. No matter how much ye love yer husband, nor how much ye want the bairn, there comes a time when ye could cheerfully strangle the man for what ye must go through to bear his child." She patted Ariana's shoulder. "But in the end, when ye hold the wee bairn in yer arms, ye are filled with God's love. Trust me. 'Tis true."

All that night Ariana continued to labor, the hours passing without relief. She began to wonder why her labor was so long, and by dawn, she was certain something was wrong.

The pain came again and the muscle spasm increased in intensity. Ariana grabbed hold of the linen and squeezed until her joints ached. Tears slipped from her closed eyelids. She could not do this.

Wave after wave of tightening agony repeatedly descended, knifing through her unendingly. The pressure in her back, stomach, and ribs was unbearable as it rippled through muscles. Her screams echoed in the room, until she was too weak to moan. Her hand latched onto Jessie. "What is wrong?"

Moire lifted the lady's night smock, and examined her. Her fingers probed the swollen stomach ever so gently. "I think the babe is breech."

"Listen to me," Ariana gasped. "Ye must reach in and push the child up the birth canal and turn it around."

Jessie shook her head. "Nay, my lady, that could kill the baby."

Moire looked at the lady, neither agreeing nor disagreeing.

"If ye dinna do as I say, I along with the bairn will perish."

Jessie's face paled, and she stumbled back, bumping into Gavin.

He stepped forward. "My lady, tell my sister what to do, and I will assist her."

Ariana closed her eyes, summoning up the strength to talk. She rasped out her instructions, then asked for something to grip.

Her face grim, Jessie marched forward and took hold of Ariana's hands.

Sweat poured off Ariana as the contractions came, one after the other without respite. She could not think beyond bearing the pain as Moire did her bidding. Her thoughts became memories tinged with the excruciating torture she endured. Everything seemed surreal except the all-consuming, all-encompassing agony. Labor took up the whole of her energy, the whole of her life. She seemed to swim in a sea of torment. Wave after wave of spasms crashed over her, taking her breath away.

Tears again slipped from beneath her eyelashes, wetting her cheeks. Then a gentle warmth suddenly filled her. Love flowed through every vein, easing her pain and fueling her with strength. "Christophe," she whispered. "You are here." She opened her eyes and although his beautiful face was missing from those hovering over her, she knew

Christophe had joined her. Whether it was wishful thinking or not, she accepted her belief without question. It calmed her. There were times when she actually felt his hand gripping hers. "Stay with me," she implored.

Jessie's voice drifted to her from far away. "I willna leave ye."

"My lady," Moire said. "I have done as ye say. Now it is up to ye and God."

Tears filled her eyes as dawn's light lit the sky. She pushed and felt the unbelievable pain tearing her in half, then she heard a frenzy of voices. "Again, my lady," Moire urged. "The bairn is in the right position."

She strained, bearing down until she felt the child pass. The agony was over.

There was a hush as Jessie released Ariana's hands, and moved around to join her daughters. "Good Lord!"

Silence reigned and Ariana lifted her head. "What is it? Is the baby well?"

Panic assailed her as she caught the dour expressions. Was she wrong? Had she delivered a premature child?

Jessie's face blanched as Gavin looked up. "My lady, the bairn is fine."

A slap, followed by the soft infant cries of a newborn, shattered the silence.

Instead of elation, fear filled her. Their faces were too solemn. They were lying. "What is wrong?"

"Nothing, my lady. Ye have a healthy strong lad." Moire's soft crooning voice filled the air. She beamed and held him aloft.

"Oh, he is beautiful," Ariana cried, seeing her son. She knew why the others had been silent. She had been right. Christophe's dark hair crowned the little one, and everyone stared. He was full weight, not early.

Gavin took hold of the baby as Jessie and Isla cleaned the wee bairn up. When the little child was bathed and wrapped in a warm blanket, Isla handed Ariana her infant son.

Her heart burst with love as she cuddled the tiny babe to her breast. "Oh, he is truly the most beautiful baby, is he not?"

Gavin cleared his throat. "Aye, he looks like . . ."

"My grandmother," Ariana supplied, knowing they wondered how a redhead and blond could produce a child so dark. Robb would also wonder, but she put the disturbing thought from her mind.

"Welcome, my son," she cooed, placing a tender kiss on the child's little forehead. Never had she felt such love. So consuming. So protective. "It does not matter if yer dark looks are strange among these fair people. All that matters is ye are healthy and alive. I thank God ye had such courage to survive the difficult birth."

Gavin turned away and suspiciously wiped his eyes. After a deeply inhaled breath, he straightened his shoulders and reached out for the baby. "May I hold the future laird?"

She nodded, knowing he had accepted her son.

He took the babe into his arms and gazed down at him in awe. "Aye, yer a brawny lad to be sure."

The tense air subsided as Gavin held up the child. " 'Tis a proud day for the MacGregors. We do indeed have a fighter."

Jessie beamed. "Aye, we will have to show the bairn to the clan." She started to cover the baby's dark hair, but Gavin stayed her hand. "He has the dark coloring of his grandmother. 'Tis a proud heritage he bears."

Tears misted Ariana's eyes as she looked at Gavin. His gaze met hers and from that moment on they shared a bond. Her son. She smiled and turned to the baby as he let out a loud, lusty cry. Christophe's thick raven hair and intense, dark blue eyes marked him as his son. A miracle of life and love had occurred as her baby, not her counterpart's, lived. She watched the baby's chest rise and fall, a breathing marvel of the love she and Christophe shared. A lump formed in her throat as she sent her gratitude heavenward. "Thank you." Then she closed her eyes, silently entreating God for Christophe. How she needed him. Her throat thickened, and she swallowed to stave off the threatening tears. Christophe would return. She would not think otherwise.

After Gavin walked to the window and held up the baby for the clan to see, Jessie retrieved the child from him and handed the bairn to her. "The little mite will need to feed soon."

As Ariana accepted her son, she heard a whisper-soft voice in her ear. Her heart swelled. She had not dreamed Christophe's presence. "I'm so very, very proud of you, my love." The voice grew louder as she drifted off to sleep. A smile graced her lips as she snuggled down into the thick covers, her babe nestled in her arms.

"She looks like a wee angel," Isla said, though a frown marred her brow as she stared at the bairn. She leaned toward Gavin. "What will the laird think of the dark hair?"

He stared at his sleeping mistress. "If he is a wise man, he will thank God for his blessings."

Christophe looked at his child. Pride filled him. "A son," he whispered in awe. He hovered over the sleeping infant, saddened but aware that his son did not know of his presence. Even so, he reached out to him, and to his way of thinking, his baby actually responded to his spiritual touch. Then, he moved next to his wife. Poor, sweet Ariana. His heart filled with love and understanding as he drank in her beauty and courage. He could feel her need for him in every inch of his essence. "I will never leave you, my love," he said, affirming his vow. "Never."

She stirred in her sleep. A soft smile spread across her lips as

*she hugged her pillow tight, snuggling down into the deep, warm
folds of the coverlet. He reached out. His touch, light and feather-
soft, covered her tear-stained cheek. He longed to hold her. To
whisper his love. His kiss grazed her lips as they parted in sleep.
An ache of longing filled him. He turned away, needing to end
his torture. Until Robb MacGregor's spirit found peace, Christophe
was resigned to this cold netherworld of neither being nor doing.
Refusing to feel sorry for himself, he centered his thoughts on a
solution. He had to push Robb MacGregor to seek his closure. It
was imperative. One last look at his sleeping beauty and son
confirmed his resolve. Though his spirit left her, a part of his heart
remained as he traveled back to his counterpart's side.*

Robb MacGregor's victorious return to Castle Mac-
Gregor heralded great joy for the clan. The whole village
cheered as he marched his triumphant army through the
streets and past the gates with their vanquished captives
trailing behind. The whole shire was alive with pride and
joy.

A thunderous applause rose up when he dismounted,
and a surge of pride filled him as he held up his hands.
"With our enemy fallen, we now have the slaves we need
to do our bidding."

A deafening war cry sounded and again the men
cheered. The conquering army beamed as they also
accepted the clan's gratitude.

As Robb faced the crowd, accepting their adulation, his
gaze scanned the familiar faces. He suddenly became aware
of the wounded soldiers in the castle guard. "What has
happened?"

Gavin ran up and bowed. "My laird, we were attacked.
We sustained losses but with the help of Laird Maclaren,

and the expert battle advice from yer wife, we carried the day.''

MacPherson beamed, joining Robb. ''Yer wife is a wonder, is she not?''

Brodie Maclaren and Gavin nodded their heads, but Robb MacGregor did not echo their praise.

''Who attacked?'' he asked, his face suddenly hard.

''The Fraziers.''

Rage, as black as night, soared through Robb. By his wounds, he would see that man punished! His eyes narrowed as he turned to Gavin. ''Tell me the whole of it.''

He listened to the report, his fists clenched in ill-suppressed anger. ''They have gone too far!''

''Aye, my laird, but we showed them no mercy,'' Gavin said, raising his hands to those that defended their home.

A roar of proud voices rent the air, and Robb's anger dissipated.

Morag nodded in approval, her voice raised in agreement. She grabbed a bouquet of dried flowers from a servant and approached him and bowed humbly. ''My laird, I returned home as soon as I heard my clan had been attacked. I offer my services and promise never to disagree with ye again. Might I be permitted to return home permanently?''

He accepted the flowers, though his gaze was cool. ''Aye,'' he replied, knowing clan loyalty ran high. Though he wished otherwise, he could not deny the woman now.

Morag curtsied again, her smile blossoming into a radiant expression he had never seen on his aunt.

Robb looked over the crowd, his eyes searching every face for the one he missed most. At her absence, his thoughts turned dark. ''Gavin, send for my wife. She must attend the wounded.''

''My laird, yer wife is abed. She has given birth to a fine son.''

"A son? 'Tis too early. Is the lad healthy?"

"Aye." Gavin smiled.

"A son." Robb's features softened, despite his distrust of her.

Laird MacPherson slapped Robb on the back. " 'Tis a lucky man ye are."

Robb did not return his smile. "We shall see, MacPherson. We shall see." He marched down the line of captives and pulled Cailin from her family. "Come with me."

MacPherson frowned as he fell into step beside Robb, who dragged Cailin behind him.

Morag ran after her nephew, and grabbed hold of his sleeve. "My laird, might I come with ye? I have not been permitted in yer chamber."

He rounded on her so fast she stumbled. "What are ye chattering about?"

"Yer wife would not permit me to see my great-nephew. I so wanted to see who the child resembled most, our family or the MacPhersons. I have heard from the servants that the child is as different from a MacGregor as day is to night. Lady Ariana claims her baby's dark hair favors her grandmother."

He raised an eyebrow at his aunt's words. A nasty suspicion formed as his worst fear surfaced, but he would never give credence to it in front of the clan. "Morag." A familiar rage filled him, but he tapped it down. "If ye wish to cause trouble, I will have ye sent back to the convent."

Her face blanched at the softly spoken threat. "My laird, I meant no disrespect. I merely wished to see my grand-nephew."

MacPherson scowled. "Send the woman away, and have done with it."

Robb ignored him. Turning away from his aunt, he proceeded down the hall, pulling Cailin in his wake. At his chamber he pushed her inside, where he found Friar Peter in attendance, along with Jessie and Isla.

He marched over to the bed where Ariana sat propped up on cushions, nursing the baby. He moved the blanket and looked down at his son with a critical eye. A fist of anger slammed into his gut. His hand touched the black hair of the bairn's pate and his features tightened. "Ye would try to pass this bastard off as my son?" he asked, knowing a betrayal far worse than any before.

"He is no bastard." Though fear clouded Ariana's eyes, she raised her chin as she cradled her child closer to her breast.

He pointed to the child, disdain in his eyes. "Ye expect me to claim a child with raven hair as my own?"

Ariana tenderly smoothed the baby's dark hair. "My grandmother had the same color hair, Robb."

"Aye, she did," MacPherson said.

Ariana's head snapped up, clearly surprised by her father's support. Her features suddenly relaxed as she held her hand out to her father.

Robb pointed an accusing finger at Ariana. "I dinna believe ye, nor do I believe that child is mine."

MacPherson's hand closed on Robb's arm. "No matter what ye think, ye must claim the baby for the clan's greater good."

Robb understood politics, but it ground his pride into the dirt that he would have to accept a child not of his loins. He shook off his father-in-law's hand.

"Bitch," he breathed, staring at her wounded expression. Disgusted by her act, he turned to the friar. "Have ye christened the bairn?"

"Nay, I waited for the father's approval."

Robb MacGregor turned back to her. "Give me the whelp."

She turned her shoulder away, cradling her son protectively in her embrace.

He reached down and tore the child from her arms.

"Robb," she cried, reaching out for her baby as MacPherson held her back.

Robb laughed at her fear, and held the baby just out of her reach, holding it as though it were a pile of manure. "The clan has an heir."

She relaxed slightly. "Aye," she said, leaning back into the pillows, but her gaze remained intent. "And his name?" she whispered.

He looked to the dark-haired infant, and knew he could not name the child. His jaw tightened as he placed his son into the pallet, then wheeled on his wife. "Name him whatever ye wish," he rasped out, then paused, his blue eyes like twin flames as his gaze bore into her. "Perhaps it would be fitting to name him after . . . his grandmother."

She visibly swallowed under his gaze, then turned away from him. "Friar," she breathed. "My son shall be called Andrew, after Scotland's patron saint."

"My lady, I will christen him now." He walked over to the pallet and motioned for Robb to pick up his son.

Robb refused. MacPherson glared, muffling a curse under his breath as he lifted up his grandchild into his arms.

Friar Peter poured a little water over the child's forehead as he said a baptismal prayer, then made a small sign of the cross with his thumb on the baby's forehead, followed by a gentle kiss. "Welcome, Andrew."

Robb watched with smoldering anger as MacPherson carried the baby back to Ariana, and placed him into her arms. "Ye have done well, daughter. The clan has a future laird." He leaned down to kiss her cheek.

She raised her gaze to him, her eyes bright with unshed tears. "Thank ye, Father."

MacPherson glared at his son-in-law. "Come and hold yer heir."

Robb's eyes narrowed, but he made no move to join them. The insult was clear.

Ariana touched her father's sleeve. "Please, dinna force the issue."

Robb tightened his jaw. How dare she act the wounded party. He marched over to her bedside and stared at her, forcing her to meet his gaze. "Know that I will never forgive ye for this betrayal. Every hour of every day ye and the boy will pay for this affront."

She gasped, her eyes wide. "Ye would take out yer revenge on an innocent?"

"Robb MacGregor." MacPherson stepped toward his daughter. "Ye go too far."

Robb turned to his father-in-law. "Dinna interfere between a man and his wife."

MacPherson sighed and stepped back, his gaze filled with regret as he stared at his daughter.

Robb walked over and grabbed hold of Cailin's hand, pulling her against him to face Ariana.

"Know that I want nothing from ye. If I must have a woman to slake my desire, I will find my solace on this one." He pushed Cailin forward.

Ariana's mouth nearly dropped open. She stared at the girl's tear-stained face, and felt guilty because relief overcame her compassion. Unable to hold her gaze, Cailin stared at the floor.

"Attend yer mistress," Robb said, causing the poor girl even more humiliation.

" 'Tis not necessary," Ariana said.

He leveled cold eyes at her, and smiled when she shivered. "If I must live with another man's child, then ye, dear wife, will live with my mistress."

Her fear fed his anger. He drove the point home. "From

this moment on, ye are here on my good sufferance. Do one thing to displease me and know I will throw ye and that"—he pointed to the baby—"bastard out in the cold."

She drew the child to her bosom, and kissed his forehead. "Ye willna have any reason to harm the bairn," she said, fire in her gaze.

"See that I do not." He left the room, leaving those behind in a wake of pain.

Morag beamed as she pulled away from the master's chamber door and scurried down the hall before the laird stormed out. She rejoiced at the turn of events, and waited all day long to get Cailin alone. Unfortunately, the laird did not allow the girl any spare time. Once she had waited on the mistress she was summoned to the laird, who had taken up residence in another bedchamber.

For a week Cailin's routine was the same, her days were spent with Ariana and her nights in Robb's bed. Every day Morag would catch glimpses of the girl, her shoulders stooping with each passing hour. At mealtimes she refused to meet anyone's gaze, her eyes sunken and dazed. Finally, after a fortnight, Morag managed to corner the girl when she was sent to fetch the friar. She cuddled and comforted poor Cailin. "Ye are not responsible for this. 'Tis the bitch up in yon bed who carries the blame."

" 'Tis not the lady's fault." Cailin lifted her sorrowful eyes.

"Oh, but it is." She held the girl's face up. "If ye only had a protector."

"Aye, but my family are wounded and enslaved."

Tapping down her irritation at the chit's interruption, she nodded. "I know. Ye must be heartbroken. I tried to warn ye about the mistress, but she had ye fooled. Just as she fooled everyone else. If only ye had listened to me, it would not have cost ye yer position and family."

Tears rolled down the girl's pale cheeks. "I was to be the wife of Robb MacGregor." She hiccupped. "I would have been respected. Instead, I am shunned."

"Aye, 'tis nothing worse than to be a leman." Morag's voice drove the humiliation home like handfuls of dirt on a coffin.

Cailin shuddered with dry sobs. "What can I do?"

"If ye trust me, I can restore all ye have lost."

Though wary, the helpless young woman looked up at Morag with interest kindling in her eyes. "How?"

Morag smiled and leaned forward. "If the mistress and her bastard were gone, then ye could take yer rightful place."

Cailin's eyes widened and she tried to pull away, but Morag held her tight. "Think on it, my dear. Think on it the next time ye must wait on her, then service her husband. Dinna ye believe ye deserve more? Why, the woman robbed ye of yer rightful place."

Cailin shuddered again. "I couldna harm her."

"Ye dinna have to. Just help me deliver her to her enemies, as she delivered ye to yers."

"I dinna know," she stammered. " 'Twould be wrong."

"No one would be the wiser and ye would assume yer rightful status."

Morag watched conflicting emotions flicker across the girl's face. Stupid child, that she had the feelings at all. "Think of all the good ye could do as the lady of this shire," Morag added. "Yer family would have an ally and ye could eventually persuade yer husband to free yer people. 'Tis much a wife can do."

Hope glimmered in the girl's eyes. "I would be a hero," she breathed, squaring her shoulders.

"Aye, and all that stands between ye and glory is one

insignificant woman and babe. Not so much really. Not so much at all."

Morag watched the acceptance chase the distaste from Cailin's expression. "Aye, I couldna be blamed for righting a wrong, could I?"

"Nay. 'Twould be yer Christian duty to do so."

Cailin drew a deep breath. "What is it ye require?"

CHAPTER FOURTEEN

Frazier's broken, wounded party rode back to their land. He had barely escaped the MacGregors' defense. Damn MacGregors, they had more allies than a king deserved! He wielded his horse up the drawbridge and dismounted, calling for the healer. His force had sustained many casualties.

As he watched his men being treated, condemning stares met his gaze. His stomach lurched. Once again, he had erred and erred greatly. If he didn't have a victory soon, his ally and men would desert him. He turned and trudged inside the castle. Throwing his sword on the trestle table, he sat down and pushed away the platter of food placed before him. He rubbed his coarse beard, feeling vulnerable and exposed. The warmth of the fire burned before his unseeing eyes as he poured himself a healthy portion of ale and propped his booted feet upon the table. After his seventh horn, he began to relax.

The heat of the fire and the potent drink had lulled

him into a half-sleep when a soldier ran in and handed him a crumpled missive.

The words swam before his eyes, and he had to strain to read the missive. His feet slipped off the table as he fell forward in his chair. "By His Wounds," he cursed. Robb MacGregor had taken the Drummond stronghold. Not only was his enemy victorious, but Lady Ariana had delivered the clan an heir. Their growing power threatened everything he coveted. The clans had started to align themselves with MacGregor.

God's Teeth, Morag's plan was the only one that might see the day won. His anger rose that she had been right and he wrong. But before he took any action, Morag would become his bride. He would have some insurance before he murdered a lady and her bairn.

He had an image to uphold; already his tactics were being questioned. He could eliminate the parents without arousing too much animosity, while Morag disposed of the infant. It was her idea. Therefore, 'twould be her crime, and her sin.

He still paced the floor when Elspeth came down the stairs. "What have ye done now, brother?"

He rounded on her. "Woman, mind yer own affairs. Father may have left ye the castle and the lands, but the men follow me."

"And will they follow ye into Hell?"

"If need be," he snapped, his tone surly. "I will rid the land of MacGregors. Ye should understand that more than anyone, sister."

"Yer hatred will destroy ye. If Laird Campbell ever learns ye were the one responsible for poisoning the water, then ye will lose his support, and everyone else's for that matter."

"And who, dear sister, will tell the Campbells?" He walked around her, his gaze hard as he stopped in front of her and poked his finger into her chest. "Ye or yer little friend?" He turned and stared at Elspeth's lover until the woman left the room.

Elspeth raised her chin and met his gaze. "I am loyal to our people."

His harsh laughter filled the air. "See ye remember who yer people are." He returned to the table and lifted his drink. After guzzling down the whole brew, he belched, then wiped his sleeve across his mouth. "Laird Campbell believes it was the MacGregors who spoiled the water."

She shook her head. "Yer hateful pride will be the clan's downfall."

The fire burned high in the great room of Castle Mac-Gregor as the family gathered there after dinner. Andrew slept soundly with Isla and Iona watching over him in the master chamber as Ariana picked up her sewing and ignored the tension in the room.

Robb MacGregor opened the missive from his neighboring clansmen and read the note. "We are invited to a wedding celebration of Laird Ruthven's daughter."

The name meant nothing to her until she looked up and saw his raised eyebrow. A memory suddenly surfaced. 'Twas the rival clan she had saved from the plague. "Are we going?"

He picked up his sword and began to clean the blade. "I will have to keep good relations with the clan. But I see no need for ye to make the long journey."

Though his reply was evenly spoken, Robb's distaste coated every word. She overlooked his displeasure. She would not be baited into an argument.

Morag stood up from her place before the fire. "I know ye neither want nor appreciate my opinion, but my laird, I beg ye to reconsider. Laird Ruthven will take great offense if the one he has extended the invitation to is not there."

She stared pointedly at Ariana. "I can see to the bairn while ye are gone."

Ariana's heart went cold. "If I go, dear sister, my baby will accompany me."

Morag's chuckle was not warm. "Quite the mother hen, are ye not? Do ye not trust us with yer child?" She pulled Cailin next to her. "But dinna fear. I raised Robb when his mother deserted him. Yer bairn is in good hands." Morag's eyes filled with a cold, almost eager light, making Ariana shudder.

"My child stays with me. I am sure ye would feel the same about yer babe. No doubt, ye didna leave the care of Robb to someone else."

Clearly displeased, Morag pursed her lips. "Dinna make yerself a slave to the bairn."

Robb held up his hand. "Enough, both of ye. If Ariana goes, she will take the boy."

Morag started to protest, but his gaze stopped her. "As ye pointed out, Aunt, it would be a snub not to go as a family."

"That is not what I meant."

He raised an eyebrow. "I dinna care."

Despite the strain between them, Ariana could have kissed him for denying his aunt the care of her son.

He continued to polish his sword as though the women did not exist. His disinterest didn't fool Ariana. She had caught that pensive look in his eyes, when he thought no one was looking. What devils haunted him? Did he wonder about her? Did he know he had died?

He looked at her, and she shivered under his intent scrutiny. Each time she intercepted his speculative study, it unnerved her.

His anger and rage were evident, but was it possible that he could be reached. "Husband, might we have a word in private?" she asked, leaning forward in her chair.

"I am busy. See to yer woman things and leave me be."

So much for tact. The man was as dense as a post.

"Very well, my laird." She picked up her sewing and headed for their chamber. It had been a month since Andrew's birth, but she was still exhausted. Gavin took her arm and chivalrously helped her up the stairs.

At her door she turned to Gavin. "Thank ye, Gavin."

"I am close, should ye need me."

His meaning was not lost on her. Morag, Cailin, and even her husband treated her with a coldness that was evident.

"I am truly blessed to have such a friend." She squeezed his arm.

Before she could enter her room, Gavin stopped her. "My lady, would ye tell Isla I will walk her to her chamber?"

She smiled. Although she valued Gavin's friendship, she had noticed his growing interest in Isla. "Aye, but her twin is also inside. I am sure they value yer attention," she said, noticing just before she entered her room that his smile faltered slightly at the prospect of a chaperone.

Once inside her chamber, she dismissed Iona and Isla, then walked to the cradle where her tiny son slept. Every time she looked at Andrew a warmth filled her. He was truly a great gift from God. She had been privy to two miracles prior to Andrew's birth, but standing before this perfect creation humbled her. "Thank you," she whispered.

She arranged his cover, then climbed into bed and closed her eyes. "Christophe, I pray ye can hear me. Remember, the lifetime when you were called Drew, I couldn't name our son after a Norman name, but thank goodness you had a Scottish name. Hurry back, our son needs a father."

"Beware of Alastair and Morag! They are planning on killing ye!" Christophe silently raged against the cosmos for his inability

to be heard. He hovered over them trying everything he knew to reach his love. But she was oblivious to him as she tended to their child. Compassion suddenly filled him as he watched her lovingly care for their child. Sensing her loneliness when she retired, he ached to hold her. He heard his son's name and smiled. "Drew," he whispered, approving of her choice, but she closed her eyes and drifted off to sleep. Why couldn't she hear him? Frustrated, he went to the husband and moved around him, swirling faster and faster, causing the man's hair to stand on end.

Christophe rejoiced when he saw Robb rub his arms. 'Twas a bittersweet victory, for he faced a horrible dilemma. If he could not protect Ariana, he might someday have to throw her into the arms of his counterpart. The pang of jealousy tore through him, but he endured the pain. For now to keep Ariana and Andrew safe, he had to enlist Robb's aide.

"Dinna leave them alone. They must not be left in jeopardy. Protect them." He circled around and around until Robb stood up and went to his room. Christophe followed, his heart heavy when he saw the woman who waited in Robb's bed. Laird MacGregor's halo seemed slightly tarnished. Cailin's tears were too much to bear, and Christophe waited in the anteroom until the woman had fallen asleep. During that time he questioned the wisdom of leaving his family in the hands of such a callous man. But he had little choice. Robb could protect them. He reentered the bedroom to find the man finally asleep. Ah, yes, dreams. Dreams gave him the clearest connection. He talked, screamed, conjured up brutal scenarios. Let him see the guilty parties. Let him see what Christophe knew. Let him hear the words Christophe had listened to.

Everything he had witnessed, he conveyed to Robb MacGregor. He used his newfound power to the limit. He prayed the man paid heed to the message. When he had imparted all he could to his counterpart, he revisited his wife.

No matter how he tried to reach her, she seemed oblivious. All night he worked to summon some response from her. Some sign that would show she understood the peril or even acknowledged

*his presence, but though he entered her dreams, she remained
unaffected. Her sleep was placid, her breathing regular, which
made him redouble his efforts. Once again, she slept through his
contact like an angel at peace. A horrible fear rose up within him.
Was he losing her?*

A fortnight later the Maclaren clan guarded the walls
under Gavin's command as the MacGregors marched out
of the castle in full regalia. Robb MacGregor, with Lor at
his side, led his entourage into the brisk air, heading his
men toward the Clan Ruthven.

In the center of the procession, Ariana sat in a cart with
Andrew, Isla, and Iona, yet she had strange misgivings as
she watched Robb lead the column. Since Andrew's birth,
Robb had kept his word and slept elsewhere. Though
thankful for his decision and the courtesy he offered, she
sensed he fought against himself and against his nature to
do so. Lately, when she caught his brooding stare, she felt
like a tightrope walker, balancing a long pole on a very
high wire. One slip and she would fall from her lofty perch
toward certain death. But she put her apprehensions aside.
She would rather be with her son and traveling in the
company of her husband than left behind at the castle
with Morag. Either way, an eerie premonition settled over
her. Where was Christophe? She wanted to run and hide
with her son, but could not. She raised her chin and looked
forward. Better to look confident than not.

Robb MacGregor had a large group of men for protection. This was no small caravan.

She only hoped that when they arrived at the Ruthven
castle, the poor laird would not think their force one of
invasion. Mayhap, that was why Robb MacGregor had mustered out such a force. She put the thought aside. She
hoped he would not attack the Ruthvens.

*   *   *

Morag smiled when she traveled to meet Alastair. With everyone away, she brazened her way to the Frazier castle. He met her in the courtyard at the witching hour. Her teeth shone in the darkness. She lunged into his arms, kissing his cheek. "We can have it all. Ye will attack the castle."

He held her away from him, and stared into her eyes. "Are ye mad? I have already tried."

"I know, but storming the castle was a mistake."

"Woman, ye try my patience. I have failed once to take the castle. My men will balk at another charge."

She chuckled, a sound that was more a purr than a laugh, as she stroked his cheek. "Only a small contingency of Maclaren soldiers have been left."

He slapped away her hand. " 'Twill be the same outcome. The defenses are too heavily guarded."

She nipped his throat with her sharp little teeth. "I will open the gates. After ye overpower the guard, we can wait for my nephew and his family."

He captured her straying fingers. "They still outnumber us."

She stabbed her finger into his chest. "Alastair, must I do everything? Ye are the man."

His face darkened, but he remained silent.

"Ye will have the advantage. Once they enter the courtyard, yer men, who will be on the walkways above, will rain arrows down upon them. 'Twill be a quick slaughter."

A slow smile of dawning lit Alastair's features. "I underestimated ye, my love." He pulled her to him, smashing her lips in a harsh kiss tasting of bruised pride. When he lifted his head he stared at her swollen lips, satisfied with the results. "Someday, my love, ye will drive me beyond myself."

She chuckled. "Ye do not scare me."

"I should, my love. For there are times I hate ye more than I love ye."

She looked deep into his eyes. "Then, my love, I will have to find a protector."

His hands wrapped around her throat. "Dinna even jest with me, my love. For if I ever thought that ye would play me false after this lifetime of waiting, I would make sure no man ever enjoyed yer charms again."

Her eyelids fluttered downward as her hands roamed down his chest. "Do ye really want to hurt me?" she rasped, moving closer and slipping her hands beneath his tunic.

He sucked in his breath, releasing his hold on her, while her hands fastened onto his manhood. "God's Teeth, woman, ye are a witch. Ye leave me powerless in yer hands."

A look of ecstasy crossed over her features as she envisioned his neck between her hands. Her hold tightened and his breathing became labored.

His eyes glazed. God, but he was easy to control. Such a simple, stupid man.

After he found his release, he stared into her eyes. "Dinna think I am not onto yer game, Morag. I know the only time ye enjoy mating is if ye are the aggressor."

Her eyes grew rounded as she feigned innocence. "It is obvious ye know nothing of ladies."

"That may be, but whores are my specialty." When she tried to pull away, he grabbed her. "Ye will marry me tonight. I will take no more risks until ye are my legal wife."

She wanted to scream *Never!* but wisely held her tongue. *Patience,* she silently counseled. *Patience, else all will be for naught.*

* * *

Elspeth pulled back into the alcove as the two lovers made their way through the castle to her brother's chamber above. Torchlight spilled onto her worried features when she stepped from her hiding place. "Dear God, how can I warn my son without betraying my clan?"

The Ruthvens' wedding was one of pomp and ceremony. Though the bride and groom were supposed to be the center of attention, the moment the MacGregors stepped into the room all eyes turned their way.

Robb MacGregor, dressed entirely in austere black, made a startling figure. But 'twas not he who garnered the most interest. 'Twas his wife, Ariana. Embarrassed by the attention, she lowered her eyes to her baby. Although she had lived three lifetimes, nothing had changed. She still hated being singled out.

Laird Chalmer Ruthven came over and bowed before her, giving her homage.

Robb MacGregor's face grew red with anger. A laird never bowed before a woman, and especially not before another man's wife. Stepping forward, he pushed Ariana behind him. Arms crossed, and legs braced apart, he stared down at his host, forcing the man to acknowledge him.

Voices twittered in the background while avid eyes and lusty natures waited for the confrontation to come. The laird's shoulders straightened and he drew a deep breath, expanding his big barrel-like chest.

Ariana cuddled her baby, astutely aware of what was taking place. Placing Andrew on her shoulder, she stepped around Robb MacGregor, ignoring his cold stare. "My laird, I am sure ye are so overwhelmed by the wedding ceremonies that ye forgot protocol. Might I introduce my laird and master? Robb MacGregor."

The tense moment evaporated when Laird Ruthven took her laurel wreath, and smiled. "Aye, my lady." He bowed before his guest. "Robb MacGregor, ye are welcome in my home."

The tension left Robb's face and he nodded his head. "Aye, 'tis a rarity indeed to be here."

"Nay, the rarity is yer good fortune in yer marriage." A cheer of approval went up from the crowd. Ariana's fame had spread far and wide. She had saved many of those within this room, as well as others who were relatives of those who had received her treatment.

Robb MacGregor let a rare smile show. No matter his personal life, he did not underestimate the value of having an important wife.

Ariana lifted her face to his. She could see pride and also calculation. She did not like the latter in the least. There was nothing in his handsome face that reminded her of Christophe. A tight loneliness squeezed her heart. Was Christophe gone? She had not felt his presence for weeks. Her stomach quivered as Robb smiled at her. A handsome man, he knew his attraction. The man's magnetism reached out to her and she gasped at his effect on her. He leaned down and kissed her cheek. Her skin tingled from the cool touch of his lips.

His eyes smoldered with a strange detachment. He wanted her, but even so, he kept himself aloof. The idea chilled her. This man was dangerous. She abruptly turned to their host. "I am honored that ye have invited us."

"My lady." He waved his hand to the side. "If ye would follow my wife, Lady Lilias, she will see to yer needs."

Lilias was a small woman with white hair and frail, thin

features. Despite her advanced years, her steps were surprisingly spry, her eagerness contagious. "Aye, yer bairn is a beautiful sight. Do ye think I could hold the child?"

Proud of her son, Ariana smiled. "Aye, it would be so helpful especially when he is crying."

Lilias laughed and reached out for the bairn. Both ladies walked together, making their way to the chamber upstairs that had been set aside for the MacGregors. At their room a guard bowed and opened the door. Ariana saw the single bed and experienced a moment's pause. She put the thought of the sleeping arrangements out of her mind and turned back to her hostess.

"Why is there a guard?"

"My lady, it is a precaution my husband deemed necessary."

She smiled at Lilias. "Yer husband is a wise man."

Lady Ruthven chuckled. "Aye, he is, but dinna let him hear the compliment. He would be impossible to live with after hearing such praise."

The thin woman's expression of mock horror made Ariana laugh, and she knew this trip had started off on the right foot. She remembered the woman from her first visit, when the illness had ravaged the castle's occupants. Now, however, Ariana was pleased to see her, healthy and robust. "My lady, we all owe ye our thanks," Lady Ruthven said.

Ariana tried to brush off the compliment, but the woman would not be stopped. "Ye may not remember me, but I wish to thank ye. Without yer help my own bairn would have died. My husband too."

"Oh, but I do remember ye very well," Ariana said. "But I did nothing more than anyone else would have done."

"Nay, my lady, it is what a saint would have done. We all think of ye as such. Ye will never have anything to fear on our land or from our allies."

Embarrassed, Ariana took Andrew from her and walked

across the room to lay her child on the small pallet next to her bed.

"God has rewarded ye with a beautiful bairn for yer good deeds."

Ariana smiled. "Aye, I am truly blessed," she admitted, touching her son's baby-soft cheek, then covering him with the small coverlet.

Isla and Iona unpacked the laird's and lady's things while Lady Lilias pulled Ariana after her. "Come, I wish ye to see my daughter, Lorna, the girl ye saved."

"I dinna save her. God did."

"As ye say. But if ye had not come to us, I am sure we would have perished from the disease."

Ariana shook her head. There would be no convincing this woman that she was not a saint. *Why try?* an inner voice counseled. Such notoriety could keep her and Andrew safe.

When they entered the chamber down the hall, the bride took her breath away. When Ariana had last seen Lorna, she was a thin, hollow cheeked patient, flushed with fever. Now her face radiated health with pink cheeks and a sparkling smile. Not to mention that her tunic showed all the curves of a budding young woman. She was breathtaking.

"My Lady Ariana!" Lorna said, falling down into a deep, respectful curtsy. "Ye honor me by attending my wedding."

The heat of a blush stained Ariana's face as she waited for the girl to rise. But Lorna had her head bowed in respect and showed no signs of rising. "Here, let me help ye," Ariana said, clasping the girl's hands and pulling her to her feet. "Congratulations, Lady Lorna. I am honored to be here. Are ye ready?"

"My lady," Lorna whispered, leaning close so no one could overhear their conversation. "Could ye give me a potion? I would like to conceive on my wedding night."

Did these simple folk really think she had such powers? If they did, it could be a dangerous assumption to let stand.

She touched the girl's cheek and smiled. "God decides when a child comes into this world, not I. Have faith, and love yer husband, and everything will turn out right."

Relieved satisfaction crossed the girl's pretty face. "I told my maid as much, but she insisted I ask."

"And so ye have." Ariana chuckled, then squeezed the girl's hand. "Good fortune," she added, then left the bride to finish her preparations.

Though the hallway was cool, suddenly a comforting warmth filled her and she knew that somehow Christophe had rejoined her. She closed her eyes and whispered his name before she preceded to the stairwell. "Thank God," she murmured, seeing the intimidating presence of her husband below. He looked angry. "Stay with me," she gasped as she descended the steps to join Robb. The room overflowed with dignitaries, and tension. Animosity hung in the air as different points of view made their way into the conversations that flowed throughout the room.

The buzz of voices slowly lessened, then eventually stopped, as one by one the crowd noticed her presence. To distract the attention from herself, she pointed to the balcony above. "The bride is on her way." But the silence remained, and her soft footsteps echoed across the stone floor as she made her way to Robb's imposing side.

His features were tight, his eyes cold as he stared at the other chieftains whose colors had long since drawn hatred from his clan. She slipped her hand into his, and felt the ice-cold chill of hatred and retribution flow over her. She gazed up at him. Lord, let him forget, so that he may heal. When he turned his gaze on her, a chill raced up her spine. His heartless eyes shone with ill-concealed malice. Swallowing, she looked away. It would take little provocation to raise Robb's ire.

Tension built within her as she waited for the bride. The murmur of soft voices lifted from the gathering as Laird Ruthven raised his hands. "Welcome, one and all. Today a truce has been called so all might enjoy the day. If any man here canna abide by that, then he must leave now."

When no one moved toward the doors, the laird smiled. "Then let the wedding proceed." He nodded toward the musicians, and they began to play their lutes and mandolins. A door overhead opened and closed as the bride stepped from her room. Though her soft steps were drowned out by the music, she soon appeared at the head of the stairs.

Her bright smile gave no indication of the tension in the room. She walked down the steps, her eyes focused on her groom. He lifted his chin and watched her every move, his face solemn.

Lord, please give her some encouragement, Ariana silently prayed, knowing too well the tension of that long walk. Each lonely step could be filled with self-doubt or terror, which a smile could relieve.

Ariana could have strangled the bridegroom. Stubborn Scot, he neither smiled nor looked away as the bride took her place at his side.

The friar started the ceremony, and she again heard the words that had bound her to Robb MacGregor. He stood like an unfeeling statue at her side, neither acknowledging her or the vows. A pang of regret sliced through her as Angus's gentle face drifted through her thoughts. His kindness and compassion lived in her heart. Unlike Robb's behavior. Indifferent and unfeeling, Robb was her husband.

Her words washed over her, reminding her that this was not her Christophe, but even with MacGregor's cold presence at her side, a warmth still resided in her heart. She remained unaffected and unafraid of the harsh man

who was, in fact but not in deed, her husband. His vacant
gaze strayed to hers. The man without a soul studied her,
and not one flicker of emotion showed within his brooding
eyes. She held his gaze, and it was he who looked away.
Had she imagined his approval earlier? It was at times like
this that she wondered what, if anything, her counterpart
had seen in this man. Besides his devastatingly good looks,
he was too cold and aloof for what she wanted in a man.
But Ariana believed that her counterpart had fallen deeply
in love, and had risked much to be with him. Ariana hoped
that Robb's troubled soul would find peace soon.

Suddenly, Robb smiled, a true, unguarded smile at something Lilias had said, and she knew why it could be easy
to love Robb MacGregor. He had a duality of dangerous
masculinity and boyish charm that was impossible to resist.

For a moment, she lost track of where they were and
gazed into the most intriguing blue eyes she had ever seen.
Warmth burned within his gaze, not of love, but desire,
and she looked away. What in God's name was happening?
Was she becoming attracted to the man?

Besieged by guilt, she swallowed and reminded herself
of her true love. Christophe would not desert her, nor
could she desert him. He would move heaven and earth
to return to her. Even now, she felt his presence. Shame
colored her features as she viewed the wedding couple as
they accepted their congratulations.

Robb took her elbow, startling her as he escorted her
forward. He offered his hand with dignity and honor to
the groom, then bowed gallantly before the bride. She
didn't know what she'd expected from Robb, but chivalry
was certainly the last thing she'd envisioned him showing.

As though knowing her reservations, he smiled at her,
before presenting her to the couple. She managed to offer
her well wishes, then moved along to let the other guests
in line come foward.

A servant approached her and bowed. "My lady, I say prayers in yer name every day." The maid knelt before her and kissed the hem of her gown.

This simply had to stop. "Please, dinna do that," Ariana said, pulling the girl to her feet.

Robb cleared his throat, and the maid whitened. "Forgive me," she whispered, and scurried away.

"Robb MacGregor," a voice called out, and his face drained of all color as he turned.

Fire burned in his eyes. "Ye dare approach me?"

Ariana held her breath, recognizing his mother, Elspeth MacGregor.

"Please, ye must listen to me. Ye are in danger."

"Begone! Ye have no loyalty in yer heart or soul."

Ariana placed her hands on his arm. "Laird Ruthven has called a truce. Ye must honor it."

He shook free of her hold. His fists clenched at his sides.

Elspeth lowered her voice. "Please, Robb, listen to me. I betray my brother to warn ye of a trap."

His stance stiffened. "I am not surprised. Ye betrayed yer husband and son."

She blanched, but raised her chin, dignity and honor shining in her eyes. "Aye, ye are right. I deserted him, for I could not bear a life I had not chosen. But know that my heart broke when I had to leave ye. Yet I loved ye too much to take ye with me. Ye see as much as it hurt, I knew yer father would make a better parent than I."

He looked at her as though her words meant nothing. His eyes narrowed. "Why should I believe what ye have to say?"

Tears dampened her lashes. "This is different. This concerns our clans. I only wish for peace."

Ariana held her breath as anger and indecision flickered in Robb's eyes. If only he'd take the laurel wreath. He might find peace.

Lor approached, interrupting them before Robb could respond. "My lady, would ye honor me with a dance?" He held out his hand to Ariana, and she reluctantly accepted. Her gaze remained on Robb and Elspeth, their faces mirroring the anguish in their souls.

As she danced, she repeatedly peeked around Lor's broad shoulders to study Robb and Elspeth.

"My lady, are my steps hard to follow?"

Her face flushed. "Forgive me, Lor. 'Tis not yer dancing. I am merely distracted."

He smiled. "Good. For a moment I feared I would step on yer toes if ye dinna try to keep them out of my way."

Why, Lor had a sense of humor. The discovery amazed her. Chuckling, she concentrated on being a better dance partner even though she longed to return to Robb.

She held back a sigh of relief when the music finally ended and Lor escorted her back to Robb's side.

"Liar," Robb spat scornfully, just under his breath.

Ariana heard the tail end of the conversation and her heart sank.

Lady Elspeth shrank away from Robb's anger, but her gaze remained on him, her sad eyes full of need, and want. "What I told ye is the truth. As Laird MacGregor ye must put yer personal grudges behind and heed my warning."

Hearing the earnest plea, Ariana touched his sleeve. "My laird, yer mother is right."

Rage burned in his eyes as he turned from Elspeth to Ariana. "Ye dare take this woman's cause? Ye may have won my enemy's heart. Would that ye could do so for me."

Ariana stepped back. This wrath was more than Robb's hurt pride rearing its ugly head. She had a feeling a deep wound had been opened tonight.

"Ye have everyone fooled by yer angelic countenance," Robb sneered at Ariana.

Elspeth stepped forward. "Robb MacGregor, ye may

have reason to hate me, but yer wife has done nothing to earn yer wrath.''

He rounded on Elspeth. "Dinna defend her. Her betrayal was worse than yers.''

Robb's pain had poured out. Ariana drew a deep breath. "Ye have never forgiven me, but I say now, ye have misjudged me. The only slight is in yer heart.''

"I have seen yer true colors,'' he ground out. "Ye are like this woman.'' He pointed to Elspeth. "No honor.''

Elspeth squared her shoulders and met his angry stare. "Ye see only what ye wish to see. Nothing more.''

His face reddened, but he glared at her until she glanced away, blocking out his anger and foolish pride.

"Begone, Elspeth Frazier,'' he then said to the older woman.

Ariana's eyes widened at the rude dismissal.

Elspeth raised her chin. Dignity and stoicism showed as she bowed her head and sank down into a deep curtsy.

His hand began to shake. "I said begone!''

Elspeth's eyes sparkled with unshed tears as she turned and moved away.

"Robb,'' Ariana whispered.

"Dinna say one word,'' he warned. "Ye dinna know the pain that woman caused, not only to me, but to my father. She is nothing but evil and trouble. I forbid ye to see her.''

Forbid. The word echoed in her mind with a nasty reverberation. "I am not a child,'' she muttered under her breath. Every inch of her cried out against such a dictate, but she remained quiet, seeing his anger seething beneath the surface. This was not the time to broach such a matter. When he calmed down, she would talk about the subject reasonably. Squaring her shoulders, she nodded.

"I mean it, Ariana, I will not tolerate disobedience in this matter,'' he warned.

She drew a deep breath and faced him. "My laird, ye have no reason to doubt me."

His eyes narrowed, his expression growing terrifying. He pulled her from the crowd. "Ye tricked my father into marrying ye. And deceived me by bearing another man's child."

Her heart raced. She knew very little of her counterpart. "Did I? Are ye so sure?" Before he could voice more, she sadly shook her head. "No more, Robb. Ye canna control my thoughts, nor my heart. They are mine and mine alone."

"Dinna push the matter. I will have yer word that ye will not speak to this woman."

There was little help for it. She either had to give her word, or openly defy him. She could not afford to alienate him at this point. "I give ye my word I willna talk to her."

The moment the unwanted words left her mouth, she felt she had made a grave mistake. But 'twas done and she was bound to her pledge.

He smiled, but the expression was cold. Calculation lived in his eyes, and she felt like a peasant under sentencing. His stare lasted for what seemed an eternity before he looked away. "Ye must mingle, but remember I will watch ye. If ye dare break yer word, none will save ye from my wrath."

She shook her head. "I wonder, my laird, if it is me ye hate so, or yerself."

He raised an eyebrow. "My lady, ye only need to concern yerself with pleasing me, not how my thoughts work. As ye said, yer thoughts are yer own. Well, so are mine." He walked away, but she knew that no matter where he was his gaze would follow her. 'Twas a test she dared not fail.

As the music filled the air, Ariana caught sight of Elspeth talking to a maid. It broke her heart to see the look of defeat on the woman's face, but she turned away, feeling her husband's gaze on her. When she glanced up he appeared to be deep in conversation with one of his guards, but she knew he still watched her.

A strange urge came over her to seek the woman out. Almost as though a spirit whispered in her ear. She heard the word *listen*. Dear God, did Christophe want her to know the story?

Her stomach roiled as she looked at Robb. She had just given her word not to speak to the woman. Could she dare break it?

She closed her eyes, trying to concentrate on the inner voice, but the music increased and she was jostled by jovial merrymakers. She needed to leave the festivities. Solitude might offer her the answer she needed.

As if in answer to a prayer, Isla approached her. "My lady, the bairn is bathed and only needs to be fed."

Thank goodness her son needed her. She quickly explained to Robb before leaving the great room.

As she climbed up the stairwell she felt a shiver of apprehension. Lord, what was this eerie feeling that hung about her like a damp cloud of doom.

She desperately tried to empty her mind of all thoughts so any impressions might materialize.

In her chamber she nursed her son, rocking him gently in her arms. He finished nursing and fell asleep. She continued to rock him, and let her thoughts drift. While she was crooning a soft lullaby, a voice echoed through her mind.

She knew the voice, and closed her eyes to concentrate. Was it her overactive imagination, or had she really heard Christophe's voice?

She lingered in the chair, when she should have returned to the wedding. Though she tried to hear him again, silence only closed in around her.

* * *

Christophe hovered over his wife and child. He knew she sensed the danger. If only she would nap, he could try to communicate with her. He whispered continually for her to rest, and thought he had succeeded when she smothered a yawn and laid the baby down.

Ariana lifted her hair and stretched, looking longingly at the bed. She took a step toward the pallet, then stopped when someone knocked on the door.

Christophe's elation turned to despair when she opened the door and Robb filled the entry. "What is keeping ye, wife? There are many downstairs who wish to see ye."

"My pardon, my laird, but I just finished feeding our son."

"If he takes this long to nurse, then let the wet nurse we brought along attend to him."

She stepped back. "As long as I can, I will nurse my own. I willna budge on this."

Christophe proudly smiled at her spunk.

Robb looked at her as though he could not believe she had asserted herself. "In this I will allow ye some latitude. For it is said that a mother is very protective of her young. Until now, I suspected it was a false rumor."

Ariana looked at him, amazed. "I am sorry yer life was not as kind as it should have been."

His features closed. "Dinna waste yer pity on me, woman. I learned my lessons very well indeed."

Ariana sighed. "Mayhap, ye did, but the experience has blinded ye to warmth."

With a deep growl, Robb pulled her into his arms and smashed his lips against hers.

Startled, Ariana cried out.

Christophe's feelings churned into a mass of knots. He wanted to tear them apart. Ariana did not fight Robb MacGregor, and although he knew she could not, a part of him raged against her passive behavior.

When Robb MacGregor lifted his head, he stared down at his wife with hot desire.

She shivered in his arms.

Damn, Christophe thought. He had to break the mood, he had to rescue her from Robb's masculine allure.

"Trust," he whispered in Robb MacGregor's ear. "Do ye really trust her?"

Robb raised an eyebrow, his gaze hardening as it scanned her face.

"What is it?" she whispered shakily.

"I almost forgot that ye canna be trusted."

She turned and pushed out of his arms. For just a fleeting moment Christophe felt a twinge of remorse. But he had done what was best. He had to protect her.

Ariana stomped down the hall, and Christophe rushed to keep up with her. He could feel her angry bewilderment. It was imperative he find peace for Robb MacGregor before it was too late for him to reclaim the body. What if she thought him gone forever and forgot about him? What if she fell in love with his counterpart? He couldn't bear it. It would make him insane.

"I love ye," he whispered, dying to touch her warm flesh, to taste her sweet lips and smell her womanly scent. He called her name, over and over—a soft litany echoing from his heart to hers. His memories surfaced of their love, the sweet times shared in gentle contentment, the hot passion that joined their lives together as one. His heart cried out to hers. "Listen to me, hear me. Believe in love. Believe in me."

Ever so slowly, he watched her face relax into a calm expression, and a smile teased her mouth. Whether it was because he had reached her, or because she entered the great room, he would never know.

CHAPTER FIFTEEN

Remarkable, Ariana thought, staring up at her husband's smiling face as he twirled her around the dance floor with precision and grace. No one would ever guess they had exchanged cross words. Elspeth Frazier's gaze followed them as she moved on the outer circle of the festivities. Under the intense scrutiny, the hair on Ariana's neck raised. Although she wished to seek Elspeth out, she could not.

The opportunity arose later that evening when the minstrel announced a lady's dance. Elspeth pressed a piece of paper into Ariana's hand when they met in line.

Ariana's gaze flew to Robb. Thankfully, her husband's attention centered on their host, not on her. Relieved that he had missed the note's transfer, she quickly hid the missive in her tunic. All night, she felt the thin piece of paper against her skin, and itched to read it.

Her heart raced when Robb pulled her into his arms, and the paper crinkled in his tight embrace. She held her breath, but he failed to hear the damning sound as he whirled her around the floor.

"Is something troubling ye?"

Guilt flushed her face. "Nay, 'tis all the dancing that has worn me out."

"Then perhaps we should retire to our room." His smoldering gaze fairly scorched her.

Her heartbeat quickened. Up until now he had spent his nights with Cailin. Her throat tightened as she dampened her lips. "Now?"

"Aye, now."

The room spun around as she stared up at Robb's handsome features. The firelight shadowed every strong plane and hollow in his face. In the flickering firelight, golden streaks highlighted his light hair and his bright blue eyes sparkled. Her breath froze as a slow seductive smile slipped across his firm lips, revealing even white teeth. He bent his head to nibble on her ear, and goose bumps covered her arms.

She trembled as his breath wafted across her neck. She closed her eyes and summoned her resistance against his dangerous and disarming assault. He was not Christophe.

He brushed a curl from her cheek in the same way that Christophe had done. His hand traveled to her neck, his fingers grazing her skin. Just like. . . A shiver of excitement raced up her spine. Dear Lord, was it possible? Her eyes flew open. She looked at him, and her breathing quickened. For a heart-stopping moment she thought Christophe had returned. But when she gazed into his eyes she knew it was Robb, not Christophe, who stood before her, desire in his eyes. Oh, Lord, what would she do?

"Please, I think we should remain a little longer. It would be bad form to leave before the wedding couple." *Christophe, where are you?*

His husky chuckle reminded her of Christophe. If she

closed her eyes, she could almost imagine him here with her.

"Bad form, Ariana? Do ye fear others will realize what a wanton woman ye are?"

Stunned by the sudden sarcasm, she stiffened for a moment thinking she had imagined it. One look at his harsh features confirmed his change of heart. Though relieved the sexual teasing had ended, she wondered what devils rode this man.

"Yer moods shift with the wind, husband. Either ye hate me, or ye do not. Which will it be?"

He released her. "I own ye. That is enough for me."

Liar, she thought. He desired her, but his stubborn pride had returned. Encouraged by the knowledge, she laid her hand on his arm. "Hate me if ye must. But dinna hate wee Andrew."

His eyes turned cold. "Ye dare bring him up."

"Robb, if ye do not find peace, ye will make the same mistake as yer parents. Ye will raise yer son without love."

The only visible sign that he had not turned to stone was the muscle working furiously in his cheek. "I know the guilty party," he hissed.

She raised an eyebrow. "Do ye?"

Rage darkened his eyes, and trepidation surged through her. He gripped her hand in a painful hold. "Make no mistake, wife, I could kill ye for what ye have done."

She swallowed, but refused to look away. "Robb Mac-Gregor, ye are hurting me."

He thrust her hand away and opened his mouth to speak, but the music stopped. Clamping his jaw shut, he took several deep breaths. Within moments iron control slipped over his features as he surveyed his surroundings.

Laird Ruthven came up to them, his hand extended. "Join me in a toast, MacGregor."

Robb shook the man's hand, and was pulled away to

share a drink. He looked back over his shoulder once, and the message in his eyes upset her. He had plans.

She wanted to read the missive hidden in her tunic, but instead massaged her fingers and looked down at her hand. Her amber ring glowed in the warmth of the candlelight. A mental image of Christophe returned. She envisioned him when he'd put the ring on her finger for the first time. He had been a magnificent warlord, so strong and so masculine. Her gaze strayed to Robb MacGregor. A chieftain and Scottish laird. In his own way there were similarities, but there were also many differences. *What now?* she thought. *What am I to do?*

The music swirled around her, forcing her melancholy away as she was beckoned into another round of dancing. Lor escorted her in a dance, and when they left the floor she was asked to dance by several other lairds, all of whom had benefited from her cure. As the night progressed, her mood gradually lightened. The ale and good wishes flowed as the celebration continued. She was out of breath when Laird Hay led her over to the chairs. "My lady, would ye wish a chalice of wine?"

"Nay, my laird, but thank ye." She fanned herself as she watched the merrymakers. The joy on the bride's face and the pride in the groom's smile drew her attention like a magnet.

"By yer leave, my lady." Her escort bowed, and she longed to sneak away to read the missive. But no sooner did he leave than another clansman claimed her for a dance.

She danced several more dances before she sought some refreshment and a quiet corner. Life, she thought, was meant to be enjoyed. Her eyelashes fluttered closed, and memories so achingly sweet and rich washed over as she remembered her extraordinary lifetimes. They seemed so long ago. Her eyelids opened and her gaze moved to her husband. In the blink of an eye, your life could end, or start anew. She would not worry about Robb MacGregor. Whatever happened, she would take it in her stride. Andrew's survival depended on her. Christophe would expect her to protect their child at all cost.

With her decision made, a much needed calm washed over her.

A hand extended into her line of vision, and she looked up to see Robb's smiling face. "My laird?"

"My lady, a dance, if ye please."

Christophe? she wondered, then dismissed the hope. She placed her hand in his and felt his firm clasp. He was as much an enigma as Christophe had been.

He pulled her close. His breath wafted across her cheek, and the strong scent of spirits assailed her. "What were ye thinking about a moment ago?" he asked.

She sighed, knowing he was feeling his drink. "I was thinking about life and how lucky we are for every precious moment God gives us."

He pulled back, a puzzled frown marring his handsome features. "Ye never cease to amaze me. I dinna know if ye are really sincere or the greatest fraud of all time. Tonight, I intend to find out." He pulled her back into his arms. A kiss away from her lips, he whispered, "Show me yer heart."

She swallowed. Her resolve was going to be extremely hard to keep. She pulled back and the rustle of paper sounded.

He raised an eyebrow, then slipped his fingers into the side of her tunic. Suddenly, the paper missive slid out of the thick folds of cloth, and fell into the rushes.

She held her breath as he leaned down and picked it up.

"What is this?"

She stared, unable to explain as he opened the folded parchment.

His face darkened as he scanned the note. Then he glared at her, blue fire shining in his eyes. "Ye dare defy me?"

Her mouth went dry under his condemning stare. "Yer mother handed it to me. I have not had time to look at it."

"So ye say." He crumpled up the note and threw it into the hearth.

With a sinking heart, she watched the note flame and curl into ash. " 'Tis the truth."

He pulled her from the main room into an antechamber. Once inside, he released her and shut the door. When he turned to stare at her, his disgust set fissures of fear through her nerves. "What a wife I have. A woman of deceit and defiance."

"Ye forbid me to talk to her. I didna speak to her. I have no control over what others do. She handed me the missive."

"Why didna ye hand the note to me?"

"Why should I spoil yer mood? I intended to read it and if I thought it would not anger ye, then I would have turned it over. If, on the other hand, I thought it would upset ye, I would have thrown it away."

"Ye expect me to believe ye?"

"If our situation were reversed, Robb, and ye found yerself married to a volatile mate, would ye have risked yer spouse's displeasure over a mere note?"

He glowered at her, but 'twas obvious he considered the matter.

His momentary doubt emboldened her. She walked over and placed her hand in his. "Ye could crush the bones in my hand so easy. Why would I seek yer wrath?"

His eyes narrowed.

She studied his set features, wondering how to reach this tortured soul. She took a gamble. "Did ye ever love me?"

His grip tightened as he pulled her into his arms. "I remember telling ye so, but I canna remember where. Perhaps I dreamt it."

Her counterpart would have been devastated, but she raised her chin and met his angry scowl. "Ye dinna spare my pride, do ye?"

"Did ye ever spare mine?" His mouth covered hers, and his tongue slipped sensuously over her lips.

She gasped at the raw sensuality. His breath fanned over her face.

"We have always had one thing in common," he huskily murmured when their lips parted.

Her heart fluttered, for his words struck a chord within her. Her counterpart had fallen under the spell of his blatant masculinity, ignoring his selfish nature, seduced by his devastatingly attractive features and dangerous manner. She swallowed, his cool appraisal making her shiver. "What do ye want from me, Robb?"

"I want a wife. One I can trust and believe in."

"Believe in?" she questioned, wondering if one small part of Christophe remained.

"Aye, believe in." His features closed. His eyes hooded.

Lord in heaven, he wanted a truce. Was this a test? Her mind went fleetingly to Christophe. *Help me,* she silently cried.

"Ariana?"

She didn't trust Robb. No doubt politics played a part in his request, but her son's welfare depended on her actions.

"I believe in love, Robb MacGregor, I always have," she replied truthfully.

He smiled as his gaze dropped to her lips. "We will soon see."

Her nerves tingled with the course she had set. There could be no turning back. Yet the memory of her love still accompanied her on this dangerous journey of deception. She was not foolish enough to believe that she could hold this attractive man at bay. Nor was she a hypocrite. Her heart belonged to Christophe, and would be kept locked away until he reappeared. "He might never return," a small voice whispered, but she refused to listen. Christophe would come back, and when he did she would deal with her choices. Until then, she would do whatever it took to survive. She had to think of her son.

She looked up at Robb, and his face lowered to hers. His hand slipped behind her head and pulled her closer, bringing her lips to meet his. At first his kiss tasted of virile seduction and passion, then suddenly of wonder and surprise.

He pulled back, his expression puzzled. "Ye didna ever kiss like this before."

She latched onto the first excuse that entered her head. "Of course not, husband. I am a married woman now."

He shrugged and pulled her closer. Fear shot through her as he kissed her again, enveloping her in a passion that promised much, much more.

"What are ye thinking?" she asked when the kiss was over.

"I canna explain, but there are times when ye remind me of the woman I knew, and others when ye seem a stranger."

"I feel the same way about ye."

Again his lips captured hers and though she did not resist him, the fire and passion he had known were missing. His mouth traveled to her ear. "If ye dinna try to convince me that ye care, I will not hold to the truce."

He nipped her ear, then lowered his head to again taste her sweet lips, but a knock on the door interrupted them. He sighed, wanting to ignore the intruder, but knew he could not. "Enter," he commanded.

She tried to pull out of his arms, but he held her tight, running his hands over her back as the door opened.

Music and laughter flowed into the room until the door shut and someone cleared his throat behind them.

"What is it?"

Lor approached him. "My laird, forgive the interruption but. . ." He looked at her and hesitated.

"Lor, this had better be worth it."

Lor's face flushed. "It is, my laird, if I might have a word with ye alone." He bowed to Ariana, then left the room the same way he had entered.

"Tonight," Robb whispered. Kissing her hard, he turned and marched to the door. With his hand on the knob he glanced back, catching her expression, before he departed. The confused concern, masking her beauty, haunted him every step of the way.

Lor led the way through the great room, and armory. "My laird, there is news from home." He pushed open the door to a chapel lit by candles and torches. As the light flickered in the chilly draft, shadows danced across the walls. On the cold floor lay a man so bloodied and beaten, his features were unrecognizable.

"My laird," he rasped, reaching out.

"Gavin?" Robb rushed to the fallen soldier's side. "What in God's name happened?"

"Frazier, my laird. . .betrayed. . .castle." His grip slipped off Robb's tunic.

"Betrayed? By whom?" he asked as an uncontrollable rage filled him. But the battered soldier slumped back, unconscious and unresponsive.

"Send for my wife," Robb bit out.

* * *

Ariana gasped when she saw the beaten warrior. The candlelight in the chapel fell across his disfigured face, lighting the purple bruises and dried blood in flickering light. She looked at Robb. "What happened?"

"Can ye revive him?"

"I dinna know until I examine him. Who is it?"

Robb glanced at Lor. Apparently his man had not informed Ariana. " 'Tis Gavin."

Her face crumpled into a mask of pain. "Nay," she cried. "Not Gavin."

Robb took hold of her arm. "I must know what happened."

Tears burned her eyes as she met her husband's gaze. "I will do what I can." She knelt before the gentle giant and looked at his wounds. The poor man was lucky to be alive. A door opened and a soft cry sounded. She turned to see Isla, her eyes tear-laden as she rushed forward. "My lady, what can I do?"

"Get my medicines, quickly."

"Aye, my lady." She reached out to brush the man's hair from his face. "Take care of him, my lady."

A lump formed in Ariana's throat at the tender action. "Dinna worry. Hurry now."

Isla pushed Robb and Lor out of her way and ran from the room.

Ariana turned to Lor. "I will need several pans of boiled water."

"Will ye need anything else, my lady?"

"Aye, fresh linen."

He bowed and departed.

Several minutes later the maid returned with the healing pouches, followed by Lor. He handed the linen and pan of water to Ariana, then stepped back to join Robb.

Lor shook his head as he stared at his friend, then spoke to Robb. "Do ye think Gavin was attacked at the castle, or on the road while he carried a message to ye?"

Robb frowned. "I dinna know." He moved closer to the pallet, hovering over Ariana's shoulder. "Ye must revive him."

She did not look up. "Robb, I will tend the man, but I dinna know if he will regain consciousness."

He grabbed her, his fingers biting into her flesh. "Listen, wife, he must. Our home may be under attack or have already fallen. It is imperative I know."

Her heart sank. War, and more war. Did these people know of nothing else? She pulled free of his hold. "Let me see to him," she breathed.

Gavin's tunic bore a large hole where his side had been pierced by a blade, and his arm lay at an unnatural angle. His clothes were saturated in blood. That the man had lived this long seemed a miracle. "Gavin," she whispered, while starting to peel his clothes back. "Gavin, can ye hear me?"

Silence met her plea.

Ariana ignored the deep scowl on Robb's face as she tended her patient. His wounds were severe. Tears hovered in Isla's eyes as she assisted. Ariana's hands shook as she bathed Gavin. She could not bring herself to tell Isla that she feared he would die. In fact, it was hard to even meet the woman's gaze.

Gavin mercifully slept, not regaining consciousness through the ordeal as she tended his wounds.

Robb paced back and forth. Once Gavin's wounds were seared, stitched, and bandaged, Robb came to a halt behind her. "Wake him."

"I canna."

Robb ran his hand through his hair. "I must return to the castle."

Terror shot through her and she jumped to her feet. "Ye canna! 'Tis too dangerous."

"Our home is in danger."

She reached out to him, holding his arm. If he died, Christophe could never return to her. "Please, dinna go. It may be a trap."

A strange light entered his eyes. "Ye care if I live or if I die?"

"Of course I do."

His expression momentarily softened. "I should have told ye before. If there is only one woman who has captured my heart, 'tis ye."

His declaration terrified her. It sounded too much like good-bye. Tears stung her eyes. "Robb, please, ye must not go."

He peeled her fingers from around his arm. "I must."

She ran after him, and again, she grabbed his arm. "Robb MacGregor, if ye get yerself killed I will never forgive ye."

He chuckled. "There is the woman that bewitched me. For a while I despaired I would never see her again."

Then he kissed her hard. Not brutal, not sardonic, but passionate, a hint of his inner heart revealed. "Remember me."

Her heart ached as she watched him walk away. She could do nothing to stop him. She followed slowly and stood in the doorway as he entered the great room. The wedding party had retired, but the revelers remained.

Robb swiftly rounded up his men, only to be stopped by their host. "What goes here? Why are ye leaving my festivities?"

"One of my men has been injured. I suspect an attack on my home, but I have no way of knowing without going there myself."

Laird Ruthven raised his hand to the assembly. "Laird

MacGregor's home is in peril. I will ride with him. Who rides with me?"

Every laird present stepped forward. They looked not to Robb, but to Ariana. Their generosity humbled her. Robb would be safe with such a force.

He looked back at her, a small smile teasing the corner of his mouth. His attractive face took her breath away. Robb MacGregor's charisma reached out to her, daring her to come near. She sighed as she watched him walk away. Never again would she wonder why her counterpart had fallen in love with this man. Devastatingly handsome and dangerously attractive, Robb MacGregor could, when he chose to be charming, make any woman's heart beat faster.

"God go with ye," she whispered.

Robb MacGregor's upheaval began the moment he left the Ruthven castle. His ambivalent feelings toward his wife swirled in his mind, but he buried his doubts. Inside, thoughts and emotions battled for ground. His mother had warned him of the betrayal, and Gavin had confirmed it. But what about the trap? What was it? Elspeth said he would be walking into one. Did he dare believe her? Hatred swirled in his mind, taunting him, reminding him of his childhood, when trust had been destroyed. Bitterness surfaced. Yet in the midst of his anguish, his mother's voice sliced through the years of anger, warning him. He ignored the struggle, ashamed of his loss of control. Never had he experienced such doubt or uncertainty.

An inner voice sounded in his head, thundering through his thoughts. "Beware."

He turned to Laird Ruthven, his head aching. "What do ye think?"

"Can there be any doubt?" The laird sighed. " 'Tis Frazier."

Rage returned, swift and harsh. He could barely see through the red haze that overcame him. His mother's abandonment, his father's betrayal, the deception of the clan. He hated them, hated them all with a force that was unexplainable, and undeniable. He would avenge himself and his clan, but he sensed there was more, much more. He pushed the anger deep in his gut. When he met Alastair he would unleash his hatred. A calm settled over him, but a soft whisper of warning circulated. *"Beware."*

Laird Ruthven pointed to the west. "Look. Ye have company."

Another laird loyal to his wife rode toward them. "I will stand with ye," Laird Dunn said.

Suddenly, his ranks had swelled to twice the numbers. He now had over six hundred men. He wondered if he could not take his castle without a siege and with few losses. Though he would never admit that his mother's warning lay at the base of his decision, he now had an advantage. He turned to his fellow chieftains and motioned them to join him.

The lairds rode their horses up the ranks. When they stopped in front of him, Robb raised his hand. "In case it is a trap, I have a plan. What say ye about an attack? They would not suspect it."

"What if yer men are on the walls? Ye would be putting them in jeopardy," Laird Ruthven said.

"I can send a rider in to see who stands guard. If Alastair has taken my home, I doubt he would man the walls with MacGregors."

"Aye," Laird Dunn said. "If the man does not return, we know yer castle is in enemy hands and yer men in the dungeon."

Laird Ruthven smiled. "Let us have this business done."

Robb MacGregor took hold of each chieftain's hand. "I pledge ye my loyalty, though I ask that Alastair Frazier's demise be left to me."

"Aye, kill the bastard," Laird Dunn said as the others agreed.

"I will," Robb vowed, then again outlined his strategy, making sure everyone understood the plan. Once the battle positions were assigned to each chieftain, they marched to MacGregor's land. Every hamlet they passed through added men to their ranks, all in gratitude to Lady Ariana.

Robb MacGregor was not surprised when Laird MacPherson joined him. "I hear ye need assistance."

"Aye."

"My daughter?" he inquired, his gaze direct.

"She is safe at Laird Ruthven's."

MacPherson raised a brow. "I hold ye responsible for her safety, as well as the safety of my grandson."

"No one will harm the lady while she is under my protection."

MacPherson nodded and together the large force of men, united by Ariana's unconditional charity, headed to rescue her castle. At nightfall they camped in a valley just south of the MacGregor castle. Small campfires were built and the men gathered around them, talking in hushed whispers. Their thoughts of home and family intruded on their minds, as they always did the night before a battle.

Robb dispatched a soldier to the castle. "If ye dinna return by dawn, I will attack."

Dressed as a peasant, the lone soldier walked off toward the castle.

During the night, Robb MacGregor contemplated his life. For the first time he admitted his love for his wife. He closed his eyes and asked forgiveness for all the times he had hurt her. He sighed. Once the campaign was over he would never leave her again. He had found his heaven, and he cherished it. The stars overheard winked down at him as he closed his eyes. He would give her his heart and his love. With a woman of her courage and integrity, he was safe. He knew that now, even though the proof had always been before him. His wife, Ariana, belonged to an elite class. She was an angel.

No sooner had he closed his eyes than he dreamt of her death as they had fallen over a cliff. The call to arms sounded. In a blinding flash, he knew: He had wasted his life and been called back, not to avenge the innocent, but to forgive the past. Then the thought faded as he came fully awake. He stretched, but the uneasy feelings of his dream haunted him. Distant thoughts lay just out of reach.

He sighed, and ran a hand through his hair. His soldier had not returned. It appeared his mother had been telling the truth. Even so, he would have proof before he believed her. Trust was hard-won. Today he had a battle to wage.

CHAPTER SIXTEEN

Christophe hovered over the advancing army. Every ounce of his being, every sense, screamed for them to be aware of Alastair's treachery.

He shadowed Robb MacGregor. Christophe hoped that once Robb killed Alastair and Morag to avenge his and Ariana's murder, his spirit would at last find peace, and eternal rest. Only then did Christophe feel his spirit would return.

Suddenly, he felt the undeniable pull of a greater force. He was moving away from the army, away from keeping Robb MacGregor safe. "No," he cried, twisting and turning against the tow. Though he fought against the powerful force, his efforts were as ineffectual as a storm-tossed leaf. "Damn it, I must stay," he cursed, railing against fate as he was whisked away. He struggled, watching helplessly as the ground moved beneath him, sliding past with incredible speed. He rose higher, soaring over snow-blanketed moors, tree-covered forests, vast stretches of mountains to finally hover over a valley where a castle rose into the sky. His senses reeled as he recognized the structure; he had been there before.

Suddenly, he moved toward the fortress and found himself in the Fraziers' castle.

Alastair gripped Morag's face in a viselike hold. "Yer nephew marched with a multitude of soldiers. My source said Robb Mac-Gregor knew of the trap." He pushed her away in disgust, then circled her like a falcon homing in on his prey. "How is that, Morag?"

Dear God, they ~were here. Safe. How would he return if his counterpart could not find peace?

"I dinna know. But ye deserted the Campbell. Yer allies are left to defend the MacGregor castle."

"Campbell's loyalty was waning. I can find allies in Normandy. My dear, we have only one option now. Forget about ruling our two castles. I have a plan, for ransom."

Before Christophe could hear more, he felt the pull stronger than ever. "No! I must hear what they plan."

Ariana attended Gavin, who still had not regained consciousness. Isla hovered over the handsome Scotsman, her concern evident.

Iona rocked the baby and leaned forward, speaking her fears aloud. "I hope Brodie is well."

"And Mother and Father also," Isla said, finishing her sister's sentence.

Ariana nodded in agreement. Standing, she began to pace. Robb had been gone only a short time, yet a terrible premonition descended. She could barely sit for the eerie feeling that overcame her, fraying her nerves.

When news came that Cailin had arrived at Ruthven, Ariana flew out of her chair to meet the woman.

Cailin, her face dirty, her clothes tattered, stumbled into the main hall looking tired and frightened. "My lady, yer husband has been wounded. His aunt sent me to summon ye home."

Ariana gasped. "Wounded?" Her heart sank as her worst fear materialized. Pinpricks of light flashed before her eyes, but she took several deeps breaths to gain her composure. Though terror surged through her, she walked across the room and put her arm around the poor shivering girl. "How serious is his injury?"

Cailin pulled back to face her. "I dinna know, but Lady Morag said ye must hurry. Yer guard is waiting."

"Ye were the only woman traveling with the entourage?"

"Aye, I am a servant now."

"That is no excuse for Morag to endanger yer life."

Cailin lowered her gaze, and Ariana squeezed her arm. "There, there, we will sort this out when we arrive home. Come sit by the fire and warm yerself."

"How do the villagers fare?" Isla asked, her face pale.

"Well," she hedged. "Laird MacGregor's victory freed them."

"And the soldiers?" Iona asked.

"I dinna know." Cailin looked away.

Ariana squeezed Iona's hands. "Dinna worry about Brodie Maclaren. I am sure he is fine."

When Iona nodded, Ariana went to the door and asked a servant to fetch Lady Lilias.

Several minutes later Lady Lilias rushed into the room. "My dear, I heard, I will have my men escort ye home tomorrow morning."

" 'Tis no need." Ariana hugged the lady. "Lady Cailin has brought my escort."

"But 'tis almost sunset." Lady Lilias pulled out of the embrace and stared at the determined features. "Very well. I shall have the kitchen pack some supplies."

Ariana nodded, then picking up her son from the cradle, she looked to Isla and Iona. "Come, we must hurry."

At the great room entrance, Isla touched her arm. "My lady, might I stay and nurse Gavin back to health?"

Ariana's gaze drifted to the man still asleep. She prayed Robb was not in the same state. "Aye. That ye must."

She rushed through the castle, entering her room with Iona behind her. "Just pack my medicine and Andrew's case. Lady Lilias can send my belongings later."

While Iona carried out her wishes, she laid Andrew on the bed. "We will be home soon, Andrew," Ariana cooed, changing him and bundling him up in several warm blankets before covering him in a small fur robe.

"My lady, ye must be better prepared," Iona said, throwing Ariana's fur mantle over her shoulders and grabbing a warm fur for herself.

The icy bite of winter took Ariana's breath away when she walked into the courtyard. She snuggled Andrew within her arms, sheltering him from the cold.

It was near dusk when under a weak winter sun, Ariana left with a small party of men, Cailin, and her maid Iona. She did not recognize the soldiers, but then they could have been from any clan who supported her husband. However, Cailin's father and brothers were among the men. With the clansmen busy, it made sense that slaves would round out the caravan, but their presence did not instill confidence.

The journey home moved slowly and the route was not familiar. When she asked about the direction, the man leading the column bowed, but she caught a hint of impatience. "My lady, we are trying to avoid attack."

"Do ye expect one?" she asked, pulling her sleeping baby protectively against her.

"The possibility exists. I have my orders about yer safety."

"Very well," she conceded. "But we must hurry."

"I canna increase our pace until after we have cleared the forest."

She pursed her lips together, neither liking or understanding the man's indifference. "When will we be able to travel the most direct route?"

"In the morning. By then we should be past any enemy clans."

She bristled at his brusque tone as she watched him return to his position. The Drummond men smirked at her irritation, but quickly averted their gaze when she glanced their way. She was about to call the leader back, when she noticed a break in the woods up ahead. Quickly, the dense trees fell away, revealing an open road, and without a word the leader raised his hand and signaled the column to increase their pace.

Impatient, but satisfied with their progress, Ariana thought of her husband. Robb would not die. She would be in time to treat his wound. Even though she repeated the litany, a strange foreboding overcame her. Though apprehensive, she refused to give in to fear. She could not afford to panic.

They made camp only an hour after leaving Ruthven's castle. She shivered in the night air, chilled to the bone. After warming herself by the fire, she quickly ate her meager supper of oakcakes and tea, then retired to her tent for the night.

" 'Tis time for yer little angel's feeding, my lady." Iona handed Andrew to her, then ushered Cailin through the open flap. "We will be back after we have a little supper," she added, then pulled the flap down behind them.

Andrew nestled close to her, unaware of the chill and her fear. She smiled at the precious bundle in her arms. He was so perfect, so loving. After Andrew finished nursing, she changed his clothes and rocked him to sleep in her arms. As Andrew drifted off, her thoughts wandered to Christophe. Within the privacy of the quiet tent, she concentrated on her love. Desperately, she relived their life together, remembering all the sweet moments they'd shared. His gentle touch, his passionate kisses, the deep resonant sound of his voice, the comfort of his arms when she needed to be held, the kindness of his soul. She closed her eyes, searching for, but unable to find, his presence, and a great loneliness engulfed her. For a moment she feared his defection. What would she do if he never returned to her? The more she thought of him, the lonelier she became. A terrible melancholy descended, bringing tears to her eyes.

Forcing her emotions back, she laid Andrew beside her and settled down to sleep. Cailin and Iona entered the tent and quickly wrapped up in their fur robes to sleep. Ariana awakened just before dawn to feed Andrew. She had barely fallen back asleep when a loud scream awakened her. Terror sliced through her as she scrambled to her son and cradled him against her breast.

"Frazier is here." Iona rushed into the tent and huddled next to Ariana, whimpering in fear. Strangely, Cailin didn't cower. After Iona's crying stopped, noise ceased. There were no screams of battle, just eerie silence.

In the hush, their tent flap was ripped open and Alastair Frazier reached in, grabbed a handful of Ariana's hair, and yanked her forward. Defenseless while she protected her child, pain exploded in her head as he pulled her out into the cold morning.

"Ye are now my prisoners." He pointed to Cailin. "Take the child."

"Nay," Ariana screamed, clutching her baby to her bosom.

He pulled her close and hit her face with the back of his hand. "Dinna cause any more trouble or ye will never see the urchin again."

Cailin tried to reach for Andrew, but Alastair had a guard rip the child from her arms. Andrew started to cry as the guard thrust the baby into Cailin's arms.

"Nay," Ariana screamed, clawing at him to gain her freedom.

He held her back and chuckled cruelly. Tears burned her eyes as she watched her son being carried away in the arms of another. Her face stung, but she lifted her chin. Hatred unlike any she had ever known filled her. "If ye harm my bairn, no power on earth will stop me from killing ye," she spat, glaring into his eyes.

He stared at her, then threw his head back and laughed.

The ugly, mocking sound grated on her nerves, and she knew she had encountered true evil. He grabbed her and hauled her after him, nearly dragging her across the ground. When they reached the horses he threw her upon the saddle. She reached for her child, thinking once she was astride they would return Andrew, but Cailin ignored her as she clutched the baby to her bosom.

Frazier took Cailin's elbow and carefully helped her over to a horse. "Ye have done well." He took Andrew while Cailin mounted then handed her the baby.

Ariana's blood turned cold. Cailin had helped them. Her baby resided in the arms of a betrayer. Andrew's plaintive cries broke her heart. She glanced around, suddenly becoming aware of the undisturbed camp. She had fallen into a trap.

Alastair motioned for the guard to bring the maid. Iona's cries captured Ariana's attention. Cailin's brothers, those two burly oafs, dragged Iona from the tent. Ariana held her breath when Alastair approached. "Yer mistress no longer needs a maid." He pulled his sword from its sheath and put the blade to her throat.

Iona's eyes widened as she stared at the man. Her gaze slanted beseechingly to Ariana.

"Dinna look to her, she canna help ye."

Ariana quickly nudged her horse forward. "Wait! If ye kill her, who will learn of yer brilliant scheme? But if ye allow her to tell that I and my son are alive, others will know of yer daring.''

He considered the matter.

''Dinna listen to her,'' Laird Drummond demanded as he rushed up.

Alastair stared incredulously at the man. ''Ye dare issue orders to me?''

He turned to Ariana, sheathing his sword. ''Ye have a point.'' He then looked at Iona. ''Go,'' he bellowed. ''Tell them all who has the lady.''

Iona scurried to her feet. She glanced at Ariana, a grateful expression gracing her features, then turned and ran from the camp.

Ariana's shoulders began to slump in relief until Alastair looked at her. His expression sent a chill down her spine. His twisted, disgusting actions were proof of his insanity. She sensed that fear fed his need for power. She held his gaze for as long as she dared before finally looking away, only to encounter the hateful glare of the Drummond men. Their gazes were no longer sullen, but vengeful.

Laird Drummond walked by her. ''Not so high-and-mighty now, are ye, my lady. Thanks to my little Cailin, we will soon have our position back. Yer husband's death will be my rebirth.''

Although fear sliced through her, she sighed as though bored with the matter.

As they traveled, Ariana turned several times to check on her son. Though Cailin had betrayed them, she lovingly cared for Andrew. The ride was hard. Frazier did not make allowances for the women or the baby, pushing the entourage until the horses needed a rest. Every muscle in her body ached when they finally called a stop at noon.

Alastair dragged her from her horse and over to the small fire. Cailin handed her Andrew, who was ravenously hungry. After she had loosened her tunic and pushed aside her smock, he latched onto her breast and began to suckle hungrily. Cradling her child, she ignored everyone around her while looking about the circle of the fire. No possible avenue of escape presented itself; too many soldiers walked the perimeter of the fire.

The flames grew, and at last the fire began to warm her. She sighed, feeling the heat after the long cold ride. "Where are we going?" Her gaze met Cailin's.

"To Laird Alastair's home."

Though she expected as much, she dreaded the prospect. "I see. And then what will happen to my son?"

Cailin's eyes rounded. "I willna let anyone harm Andrew."

"Really? How, my dear, will ye stop them?"

Cailin looked puzzled.

"Do ye not see? They are using ye. My son will lose his life when they decree. I would imagine as soon as he outlives his usefulness."

Cailin blanched. "They would not harm a baby."

"My son stands between them and what they crave most. Power."

Cailin shook her head and backed away. "Ye only say that to enlist my help. For once, my family needs me, and I intend to improve their position."

Ariana shook her head at the little fool, watching her dash toward her horse and her waiting family. Ariana would have to find a way to save Andrew. 'Twas clear Cailin would not interfere.

The short rest ended, and too soon Alastair snatched her child from her arms and handed him to Cailin as they mounted their horses. They rode the rest of the day. The stars shone bright in a cloudless sky before they finally stopped to make camp.

The wind howled, cold and unfriendly as it stung her cheeks. Exhausted, Ariana dismounted. Her knees gave way and she sat on the ground, not moving until she could muster the strength to stand back up and walk. Her muscles quivered and the pain of spasms radiated up her legs, but she ignored the anguish as she readily accepted her baby, then sat by the fire to feed him.

As Andrew nursed, she carefully inspected him. An extra blanket covered him. Thankfully, Cailin had kept him well sheltered from the elements. Ariana rocked him gently as he ravenously kneaded her breast to appease his hunger. She closed her eyes and concentrated on the moment, not permitting the sound of her abductors or the reality of their danger to intrude on her thoughts. She needed to focus on her baby.

A short time later, a plate of unappetizing fare was thrown at her feet. As much as she would have liked to throw the food back in their faces, hunger goaded her to eat. She needed her strength. As she chewed the tough meat, she deliberated on her chances of survival. The night crowded in on her. She had to escape.

Her gaze traveled the perimeter of the camp, taking in the number of guards. Could she slip by them with a child in her arms? She would have to if they were ever to gain their freedom. She mentally calculated her chances. If Andrew were quiet and the guards overly tired, it was possible.

A shadow fell over her, blocking out the light of the fire. "What are ye planning?" Alastair asked.

Her heart lodged in her throat. She looked up at him and brazened out his stare. "I am imagining yer death."

His lips thinned into a twisted smirk. "Yer husband wilna be able to kill me."

"Who said anything about my husband?"

"Ye?" He scoffed. "Ye think ye could kill me?"

"I said I was imagining yer death."

"Forget such nonsense, woman. There is nothing ye can do."

She continued to cuddle her child. Placing Andrew on her shoulder, she patted his back, while gently rocking him in her arms. "To see yer demise with a baby in arms has me sorely disadvantaged, but dinna worry," she said. "I will find a way."

She met his gaze, letting him see maternal determination. His expression hardened as he considered her words. Never once did she flinch as she stared him down.

When Cailin returned and reached for Andrew, Alastair stayed her hand. "Let the whelp stay with his mother."

Elation swept through Ariana, but she wisely lowered her eyes. She had won that round, but knew there were many more to go.

"But ye said I could care for the child," Cailin whined.

"Dinna challenge me, woman."

As soon as they walked away, Ariana huddled with her baby on the ground. The wind rose and she shivered. Cocooning her son against her, she wrapped her cover over Andrew, trying to shelter him from the biting air. Visions of rescue wandered through her mind. Would Robb MacGregor risk his life and limb for a child he feared not his own? Dear God.

Christophe, where are ye? She had not felt his presence since she started on this horrendous journey. She prayed he was all right. Andrew whimpered fretfully, and she made him as comfortable as possible, then closed her eyes. The sounds of the night filtered around her, but she barely noticed them. She had but two things on her mind. Her son's safety and escape.

When the moon rose overhead, she peeked through her closed lashes to find the guards falling asleep at their posts. She shifted slightly. Nestled snugly in her arms, Andrew stirred, but did not awaken. She slowly shifted him to a

sitting position, as if she was feeding her child. Her covert
gaze searched the ground. The men were fast asleep. Holding her breath, she made ready to get to her feet when a
twig snapped behind her.

She did not have to look. She knew it was Alastair.
Instead, of lying back down, she adjusted her tunic to let
Andrew nurse. Though half asleep, he rooted around and
immediately began to suckle. The hair on the back of her
neck stood on end as she felt the man's gaze bore into
her back. She swallowed her revulsion.

The moon slipped behind a cloud, bathing her in shadows. Relief flowed through her as the night's ebony arms
embraced her, shielding her from Alastair's lascivious gaze.
Never had she found such comfort in the dark.

He cleared his throat, his cough hoarse. "Get to sleep,
Lady Ariana. Tomorrow will be demanding."

Her eyes closed. She nodded, unable to trust her voice,
unwilling to give credence to his suspicion.

When Andrew had his fill, she covered her breast and
kissed his tiny dark head. "Sleep, my darling." Cradling
her babe close, she curled up upon the cold ground, and
pulled her mantle around them.

She heard Alastair move off, and looked up at the canopy
of stars, watching the moon slip from beneath its shelter.
"Help me," she whispered.

The vast star-studded night stared down at her, beautiful
and immense, but the heavenly answer she sought did
not come. Staring up at the millions of stars and planets
twinkling overhead made her feel all the more alone. Christophe's dear features floated through her mind, and a
sharp pain stabbed her heart. He was gone. Her eyes stung
with unshed tears as a life without him loomed before her.
Andrew suddenly nestled close to her, his tiny fist grasping
her tunic. She smiled at his determination, and blinked
the moisture away. Christophe would always be with her.

The chill in the night air turned bitter. She huddled her child close, protecting him from the biting wind. He slept comfortably against her, unaware of the danger or her fears. His little fist still clutched her tunic as his soft, warm breath whispered across her skin. Her hand curled protectively around him, tucking his body closer to her heart. She closed her eyes. They were alive. They were safe. That was all that mattered.

Her dreams left her exhausted and drained. Although she could hardly summon the energy to rise, she crawled to her feet and stretched the aches away. Cold gray clouds covered the sky, and before the dawn broke snow began to fall. She removed her mantle and wrapped it around Andrew. Teeth chattering, she ate a cold breakfast, then fed Andrew.

"Fool," Alastair spat when he noticed her shivering, but he did not take the child from her, nor offer her another wrap.

It was Cailin who brought her a fur wrap a short time later.

When she hesitated to wear the gift, the girl pointed to it. "Please, put it on. Ye gave yers to the bairn." Her eyes lowered in what might have been shame. "I dinna wish ye any harm, my lady. But I must help my family."

Ariana nodded and silently accepted the covering, placing it about her shoulders. At once it helped warm her numb muscles. When the soldiers were ready to go, she mounted her horse, tucking Andrew within the folds of her fur.

They rode hard toward the Frazier castle. The snow stung her face like a thousand needles, but she blocked out the pain, ignoring the numbness of her body after hours passed in the saddle. The animal's hooves tore up the earth as they thundered across the moors. At noon she saw the dark Frazier castle loom up against the gray storm clouds in the distance, and her heart caught in her throat. She cradled her son next to her breast, struggling to maintain her balance on the fast steed. Her fingers had lost all feeling, and the idea of dismounting from this beast filled her with dread.

When the gates opened to admit their party, the hairs on the back of her neck prickled. Now that she was in the enemy's stronghold, she was totally at their mercy. She kissed her son's head, and drew him closer. When Cailin held out her arms for Andrew, Ariana turned away, cradling her child in her arms. The woman might have shown her a small kindness, but she had not forgotten Cailin's treachery. A big, burly soldier dragged her and Andrew down off the horse.

Her legs wobbled, but held her upright. She hugged her baby protectively in her arms, her gaze scanning the area. The courtyard's stone walls showed signs of deterioration, as mortar flaked from between the stones.

Morag entered the courtyard from the castle. "Give me the child," she ordered, pushing Cailin away.

"Nay," Ariana said, shielding her son with her body.

Alastair stepped forward. "Give her the child."

"Nay." Lady Elspeth's voice rang out from the doorway above the stoop.

"God's Teeth," Morag snarled at Alastair. "I thought she was away at Ruthven's."

Elspeth smiled sweetly at Alastair's frown. She stepped down the stairs and into the courtyard. "Remember, brother, the castle is mine. I will take charge of my grandson. No one else," she said, reaching out for Andrew. When Ariana raised her chin in defiance, Lady Elspeth leaned forward. "I was not there for my son's childhood. I willna miss my grandson's. No one will harm the child while he is in my care, my dear. Absolutely no one!" She stared at her brother, and he looked away.

Ariana kissed Andrew's head. "I love ye," she whispered, then handed her son over to Elspeth.

The moment Andrew left her arms, a guard grabbed her and dragged her toward the dungeon. Tears burned her eyes as she watched her child being carried away in the opposite direction. When the heavy dungeon doors closed behind her, she crumpled to the ground. Battling tears, she rested her head on her knees, hugging her legs with her arms. Would she ever see her son again? What if someone else saw his first steps, heard his first words, and received his love? Did it matter, as long as he lived? Suddenly, at that moment, she knew that he would. For herself, she had doubts. A lone tear trickled down her cheek. Were these cold, dark hours her last?

No! she silently cried, denying the thought. As long as she drew breath, she would fight for every last moment of life. She had learned how precious time was. She closed her eyes and let her mind dwell on her beloved. *Wherever ye are, Christophe, I love ye, I always have. I always will.*

The depressing moaning of the other prisoners in the dungeon intruded on her thoughts. Their despair hung in the air, as strong as the dank odor of unwashed bodies. Though hope hung by a slim thread, Ariana clung to it. Nothing was so insurmountable as long as ye believed. She turned her ring, twisting it around her finger. The inscription came to mind. *Believe in love.* She did. Nothing else would sustain her. *I will not give up.* Immediately, she rose and paced the cell, rubbing her arms to replace the warmth. She concentrated on escape, and the moment she did, Christophe's face rose in her mind.

Fear melted in her heart. He would find her. He had to. She doubted Robb MacGregor would rescue her, or a child he did not think his. Her heart nearly broke with the weight of her thoughts, but she refused to succumb to panic. A cool, rational mind was needed. If Christophe could not return, she would have to rely on her own resources. In her gut, she knew Elspeth would take care of Andrew. Ariana had to find a way to protect them all. Her bairn's life rested on her resources.

Think! Think! she silently screamed. Wild thoughts flashed through her head. She could always act as a seer. After all, she knew the future. Alastair would be happy to keep her and her son alive for such knowledge. As quickly as the thought occurred, another took its place. Could she betray generations yet to come? No. She could not buy her happiness with another's misery.

She closed her eyes to still her anxiety and calm her thoughts. *He will make a mistake, and when he does ye must be ready,* an inner voice sounded. Lying down on a scant pile of filthy straw, she considered the words. Yes, finding a weakness was the only way. Whatever mistake presented itself she would use. She only hoped it was enough. She could not fail.

CHAPTER SEVENTEEN

Robb MacGregor knew every defense of Castle MacGregor. He pointed to the map, familiarizing each laird gathered around the campsite table of his plan and their part in it.

Dunn rose. "Why dinna ye just take a small party of men in through the gates? Once ye are in the rest of us will attack."

Robb had been expecting this. In theory it sounded good. They had the element of surprise. But Robb doubted an army of his size could travel undetected. Frazier would have warriors posted for intelligence. Even if they still held the element of surprise, the plan was flawed.

"Laird Dunn. If we ride into a trap, how long would it take yer army to rescue us?"

Laird Dunn looked over the area. "Five, maybe ten minutes for us to leave the cover of the trees and storm the castle."

"Aye. I agree. If there are twenty or even thirty men on

the walkways and they can fire ten arrows a minute, in five minutes fifteen hundred arrows would be shot into the courtyard." Robb held up a shield. "At that close range the arrows would pierce this shield, killing the man beneath."

Dunn sat down. "No one would survive."

"Aye," Robb said.

"The arrows will still cost us many men," Dunn interjected.

"I would wager they dinna have a great supply of arrows. They meant to trap us, not withstand a siege." Robb did not have time to institute great change, but he had a few ideas that would insure them success. He held up the shield again. "Laird Dunn is right when he said we will lose a great deal of men to arrows. So I want each soldier to line his shield with sod." He cut a deep piece of turf with his dagger and placed the ragged square on the inside of the shield. Then he wound a piece of material around both the shield and the sod. "Laird Dunn, would ye be so kind as to take yer bow over to that ridge and fire an arrow into my shield?"

He held the shield up, and turned to the lairds. " 'Twill be heavy, but it will insulate the shield and absorb the arrow tips."

Laird Dunn waved his hand that he was ready, and Robb nodded.

Suddenly the arrow whizzed through the air and embedded in Robb's shield. Robb turned the shield over and the lairds crowded in to inspect it.

" 'Tis a wonder," Laird Dunn said as he joined them.

MacPherson nodded. "Robb, yer plan has merit. I yield to yer command."

Robb MacGregor gave no sign of his fears as he faced the other lairds. Though they had joined him, they might not accept his orders.

Laird Ruthven extended his hand. "I too will follow ye."

After the first show of support, each laird at the table accepted his strategy.

An hour later, he walked though the cold brisk morning, confident and ready. The bite of the wet air reminded him of the hardship ahead. He knelt in the dirt and said a short fervent prayer. Then he mounted his horse and with his hand raised, led his men to destroy his home's defenses.

The instant they approached the high stone edifice of Castle MacGregor, the arrows rained down on them. With the improved shields, arrows harmlessly struck and stuck like quills on a porcupine's back. They waited several hours until the barrage of missiles thinned, then continued over the moors, relentless in their quest. If every laird followed his lead, the castle could be taken.

A voice thundered within his head. "Elspeth had told the truth." He pushed the thought aside. Not until there was no doubt would he let himself believe her. If she had indeed warned him of the truth, he would, by his very soul, forgive her for deserting him.

The call to arms sounded. Legion after legion of Scotsmen loyal to the MacGregor clan joined the army, marching at the right and left flank. The lairds looked to him for direction. He raised his hand and gave the command. War cries sounded. Sword in hand, he charged straight ahead, leading the bulk of the attack. He reached the base of the gates unscathed, and stormed the castle walls. Wave after wave of Scotsmen followed after him. By noon the base of the walls were surrounded, but men screamed in agony as they were impaled or burned by boiling oil. Ladders were raised and rested on the stones, allowing the men to scale the walls. The first wave of soldiers over the wall were hurled back and fell to their deaths.

As he watched the men dying around him, his heart turned to stone. Frazier had dared invade his home while he was away? A terrible rage consumed him, devoured him.

A moment before he'd feared the wall would hold, but suddenly the strength and valor of three men surged through him.

Charging up a ladder, he leapt over the wall, and all who watched him immediately followed his lead. After landing hard and somersaulting to his feet on the walkway, he met the first soldier. Adrenaline pumped through him, his heart racing as he held the castle soldier off until the man behind him climbed over the wall. Wielding his sword, he pushed the sentry further back, allowing his numbers to swell on the wall.

His tactic of occupying the sentry to protect the invading men allowed his army to flow over the battlements, and join the fight.

At times he had to fight three men, courageously furthering his cause. His Scots rallied to his war cry, and pushed the enemy closer to defeat. The fight lasted only an hour before his forces finally overran the walls. Once inside the battlement defenses, they fought their way to the gatehouse, only to find the mechanism to raise the heavy portcullis had been destroyed. The rest of their men would have to climb up the way *they* had. By midafternoon, all their forces had infiltrated the castle's defenses.

A Campbell soldier managed to slip his sword beneath Robb's guard and sharply slice his arm. The wound stung, but it sharpened his instincts, and he charged the man to quickly run him through. He tore off a piece of his kilt and wrapped the plaid around his forearm. The blood quickly soaked the makeshift bandage as he raised his sword and stormed down the steps into the thick fray.

His men swelled behind him, their war cries sounding as swords clashed and agonized screams rent the air.

Cornered in the courtyard, the enemy fought back-to-back, but men fell and were trampled as the fighting continued. Not until dusk did the army surrender.

Firelight shone on the dirty, beaten soldiers. Their eyes were vacant, their faces expressionless. Robb noticed that every soldier taken prisoner belonged to the Campbell clan, not the Fraziers. A nasty suspicion formed in his mind as he ordered his men to free his people from the dungeon. After unsuccessfully interrogating the enemy, he searched every room, but could not find Alastair.

MacPherson ran up the dungeon stairs. "Robb, come here." Behind him two soldiers carried someone up from the dungeon. It was Brodie Maclaren. Unable to stand, the lad looked half-dead, beaten to a pulp.

"My laird, yer aunt betrayed us," he gasped. "She opened the gates for the invaders. When Frazier heard how many men marched with ye, he fled our castle, abandoning the Campbells to hold the defenses alone."

Robb clenched his fists. "Where did he go?"

He shook his head. "I dinna know."

Robb pressed the soldier's shoulder. "Rest easy. Ye have earned my respect."

Brodie reached up and offered his hand. "My laird, I give ye my allegiance."

Robb shook the man's hand, then moved aside when Jessie knelt before the wounded soldier to clean and wrap his wounds.

Disgusted, Robb MacGregor stared at the carnage around him.

MacPherson joined him. "Alastair Frazier's cowardly action, 'tis shameful."

Robb nodded his head, an idea forming. "Let the Campbells return home."

MacPherson raised a skeptical brow.

Robb grinned. "They will carry the tale of Alastair's betrayal to their chieftain, Laird Gregor Campbell. He will be honor-bound to hunt Alastair down for his treachery."

"Ye no longer seek revenge?" MacPherson asked.

Strange, but the rage had dissipated. He shook his head, unable to explain. "Frazier will die. It matters little by whose hand."

MacPherson gripped Robb's shoulder. "Today ye have shown yer father's wisdom. I will send a rider to have Ariana return home."

Robb watched his father-in-law walk away, and a peace unlike any he had ever known filled him. He turned to Lor. "Have the men take their meal and rest."

After he had met with his allies, Robb retired for the night. As incredulous as it seemed, his mother had told him the truth. And thanks to her honesty, he had been victorious. He closed his eyes, and finally forgave her. Immediately, the pain of all the years washed away, and his spirit healed from the childhood scars. Instantaneously, he fell asleep and dreamt of his love. Ariana stood highlighted in a brilliant light, surrounded by wispy clouds. "Robb," she called out to him. She glided closer, and in her arms was their son, a blond baby with deep blue eyes. Understanding washed through him, cleansing his soul.

"Forgive me." He reached out to her, and suddenly, his spirit floated up into the light. An avalanche of emotions poured over him as his soul merged with hers. "Thank you, my love." He glanced back to his body, bidding his earthly bonds farewell as he joined his beloved and their son.

Suddenly, Christophe's soul passed through him to float downward. Robb smiled, watching Christophe's spirit slip back and awaken the body. His counterpart would live once again.

"Poor bastard," Robb whispered, wondering if the man could restore all the damage that he, Robb, had done.

An incredible warmth rushed through Christophe as he hurtled through time and space. Abruptly, the journey stopped, ending in a large, dark room, which he instantly recognized. A fire burned low in the hearth, giving the MacGregors' master chamber a soft glow. Robb MacGregor slept in bed beneath several fur pelts, safe from the night's chill. Christophe stared at his counterpart, envying the man. "God, send me back." Then, instead of hovering and watching as he normally did, he began to move forward. Realization struck and joy rushed through him. "Thank you," he whispered. He could save his beloved.

Just before he entered Robb's body, the departing spirit left. There was a brief moment when their spirits touched, shared a millennium of memories, then parted. In that instant, Christophe learned he had been wrong when he assumed Robb MacGregor needed to avenge his death to find peace. His quest had been to learn forgiveness.

Christophe floated downward and slowly awoke in Robb's body. He inhaled the sweet taste of air, felt his lungs expand, and reveled in the gift of life. He flexed his arms, relishing the incredible feeling of movement with form. "Thank ye," he whispered again, then added, "Be at peace, Robb MacGregor. I will do yer name honor and wear it with pride."

When the lingering cobwebs finally dissipated, his thoughts turned to Ariana. Lord, she was in danger. He jumped out of the bed, threw on his kilt, and stomped into his boots. With one arm in his smock and the other searching for the sleeve, he reached for the doorknob.

His footsteps echoed on the stone steps as he swiftly marched through the castle. Dawn was breaking when he roused his troops. Walking among the men, he shook the lairds awake. "Get up."

"God's Teeth, MacGregor," MacPherson cursed as he pushed the sleep-tousled hair from his eyes. "Have ye lost yer mind?"

Robb glared at him, and the others who grumbled at the early morning awakening after a night of celebration. "We have to march on Frazier," he said.

MacPherson rose off his pallet and braced his hands on the trestle table before him. "Why? Last night ye were willing to let Campbell wreak havoc on the man."

"Because . . . "

Before he finished, Lor escorted Iona into the great room. "My laird, the Lady Ariana is not at Laird Ruthven's castle." Lor helped the exhausted maid forward. "Tell him," he ordered.

Iona curtsied before Robb and started to weep.

Laird Ruthven stepped forward. "Of course she is not there. Laird MacPherson sent a man to fetch her."

Lor turned to him. "Nay, my laird, Lady Ariana was tricked into leaving Ruthven Castle."

Iona sniffled and nodded. "Aye, she left with Lady Cailin Drummond. They were to return to Castle MacGregor. She was told that Lady Morag sent for her because Laird Robb MacGregor was wounded." Tears filled her eyes. "It was a lie and Alastair Frazier kidnapped her." She turned to the other lairds, and her eyes widened when she saw Brodie by the fire. "Brodie," she cried, and ran to the injured warrior's side.

"Morag and Alastair," Laird MacPherson concluded.

"Aye," Robb said. "That is why I have roused ye."

"But how did ye know?" Laird Ruthven asked.

Robb looked at the lairds' puzzled faces. He knew the importance of his answer. He was about to say he dreamt it when MacPherson stepped forward.

"No doubt ye sensed it. I often know when my wee wife is in peril." Laird MacPherson glanced around the room. "Didna ye ever sense when yer loved one has need of ye? We Scots have an uncanny way of knowing when our family or friends require help."

"Aye," Laird Ruthven said as Laird Dunn nodded. The matter was easily accepted.

"We march on the Frazier castle immediately," Robb said.

"Aye, muster out the men."

MacPherson stepped forward. "I will send word to Laird Campbell. He might even join us."

All the chieftains moved to ready their men. Robb watched the early morning preparations, and mentally planned his strategy.

Jessie bustled into the room with a platter of hot bread. She cried out the instant she spotted her daughter. "Malcolm, come quickly, yer little girl is home."

Iona explained that Isla was safe at Ruthven's castle caring for Gavin. They hugged briefly before Jessie rushed to put out a meal of cold meat and cheese.

Robb watched the family's touching reunion, and felt a pang of poignant envy. "Malcolm."

The man quickly left his daughter and joined the laird. "Aye, my laird."

"Lor must come with me. Gavin is injured and so is Brodie. I want ye to take command of the castle troops."

Malcolm beamed at the high honor. "Aye, my laird. I will see to yer castle and all that reside in it."

Robb clasped the man's shoulder. "I will rest easier knowing ye are caring for my clan." Robb would leave, knowing that the older warrior would be safe with his family. Enough men had died in this war.

After the quick meal, the men gathered in the courtyard and the horses pranced as Robb raised his hand, then pointed toward the north.

Once the column of men cleared the gate, Robb's thoughts turned to his adversaries, Morag and Alastair. He knew what they had wanted—power. Only one family had stood in their way—his. Now they needed wealth.

Robb had two scores to settle now, not just for himself, but for his counterpart.

The ground fell away beneath them as they rode toward Frazier's land. With every hoofbeat, his anger intensified and worry for Ariana grew. They rode into the snow-covered moors of the north, but he neither felt the cold, nor acknowledged the hardship.

By midafternoon, gray storm clouds gathered overhead as Laird Gregor Campbell's army joined their ranks. "I willna let the cowardly cur live."

Robb accepted Laird Gregor's hand, and by so doing, the animosity ended. For the first time in years a peace existed between the clans. With the addition of the Campbells, an army of immense proportion marched several leagues to reach the Frazier stronghold.

Once there, Robb surveyed the crumbling structure and ill-manned battlements from a snow-covered hill overlooking the valley. Laird MacPherson, Laird Ruthven, Laird Dunn, and Laird Campbell rode up behind him and dismounted. Their footsteps crunched in the frozen snow as they approached. The other chieftains waited with their men for a report.

"A siege is the only way." Laird MacPherson pointed to the walls.

"Aye," Laird Ruthven agreed. "Many will lose their lives, but we have little choice."

Robb leaned forward. He knew Alastair needed a ransom, but he could not tell them how he knew it. "Mayhap we can make Frazier an offer he would consider."

The men looked stunned.

"A siege is the only way," Dunn emphasized, but Robb cut him short.

"Laird Dunn. Ye thought riding into a trap a good idea until I showed ye another one."

The other lairds chuckled as Laird Dunn glared.

Robb looked at the lairds. "My wife and son will die in a siege. Bear with me while I explore other alternatives."

Approval shone in MacPherson's eyes as Ruthven nodded.

Laird Campbell clamped his arm around Dunn's shoulder. "Would ye not do the same for yer own?"

Dunn shrugged his shoulder, then looked Robb in the eye. "What do ye have in mind?"

"When Frazier sees our strength and that Laird Campbell has joined us, he will know there is no place in Scotland to hide from our retribution."

"Aye, that be true," Laird Campbell said. "He will have to flee to survive."

"Exactly," Robb said. "And to flee he will need money."

"A ransom?" MacPherson asked.

"I willna pay the cur," Dunn said.

"Ye willna have to." Robb pointed to the towers. "If he thinks I will pay a ransom, he will let his guard down. When he does, I plan to sneak into that castle and free my wife and son."

"What do ye want us to do?" Campbell asked.

Robb took a deep breath. "Agree to follow my lead whatever it is. And"—he paused—"if I fail in my rescue attempt, pledge me ye will continue in my absence."

" 'Tis a good plan." Campbell slapped him on the back. "We have nothing to lose by trying it and everything to gain. I say well done."

"Aye," MacPherson said.

"Tell the men to surround Frazier's castle and build their campfires now," Robb said. "I want Frazier to know how many men are here. Display the banners."

Dunn stepped forward and thrust out his hand. "I will take yer decision to the other chieftains who have accompanied us."

"Tell them I am grateful for their support."

At early evening a messenger rode out to the camp under

a flag of truce. "My laird, Laird Frazier wishes ye to come to the gate."

" 'Tis a trap," MacPherson cautioned.

Robb brushed the warning aside, and turned to the guard. "Tell Frazier that I and several of my chieftains will be there. If one aggressive move is made during this talk, there will be no mercy shown to anyone."

The guard nodded and rode off. When he had cleared camp, MacPherson objected.

Robb rounded on the man. "We have a part to play. Remember that."

Robb, Campbell, MacPherson, Dunn, and Ruthven separated from their army and rode slowly toward the stronghold. Robb stared up at the imposing gray stones with a soldier's eye, seeing only its weaknesses and strengths. His gaze traveled to the defenses, undermanned and ill-placed. He mentally timed the guards that walked the battlements.

At the base of the castle near the gate he stared at the ramparts. "Frazier!" he bellowed, his frozen breath hanging in the breeze. "Ye wanted to talk!"

Several minutes went by before Frazier's gravelly voice answered from the walkway above. "Aye. I will exchange yer wife and son for a ransom."

"A ransom?" Robb asked, feigning surprise.

A scream sounded as a woman was dragged over to the wall and pushed forward. "Aye, a ransom of ten gold bars and a chest of jewels," Alastair demanded.

His blood ran cold as he watched Ariana standing at the wall's edge dressed only in her thin tunic, her hair wildly blowing in the wind. Her hands pummeled at the chest of the guard, who handed her to Frazier.

Alastair yanked her hair back. "Ye will leave with yer army and return in three days alone with the ransom. When I have the payment in my hand, I will return yer wife and son."

Robb tightened his fists.

"Robb." Ariana struggled with her captor. "They have our son." Her hysterical voice sailed out on the wind.

Robb pointed to his forces behind him gathered on the snow-swept moors. "Look on yonder field, Alastair. 'Tis an army of many chieftains. Look ye at the men I have brought."

Alastair's gaze scanned the full length of the army, and he seemed to falter. Robb held silent, hoping he could bluff the man with a show of power.

As Robb weighed the outcome, Morag's face appeared over the rim of the walkway. She dangled his son over the icy wall, gripping him by his heels. Robb's heart lodged in his throat. He stared at his son, swaying precariously over his head, and could barely breathe. The poor infant's plaintive wails rode the wind.

"God in heaven," MacPherson whispered.

"No," Ariana screamed, fighting and clawing to get free. She raked her nails down Alastair's face, fighting to reach her frightened baby.

Alastair roared, and his meaty fist sent her crashing to the stone walkway.

"Gouge his eyes out," Campbell muttered as Ruthven scowled fiercely and Dunn's hand covered the hilt of his sword.

Robb clenched his fist, praying for strength. His wife struggled to her feet, her face bleeding, and again tried to reach for her child. Rage, unadulterated and raw, sang through his veins. No force on earth could stop him from killing Alastair and Morag. The warriors with him were silent. They stared in horror at the wall.

Alastair dragged Ariana closer to the wall's edge. Her face was swollen, her eyes terrified.

Morag's high-pitched nasal whine rent the air, like a

witch's wail as she gave Andrew a shake. "I would not hesitate to kill yer wife and son, nephew. Have no doubt."

"Enough!" Fear sliced through Robb, as he turned his horse and signaled the lairds to return to their men. "I will withdraw and return alone in three days with yer ransom."

Morag pulled the baby back and shoved him at Ariana, who clutched him to her breast. She laughed as the men rode away. "Ye see how easy it is, Alastair."

Robb's stomach churned as he marched his army from the frozen land to lull the Fraziers into a false sense of security. He knew from experience that Frazier had spies. As he rode, he thought of his wife. Ariana would think he had abandoned her. As far as she knew, his counterpart lived. He could not lessen her pain, but he would rescue her, and when he did he would keep her safe forever. He could not spend another hour on this earth without her.

A light dusting of snow fell before they reached camp. That evening, Robb met with the chieftains. They gathered around a small campfire as the cold wind swirled the snow about their feet. Huddled in warm wool plaids and sipping mulled ale, they focused their attention on him. Tension mounted in the air as he scraped a stick through the snow-covered dirt. He knew the Frazier castle as well as his own. He had been there enough times as a spirit. "I will lead a small party of men back." He looked at his fellow chieftains, then pointed the stick at an outline. "Here is the castle. I will take my party to the wall and scale it. Once the sentries are subdued, I will let the others in."

"How many men will ye need?" Ruthven asked.

Robb considered the question. "Only a score."

"Twenty men?" Campbell asked, his expression skeptical.

"A small party will accomplish what a large force never

could." He looked at the roiling storm clouds. "There is no moon tonight, and we will be able to approach without discovery."

"How?"

"If the men dress in light fur robes, they willna be seen crawling over the snow-swept moors."

Campbell digested the idea. "How will ye scale the wall?"

Robb produced the rag-covered grappling hook he had fashioned. "I will scale the wall with this."

Laird MacPherson took the hook and examined it. "Ingenious," he said, then passed it around.

"MacGregor's plan has merit," Laird Ruthven said, seeing the advantage of subterfuge. "Using wit instead of brawn would throw Alastair off."

The chieftains talked among themselves as they examined the hook.

Robb stood up. "I will only ask for volunteers."

Laird Dunn slanted a brow. "Are ye questioning my loyalty or bravery?"

"Neither. I know ye are a man of yer word." His gaze scanned the circle. "But none of ye promised to see this to the end. And by all accepted standards of conquest, a siege would be what ye expected."

The chieftain smiled and extended a huge hand. " 'Tis to the end or nothing."

When Robb accepted it, the dissension ended.

Laird Campbell slapped him on the back. "Aye, yer idea will have the element of surprise and I believe will succeed. 'Tis a brilliant strategy. I, for one, join ye."

With those words of praise, the other lairds all agreed.

"I will not be left behind," MacPherson said.

"Nor I," added Laird Ruthven.

"We will go in at midnight."

After the lairds left to inform their men, Robb stared at the fire.

The darkness crowded in on him along with his thoughts. Every time he pictured Ariana with that monster, his heart raced. And the image of his son hanging over the wall tightened his gut into a hard knot.

He closed his eyes in a vain attempt to block out the scenes, yet they came back more vividly than ever. He fisted his hands, remembering the abuse Ariana suffered at Alastair's hands. Wave after wave of fury overtook him, and he finally understood his counterpart. Though the air was bitter, sweat covered his body, and he could not erase the images. Large cold flakes covered his hair and face, intruding on his thoughts, and he looked up. "Thank ye," he whispered as the snow began to fall in earnest. With the weather change, visibility would be greatly impaired. He concentrated on every detail in his mind until it was committed and recommitted to memory.

He would attack, and he would squeeze the life out of his enemy.

He would not allow himself to think of Ariana again, only the upcoming battle. A battle he could not lose.

So many men volunteered that Robb had to choose only a handful from the assembled ranks to accompany him on the daring mission. The rest would remain in camp, waiting to invade the castle should he succeed. There could be no mistake tonight.

At the appointed hour Robb stood before his men in a blinding snow. "Not one sound can be made for this plan to work. Remove anything on yer person that can make noise. No chains can be worn. The only metal allowed is yer weapon." He had Lor hand out the light-colored fur robes. "Cover yer plaid with these."

Once the men had wrapped their plaids in fur, and removed their bands and chains, leaving them with Lor, who handed them to the friar, they quietly filed out of camp.

Robb MacGregor led his men back to the Frazier stronghold.

"My laird, where do ye want us?" Lor asked.

"Over there"—Robb pointed to the castle's portcullis—"is the weakest point."

Thick white flakes blessedly continued to fall. The men crawled on their bellies across the white moors and up to the base of the castle. Camouflaged beneath the light fur, they were invisible in the heavy falling snow, and blended into the landscape.

Once in position, Robb threw a rope up the wall. The hooks were wrapped to muffle the sound. It took three tries before he finally anchored the rope. Though his hands were numb, he quickly tested the rope with his weight. Halfway up the rope, Robb heard the sentry overhead and froze, hanging suspended on the castle's face.

His men silently lay facedown in the snow, and remained still until the guard passed. Robb held his breath, waiting for discovery, but the guard walked his post, looking out into the falling snow that covered the moors, instead of down, failing to see what was right beneath his nose.

As soon as the sentry moved to the far end of the wall, Robb climbed up the rope and slipped over the wall. Crouching down, he waited for the guard's return. When the guard passed by, Robb easily dispatched the man, and quickly stripped him. Two more men made it up the rope as Robb donned the sentry's clothes.

Once disguised, Robb walked the wall, meeting the other sentry without making a break in the routine.

As soon as they had the rest of the men up, Robb took out the other sentry. His men crept along the wall, and quietly dispatched the remaining sentries. With the walkway secured, Robb sent his men to open the gate to let in their forces.

The army silently began to pour into the large courtyard.

Lor, Dunn, Ruthven, and MacPherson would take their forces and enter the barracks, leaving Campbell's men to capture the servants.

Robb crept silently down the dungeon steps. The torchlight flickered on the stone walls, casting eerie yellow shadows as he clung to the wall, slipping into the shadowed darkness. A guard snored loudly, but his breathing caught every third snore, almost awakening him. Robb froze in midstep, waiting for the guard to resume an even cadence, before moving on again. He continued to silently advance on the guard, stopping each time his snores lost their even rhythm.

Suddenly, as though aware of Robb's presence, the guard snorted, blinked, and sat forward in his chair. His eyes fully open, he stared at Robb.

Robb's lightning fist sent the guard back to sleep. He pulled the keys from the man's belt and ran over toward the darkened cells. "Ariana," he called.

"Robb," a faint voice echoed in the shadowed light.

"Ariana, where are you?"

"Here," she called, her voice growing stronger.

He moved down the row of cells swiftly, not stopping until he arrived at the one that held her. The instant he jammed the key into the lock and threw open the door, she lunged into his arms. Her body quivered as she held him close.

"I feared ye had left me and our child."

His hand shook as he gently smoothed the hair from her face. "How could ye think I would commit such a cowardly act? Dinna ye believe in me?"

Her tear-streaked face met his. She peered closer, her lips trembling. "Christophe?" she whispered. "Is it ye?" She caressed his face. "Dare I hope?"

"Believe in love," he whispered, knowing she had never stopped loving him. He placed his fingers over her lips. "Remember, ye must think of me as Robb."

"Oh, thank God," Ariana cried, collapsing into his arms. "Ye are back." Tears coated her lashes as she suddenly kissed his face. "I'll never ask God for another thing."

He smiled. "I know."

Then just as suddenly, she pulled out of his embrace. "Alastair has our child. He would not allow me to have our son."

His face grew stiff. "Where are they keeping him?"

"I dinna know. Cailin brings Andrew to nurse, but she never says anything. I know that Elspeth rescued him from Morag, but I dinna know where she sleeps. They may have even taken him from her by now."

"I will find him, after I have seen ye to safety."

"Nay! We started this journey together. Together we will finish it."

He took hold of her shoulders. "Ariana, ye must be out of harm's way."

She pulled free and faced him. "I will not be separated from ye again. We will search for our child together. In this I will not be swayed."

"Now there is the woman I fell in love with. For a time, I feared I would never see ye again." He took her arm, and together they marched up the stairs. The sound of fighting could be heard in the barracks outside. They crossed the great room, and he pushed her behind him as he edged up the stairs to the sleeping apartments above.

Torchlight flickered and shadows danced on the walls as they climbed the narrow circling staircase. The stone walls were cold, the castle damp. Once upstairs, Robb pushed open the first door on his right and found his enemy, standing naked in the room, his manhood at the ready. Morag screamed and wrapped a fur robe around her nudity as she dashed from the bed to a small anteroom.

Heedless of his state of undress, Alastair smiled wickedly. "Have ye come to feel the prick of my lance?" He picked up his sword and ran to meet Robb.

"Find our son," Robb called to Ariana as he moved to meet the attack.

Ariana glanced around the room, but her son was not there, nor was he in the anteroom. She started to follow Morag, but the men blocked her path. The connecting room might open to the hallway. She spared Robb one last glance, then rushed out of the room and down to the next chamber.

Behind her she could hear the battle below winding down. She gripped the doorknob, having no doubt that Robb would defeat Alastair.

The cold handle slipped through her fingers and she regrasped it, and opened the door. Inside she found Morag quickly dressing.

"Where is my son?"

Morag turned. Her cold, lifeless gaze sent a chill up Ariana's spine. "Yer son is dead."

A deafening roar rushed to her ears, and her heart lodged in her throat. "Nay," she declared as she moved closer to her nemesis. "Nay, ye lie. My son lives."

Morag threw back her head, and laughed. It was an evil wicked cackle.

Ariana drew back her hand and slapped the woman's face. "Tell me where my child is!"

Morag raised her hand, fingers spread and nails poised to rake nasty scratches, but Ariana blocked the attack to her eyes. She grabbed Morag's hair and yanked her head back, while wrapping her fingers around the woman's throat. "I asked ye a question. Where is my child?"

Morag's eyes bulged as she struggled within her grasp.

Ariana tightened her hold. "I said, where is my son?"

Morag began to whimper. "Lady Elspeth has the bairn."

Ariana released the woman so hard that she fell to the floor.

"Which room?"

Clutching at her throat with one hand, Morag pointed to the room across the hall.

Ariana rushed to the far door and threw it open. "Elspeth?" She entered the room, her footsteps echoing in the cold, dark chamber. Her blood froze at the sight of the empty apartment.

"Andrew," she whispered, then turned and ran from the room. She had to find her son. She saw Morag turning a corner ahead of her. Dear God, Morag was going to the tower. She followed the woman up the steep stairs.

"Morag, stop!"

Harsh laughter floated down to her. "Ye fool." Morag's voice echoed off the walls, taunting Ariana's mistake.

Her heart raced as she ran after Morag. She reached the tower and watched her enter a room.

"Morag!"

She skidded to a stop just inside the room. Andrew's cries broke the silence as Morag ripped him from Elspeth's arms.

"Come in, Ariana. Come in and watch yer son's death." She brandished the dirk against her baby's throat.

Trembling, Ariana choked back her fear, and although she had vowed never to ask God for another favor, she sent her prayer on its way. Ever so slowly, she stepped into the room, her gaze never leaving Morag's face. "If ye kill him, ye will never be able to escape. Do ye really think Alastair can defeat Robb?"

Morag's eyes narrowed. "Ye would say anything to save yer child."

"Aye, I would, but this happens to be true. The only

thing keeping ye alive is my son." She crept closer, her movements calm as she watched Morag.

Morag's face paled. She glanced at Elspeth. "Ye will come with me." She held the dagger to Andrew's throat and started forward. "Move out of my way."

When Ariana did not move away from her path, she raised the dirk. "Do ye think ye can reach me before I plunge this into his heart?"

Ariana moved aside. She watched helplessly as they walked from the room. Once they were through the door, she followed them. The sounds of the fighting had ceased from below, but she could still hear Robb and Alastair fighting with swords in the bedchamber.

"Go to the master chamber," Morag ordered Elspeth.

The men were cut and slashed as they parried and thrust their weapons. Suddenly, Robb disarmed Alastair. He pressed the tip of his sword to Alastair's throat.

As Elspeth stood in the shadows, Morag held the dagger to the child. "Robb MacGregor," Morag screeched. "If ye want yer son to live, ye had best release Alastair." It was an order.

Robb glanced at Morag, and his face paled when he saw the dagger pressed to Andrew's neck. He dropped his sword instantly. His eyes narrowed as his gaze slanted to hers. "Ye will die for this."

She laughed. "I should kill ye now, but yer men may not be so sentimental about this brat." She turned to Elspeth. "Get yer brother his kilt."

Suddenly, Andrew's cries filled the air.

Robb took a step toward Andrew.

"Careful," she warned.

Alastair wrapped his kilt around him and reached for his sword. "Kill the whelp," he rasped angrily.

"Nay," Morag snapped. "This little bastard is our way out of here, and we can still claim the ransom from Normandy." She backed up into the hallway and glared at Ariana. "Stay where ye are, or I will cut his throat."

The dagger gleamed in the firelight.

Ariana's hand slipped into Robb's as he joined her.

"Elspeth," Morag screeched. Elspeth ran out, and Morag thrust the baby into her arms. She carefully cradled the baby as Morag and Alastair guided her down the steps at knifepoint.

Once they were in the main room Robb's men stared at them, but none dared to advance. MacPherson raised his hand. "Where do ye think ye are going with my grandchild?"

"Get out of the way or the wee cur dies," Morag said, waving the dagger in plain view.

MacPherson glared. "Where is my daughter?"

"Here, Father," Ariana called out as she and Robb descended the steps, though her gaze never left her baby.

Alastair and Morag shoved Elspeth forward, toward the door. A maid stood to one side, her eyes wide with fright, her gaze fastened on Elspeth. Alastair turned and glared at the men who had taken over his castle. "If anyone tries to stop us, I will gut the brat."

"Cailin," Morag called impatiently.

The girl appeared from the armory, her face dirty, her hands wet with blood. "They killed my family."

"Get over here and help us."

Cailin looked up, her eyes glassy. Dazed, she walked docilely across the great room through the throng of men. "But my family are dead. Ye said it would be all right. Ye promised if I brought Lady Ariana here, everything would be put to right."

"Silence!" Morag yelled. "Get some food packed."

As she walked toward Morag, Cailin turned to Ariana.

"Forgive me, my lady." Her eyes were sad. Then she looked at Morag, and began to laugh. The sound of a madness echoed in the room. Without warning, she raised a dagger and charged Morag. "Ye are the reason my family is dead!"

"Alastair!" Morag screeched.

He turned and raised his sword, catching Cailin in the breast.

She dropped to the floor, a gurgle sounding in her chest.

Sickened, Ariana turned away, blocking out the sight. Poor Cailin. She had believed them, and it had cost her life.

"Hand the bairn over." Morag reached out for the child.

Elspeth turned her body away from Morag, shielding the baby in her arms. "Nay, ye willna harm him."

Morag threw her head back and laughed. "How will ye stop me?" She advanced again, her eyes glazed.

Suddenly, her scream rent the air as a look of utter surprise crossed her face. She turned, and a wicked dagger protruded from her back.

"Ye," she whispered.

"Aye." The little woman stepped out of the doorway into view.

"Done in by a . . ." Morag gasped for air, her face turning toward Elspeth. "Yer maid."

"Aye," Elspeth said. "And my lover."

Alastair grabbed Elspeth before she could flee. "Sister, dinna test my patience." He spared his dying lover only a momentary glance, yet fear flickered in his glance. He placed his sword to the child's neck. "Dinna think I willna kill the bairn."

Elspeth shrunk away from his menacing features. " 'Tis over, brother. Ye must stop this madness."

Robb squeezed Ariana's hand, then stepped forward. He laid his sword in the rushes. "Take me as yer hostage. Leave the woman and child."

"Nay, ye willna risk their death."

"If ye take me, no one will pursue. I will leave orders ye are to be left alone. Ye must flee Scotland. No one will offer ye sanctuary."

Alastair's eyes looked wild as he stared at the other lairds.

Dunn stepped forward. "Aye, ye have burned all yer bridges now."

Alastair's face drained.

Ruthven's deep voice broke the silence. "I will hunt ye down."

Campbell raised his sword. "I will never forgive yer abandonment of my clansmen."

Alastair appeared to consider the idea, and Ariana's heart skipped a beat. They were winning him over.

He pointed to her. "Come here and take the bairn."

Ariana eagerly crossed the floor and reached for her child. The moment the baby lay in her arms, he hauled her close and laughed. "Now I have three hostages."

Her gaze met Robb's, and anger lived in his heart as he watched her being dragged away.

"Dinna follow," Alastair warned. He walked down the steps, the sword point pressed into her back, and ordered three horses.

The men followed, the lairds, standing on the stoop, waiting and watching.

Elspeth gave Ariana's arm a comforting squeeze before she fell into Alastair, breaking his hold on Ariana.

Before Alastair could rise, Robb leapt from the stairs and tackled the man. The lairds crowded around the two men, blocking Ariana's view. Cradling Andrew, she approached the tight circle, but no one made room for her. She hovered, moving back and forth to catch a glimpse. She could hear shouted encouragements, but could see nothing.

After what seemed an eternity, a cheer went up and Robb suddenly appeared through the ring of men. Behind him, Alastair lay beaten and bloody on the ground. As Robb approached amidst the cheering crowd, Alastair suddenly pulled a dagger from his boot and leapt to his feet.

"Robb!" she screamed, her heart in her throat as Alastair charged with the knife raised.

Robb turned, blocking her from harm with his body. In the nick of time, he fended off the weapon, catching Alastair's wrist. The lairds watched, but no one made a move to help him. The two men wrestled on the ground, the weapon's blade catching and flashing in the firelight as it hovered at Robb's neck. She ran over to her father. "Stop this."

Laird MacPherson pushed her behind him. "Now Ariana, ye must have faith in yer husband."

She was about to kick the stubborn Scot when the cheers stopped. In the eerie silence, she turned to see that Alastair had pinned Robb, and the knife lay somewhere between them. A scream caught in her throat as both men lay still. Tears burned her eyes as she took a step forward. Suddenly, Alastair moved. She held her breath, clutching Andrew to her breast as Alastair gasped, the knife embedded in his chest, then rolled off Robb and lay faceup.

Tears slipped down her face as Robb struggled to his feet and staggered over to her. She flew into his arms. Crying and laughing, she smothered his face with kisses. He hugged her, kissing her hard on the lips. The moment was sweet, tasting of love and life and joy, but far too short as he raised his head and stared at her. "God, I love ye." He kissed his son. Then he turned to his mother. "I owe ye my gratitude. I am in yer debt, *Mother*."

Her eyes glistened. "Thank ye, son."

Robb gave her a kiss on the cheek. "Ye have saved my family. 'Tis I who owe ye."

Ariana had a lump in her throat as she watched mother

and son heal the rift that had plagued this family for so long.

He turned to Ariana. "I think it is time to get out of the cold."

The lairds cheered as he took his son in his arms. "Ye, my little lad, have had quite an adventure. But until ye can wield a sword, ye best let yer parents fight yer battles."

Andrew's squeals of delight joined those of the celebrating army. As Robb escorted his wife inside, he bent down to brush a kiss on her cheek. "I believe in love. I believe in ye." His gaze traveled to the men raising their cups in a toast and calling his name. He sighed, and turned to Ariana. "I willna be long with the lairds, but I must make an appearance. Wait for me."

"I have waited for ye through three lifetimes. Ye have ten minutes," she warned, and had the satisfaction of hearing Robb's hastily delivered apologies to the lairds as he followed her upstairs.

EPILOGUE

Laird MacPherson and his wife, Lady Ruth, arrived at MacGregor Castle and were greeted by Lady Elspeth. "She has not yet delivered her child."

Laird MacPherson scowled fiercely as he escorted his wife into the great room.

He accepted a tankard of ale from Lor as Gavin and Brodie paced by the hearth. After he had quaffed half the contents, he turned to his wife. "Go to Ariana, Ruth, and tell her to hurry."

"My dear, this is not a campaign." Lady Ruth shared a smile with Lady Elspeth as they ascended the stairs to the bedchamber.

Once inside, Lady Ruth heard her daughter's plea. "I am fine, Robb. Really."

Quickly assessing the situation, Ruth laid her hand on Laird Robb's shoulder. "Yer needed downstairs."

"Why, is there trouble?" He turned. Worry lined his face.

"Nay, there has been peace in yer land for over a year, but I dinna think yer father-in-law can stand the wait."

"Go," Lady Elspeth urged.

Indecision flicked across his handsome features.

Ariana reached over and squeezed his hand. "It will be hours."

"I missed our son's birth, I dinna want to miss this one."

"Ye will be called," Lady Elspeth assured him.

The moment he left, Ariana breathed a sigh of relief. "I am ready."

Two hours later, with Robb at her side, Ariana cradled her beautiful daughter in her arms. "God has gifted us with another miracle."

Tears of joy warmed her eyes, and she smiled as she watched her husband hold his finger out to their daughter, amazement on his face when she latched on for dear life. "Strong grip. What shall we call this little mite?"

"Regan," she breathed.

"Regan and Drew. 'Tis perfect, my dear. Are ye going to give her yer ring when she reaches adulthood?"

"Aye, I hope she is as lucky as we were . . . "

"And meets her soul mate," he said, finishing her sentence, gazing down at her with love and tenderness.

She reached up and caressed his cheek. "My life, my love, my friend, ye are my heart's desire."

Robb leaned down to kiss her. The moment his lips touched hers, they created a heat. She moaned under the sweet passion of his love, and knew she had found heaven's reward.

Visit Marian Edwards's Web site for up-to-date information about her upcoming books, book-signing events, workshops, seminars, and television, radio, and personal appearances. Marian loves to hear from her readers. She has received fan mail from as far away as Japan, and she answers readers' questions about her future releases. Both her home page and E-mail are listed below:

http://home.att.net/~MARIANEDWARDS

MARIANEDWARDS@WORLDNET.ATT.NET

BOOK YOUR PLACE ON OUR WEBSITE AND MAKE THE READING CONNECTION!

We've created a customized website just for our very special readers, where you can get the inside scoop on everything that's going on with Zebra, Pinnacle and Kensington books.

When you come online, you'll have the exciting opportunity to:

- View covers of upcoming books
- Read sample chapters
- Learn about our future publishing schedule (listed by publication month *and author*)
- Find out when your favorite authors will be visiting a city near you
- Search for and order backlist books from our online catalog
- Check out author bios and background information
- Send e-mail to your favorite authors
- Meet the Kensington staff online
- Join us in weekly chats with authors, readers and other guests
- Get writing guidelines
- AND MUCH MORE!

**Visit our website at
http://www.zebrabooks.com**